SUMMARY

When Death pays a visit to Ramona's shop, it seems only polite to invite him in. Particularly when he has intense green eyes and can kiss like that...

A Grim Reaper knows when every living thing will die. But Silas can't see Ramona's death. It's one of many reasons the Chaos witch intrigues him. She's the antithesis of order, but when a dire threat to a single soul reveals a deeper attempt to ruin the order of life and death in the world, her power might be the key to making things right.

If they survive the evil that wants to destroy everything that matters to them both, Ramona wonders if she's finally found the male who won't run from who and what she is. Suddenly the term "Death is the only certainty in life," isn't a threat—it might be a promise.

ARCANE CHAOS

An Arcane Shot Series Novel

JOEY W. HILL

Arcane Chaos

An Arcane Shot Series Novel - Book #3

Copyright © 2022 Joey W. Hill

ALL RIGHTS RESERVED

Cover design by W. Scott Hill

SWP Digital & Print Edition publication June 2022 by Story Witch Press, 452 Mattamushkeet Dr., Little River, South Carolina 29566, USA

This book may not be reproduced or used in whole or in part by any means existing without written permission from the publisher, Story Witch Press, 452 Mattamushkeet Drive, Little River, SC 29566.

Warning: The unauthorized reproduction or distribution of this copyrighted work is illegal. No part of this book may be scanned, uploaded or distributed via the Internet or any other means, electronic or print, without the publisher's permission. Criminal copyright infringement, including infringement without monetary gain, is investigated by the FBI and is punishable by up to 5 years in federal prison and a fine of $250,000. (http://www.fbi.gov/ipr/). Please purchase only authorized electronic or print editions and do not participate in or encourage the electronic piracy of copyrighted material. Your support of the author's rights is appreciated.

This book is a work of fiction and any resemblance to persons, living or dead, or places, events or locales is purely coincidental. The characters are productions of the author's imagination and used fictitiously.

The publisher and author(s) acknowledge the trademark status and trademark ownership of all trademarks, service marks and word marks mentioned in this book.

The following material contains graphic sexual content meant for mature readers. Reader discretion is advised.

Digital ISBN: 978-1-951544-21-8

Print ISBN: 978-1-951544-22-5

ACKNOWLEDGMENTS

Many thanks to the following for helping me with the random things that come up in the writing of a story:

First, to Lisa W, for giving me a recent firsthand account of your visit to the Tomb of the Unknown Soldier in Washington D.C. I hope to make it there myself one day.

Second, to Mary C-P, deep appreciation for reviewing the parts of the story related to looms and weaving. This is a skill that's on my bucket list, right alongside fencing. However, since I haven't gotten around to it, it was essential to have someone take a look at my research results and tweak where needed. Her knowledge transformed key scenes into a much better read. And thank you, Donna S, for connecting us!

As always, any errors are my own.

Because of where this story goes, I also want to offer a thought to the universe for all of us, myself included. A hope, really, for the day when we lay down the weapons of hate and fear, not simply from the exhaustion of futility, but because we finally understand how all souls are connected.

CHAPTER ONE

"*You'd* have the greenest eyes I've ever seen, if they weren't gray."

Before Silas turned toward the thoughtful, amused voice, he knew three things about the woman.

She was a witch.

She served Chaos.

He'd let his eyes be whatever color she wanted.

He checked his mental timeclock. He wasn't due to Reap Calloway "Cal" Horscht's soul for another twenty-five hundred heartbeats. Approximately thirty-two minutes. He could hear it in his head, grains of sand falling through the hourglass.

He couldn't be late for this one. Cal was a new soul, and death would be sudden, a heart attack. But Silas had a few minutes. Or heartbeats, as it was. And she'd noticed him. Enough to know his true eye color was green.

Most people saw gray when he was visible to them. Or blue. Or brown. It depended on what was in someone's heart. What they needed to see. His true form brought a person face-to-face with their own mortality, and that often didn't go well.

He turned toward her.

Her voice had been girlish and sultry, a mix of maiden and woman. The lavender-tinged silver eyes shifted in color, probably because of the dappled sunlight coming through the two pear trees planted in front of her store.

She was slim and barefoot under her blue wooden store sign. *Toys, Teas, Herbs and Magic* it proclaimed, the debossed letters gold-painted and in a font style that evoked Vikings and runes. It fit. She could have lived among them, the village *völva*. Benevolent with a core of steel.

Strong, gentle women were often underestimated because they didn't meet a fight with a raised sword. *They* were the blade, the one who would withstand the blow, prevail, bring a battle to an end with their inexorable will and earth-deep understanding of the disturbing depths of the human soul.

Despite her thinness, the lack of curves, a man's attention would be caught by those eyes, his lust aroused by the mane of thick hair she possessed. Worn loose, it poured out in fist-tempting waves to her waist, draping her narrow shoulders and the freckled, pale skin of her arms.

The tiny bells on the tasseled drawstring of her flowing skirt chimed as the breeze rippled the folds. Her purple T-shirt had sparkles that said *Embrace the Magic*. No bra. The hint of her nipples brought to mind the flourished tip of soft serve ice cream. The heat of his mouth shaping it, his tongue savoring the taste and response it gave him.

Sex was important. It maintained vitality, kept the bonds between him and the rest of the world strong. No matter that he belonged to the most isolated race in the universe, he was still connected to all life. It was essential for a Reaper to remember that, since a soul was most aware of life's meaning when they stood in Death's shadow.

All in all, a valid set of reasons for giving the woman who'd spoken to him a closer look.

She stood next to a wheeled wooden display she'd pushed out onto the sidewalk. The bins on it were loaded up with whimsical toys. Rubber balls painted with the faces of gargoyles, grinning maniacally. Tasseled wands for child fairies, satin ribbons fluttering in the wind. Wood-burned rhymes spiraled around the handles, playful spellcraft. Harmless, but not meaningless. Energy vibrated along the shafts. She had baskets of wind-up metal toys, and one of them, a bear on a painted red tricycle, clacked along the sidewalk, turning in circles around her feet.

The store fit the wider setting. The Southern town was a few miles from a larger city, the small-town elements well preserved and enhanced by the quirky, artsy shops and bistro-style restaurants along this main street. A town like this was a good place for a person who didn't blend well. Who needed the patience and setting of a slower pace to do the best she could at that blending.

The witch was still gazing at him with deep curiosity. No trepidation. She knew their paths were going to cross, and the adventure of it would be welcome.

The thought drove blood to his groin. Made him think how she'd react when he put his mouth on hers, swallowed her gasps, her energy rippling into him as he took her over, plunged deep, so her soul would open and see his.

But when their eyes met, something else shot through him. A startling revelation.

Before he could confirm it, she sighed. "For want of a nail," she said ruefully, resignation capturing her intriguing gaze.

With a groan and a harsh squeak, one wheel shot out from beneath the display. As the wooden structure lurched toward that unbalanced corner, the bins fell, their contents tumbling out onto the sidewalk and rushing in every direction. Including toward him.

When she'd pushed the display out of the shop, Ramona already knew something was off. She didn't anticipate it being something so pleasing that her female side elbowed her concerns out of its path to indulge a closer look.

I want that.

He was two stores up, in front of Bygone Treasures, Cordelia Sun's antique shop. Cordelia's current window display included a French dining table made of walnut, circled by four apple-green velvet upholstered chairs and topped by a low-hanging chandelier. She made it seem like her shoppers were peering into someone's home, inspiring purchases of those same items.

She routinely clucked over Ramona's eclectic and disordered

window. *"Strategic clutter is essential for a shop, but it* must *have a theme. A subtle order."*

There *was* a theme to Ramona's offerings. And her shoppers didn't seem to mind when the thread of that theme got snarled up in an unexpected knot here and there. She'd told Cordelia as much. In a friendly way, because they *were* friends, the fellow shopkeeper kind.

That said, if Cordelia came out to lure in the intriguing male, Ramona would ruin her perfect shoulder bob with a pint-sized tornado. When he looked her way, she felt the trigger pull, low in her belly. One testosterone-fueled, estrogen-answered shot.

Her friend and sister witch Ruby would appreciate the metaphor, because Ruby operated the local gun range and firearms shop. Raina, the other member of their coven trinity, would fully understand it. Because Raina was half-succubus and she ran the one and only local bordello, discreetly located in an antebellum home outside of town.

If she were here, she would already have given Ramona a healthy shove toward the stranger.

His face was strong and angular, skin stretched taut over bone, making those remarkable green-yet-gray eyes deep set. His walnut-colored brows gave them a fierceness that eased when his forehead did, turning the warrior into a sexy librarian. All he needed were wire-rimmed spectacles.

His firm mouth showed resolve and clear purpose in an unclear world. It proved he'd fought more than a few battles to get it to that shape. She felt compassion toward him for that. Those battles left wounds that didn't always heal.

His jeans liked his lower body just fine. Against the morning's slight chill he wore an unzipped hoodie, a dark cotton T-shirt beneath. Nothing had a visible logo, no art on the shirt. She suspected the clothes were generated from ones he'd seen, suited to his preferences. No wasted time on more authentic details, like labels or designs.

She couldn't tell exactly what he was, but she knew for certain he wasn't human. Or a shopper.

Pleasure shoppers didn't shop alone, and they would linger, in no particular hurry, chatting about where they might eat lunch. Quick gift buyers were usually locals.

He could be waiting for someone, but his body language didn't telegraph that. As he'd studied the window, he'd had his hand pushed into a pocket, and rocked forward and back on thick tread shoes. She thought he was a man killing some time before he had to be somewhere.

On occasion, an item would catch the eye of a non-shopper like that, resulting in an impulse buy. A thought that thrummed through her when her comment drew his attention and his gaze sharpened with distinct interest.

When a man saw her beauty, he'd make the automatic sexual assessment. If he was available and not an asshole, he'd be appreciative but uncommitted until he read the right signals. The look was an indulgence, not an investment. Particularly if her behavior didn't encourage it.

Then there was the kind of man who looked at her like this. If she'd anticipated the force of his energy, she might have given more thought to the consequences of opening her mouth. Great Goddess, really, what *was* he? It was something she'd never encountered before. It unbalanced her, made her feel like...

Damn it.

She'd learned long ago not to fight or regret it, and to follow it where it led. A Chaos witch came into the world with one guiding aphorism for her life. It might as well be tattooed on her ass. *Make your plans and watch God laugh.*

Even so, it would have been nice to indulge a longer look, an exploration of that unique energy, before the Chaos inevitably sent him on his way.

"For want of a nail..." She sighed.

She'd noted the wheel was loose when she'd pushed the display out here, had intended to tighten it before he'd distracted her. So she could blame it on him.

She grabbed for the shelf to keep the sudden weight shift from taking it all the way over. Eight bins toppled out, and one of them contained balls. Of course. At least the grinning gargoyles looked cheerful, bouncing across the sidewalk, some halting in the pine bark around the pear trees, but too many spinning elsewhere. Off the curb, into the street, rolling under parked cars.

The wind-up toys clattered to the ground. A couple frogs hopped a few steps across the pavement, the sun glinting off the painted green metal. The horses treaded air when they ended up on their sides. The tricycling bears trundled off, though they wouldn't go as far as the balls.

The traffic on Main Street hesitated only long enough to be sure they wouldn't run over anything. After toeing her concrete pig doorstop over to the display to keep it upright, Ramona shoved her feet into her zebra-striped sneakers and headed toward the road.

As she began to step out between two parked vehicles, an SUV and a jacked-up pickup, her elbow was grasped. A truck trundled by. It wasn't going fast, but its driver was scrolling through his phone, looking for his delivery address. Two gargoyle balls were flattened beneath the big wheels.

After he passed, they shook loose from the treads and reinflated, distorted faces snarling at the offense. One rolled to Ramona and bumped the side of her foot. The shoe's canvas was thin enough she vaguely felt it, but her sensitive nerve endings were attuned to the fingers gripping her arm.

When she lifted her gaze to the stranger's face, she found his green eyes could rob a woman of speech. Maybe permanently. Why waste time talking in a gallery, when focusing on the art could give you everything? His prominent bone structure, the brow and jaw, the sharp cheekbones and deep-set eyes, were the best work of a master sculptor.

"Your hair," he said, "would be the reddest I've ever seen, if it wasn't spun gold." His gaze shifted over it. "Now it's both. Like fire."

Sunlight could do that, but the sudden smoky scent told her he'd set off a reaction from her she had no time to quell.

He had a strand between his fingers, so he saw it shimmer, then spout flame. He didn't snatch his hand back. Before she could protect him, he'd closed his hand around the fire, taking the heat into himself. She saw the brief spark in his gaze, then it was an ocean hue again. Her throat went dry.

"It was the color of earth at one time," he noted, still apparently speaking of her hair. His lips curved. "It's been green, too. And blue."

"All the crayons want their turn," she managed. "I need to collect the toys."

"Some bears went that way." He nodded toward Cordelia's. "I'll get them. Mind yourself before you step out."

Whoa. The way he said it, his voice measured and calm, the steady look he reinforced it with, gave her a serious pause. And aroused the contrary part of her that wanted something she couldn't have, because it didn't exist.

A male who could Dominate chaos, give her even just a careful taste of the surrender she craved.

But he seemed careful, didn't he? He'd just kept her from stepping out in front of a truck, after all. Though in truth, what he'd done was save the driver, from a massive fender bender with the chain of parked cars along the street. Chaos tended to be protective of her.

Much as he'd seemed to be.

As he turned to do as he'd indicated, Ramona discovered he looked pretty damn good from behind. There wasn't a lot of bulk to him, but he had swift grace and a dense power.

When she recovered enough to scamper off and grab gargoyle balls, she could sense Cordelia's exasperated disapproval through her side window. Normally, she would have been the first to come out and help Ramona. Being as sharp as any female friend could wish her to be, Cordelia wouldn't interrupt whatever possibilities were playing out between Ramona and the stranger. Much as she often chastised Ramona like she was an untidy child, she also routinely asked if Ramona had found someone "nice," because she deserved that, she "surely did."

Other pedestrians were collecting the toys. She righted one of the bins, depositing balls in it before moving with a smile toward a couple bringing her another armload. Then she did a double take.

"*Raina.*"

The last person she'd ever expect to see in town. Since Sweet Dreams employed a dozen sex demons, the bulk of Raina's energy was required to maintain the spellcraft there. It allowed her demons to pass as humans and feed from her human clientele without killing them. It didn't leave much extra for the shielding her succubus nature would need if she came to town for a casual shopping day. As such, she rarely visited anywhere as populated as this. But here she was.

The power that disguised Raina's appearance wasn't her own. The question of who had provided the concealment was answered in the same look and brought a greater shock. Plus a surge of anger.

Mikhael Roman. A Dark Guardian. A powerful being Raina had

once said needed to have his testicles roasted in hellfire *and* his anus injected with hot sauce.

Was Mikhael here for Raina? If so, Ramona needed to protect her coven sister, get her away from him.

But since her impulsive magic could reach nuclear levels if she let strong emotions take over, she took a vital extra beat to review the situation. First, would Raina have taken the time to pick up toys and bring them to her if she was in danger? Second, she evaluated the body language between Raina and Mikhael.

Yes, something as hot as hellfire was happening. But not the type associated with that kind of torment.

"I'm confused," she said. "Normal for me, but really confused."

Her green-eyed stranger had come back to her side. For her next shock of the day, she saw Mikhael offer him a slight nod. Acknowledgement. The respect of a peer.

Double whoa.

Was he a Guardian of some kind? No, she'd recognize that. Ruby was mated to a Light Guardian, and despite being different sides of the coin, Mikhael and Derek had a common energy current.

Then the stranger's gaze shifted to Raina, and Ramona could tell he saw through her shielding. Ramona suppressed a pang of regret. *C'est la vie.*

She told herself she wouldn't hold it against him. The succubus blood made it impossible for a male not to be ensnared by Raina. Combine that with the whole physical package—Raina's long dark hair, lush body and moist, full lips—a man would think of sex with her even standing waist deep in fresh horse manure. Or naked strippers.

But as he made a polite comment or two about the toys, he merely nodded courteously to Raina. Then his attention was fully back on Ramona.

Today was full of more surprises than even her norm. She wanted to get some answers. She wrapped things up with Raina and tossed out some inane prattle about good places for a visitor to eat in the area as she drew the male back toward her store.

As she did, she threw a look at Raina that said she'd want details later about why she was running around with Mikhael Roman. Ruby was going to have kittens. And fucking hell, to say nothing of Derek.

Raina's look and quirked lips said, *"Right back at you, sister. And by the way, make sure there are* lots *of details to give."*

While her professional life was saturated with it, Raina was always more than willing to talk about sex. Remembering the way the male's green eyes had penetrated her to her toes, Ramona wasn't going to claim she was above such things.

She just had to go without sex a lot more than Raina did.

At the entrance to her store, he held the door open for her. Once inside, she put down the rest of the toys she'd gathered on a long display counter. A couple of the windup ones had been damaged, so she separated them for transfer to the discount shelves in back.

As he turned to study her store's interior, he shrugged out of the hoodie and folded it over his arm, revealing the curve of biceps, the flex of his shoulders. His back tapered down to his waist, and she'd already seen the ass beneath the denim looked good, though a second verification never hurt. If she touched his nape, would the heated flesh be slightly damp? His thick brown hair, short with a mix of earthy shades, curled a little, making her want to feather her fingers over it.

She pulled her attention to what he was looking at, trying to read his impressions. Cordelia said Ramona could fit the universe in a shoebox, with room for extra laces. No matter where one looked, the store had something to see. Kites hung from the ceiling, drifting with the help of a fan. Shelves held toys, games, magic implements, potions, crystals. Tea. One section was for teacups, placed high enough to avoid tiny hands, though Ramona had put less breakable, sturdy ceramic ones down a little lower.

As she took the damaged toys toward the back, he followed her, more slowly. Opposite the discount shelves were the displays with her hand-woven linens. Blankets, towels, rugs. Tapestries. He took a closer look at one with a navy-blue swirly pattern, marked with tiny white dots, stars in a night sky. A giant rabbit woven of fuzzy thread danced against it.

When a whistle drew his attention upward, a toy train chugged into view on the track that ran through the store, several feet above the heads of her visitors. Steam came out the engine stack as the locomotive wound its way past the linens and disappeared.

"You sell trains, too." Inside, his voice became a deeper hum, one she felt in her bones.

"No. Not directly. The vendors swap inventory to help all our sales, but the train seller gave me this one. I convinced the mice in his walls to live somewhere else. The track rearranges itself into different routes throughout the store. I let it decide how it wants to go."

With this male, there was no reason for her to pretend not to be the witch he knew she was.

"So all types of magic can happen here."

When she didn't immediately answer, he turned to look at her, expectant. His expression reminded her of his tone when he'd told her to mind herself. Her stomach fluttered.

"Yes." As she put the broken toys on the discount shelf, she looked at the plaque mounted beside the entrance to the private back rooms. *Come to earth like an angel's feather. Leave the same way.*

Crescent, the Fae pixie female who'd raised her, had said she thought Ramona's soul had come to earth like that. Soaring in wild patterns that only she could see, always ready to take off and soar again.

She turned to find him standing behind her. His piercing eyes, touched by something fierce, made her wonder if she should have stayed closer to the sunny street. Or at least left her front door propped open.

She wasn't easily rattled. But this concentrated stillness, holding her in one fixed point while the rest of the world spun around them, didn't happen to her. She was one of the things that spun around the fixed points.

Inside that unexpected place, she found a throbbing center of singular want. Something elusive and out of reach for a Chaos witch. Usually.

He was tall, but she lifted her hands, framed his head, shaped it without touching. Spreading her fingers like bird wings, she swept them back, as if pulling any energy away that concealed him from her, who he was, what he wanted. All she felt was the clean heat of a man's hunger. The weight of it, while daunting, was a reassurance, not a threat.

His eyes darkened and he put his hand on the side of her throat.

His fingers brushed her hair, curving under it, firm pressure against yielding flesh. As she stared up at him, he held there, still. Waiting.

Moistening her lips, she lowered her gaze to his chest. A hard vibration went through her as his energy changed, responding to the message she'd just sent him.

His forefinger slid against the main artery in her throat. The pressure increased, so she could feel the blood rushing, the beat of her heart, as her body responded. His thumb moved to her lips, a stroke. He had a large hand, so could do both without straining, his fingers still caressing the sensitive skin of her neck.

His gaze traveled over her features, down. Back up.

"Say what's in your mind, witch."

A man used to holding authority, wielding it, but not with malice. The surety in his touch was like an ocean. If an army was placed before the sea and told *defeat this*, there'd be no starting point. Its power was too vast. Permanent. Binding.

"Say what's in your mind," he repeated.

"My lord is my shepherd, and in his presence, I shall do nothing but want."

She didn't know why certain words came to her, but whatever she'd said had a decided impact. A flash of surprise, then naked desire. A soft moan escaped her lips as his grip tightened.

"I've been called a shepherd before." He gave her a smile as old and breathtaking as Earth's first day. Then his gaze sharpened again, that blade she wanted to cut her everywhere. He dropped to a knee, his hands leaving a tingling caress along her shoulders, her upper arms, coming to rest with heated palms on her forearms.

Things in her stomach took flight. She tried hard not to think the word, but there it was, and so as he acted, they became part of this.

Dragonflies. As within, so without. They were darting around them, iridescent wings picking up the green in his eyes, the purple of her clothes, like living accessories.

He noted them, and seemed pleased by the response. His attention shifted to her breasts, small mounds beneath the sparkling words on her T-shirt. The taut points stretched the fabric. Being so small, she often didn't concern herself with underwear for them, though that scandalized poor Cordelia.

The male studied her nipples beneath the cloth. He absently

brushed a perched dragonfly off his cheek before he leaned in to press his lips to one covered peak.

His mouth was like a bee's legs on a flower, a teasing dance. His hands had shifted to her waist and held her still, command in his touch.

She could call the power of the Goddess, and that power knew just how potent surrender to a lover's touch could be. She didn't know him, but trust in a cocoon of heat, in a corner of her shop, didn't have to reach far.

All this surrender required was accepting this blink-of-time remarkable magic, where two souls opened and heard each other's language.

Before the noise of the world intruded again.

She heard a third heartbeat. Hers was erratic. His was smoother, but gaining ground like a wolf increasing pace toward a target. She saw some wolf in him. The third heartbeat seemed to be coming from him, too, like the ticking of a pocket watch.

He was still staring at her, as if getting to the bottom of something. "You are difficult to read," he said at last. "Perhaps it's the Chaos magic."

Her desires were as evident to her as her brightly colored wind-up toys. "Really? My antique store neighbor would say I was being too obvious. Terribly unladylike."

He looked startled, and she bit her lip. "You weren't talking about that."

"No." But when she would have tried to slip away, regain her composure, the grip of his hands and eyes kept her with him. "There is nothing in this world, or any other, more welcome and appropriate than a woman's desire."

How many other worlds had he seen? With how many women in them? What did that have to do with this? *Shut up, Ramona.*

As he kissed her right breast again, her hand brushed his forearm. Short, dark hairs, his skin rough beneath them, a contrast to hers. She explored it, one finger sliding along his flesh. She watched his hands under her shirt, warm palms against her abdomen, thumbs on her rib cage, other fingers gripping her above her lower back. Demanding, overwhelming. She'd give so much to let a man take her, all the way to the core—sex, heart and soul—and bring her satisfaction.

But that heartbeat...

"I don't want to seem nosy," she ventured on a humming note. Her fingers dug in as he nuzzled, teased, did something amazing with his tongue over her clothes that had her dropping her head back, sensation washing through her chest, her aching nipple. She wanted to be suckled, bitten, kissed. She wanted him there forever.

She was amazed at how easily he held her, steadied her. Normally, the more aroused she became, the more her magic would spin up and cause all sorts of problems. Not the least of which was an end to the pleasure.

Thump-thump. Thump-thump. This time, her own mouth would have to take the blame. She found the thread of her question. "Do you have two hearts?"

Those brilliant eyes lifted. But as he registered her question, they lost focus on her and turned inward.

An expression crossed his face that sank her heart like the Titanic. He looked like a man woken up from a dream, realizing he couldn't afford even another moment in bed. She'd lifted her hand to brush the silken hair at his temples, but before she could, he rose and stepped back, giving her a hard, searching look.

Friend or foe? That was what he was trying to determine. Whatever it was she'd detected, he hadn't expected her to have that ability. In the shift, she saw he had powers that could end her. Sending Raina on her way suddenly didn't seem as sensible.

But as unsettling as facing that dangerous judgment was, it still felt better than when his attention left her entirely. His total concentration had felt so wondrously real and strong.

Chaos was always ready to remind her nothing was in her control, especially the things she most wanted to hold onto. No surprise, she heard a loud crack outside. A jarring series of crashes as wood hit concrete and splintered, more bins toppling. Another loose wheel had broken free, dumping the whole thing on the sidewalk and likely destroying the display's use entirely.

For want of an army, the war was lost. But it all started with a nail.

Being lonely was an emptiness. If she treated it like a pool, it would fill with pain, drag her into its depths to drown or worse— wallow. So instead she treated it like a room, and she was the house. It was just one small part of everything else she was. It helped to think of it that way.

"I must go." He bowed to her, an absent-minded courtesy over-shadowed with urgency. That beautiful desire he'd given her had galloped away like a wild horse. "Goodbye. Thank you."

"Goodbye." It was kneejerk, an inane parroting of his own farewell. But he was already gone, as if he'd vanished right in front of her.

He hadn't. The shop bells were chiming, telling her he'd passed through the door.

She hated herself for it, but she ran there to look for him. He was crossing the street, long legs eating up the ground. He disappeared in the alley between the movie theater and Peterson's Hardware.

He didn't look back.

She glanced down. A dragonfly lay on the floor of her store, tumbled from wherever it had been perching. Her magic had called them to her, and this one had been in the last minutes of its short life span as a flying adult. An amazing flight, over in an instant.

Her skin was still vibrating, her lips tingling. She passed her fingers over them, hugged herself, not ready to let go of his scent, the feel of his touch.

But life went on. At length, sighing, she scooped up the dragonfly and stepped out, letting the wind have him. Then she began cleaning up her sidewalk. This time, he hadn't stayed to help.

But Cordelia was already coming out to do so. Ramona had friends. She had a life. A house of many rooms, and she was always adding to them. It had been a nice moment. She'd store it as the wistful memory it would become. She'd be holding onto those green eyes for a while.

She'd let the rest of him hold onto her, if only in her dreams.

CHAPTER TWO

*H*e'd hurt her. He was wrong for doing that. But hell, he'd lost track of time. That *never* happened to a Reaper.

He'd intended his time with her to be mutually pleasurable, no strings. But the first time she met his gaze, she'd unbalanced that idea as surely as the wheel shooting out from beneath her display had toppled those bins.

The knowledge that was always there for him, for any Reaper... wasn't.

If someone crossed his field of vision without direct eye contact, he could shield himself from the information if he wished. But if he looked into someone's eyes, the book of their life opened to the final page.

Their gazes had held. One beat, two beats.

Nothing.

Instead, he'd discovered the first chapter of their paths crossing. He'd found dragonflies. Magic. The scent of tea. Sunlight sparking off golden hair that turned into red-orange fire.

Dance with me in the storm.

I will never give you harm.

She'd been murmuring that as he followed her into the back of her store. Even as she carried her fallen toys, she'd walked lightly on her feet, had twirled twice, done a sidestep and back to center, dancing to the cadence. She didn't seem aware she was doing either the dancing or the grounding chant. He'd unsettled her. He didn't mind that.

When she'd reached up and let her hands glide over the outline of his skull, she'd been testing the energy of his intent, but the motions matched the pushing back of a cowl. Then her eyes had held him in that significant pause.

Before they lowered.

Submission was a powerful magic. She'd offered it as an invitation, not a mandate, but courage was required at that threshold. It wasn't meaningless or ephemeral. It could leave a mark on the soul. A mark became a link. Connection could become a binding, a permanent one.

Everything about her spoke of the things that made no sense to the mind, but were clear as blue sky to the heart.

Protectiveness was in his nature, but the surge of it toward the witch had been unusual. Chaos and power swirled around her. She was dangerous, a force to be reckoned with, but there was a vulnerability there, too easy to see. She could be destroyed by it.

Dance with me in the storm.

I will never give you harm.

He'd had to depart far too abruptly. But he'd left her a gift. An apology and a promise wrapped up together. He wondered how long it would take her to find it.

His inability to see her mortality might not hold the significance he'd assigned to it. He didn't know much about Chaos witches, but the very name suggested an explanation.

Then there were the two friends they'd met while gathering toys from the street. A half-succubus witch who oozed sensuality and power, accompanied by a Dark Guardian, an Underworld elite enforcer.

Guardians were among the few who could recognize a Reaper, no matter their shielding. They had no quarrel, though Silas had noted the Dark Guardian's body language became more protective toward the half-succubus, in case Silas was there for her. Interesting. Guardians rarely found a mate. Much like Reapers.

Silas wasn't in the habit of revealing himself to anyone. Keeping his cloaking in place was second nature to him. Removing it required more thought and effort.

Practice had made it that way. While he went to his dormant state periodically, as all his kind did, he didn't do it until it was necessary to recharge. He liked interacting with humans. Walking among them, enjoying their world.

Most Reapers his age didn't. They saw everything with old, tired eyes. Eventually, one day, they were gone. Instead of recharging and returning, they dissolved into the shadows of caves and remote places. They became the peaceful energy hovering in quiet spots. The spirit resting in the hollow of a lightning struck tree, or under the blanket of a creek's bottom silt.

When a new Reaper appeared in their ranks, he or she would be an old soul, but compared to the existing Reaper ranks, they always seemed fresh-faced and eager. He'd become a Reaper over four hundred years ago, but Honora, the leader of their Wake, often told him that he'd retained that quality. Since she made the observation in her flat, impossible-to-interpret way, he wasn't sure if it was a compliment. It surely wouldn't be today.

Though he was next in line to command their Wake, today he'd acted like a novice Reaper. Like any job, time management decisions were important. Sometimes terminal illnesses could wait a day or two for a Reaping, because a soul, finally uninhibited by the pain and medicated confusion of their final days, wanted to linger near family, say a mental good-bye.

In contrast, sudden death usually needed immediate guidance. The disoriented soul might hover over their loved ones, injecting them with a formless despair and anxiety as the soul screamed to be acknowledged, not realizing it had left its body.

The age of the soul could mitigate that. Once past the threshold of death, an older soul calmed down a bit, was able to lower the wall between this life and past ones, which helped them let go of the mortal form.

Like the child he'd Reaped several weeks ago. Despite its five-year-old body, the soul was on its eleventh incarnation. It had been placidly waiting for him, sitting on the hood of the police car which had responded to the hit-and-run that had ended his mortal life. The soul knew how to manipulate matter, so he'd been turning the lights and sirens on and off, perplexing the rookie officer first on the scene.

"He was upset about seeing a child's body," the soul had told Silas. "I was distracting him." There'd been sadness in the spirit's kind voice, as he acknowledged the life and family he was leaving behind, but otherwise he was calm about his transition.

A newly minted soul, their first crossing, was a different matter. Younger souls had a harder time recognizing that wall between this and past lives, let alone lowering it. Which was why he'd needed to be on time. Why he'd had to hurt the witch by leaving so abruptly. Being three minutes late could be as catastrophic as three days.

The soul could be frightened, uncertain. And unprotected, vulnerable like that, they were a magnet for a Soul Collector. A newly minted soul had a pure energy they could use to augment their own power.

Cursing, Silas increased his pace, moving through and then outside the main part of the town, using portal currents where they existed.

He landed on the street in front of Cal Horscht's home, and a jogging woman shrieked. She couldn't see him, but his energy had blown her forward several strides. That wasn't what had caused her startled reaction, though.

Damn it, he'd cut it too close.

To mortal eyes, Cal's house with its green, well-tended yard was soaked in sunshine. What Silas saw was a darkness cloaking the backyard and spreading outward toward the street. Soul Collectors liked to pollute the area they inhabited, and the first greedy fingertips of it had reached the jogger.

She'd pulled her ear buds free, had spun around to see what had sent such a wash of disturbing feelings through her. Seeing nothing, she still bolted for the safety of home, base survival instinct overriding rationality.

Silas uttered the words to shove the billowing roll of energy back into the rear fenced yard and contain it. If it had engulfed the jogger, she would have suffered a year of nightmares.

Whether he'd fucked up or not, he had one mission now. Cold rage flooded him. His battle instincts rode that surge, a waiting arsenal of skills to do what he was born to do. The shepherd protecting a member of his flock.

He called his scythe to hand. The curved blade gleamed with blue and orange flame, the fires of Heaven and Hell together. As he gripped the solid ash handle, energy rushed through it, giving the wood a red color that moved like running blood.

White flame sparked on the arched edge when it made contact. The tip was a lethal finger that would hook, draw blood, and rip through whatever flesh it touched.

Silas vaulted the six-foot privacy fence, landing just as the creeping apparition at the center of that spreading mass was spiraling into a point toward Cal's fallen body. While it wasn't the ultimate goal, the Soul Collector had a reason for laying hands on it. The cord between it and the soul was still connected. A clawed hand reached out of darkness.

A chihuahua with the bravery to deserve a much bigger frame held his ground between the fallen body and Cal's soul, yapping and snarling at the Collector as it prepared to slice through that connection and seize the cord. Typical for a first incarnation, Cal's spirit looked much like the elderly body on the ground, though his shoes were missing, ethereal toes curled into the thick grass. Unlike his body's fixed, staring eyes, his brown-eyed gaze wasn't vacant. It was full of terror and confusion.

The Soul Collector's head had emerged from the darkness, a mix between a hairless lion and bear, three times larger than either. It saw Silas, bared its teeth. With a swift movement, it sliced the cord with its talons, wrapped it around a thick, spiny wrist with a deft twist. In the same breath, the beast tried to reopen the portal to yank itself and Cal through.

Cal was airborne, crying out in fear, hurtling toward that opening, a vortex of darkness. He'd be seeing every fear of his worst imaginings, the adrenaline intensifying and compacting the soul energy he had, making it an even richer meal for the Collector.

Silas brought the scythe down, cutting the cord a foot away from Cal's spirit. He grabbed the soul around the chest with one arm, spinning them both back toward the yard. Cal stumbled free, a tumbling float and fall, because the cord that connected him to earthly things like gravity had been severed. Now it was just muscle memory. Habit. The known and familiar in a world that was anything but.

"Begone," Silas told the Collector. It crouched on the edge of the dark doorway a few feet above them. "You have no business here."

The umbilical cord had enough residual soul energy for the Collector to transform it into a barbed whip. As the creature lashed out with it, Silas blocked and sliced through the cord with his blade, but it had been a distraction. The Collector sprang over him. Landing next to Cal, it wrapped its arm around the soul's throat.

The dog attacked the Collector and cried out in agony at the poisonous contact. Silas levitated him out of the way, dropping him on the far end of the yard. The demon opened up another portal and leaped backward into it, holding Cal to him, digging into Cal's spirit flesh with those sharp claws. If they could hear it, the soul's scream of terror would have speared the heart of everyone in his neighborhood.

A new soul sounded like a child.

Silas leaped after them. He got his arm and upper torso through, but had to divert energy to keep the closing portal from severing him in half. The Collector had too much forward momentum; Silas had lost the chance to pull Cal back out.

He could let go, or he could follow him.

Silas pulled his scythe in with him. The portal slammed shut, and they were tumbling through a world of blood and lightning, a tunnel to the demon world that felt as terrible as it looked.

Offering yourself, Reaper? The whisper in his head held a million violent deaths. Hate, lost hope. Despair at a level that would hold even the mightiest down and bury them with the cold dead.

There was Heaven, the afterlife. Hell was a place of redemption, of order and logic. Punishment could be dispensed there, but those who administered it weren't evil.

Evil lay in the in-between places. It liked to lurk in the channels and boundaries of the Underworld, in its dark shadows, looking for the lost. Poised to steal them and take them back to the demon region of the Underworld. A place no one went. It was wholly theirs.

No Reaper did what he'd just done. No one from the world they'd left could win a fight in the demon world. On Day One of their lives as Reapers, they were all told that.

We do all we can to deprive Soul Collectors. But we do not, under any circumstances, follow them into their world. We cannot retrieve a soul from there. And giving them a Reaper is not an option.

There was a first time for everything, and he wasn't giving them one damn thing. He'd committed himself, and now only one goal mattered.

He swung the scythe through the rushing, hot air, now full of a choking snowstorm of ash. He found solid purchase, and won a scream. Cal's soul fell free of the Collector's grasp and into Silas's arms.

"Hold onto me," he told the terrified spirit. In a heartbeat, its primal instincts shrunk it from a man-sized form into a child, a toddler, wrapping arms and legs around Silas, burying its head in his neck, hoping to be absorbed and escape. Or at the very least, grab the illusion of protection before he woke from the nightmare. Silas was good with the scythe one-handed, even against a fast opponent, so he circled the small form of shining light with one arm and gave it a reassuring squeeze.

He'd failed Cal, and he had to make that right. No matter the cost. Doing his job well wasn't merely about pride. Nor even about the balance of the universe. Caring for each soul he was charged to protect was who Silas was. A guardian. Which was likely why Dark and Light Guardians could recognize a Reaper.

A soul had so much potential for substance, things it would earn in subsequent lives, if the soul was given that chance. Cal would have that chance.

Pain seared across Silas's back, grabbed at his legs. With a roar, Silas responded, the scythe flashing around him and Cal, turning them into a spinning star with sharp points that found purchase and drove the Collector back.

But they had reached the outer ring of the demon world, and their fall was about to meet hard ground. Others would join the Collector, coming to the foul beast's aid.

With the last spare thought he had, Silas thought of the witch. He was glad for the gift he'd left her. If they ever met again, would she still possess it? How would it change in her keeping?

If he never saw her again, he hoped she would understand he meant it, despite the briefness of their meeting. As much as one hoped a relationship could be a line, sometimes it was one dot on a blank page. A significant momentary intent, to treasure amid a whole lot of white space.

He'd told himself it was her nature that shielded him from the knowledge of her death, but about to be scalded of anything but truth, he wanted to believe otherwise.

Though their own timeline and that of their brethren were not available to them, Reapers could see the time and cause of death for every other race and species, from a Guardian to a tomato plant. With one notable exception.

A Reaper couldn't see the death of his own soulmate.

A mercy, because carrying around the knowledge of how and when the person you loved most would be taken was a cruelty beyond imagining. He didn't mind imagining she might have been that person for him, no matter how painful believing it right now would be.

As other minions rushed to the Soul Collector's aid, Silas spoke the words to charge the scythe. Then he put everything aside but fighting for Cal's soul, with all the strength the Lord and Lady had given him.

~

"What a dick."

It didn't have to be his fault to hurt. Ramona acknowledged that, even as she appreciated Ruby's solidly loyal blunt assessment.

"Why am I always surprised when a male not typically human ends up being a typical dick?" her friend continued.

"Because if you have a dick, you can be one," Raina observed, handing the almond cakes around again. Ruby topped off their wine, splashed liberally into glasses Raina had brought in a plaid-lined picnic basket. Since Ruby had recently learned she was pregnant, her glass contained apple cider. "Whether Guardian, titmouse, or garden variety homo sapiens," Raina added.

"Or Grim Reaper," Ruby confirmed.

Mikhael had recognized right off what Ramona's visitor was. He'd even found out his name, from his vast army of Otherworld contacts.

Sylvanus Pendleton, known as Silas.

Their fifteen-minute encounter had happened exactly twenty days ago, a nice round number that coincided with this month's full moon ritual; hence the offer of supportive male bashing from her two closest friends.

"Are you okay?" Ruby touched Ramona's hand.

"Sylvanus was the name of a woodland spirit, a demi-god protector. I felt that kind of energy from him," Ramona said. "Like a tree growing in an ancient forest."

He had a name like music. Sylvanus, Silas.

She didn't want to see Ruby and Raina exchange the *she's-still-messed-up-over-him* look, so she tipped her head up, looking into the branches of the trees above them. Their preferred ritual spot was a glade in the wooded area flanking Raina's house, part of her extensive property.

Just fifteen minutes. Seriously, she found it even more puzzling than they did. She supposed a Reaper was capable of making a bigger impression on a woman than most males.

Her lips twitched. She hadn't managed the full body-to-body contact that would allow her to confirm that as an appropriate sexual innuendo. But she sure could imagine. It seemed like all she'd done, every day since then. She cleared her throat. "His mother named him well. I assume Reapers have mothers."

"Still a dick," Raina said into her wine glass, the red making her lips look extra glossy. "Everyone has a mother, even if the mother is the Goddess alone. Gina wanted to know if he'd Reaped the soul of a famous person. George Washington. Chadwick Boseman. Elvis."

At Ruby and Ramona's expressions, she shrugged. "You know my sex demons are as inquisitive as babies."

Ruby snorted. "With the sexual skills of ten generations of Renaissance courtesans."

"Which is why I'm so filthy rich." Raina tapped her glass. "Say 'courtesan' again. It's so sexy in your pragmatic Agent Hill *Avengers* voice."

"Don't make me pinch you." Ruby shook her head. "He might not even know who *is* famous. Who says he watches TV or listens to music? He might just wander the ether and meditate. Become a tree in an ancient forest when he's not Reaping." She dipped her head toward Ramona.

"He has a dick, and he's interested in her," Raina said bluntly. "I think he's doing more than meditating. I suspect he's seen at least a few movies. Or read a book or two. Mikhael said Reapers are like Guardians."

"Derek says they're more like Light Guardians," Ruby corrected. "'The good guys.'"

"You know he said that just to yank Mikhael's chain," Raina retorted.

"No doubt. But even if he's a dick when it comes to a woman, it says he's a good guy dick."

Ramona sighed and stretched out on the ground, putting her head in Ruby's lap. "Let's look up at the stars."

Obligingly, both women set aside their glasses. Raina stretched out with her head on Ramona's stomach, and Ruby used one of the cushions they'd brought to support her own. Her touch drifted over Ramona's hair, finger combing out the long, wavy locks over her hip and upper thigh. Clouds drifted across the moon.

During the ritual, energy had been raised and targeted for various intents. The wellbeing of Ruby's pregnancy. The inner balance of Li, Raina's most mature sex demon. He was approaching thirty, a dangerous time for incubi.

In the aftermath of the ritual, there was always this temporary peace, an easing to the sharper edges of worries. They felt the connection to the ancient wisdom of crones, the nostalgia for when they were maidens. They also carried the protectiveness of mothers, toward whatever was given to them to protect, whether Raina's young sex demons, Ruby's coming son, or Ramona's...what?

She would have no children, would likely never have more family than what was linked to her right here and now. But that was okay. She knew her job.

Protecting the world, however that presented itself to her.

They each carried their fair share of power, and particularly when they did a ritual like they did tonight, they were aware of its influence, the responsibility for its wise use. When bestowed or earned, power always had a purpose. Whether daily purpose or world-saving purpose, it was intended for *use*, to be pushed to its limits, explored fully, worn out...

A lot like the life one was given.

Raina put her hand on Ramona's knee, tapped it. "You're so quiet. We've been teasing to help, but we're sorry he left the way he did. I know he made a big impression on you."

"I don't know what responsibilities a Reaper has, but I could tell he lost track of time, being with me." There was some balm to that, but why hadn't he returned?

Impression was a good word choice, because he'd left a stamp on her soul. Some days it felt like a boot print. Other days, it was as if he was holding her again, in that unforgettable grip. At first, she'd thought it just the resonant aftermath of an erotic encounter. She'd had actual sex that wasn't as intense as those few minutes together, though that wasn't saying much. For a Chaos witch, intimacy was a tricky proposition.

She didn't know much about the kind of extremes that she was sure Ruby and Raina had experienced. They didn't go on and on about them, but they were evident.

Ruby lost her train of thought when Derek gave her one of those penetrating looks that reflected what he did to her behind closed doors. And while the shock of Mikhael and Raina becoming a mated pair had ebbed somewhat, the erotic vibrations between them became so intense when they shared the same room, it could inspire a small snowstorm to cool everyone off.

In all fairness, Ramona hadn't *meant* to do it. When it started, she'd hoped it would limit itself to her immediate proximity, so that she could scurry out of the room with it. Instead, it had dumped three inches of snow in Raina's dining room. Amid the swirling flurries, the sex demons initiated a snowball fight that took out two teardrop crystals of Raina's antique chandelier.

In the ensuing tirade from their mistress, they'd scattered to escape her wrath. Whereas Mikhael had sat at the end of the table, comfortably sprawled, ankle on one knee. As he watched Raina threaten their lives, his dark gaze tracked the flash of her golden-green eyes, the way her voluptuous curves quivered with her indignation. Ramona had been pretty sure he had plans to take her on that snow dusted table. When he glanced her way while Raina was distracted and mouthed *Run now*, with a quirk of his lips, Ramona had prudently made her own escape.

She didn't live far from Raina's. As she'd walked home, she'd felt flakes melting on her cheeks and imagined Silas touching her face once again.

Turning her head toward Ruby's touch now, joy and a poignant despair filled her. It refused to go away. The memory of him was a ribbon wrapped around her heart, an adornment for a gift. As if her heart was the gift, or...

Whoa. She abruptly sat up, easing Raina's head off her lap before she stood. They performed the ritual sky clad and hadn't yet slipped back into the robes they'd brought, so Ramona held out her arms, watched the moonlight reflect off her pale skin, the scatterings of faint freckles she possessed.

Like the inside of a perfectly baked cinnamon roll, and likely tastes just as good. The town baker, who liked to outrageously flirt with his clients under his wife's indulgent eye, had described Ramona's skin that way. But those freckles had a more serious origin, which was what had inspired Ramona's thought process now.

"He left something," she realized. "I thought it was a feeling from me, and it is, partly. I'm making it stronger." Making her miss a stranger far more than was warranted.

Like a soul marking.

Almost as soon as she had the thought, the other two had put it together. Raina and Ramona were on their feet, kickass intent in their rigid forms.

"No..." Ramona gripped their hands. "I don't want it destroyed. I want to understand its shape. How it got there. How...I might have accepted it."

A soul marking had a lot of forms. It could be designed to melt like consumed candy, leaving a nice lingering memory, if that was all it was. But if not...

Though he hadn't looked back after he left the shop, when he'd stepped back from her, there'd been a cauldron of regret on his face.

She'd questioned that perception, whether it was just her wish that he'd felt that way, but now... He'd left her a gift. Was it something for any woman he touched, a thanks for her moment of favor or respite?

"Okay," Ruby said. "Stay still."

She laid her hand over Ramona's heart. Or rather, over Ramona's hand, because she already had her palm pressed there. "When I focus on it, it spins out from that point," Ramona said. "The stronger I feel his absence, or the more I think about him, the more I feel its hold."

Raina laid her hand over Ruby's, so she too could get a sense of what they were dealing with. Ruby was the best technical crafter of the three of them. So as she tuned into those energies, Ramona could feel them aligning, revealing themselves to the intent witch.

"It needs more than a simple Reveal spell," Ruby said, curiosity in her voice, and a reluctant admiration. "It's like an Unravel in a Reveal. For only knowing you a short time, he achieved a remarkable understanding of how your magic works, Ramona. Or his energy is just intuitively compatible with it. We can help stabilize it, but it's designed for you. You have to be the one to grasp the end and tug it free to open the spell, reveal its full nature."

Well, crap. Her magic could scramble the most stable spells better than a skillet of eggs. But it also usually worked out the way it was supposed to. Despite her being supremely pissed over her chandelier, Raina had probably enjoyed being taken on her dining room table by her powerful and handsome Dark Guardian. Right?

Ramona knew the best way to work with her magic was *not* to try and direct it. She couldn't push it in the direction she thought it should go. The way she wanted it.

That said, she still considered leaving it alone. Maybe feeling a hint of whatever this was, knowing it had been left for her, was enough. A gift that remained at her doorstep, something she could wake up to in the morning, step past as she came and went to work. Know it was there as she fell asleep.

It would be proof. But proof of what? The meaning of gifts was important, and to understand that meaning, some gifts had to be opened.

Damn it.

Fine. She took her place in their marked circle, mute acceptance, and the other two followed. They hadn't opened the circle yet, offering the proper farewell courtesies to the four quarters—go if you must, stay if you will—so little was needed to prepare for further energy work.

Because the three of them did magic together so regularly, reconnecting wasn't difficult, either. The strong hum she felt as they linked and engaged helped to reassure her, somewhat.

"Do the Unravel and feel your way through the Reveal," Ruby said, her hazel-colored gaze still gauging what couldn't be seen by the untrained eye. Raina had the same focus. "We'll fill in the gaps and if something goes haywire with it, we'll try to keep the core in place. Not the first time we've had to improvise in the face of the unknown. At least this time it's not life or death."

"If we're not building the track an ass hair's width ahead of the roller coaster wheels, I feel spoiled," Raina agreed.

"I don't want to lose it. I know that sounds idiotic, and desperate..." Had she really become so lonely she'd turn a chance encounter with an intriguing stranger into a major drama? One that thickened her throat, made her clasp the other two women's hands in fervent entreaty?

Raina touched her face. "Be easy, love. We get it. Mikhael is the world's biggest dick sometimes. It's what I'd expect from a guy over a thousand years old with a direct line to Lucifer himself. He's also everything I ever wanted in a male. Caring, protective, funny and scary intelligent. He gets my music playlists, which is the best compliment I can give a man. He knows what I need, sometimes even before I do. So a man can be a dick *and* someone worth keeping."

She shot a teasing look at Ruby. "Derek is even more of an overbearing, self-righteous prick, but Ruby refuses to kick his ancient ass to the curb for the same reason."

Ruby arched a brow. "Mikhael is older." But the tug at her lips said she didn't disagree. "Let's do this."

"Maybe try to throw a shield around it once it's revealed, so I don't obliterate it," Ramona said. Though if her magic wanted to zap it away before anyone caught a glimpse, even herself, it would. She'd have to accept that as what was meant to be.

Please don't.

Enough of this.

Ramona closed her eyes. She let the Chaos take her on a swirling ride down into her subconscious, where that torturous feeling was strongest. An arrow. She followed it, that absurdly deep sense of missing him, a winding path to her core. She should be mad at him for doing this to her, but she couldn't find any anger in herself. Just yearning.

There it was, sitting in a dark corner. It took the form of a porcelain box with a purple sparkling color like the T-shirt she'd worn that day. But when she put her hands on it, it shattered, the pieces spinning away. Her heart plummeted.

But then a glittering particle rose before her like a tiny sun. She hadn't broken the box. It had merely opened at her touch. The light drifted around her, eluded her grasp playfully. When she stopped trying to catch it, it settled on her upraised palm and became a dragonfly.

He'd done the delicate spellwork so subtly. Maybe when he was kissing her breast, his hands on her in such a distracting way...

As her fingers closed over the mote, it shimmered. Another unlocking, where her touch was the key. Golden light spilled forth, at first like the rays of the small sun, and then they began to twist into ribbons, moving in a serpentine dance around her. They encouraged her to dance with them, turn and spin. When the ribbons wrapped themselves over her arms, her upper body, she drew in a breath. Their sensual heat carried the memory of his touch, so vividly the desire for it tripled in her erratically beating heart.

"Ramona."

Slowly, she became aware they were calling to her, Ruby and Raina, coaxing her to open her eyes.

They were still holding her hands. Her arms were stretched toward them. A ribbon of fire visibly spiraled up the right one. When it reached her shoulder, it moved to her throat, wrapping around it once to form a collar that teased her pulse. The constriction affected her breathing, but not in the strangling way. The heat didn't burn her flesh, either. Instead, both sensations roused her darkest erotic imaginings, the fantasies she'd had of belonging to a male who could claim her like this.

As if hearing her thoughts, both reactions increased, just enough to shoot need straight down the center of her body.

When she gasped, she could almost hear the husky, satisfied male chuckle. The ribbon continued its spiral around her other arm. It wrapped around her waist, a thigh, down to the ankle, back up and...

She convulsed as a knowing touch passed over her sex, between her buttocks. Her knees gave out, her body offering itself to the bindings. Raina and Ruby lowered her to the ground as arousal spiked, teased. A moan came from her as the heat started a second full circuit, from the starting point at the first wrist again. She arched into the constriction, helpless to resist it.

Raina and Ruby kept their hands on hers, their palms at her back, holding her steady. Though she couldn't find words, immersed in the pleasure of the gift, their demeanor told her they knew she wasn't afraid or in distress. They remained watchful in case the spellcraft took a turn for the malevolent, but Raina's free hand stroked her hair, her green-gold eyes glowing, the succubus energy only adding to the potency of what she was experiencing.

The gift's intent wasn't to give her full release. There was a direct message to that. Silas intended to retain that pleasure for himself alone. The thought spiked in her vitals, a need for him that wouldn't ease until she saw him again.

But, Goddess... As if it knew she could take no more without that release happening, the thrumming heat and sensation started to ebb, the ribbons to disappear. Except at her wrists.

Her gaze fell upon them as the gold vanished in a shower of sparks, like the final strike of a blacksmith's hammer. In its place were two bands of script. The ink was a burned wood color, like a henna tattoo.

For only she that has my soul—one wrist—*can engage my sword.* The other wrist.

She stared at the words as Raina and Ruby helped her back into a full sitting position. Her body was throbbing.

"One of the writings of Alpha Behn." Raina's feral smile said she appreciated Silas's creativity. "'Love Letters Between a Noble Man and His Sister,' which I mostly interpreted as the author lusting after his sister, wanting to bed her, instead of his wife. But the line is beautiful, and I expect your Reaper has his own meaning behind the words. Probably sans the obvious sexual entendre about engaging his sword."

She passed a finger over the marks on Ramona's wrists, lifted a brow as Ramona shivered. "He's also got a kink flair to him. I'd say he's a presumptuous bastard, but for the nature of it."

At Ramona's curious look, Ruby explained. "It's fueled by your wishes and desires. As long as you want the marks, they will stay. If your feelings for him increase, they'll get deeper and stronger. When you don't want them, or if your feelings lessen, the marks will fade away at the same rate. We feel no coercion or manipulation to it." That reluctant admiration in Ruby's voice had increased. "It's very deft magic. Complicated."

And he'd put it in place in a matter of seconds, while giving her pleasure.

She also agreed with Raina. The sword thing wasn't necessarily a sexual reference. His protection was on her, his...interest. A message that had to mean *"I will be back."* Right?

"Your magic isn't the only thing he picked up on quickly," Raina noted. Ramona closed her hand over one of the marks, rubbed it with careful fingers, as if she might accidentally erase it.

"That's just fantasy."

"It's reality," Raina replied bluntly. "An orientation you've had to accept as a fantasy, thinking there was no man who could make it an option. I'd say he picked up that option and marked you as his. Whatever you did to him during those few minutes," she added dryly, "don't teach it to my demons. Overly attached clients are not good for business."

When Ramona touched the left mark, gooseflesh spread to where Ruby still gripped her upper arm. The heat of the other woman's palm was different from the heat in the ribbons. Ramona could feel the contrast. What was in the bands was definitely a strong echo of Silas's touch.

So where had he gone, Ramona wondered. And when would she see him again?

CHAPTER THREE

*R*uby drove her home. Ramona being at the wheel when she was unsettled could turn a vehicle into a weapon of mass destruction.

She said little, inviting Ruby's close scrutiny throughout the drive. But she had a lot to think about. Fortunately, Ruby understood that. When they parted, Ramona kissed Ruby's stomach, giving the unborn Derek-Ruby DNA peanut a blessing. Ruby touched Ramona's hair, a thanks and reminder that the love for her coven sisters went both ways.

She went up the front steps of her porch and slipped inside, letting out a relieved breath as she did. Home. The place where she never had to worry about what she was. It met her needs in a way nowhere else could.

She inhaled darkness and old wood, memory and history. The interior of her 1810 farmhouse matched the exterior. A wood stove and fireplace for heat and cooking. Screened windows for air conditioning. A kettle on the stove handled coffee and tea making. She had electricity, but she used it sparingly. A landline was accommodated by a beige-colored brick of a phone Cordelia could sell as an antique these days. Because Ramona rarely used it, the curly cord stayed bundled close to the base like a sleeping snake.

She lit two oil lamps. The light gleamed off the ivory tiles she'd layered over the scarred surface of her old farm table, the turned spindle legs of the six straw-bottomed chairs. She bought furniture created in times before complicated machinery. They did better here.

Plus, it made her feel close to her roots. She'd been raised in deep forests, places away from human civilization.

Like the universe, a Chaos witch is born without placeholders, things to define her. You must create those, project them from within.

Another Chaos witch had told her that. Prior to killing herself.

Ramona sank down on her couch and looked up at the high ceiling. A spider rested on an oblong, intricate web in one of the crevices created by the rafters.

She held up her wrists to look at them, then folded them over her stomach. Even in the car with Ruby, she kept touching the bands of ink and she did it now, her thumbs passing over them. Slow, back and forth. The words had a raised texture. She thought of his hand, holding her wrist, curved around it, his thumb on her pulse.

Because she hadn't climaxed while with Raina and Ruby, her body wanted to ride that wave back toward a crest. She wasn't averse to functional self-pleasuring to blunt the edge of physical need, but she wanted more than that. She didn't want to rush it.

She imagined him here, above her, a hand drifting over her cheek, moving to her throat. Her eyes fell half closed, chin lifting.

Take off the dress. That voice from deep in the earth, a command.

When Raina made the comment about Silas's preferences and Ramona's reaction, Ramona had defensively called it fantasy. However, as often as Ramona came to her bordello to watch, Raina had always known the shape of her desires. Desires that Ramona couldn't pursue safely with anyone.

It was at Sweet Dreams that Ramona had learned about her own preferences and what to call them. When managing one's sexual frustration and self-denial, it was important to use the right terminology.

As she obeyed the imagined command, she wanted to believe it wasn't imagined at all, that somewhere that spell connected directly to him. It didn't hurt the fantasy to believe it.

She wore nothing beneath the dress to deny him any part of her he wanted to see. Just the look in his eyes would make the bands on her wrists burn. Their combined desires would fuel them, the starting point to have those ribbons spiraling out again to restrain her upper arms, her throat. Crossing over her breasts, sliding around her small curves, plumping, tightening and lifting. Displaying her to him. He'd twine his hands in the ends of the ribbons, hold them. Hold her.

Because so much of her life was unpredictable, it made sense that a male who could bring control, enforce predictability, was a pervasive fantasy.

When Silas had been in her shop, it didn't feel as if he'd over-ridden her magic. He'd stepped into the middle of it, and her magic had been willing to revolve around him. She laid her palms on her thighs, slid them along the insides as she spread them to his gaze. An invitation.

My lord is my shepherd...

Initially, the time she spent observing at Raina's had been a practical exercise, learning how to manage sexual attraction. She was a witch, connected to the rhythms of the Earth, a woman with strong desires.

She'd quickly learned that males with that intoxicating Master vibe presented the greatest challenge to her control because...well, the irony. As long as it wasn't targeted directly at her, she could resist it. At least until she was alone and it fueled her very active solo sex life.

Even if she could go to bed with a man on a whim, she wasn't the type of person who did. But as soon as Silas had come into her shop, his proximity sent her spiraling into a vision of muscles shifting under her hands, slick bodies moving together in that rhythm that produced blissful Chaos. Because Chaos was a lack of control, and a climax was entirely that, in the right ways.

Silas's Mastery had stayed with her like the summer sun's lingering heat, a pledge it was only as far off as the next dawn. She slid her fingers over her sex, drew in an erratic breath. Those eyes, the green of lush velvet. All of it stroking her, teasing her.

I will make you come just by looking at you. Your hands and legs tied open with my gift, while my gaze alone shows you everything I can and will do to you.

He'd given her that promise in a glance. What would he give her with the rest of him?

Her hips lifted into her touch. She stroked, moaned, pleaded. Felt the rippling in her lower belly. Felt his gaze, his far too brief touch.

I'm making too much of this. But the nice thing about self-pleasuring was there was no such thing as too much.

She imagined hands tightening on her wrists, drawing them away, and stopped touching herself. She gasped as the throbbing of her flesh intensified with the frustrated jerk of her body.

No touch. Nothing but my gaze, my command. Show me how much you want me. Get wetter. Slicker. Show me.

Her hips rose and fell, straining for what her flesh and emptiness needed. Her cunt had dampened, but now, with nothing but the thought, his order, she knew it was slicker. The impact of her buttocks against the firm sofa cushion sent more shock waves through sensitive flesh.

She gripped the sofa arm behind her with both hands, breasts lifted and thrust out, offering it all to him. The ink around her wrists burned. She wanted the words branded to the bone.

Mouth, cock, touch, taste, her gasps for his ears alone, his eyes offered an exclusive feast.

Yes. Do you offer this to any other male?

Not in a while.

Never again.

For her, possession was a need, a dream. Of being the center of someone's existence, the only one to whom she'd give her body. A belonging that couldn't be questioned or challenged by any power in the universe. In this quiet place, her woman's soul might be overwhelmed by loneliness, but she was also powerful, claiming and owning the fantasy of believing in it.

Perhaps I'll forbid you to climax until I'm really here again. Order you to keep count of the times your body will rebelliously seek satisfaction in your dreams, so you wake with your release still slippery between your thighs. That way I'll know how many punishments you deserve.

I can't control my dreams.

You say that like it matters. I control everything about your pleasure.

You wouldn't be cruel enough to deny me an orgasm until I see you again.

Wouldn't I? I can be cruel in memorable ways.

He'd had a kindness, a patience that spoke to how disciplined and focused he could be. But when he turned all that toward a man's hunger, mixed it with the wolf she'd felt from him...yes. He'd had that cruelty to him. Remembering sent ripples through her core.

"Please..." Her heart thudded hard against the wall of her chest.

She wanted a man she could beg. One she could trust that much, to lay herself open, let him see how vast and deep her need was.

Keep begging, witch. It only makes me harder.

A smile in his voice, one that heated her within, took her toward conflagration. She envisioned him bringing that hardness to her emptiness, filling all of it.

She wet her lips, swallowed, writhed. Wetness dampened the tender pockets between thigh and sex. She was moaning, whimpering. Energy swirling, the curtains lifting, fitful breezes coming in the screens, the porch swing creaking, jangling on its chains.

She didn't have to stop, rein it back. Chaos magic was a toddler running amok, but she was home. Where she'd made sure it was all safe, at least when she was alone like this. Shielded and protected. No glassware to break.

"Please..."

I have you. Let it go. But do not touch yourself.

The climax grabbed her, her body convulsing. She writhed for him, dancing, her fingers clutching the cushions above her, breasts aching. All of her aching, shuddering, in a paroxysm of response that went on longer than most of her self-inflicted orgasms.

It was still over too soon, but it wasn't the end. She might be the only person in the world who stretched her sexual fantasy material out to include cuddling aftercare. She dreamed of him holding her, his hand idly stroking her hair. Though it was blonde, he'd said he saw it as red. Maybe she'd try red sometime soon.

What small talk would they share? Maybe what they'd cook for breakfast. Or things happening in her store. His Reaper shop talk. Where they might go on a play day, when they didn't have to work.

In his absence, she'd create a persona for him, a rich backstory and personal life to keep her company. A detailed fantasy of being a couple with someone.

Like what Ruby and Raina had found. Their matings had made Ramona a true third wheel, though she knew that was a pathetic characterization. If she needed anything in the world, they'd be here for her, and not just them. Derek and Mikhael considered her their family. Two Guardians, one Light and one Dark, including her inside their protection.

Sylvanus "Silas" Pendleton. She wouldn't likely see him again, she knew. He'd even designed the gift to allow for that possibility. Something that would fade and disappear with time. If she wanted to hurt her own feelings, she'd remind herself that deft spellwork had been as easy for him as a child's game. As such, it could be nothing more than an erotic thank you for the nice moment they'd shared, offering a forlorn witch pleasurable masturbation material for as long as she could keep it going.

Wow. That was an impressive piece of self-pity. The gift might not be everything she hoped it was, but she didn't accept that it was merely a token. She could choose to cherish the memory and accept what it could give her, not harp on what it left her wanting.

The thought eased the emotional slap she'd just given herself. Slowly, she centered herself again, until fantasies melted away and it was just her and the wind, the comfortable old wood smell of her house, the earthy scent of her spent body. With a sigh and rueful smile, she rose, slipped her dress back on and padded out to her back porch to sit on her swing. Bracing her hands on either side of her, she let her feet dangle and the swing rock as she peered out over her darkened property.

The nearby barn provided a loft annex to do additional energy work and experiments she didn't want to do inside the farmhouse. Learning to channel Chaotic energy, work Chaos magic, required room and nerves of steel. Flexible steel. Maybe rubber bands were the better description.

Tap, tap, tap as Buford came up the steps and bleated at her. Jumping nimbly on the swing, he collapsed his solid miniature goat bulk against her. He sniffed at her wrists, sneezed and stared at her with his clear eyes.

Buford was her familiar, the first of a small menagerie of animals that had found their way here. A cow, an elderly horse named Esmerelda, three sheep and a flock of chickens that gave her eggs. The barn was useful for them as well.

"They are strange, aren't they?" She passed a finger over one of her wrists and shivered. "But wondrous, too. I like them. Too much, probably."

Where are you, Silas? What happened? Maybe time worked differently for him, like between the Fae and human worlds. It didn't make the wait any easier.

Her thoughts had an effect on the swing. Buford settled in deeper as the rocking became more erratic. The front left corner moved ahead of the right, like when a person pushed off wrong and it jangled back and forth on the chains. She let it pass, let it play out, a minor irritation.

One night soon after the pixies had found her, she'd wandered away. They'd tracked her to a farm on the edge of their forest home. She'd been curled up against the side of a goat, among a herd of them on a warm summer night. The farmer had an electric fence, but one touch of her curious, tiny hand and it had fizzled, popped and shorted out.

As she put an arm around Buford, she remembered the solid feel of that mother goat, the musky smell, the softness of her udder against Ramona's hip. A stable heartbeat, warmth. Then the brush of pixie wings along her cheek, the touch of hands small as mouse paws. The pixies made her laugh, danced with her, led her away from the farmer's field and back into the forest.

When she was in her teens, they'd sought out another Chaos witch to guide her, but in the end, what helped her the most was accessing what lay within her. Figuring out a way to keep from going mad in front of that mirror.

The witch they'd introduced her to had not succeeded at that. Ramona's free hand curled against her knee, remembering Frieda's limp body lying across her lap. The blood drained from her wrists swirling in the bathtub.

It had taught her a vitally important lesson. If she fought it, resented it, she was missing the point. Chaos magic was her magic. It didn't happen to her. It *was* her. Part of who she was, her power to wield. She smiled, and the wind rocking the swing in an asymmetric way settled into a rhythm. Buford made a grunt of satisfaction.

She closed her eyes and reached out into the night. Her spirit rode the currents, danced with clouds, soared. The soft strips of a tattered cloak stroked her cheek as she twisted and turned. She was a cloaked witch on the wind, passing across the moon on a broom, a children's story with her striped stockings, a big wart on her hooked nose.

She could project her astral self into the ether just for the pleasure of flying, but she had a purpose tonight. Silas's being in her town hadn't been happenstance. Though she didn't know how far he might travel to collect a soul, the local papers had told her three people had died in and around their small town during the week he'd come through.

So ever since that week, she'd done this periodically, thrown out a net to see if she could snag a clue that added to her information about why he hadn't returned. Each time, she told herself she was looking for a pebble thrown into a swift river current. But she still did it.

Tonight, she caught something.

A ripple of wrongness sliced through that net. The power of it knocked her back into her body, an automatic safeguard she put into the traveling spellcraft. Her eyes sprang open and she was on her feet, off the swing and moving to the rail, Buford right with her. His eyes searched the night, his body just as tense as hers was.

She tried to grab the tail of it, see its true shape, but she already knew it was only an echo of what had already happened. But something wrong had been here, in their town. And Silas's energy was tied to that wrongness.

A confrontation.

Though she lost track of time seeking answers in the night, she couldn't learn more than that. When she at last settled uneasily back into the swing, she pulled a blanket from the top of it to wrap around herself and gathered the watchful Buford closer.

The spellcraft Silas had left on her wouldn't still exist if he had been killed. On that somewhat reassuring thought, the constriction around her heart eased, but her brow still creased as she considered the possibilities.

Whatever Silas had tangled with had been an enemy to all things that made life worth living, something that threatened the soul. But he'd taken care of it. Its energy would have lingered longer than Silas's if it had prevailed. Plus Mikhael had told Raina that Reapers had assigned divisions of a sort, so he'd have had backup.

Reassuring thoughts for his wellbeing, but leaving her only a couple possibilities for the reason he hadn't returned, choices he'd made. She would *not* act like a crazy stalker and have Mikhael dig deeper to verify his whereabouts. Or suffer embarrassment when the Dark Guardian told her Reaper business was their own, but he was sure Silas was fine.

She pushed that into the self-pity pool to hopefully drown and leave her be. At least for tonight. The threads of life were playful children sometimes, playing tag, hide and seek. Crossing the paths of other threads, sometimes getting tied up in knots.

Her gaze fell to her wrists, and a faint smile touched her lips, dissipating the lingering uneasiness. He'd certainly left *her* tied up in knots.

She would not believe it was a casual gift, an afterthought. When she spoke to the night, sincerity infused the words, their power coming straight from her heart.

"Wherever you are, Reaper," she whispered, "know that I carry your marks willingly. And I would welcome you back to my arms. I wish the blessings of the Lord and Lady upon you, so that might happen sooner than later."

In short, bring your fine ass back here, before I lose my mind.

CHAPTER FOUR

Sixteen months later...

"*How* come there are no sexy Reaper figurines?" The one she placed in her display window was a nutcracker with a terrifying skeleton face, glinting ruby chips in the eye sockets and a black cloak sewn with silver threads to pick up the glint of the scythe it carried. "Don't get me wrong. You're all kinds of intimidating, and your craftsmanship is impressive, but you don't make me want to drop my panties. If I was wearing any."

She returned to the aisle from which she'd retrieved the nutcracker. Two shelves were crammed full of Reapers. She had whimsical ones, like a battery-powered figure possessing a maniacal grin and red lights that ignited in the eye sockets. When a button concealed in his cloak was pressed, the resulting sound was caught between a desolate wind and an animal growl. Another was a ceramic birthday centerpiece, with an outstretched skeletal hand and a charming smirk on its bony face.

She also had more serious ones, like the recently purchased piece crafted by a master woodworker. The Reaper was two feet tall and the centerpiece for a front entry display of her most tempting wares. The artisan had used the grains and imperfections in the wood to give his creation a gnarled appearance. Maybe she could ask him for a commissioned piece. A sexy Reaper.

Or she could mark all the Reapers fifty percent off, an early

Halloween sale or straight up clearance. A symbolic clearing of her mind.

The missing and wanting him hadn't abated. It had grown stronger. Raina and Ruby had offered to help her remove the wrist markers, no matter that her desires were driving their continued presence. But a Chaos witch understood better than most when a magic was behaving exactly as it should. It wasn't a new lesson for her, realizing the truth could be torture.

Maybe time did work differently for a Reaper. Or he was a fucking sadist.

As her toy train did a spiraling loop above her and chugged onward, she pulled forth a quote she'd been using to keep her sane. "Time to 'either get a train of cheerful ideas, or hang myself by tomorrow morning.'" Samuel Richardson, *The History of Clarissa Harlowe.*

Being well read was an excellent way to confirm you were walking a path beaten by a lot of feet. It helped pull oneself back from total hysteria, versus being overly tempted to go over the ledge with the other lemmings.

"I guess I was right. At least the part about him not coming back." Her voice echoed through the shop, but not the way it usually did when she was by herself. It bounced off something that hadn't been there a moment ago.

She wasn't alone.

"I meant to come back."

~

She had her hand on the animatronic Reaper. When her grip tightened on it, damn if she didn't activate it. Tinny demonic growls vibrated under her touch. She pulled her hand away, but went fully still. She'd imagined whole conversations where he spoke to her, gave her commands. Talked about what kind of fertilizer would be best in her vegetable garden, or didn't that cloud in the sky look like a dragon?

But it wasn't her mind who'd just spoken to her.

She hadn't heard the door open, but she felt the wash of energy course through her shop, over her. Around her. Her pulse accelerated like the Ferrari that Raina claimed Mikhael loved even more than her.

How many times had she heard Silas's voice in her mind, knowing she was only recalling it, possibly embellishing its deeper notes, the sensual murmur of syllables against her breast, her throat? After almost a year and a half, she really should have lost the true cadence and tone, simply because that was what time did to the memory. But not a single thing was unfamiliar. It came back to her like a long-lost wish, a rush as glorious as when she'd first felt it.

"Well. You did come back. You're here, aren't you?" Her voice was remarkably even. Smooth on all the surfaces, like a concrete box.

With a bomb ticking inside it.

The frame of the shelving shimmered, and she steadied it, in that indirect way she did. Couldn't manage her magic in a straight line. Had to run at it sideways. The dense wave that had been about to topple and break everything in front of her changed direction. Went up toward the high ceiling, played havoc with her kites, making their wings rattle.

He was moving. She could see the blurred outline of him in the corner of her eye, her head slightly averted to avoid a clear image. He had been standing at the top of the aisle, and he was coming closer to her.

She slipped away, rounding the corner to stand on the other side of the tall shelf unit. She gripped the edge. "Stay there," she said. "Please."

He paused, three feet of polished wood separating them. She stared down her aisle, away from him. Her gaze fell on her white-knuckled hand. She was wearing a long-sleeved shirt today, the draped sleeves edged with lace that fell over her knuckles. Three rings. Middle finger, ring finger and thumb. A pentagram etched into a slender silver band on the ring finger. A purple stone clasped by a scrolling Celtic design displayed on the middle. She wore a man's heavy silver ring on her thumb, and she'd had to pad the inside to make it fit.

Saul, one of Raina's incubi, was a fan of the *Sons of Anarchy* TV series, about an MC club who used the Reaper on their cut. He'd learned of her interest in Reaper designs and given the ring to her for her birthday. Raina's sex demons viewed Ramona as an adored aunt.

From one angle, the Reaper carried a scythe. From another, the scythe blade looked like the Reaper's cloak sleeve, the handle of the scythe transformed into a sword he was drawing forth.

It was scary and intimidating. And kind of hot. Maybe the draped sleeves would conceal it. Not that anything could conceal the army of Reapers he was standing in front of.

The ceramic birthday centerpiece was motion activated. As he shifted in front of the shelf, it spoke in its Alan Rickman, Snape-inspired tone, the syllables drawn out with menacing reassurance. "Relax. I'm just here for cake."

Her magic tossed a Reaper dish cloth over it, burying it under the folds.

Please, let a customer come warred in her head with *Don't let anything disrupt this moment.* She didn't know why she felt so panicked.

"Is it good that I'm here?" he asked.

"I don't know." She had no idea how she was managing a normal tone. Or maybe it only seemed that way to her. Since she was having a difficult time finding breath, she could be sounding like she was about to hyperventilate. "You've been gone so long; I've created a whole life for you. Hobbies, interests, family. Friends. What you most dislike about your boss. Who is your boss, by the way?"

"It's complicated. So you've been thinking about me."

"No. Of course not." She closed her eyes. He moved around the shelf, came up behind her. She shivered.

"You're not listening," she whispered.

"I am. But I've waited an eternity to be close to you again." The roughness to his voice destroyed another layer of her resolve to hold it together. "It's made me...lose my manners."

She was standing in front of a shelf of puzzles. She'd arranged some of the boxes upright to display the pictures on front. They fell over, quiet thumps, sliding to precarious positions.

In an open space in her shop, she had a puzzle table, always with one in process. Customers with a few minutes and the inclination could try to find a few more connecting pieces. She kept the box hidden so they wouldn't know what the whole picture was, until enough pieces had been put in place to see it start to come together.

She wouldn't ask him why he'd been gone so long. She'd decided she might lose more than she could bear in knowing. She'd made peace with that decision, but it was a fragile peace.

"What's good in life is always simple." She said it aloud, because she needed the reinforcement, the reminder. The maxim routinely helped her forge a path through complicated layers of spellcraft. Or emotions.

He touched her, stroked her hair slowly, with deliberate patience. She had to be imagining the tremor in his fingers in that first second of contact. Because after that his touch held the same confidence and surety she remembered and occasionally tried to bury. But when it came to him, her memory was a dog forever off the leash, running after a scent until its heart exploded and it dropped, insensible to anything.

Lucky dog.

His voice dropped another octave, something raw and intent in the tone. "Tell me about my life, witch. My hobbies. Interests."

She grabbed for the distraction. "Rock painting. Because you travel so much. You paint them and leave them in random places for people to find." Her gaze slid to her ring. "Do you carry a scythe?"

She'd had dreams about it, the gleam of the blade, a flash of lightning across skeletal sockets, illuminating and turning them into fathomless eyes.

"Yes. It can transform into other things, too."

"Like what? And why?"

A shift to his fingers, as if he had lifted a shoulder. "Depends on the soul. I like the shepherd's crook best."

His knuckles whispered down her upper arm, setting off a ribbon of heat beneath the snug fit of her sleeve.

"Don't do that," she said.

He stilled, but didn't draw back, so she moved out of reach again, three more steps to the next section of shelves. Potions. Her gaze rested on one for adult acne.

The last woman who had purchased it had woken up after its first use to discover a blue rash staining the tops of her hands. In her dermatologist's lobby, she tripped over the mop of a custodial worker named Brahms. He caught her before she could fall. Glancing down at her hands, he'd smiled and said, "Blue is my favorite color."

They struck up a conversation, during which the rash simply faded away. They went on a date, and eventually fell in love. Which was the woman's original motive for wanting to clear up her skin problems. She had a tattoo of a blue heart placed on the back of her left hand, which Ramona saw when she was invited to their wedding.

The way to happiness, what someone truly wanted, was rarely a straight line. Before she understood Chaos magic, Ramona had tried to make potions to turn out the way they were "supposed to." When she learned she was a conduit, not a control, she'd learned the deep pleasure of watching her erratic magic do exactly what it needed to do.

But when things came too close to her own heart, it was hard not to guard it. To not be fearful about where a decision might take her. Trembling as she sensed him closing the distance between them again, she doggedly pressed onward with her description of his imagined life.

"You have siblings. Two brothers, one younger. You two older ones protected him from neighborhood bullies. Your favorite subject in school was math."

"Good choice. Sometimes all I did was count how long it had been since I last saw you. Hours, minutes, seconds. Heartbeats. I imagined it as a countdown to when I'd see you again."

He wasn't touching her this time, but he had his head dipped so his breath feathered across her ear, the tender skin of her throat. Her hair was pulled over one shoulder, leaving that side of her neck erotically vulnerable. "Why do you think I left that day, Ramona?"

It was the first time he'd ever said her name. Had he heard it that day? Maybe Raina had said it aloud where he could hear it.

She shook her head. "It doesn't matter. We don't have to talk about it. Ever."

"I'm getting the impression it's the only thing that matters. At least right in this moment." The tone of his voice shifted. A command, urgent. Imperative. "Show me."

She crossed her arms. "No. Have you earned that?"

"Turn around and look into my eyes. Decide for yourself."

"I can't."

One hand moved to her shoulder, an insistent pressure. She obeyed it, but she stubbornly kept her gaze down, staring at the planks of her oak floor. Then she saw his feet. Bare and muddy.

No. It wasn't mud. Layers of dried blood were spattered over his feet, ankles, shins. She could see through the tattered folds of a gray robe. The trousers under it were shredded up to his knees.

"Goddess." Her gaze raced upward, taking it all in. A rough twine rope belted the robe, but it was loose at his lean waist. Wide sleeves, also torn and bloodstained. Then she saw his other hand, held to his side. It was misshapen, broken. Two nails were missing.

As the startled sound of distress broke from her shocked lips, the strength he'd likely expended to chase her around her shelves, sound as in control as he'd been on the day he'd met her, abandoned him. He fell to his knees. She did her best to catch him, while his arm with the undamaged hand dropped around her waist, trying to help him stay upright.

His cowl covered his head. She pushed it back, her hands gentle, and saw the thick hair she'd remembered, only it was matted, the cowl separating from it stiffly. She stifled another startled gasp as she uncovered bone, a section of exposed skull.

"I'm sorry," he said against her abdomen. "But after...here was the first place I wanted to come. I couldn't wait. Don't be afraid." He had his forehead against her breasts. "I'm going to look at you."

She wasn't feeling fear. She was feeling rage, enough to vibrate her walls, rumble through the floorboards. Cold fury formed ice on her shelf edges. Who had done this to him?

Then he lifted his face and shock took over.

Being a witch, she was used to all the propaganda about her kind. She was okay with the modern-day holiday holdouts, like pointy shoes and hat, the latter supposedly inspired by the garb of European beer wenches. But there were the darker, more dangerous suggestions, such as witches casting curses on innocents, or making children and farm animals sick.

A reminder of how easily the wrong assumptions could be made, especially when driven by fear.

His face was like the Reaper on her ring. A naked skull, the bone the color of antique paper. But deep in those eye sockets, she saw the rich green color she remembered. There was some flesh on the right side of his face. A hint of his lips, a cheek and temple.

"Should have waited until it regenerated fully, until I looked the way you remembered, but I ended up here."

His voice, so calm and reasonable. A remarkable touch of humor, as if this was no big deal. But she heard more, too. She thought she possessed rage? Pure hellfire ran in the underground currents of his voice. The battle he'd endured to get here had been hard-fought. But that feeling was mixed with other needs, emanating from him so strongly she couldn't separate and decipher all of them.

"Silas, how can I help you? What can I do?"

That green light glowed deeper. "You know my name."

"Yes. Mikhael found it out. He's a Dark Guardian."

"Dark Guardians. Resourceful." He was still gazing at her. Even without the familiar tells, she recognized he was taking her in, every feature. "So beautiful."

"Yes, he is. Raina says he's too beautiful. It annoys her."

A glint among the green. The misdirect had amused him. Despite his appearance, that reaction held all the qualities that could touch her like a physical stroke and give her heat. The icicles on her shelves were melting, a sound like dripping rain. She felt some of it fall on her shoulder, penetrate her shirt, kiss her neck.

When stripped of everything, a soul's hunger had no normal limits. His gaze moved to that droplet, and then his unbroken hand went there. It was fully bone, but it feathered over her skin so lightly, so aware of what would give her pleasure. It was his touch. Just a different texture.

The roughness of his voice confirmed her thoughts about the direction of his. "I want to put my mouth there. Everywhere. But I guess I'll wait until I have lips again. Though biting you isn't off the table."

"Are you in pain?"

His gaze slid up to her. Instead of answering, he repeated the command he'd uttered moments before. The one she didn't want to resist. "Show me, Ramona."

She extended a trembling hand to him, the sleeve draped over what he wanted to see. "A gift should be unwrapped," she said.

He grasped the lacy hem, pushed it up.

At his touch, the heat ignited. The words had darkened over the months, a precise script in the richest dark brown against her flesh. At his regard, it shimmered with flame, the heat passing over her fingers and his.

He dropped his head down, turned her hand over and put his

mouth on her palm, her pulse. She felt that hint of his lips, but as he'd said, she mostly felt teeth. When he bit her as promised, a light graze, pleasure struck her. Her hand had fallen on his head, fingertips on bone, the heel of her hand on his damp hair.

He looked like hell, like he was torn up a million different ways. Yet he had her thinking of sex, instead of far more critical things. He seemed to need that reaction.

Chaos witches were often healers, and she was no exception. Patients had individual needs and reactions. When he moved his face to her midriff, rested it there, she curved both arms around him, holding him, a tall man on his knees. Hurting, but conveying she'd just welcomed him home in the way he needed, to start healing the right way.

It didn't end the doubts she'd had these many months, or resolve everything. She suspected he was still determined to tell her why. Eventually she'd have to hear it, because there was far more going on beyond her own concerns. Something had tried to destroy him, and maybe had almost succeeded.

"It's okay," she murmured "I'm mad and confused, but I'm glad you're here."

He smiled against her stomach. She wouldn't swear to it, not with the rain still dripping onto her from her shelves, but some of the moisture penetrating her shirt might be coming from tears. Who knew a person could cry with no tear ducts?

When he spoke, though, his voice had that same steadiness. "My apologies, but I need a place to pass out. I will be better once I wake."

"How are you not screaming?"

"I sort of screamed myself out. Plus, I'm trying to impress a girl with my fortitude. It helps when there's no muscle to give it away with twitching, or skin to show clammy sweat. Though I expect I smell like a charnel house."

At her curious pause, he added. "A vault for corpses. Like a morgue or a slaughterhouse. Sometimes I hold onto older terms, from different times."

"Like *gee golly whiz*?"

"It's *golly gee whiz*, and it's one of my personal favorites. After groovy. Or don't take any wooden nickels. That's the same as don't do anything stupid. Which I obviously did."

"Let's get you to my back room, then."

As he lifted himself to his feet, he seemed to be moving all right, if stiffly. But she was opening her healing instincts, more intimately connecting her to what was going on with his body. He was under a tremendous amount of physical duress, a combination of what he'd endured and how much energy his regeneration process was taking. She had no idea how he'd walked into her shop.

The girl *was* impressed.

They turned a corner, navigating around a tower of silk top hats, crowned with a stuffed white bunny toy, and he stumbled. He would have fallen back to his knees if she hadn't pressed up against his side, holding him with an arm around his waist. His other arm fell across her shoulders. She wished she was taller, because he was stooped in their entwined position. He gave her more of his weight than he knew he intended, but she bore up, covered it, so he wouldn't try to refuse her help.

Lady, he'd called it right. With her senses now fully probing everything going on with him, he smelled like death. Decaying, fetid death. Violent death, punctuated by tears, blood, terror.

She remembered that night at her house, all those months ago, after the moon ritual. Where she'd sensed something evil and wrong in the night.

"Is whatever you escaped coming after you?" She'd reach out to Raina and Ruby for reinforcements. They'd send it back to whatever hell it had come from, with twice as much damage as it had inflicted. People thought her a gentle witch, and she was. But no one would get to someone she cared about while she could protect them. She'd go after it until it would choose its worst nightmare rather than mess with who and what was hers again.

"Escaped? I kicked its ass. It's running from me." She heard the wry self-deprecation, liked him all the more for it.

"Not today." He gave her a serious answer then. "And not like that. No danger to you."

The cryptic comment was strained, so she decided to hold further questions for now.

She had a cot in her back room for when she wanted to catch an afternoon nap or preferred to sleep here. She eased him to the mattress, then hurried to the front to turn her Open sign to Closed and lock the door before returning to him.

He was unconscious. It startled her, but the even rise and fall of his chest, the twitch of his uninjured hand, helped reassure her. After all, he'd said he was going to pass out.

Her clunky 1950s rotary phone rang. It was a match for the one at the farmhouse, the loud jangle setting off her nerves. Even with the low tech, she sometimes had to perform magical acrobatic bait and switch tactics to keep her magic from sabotaging it. However, today it behaved, perhaps because of the urgency driving the call.

"Miss Ramona." It was Gina, Raina's youngest sex demon, who also served as her receptionist and hostess, since she couldn't serve clients unsupervised. Her ability to feed off of sexual energy could still get away from her and potentially injure them, even with Raina's protections in place. "We're trying on new role-playing costumes and doing skits to see who's the most convincing. Raina said you need to come over and—"

"She felt something off with me and wanted to make sure I was okay, without seeming like she was overreacting."

Gina paused. Before she could reply, Raina was on the phone. "The emotional blast through our Linking almost straightened my hair. What's happening?"

"He's here, Raina. He's come home."

The words matched how she felt. Though she'd stopped talking about him months ago, her wrists couldn't lie, couldn't say the connection hadn't remained, becoming all the stronger, welcoming him back to her.

Her sisters also knew how she'd suffered over it, evidenced by Raina's next words. "Tell him not to go anywhere. Ruby and I will be there shortly to barbecue his ass-dragging carcass."

"I think he's been trapped somewhere all these months. I don't know yet exactly what happened, and he says he'll be okay after he rests, but it was pretty bad." She paused. "Is Mikhael home from his last trip?"

"He'll be here by tonight, if whatever he's doing doesn't turn into a shitshow, which is what happens fifty percent of the time. Why do you ask?"

"Before he passed out, Silas seemed pretty certain nothing would be following him here, but I'm not so sure. Something feels off. I'll reach back out to you if Silas feels differently about it when he wakes, but I feel like it would be good if Mikhael could come by when he gets home. I assume Derek's still gone."

"Yes. He'll be back with Ruby and Jem later in the week, though."

Whenever her thoughts were drawn toward Ruby's young son and Derek's devotion to them, the family Ruby so richly deserved to have after all she'd endured to get them, it gave Ramona a bolstering warmth. A welcome feeling now, even though she couldn't linger over it. "All right. I need to tend to him."

"You sure you're okay? I can come over until Mikhael gets back."

"I'm a lot of things right now, but no. Thanks for offering."

Even though Ramona could feel her concern, she knew Raina would respect her wishes. When Ramona cut the connection, she returned to Silas's side.

Healing was a Chaos witch skill because the body of any species was a complex thing, with a lot of chaotic energy to it. She could tap into it, find her way to what was needed. Doing it while the patient was unconscious helped minimize their pain and discomfort.

The bloodstained cloak was unsalvageable, the rotting death smell embedded in the fibers. He must have been filtering that out for her, with the same remnants of power that had kept him on his feet as long as he'd managed. His upper body was mostly regenerated, but where blood had dried the cloak, she discovered the skin beneath had been flayed or cut from him. It explained the nicks on the exposed bones.

Her anger at the brutality wouldn't help, so she focused on what would. Warm water drawn from the tub in her full bathroom helped her loosen and free the fabric from abused skin. As she slipped the loosely knotted rope at his waist, her fingers grazed his firm abdomen, the line of hair above his navel. As Raina had said, everything had a mother.

His fingers on the one hand had been crushed, but the busy swirl of aural colors around it were evidence of the energy working to repair the bone.

No wonder he'd passed out. He'd diverted vital healing energy to get to her, speak to her, resurrect the desire between them. Did he feel he'd needed to do that to ensure a proper welcome? Had he come to her as his best choice of a safe haven?

It didn't matter. His relief at being with her, his pleasure at seeing her again, had been sincere. Plus, anyone in need could always find a haven with her. Not just sexy Reapers.

She remembered the fine grace and beauty of his limbs, his torso and hips. A noble, strong face. An interesting one. She wondered that the Goddess didn't darken the sky and boil the seas when someone tried to destroy one of Her creations this way. But maybe that was why She'd built them unexpectedly resilient, knowing her creations' penchant for destruction.

Now that he was sleeping deeply, the reconstructed skin was knitting even more swiftly, moving upward from his collar bones and throat, reconstructing that noble visage.

While what was going on with his hand was definitely an immortal's healing power, this part was different. She leaned in, studied the process. It was possible that the skeletal visage was his true Reaper form. On a normal day, perhaps the mortal covering could be shed and shrugged back on as a Transform spell.

Which meant he'd chosen to keep the mortal covering. Let it be cut and flayed from him. To confuse his enemy? Or buy time?

Pushing and adjusting his body as carefully as possible to remove the cloak, she discovered the man was far more solid than he looked. When she eventually managed it, she dropped the ruined garment to the floor, leaving him only in the ragged trousers.

Her heart tightened. Tremendous effort had gone into hurting him. A ripple of uneasiness came with the thought, because what she saw said killing him wasn't the priority. This effort was either to punish or force him to do something he wasn't willing to do.

Forming a square with her two hands like a small screen, she passed it over his body, focusing on that rectangular space. A magical form of X-ray, to probe, scan and see if there was anything her talents could do to reinforce or augment his body's own healing ability.

She paused over the center of his chest. There was something there. A dense mass, a...

It moved. And spat darkness at her.

In an instant, she was against the opposite wall, one flattened palm up in a defensive warding, the other in an offensive claw, ready to cast a counter.

For several intent moments, she waited and watched. Nothing. Silas remained unconscious. She took a cautious step toward the cot. Then another. Close enough to see a symbol now visible on his chest, the texture and color of ash soot. It set off every alarm she had, confirming why she'd wanted Mikhael.

Dark Soul magic pulsed from it.

Shit.

Did Silas know he'd been marked with a curse?

She approached cautiously, her gaze narrowing as the mark faded from view, a monster retreating back beneath the bed. The reaction had been a warning, but she sensed she'd been a distraction. Its prey held its focus.

Silas.

She wouldn't probe that area again, not until Mikhael was here or Silas was awake. While she could handle a lot of things, if a Reaper was on par with a Guardian, whatever had the power to curse him fell in line with their hierarchy and she wouldn't let pride result in catastrophe.

For now, while the curse or whatever it was lay dormant again, she'd do what she could to get him back on his feet. Then they could figure out what was needed, and who else needed their ass kicked.

Since his trousers were in no better shape than the cloak, she fetched sewing shears to cut him out of them. Settling on the edge of the cot, her hip pressed against his calf, she grasped the fabric below his left knee in a careful hand. Some people were ticklish around the knees. The tender thought helped mitigate her apprehension as she positioned the blades to cut the fabric.

In the next blink, things became far more alarming again.

Her patient shot out of sleep like a fish yanked from the water by a sharp hook. But what the fish brought into the boat made that hook look like a paperclip.

He'd told her he carried a scythe. She saw it up close and personal, conjured in a flash of heat and grasped in his intact hand. The blade was wider than the span of his shoulders. And it was notched under her throat.

Green fire blazed in his eye sockets. The lethal focus left no doubt he *had* held his own in whatever fight he'd left behind. He was the thing that gave monsters nightmares.

This wasn't that curse's doing. As her heart flailed on the edge of full arrest, a working part of her brain observed how much sense a protection spell would have made while working on a man who'd just escaped severe violent trauma.

She'd had no time to raise a counter that wouldn't harm him, but her magic didn't usually wait on her conscious decisions when her life was in peril. A vine was wrapping itself around the handle above his grasped hand, sprouting little yellow flowers and then growing cucumbers over the edge of the blade. It only took a couple seconds for them to achieve the size and weight that put enough pressure against the blade to sever the vine. Several of the vegetables tumbled to the floor. One landed on her foot with a thump.

The fire in his eyes flickered. The point of the blade eased back a spare inch. She could sense many things happening in his disoriented mind, but she'd count on him being the male she believed him to be. Months of unbridled imaginings with no information to change their direction could give a woman faith in all sorts of unlikely things.

"Silas."

At the sound of his name, slowly, that fire died back. Then, in one shift, his face was restored to its human look. Still bearing some cuts, but no open patches to show bone. Confirming her theory, he'd healed enough to use the Transform spellcraft. A power nap worked wonders for an immortal.

The scythe vanished. She'd yelped when he'd lunged at her throat, but a different sound, one of relief, came to her as he put his hand there instead. His thumb brushed the cut squeezing out tiny beads of blood.

If she'd taken a deep breath, shifted at all, the blade would have severed her windpipe. He muttered an oath.

"I shouldn't have come until I was healed."

He was trying to push off the cot. Perhaps he didn't realize how clumsily he was failing at it. Transform ability or not, his body was doing a major heal. It had no patience left for any other major activity.

He might be too strong for her to hold him, but not if they were talking the power of will. Hers for him to stay. Plus his desire not to leave, which she sensed was gratifyingly strong.

He'd put his foot on one of the cucumbers. It puzzled him enough to look down, recognize what the bumpy-textured impediment was. She scooped it up to keep it from being squished. The other two had gone under the bed. She'd get them later. They'd make a good salad. As she put her other hand on his forearm, she found his skin was warm. She wanted to stroke the small hairs layered there. Instead she gave him her best stern healer look.

"There's a variety of reasons you chose to come to me, I hope, but one was you thought you could regain your strength here. You could. Can." She pointed the cucumber at him for emphasis. "I don't care how often you whip out your scythe, you're not leaving."

He blinked at the vegetable. After a tense moment, his lips twitched. "Going to stop me, little witch?"

"Call me little witch again, and the ass-kicking you just had—I'm sorry, dished out—will seem like a picnic."

Despite the exchange, she saw the sincere struggle over it in his face. He didn't want to cause her harm. Because of that, her tone softened. "I'm all right. You didn't hurt me. You're still you."

It was that way. When you endured something horrible, you had to remind yourself, send out that challenge. *You didn't win. You may have taken everything that I loved, but you still didn't win, because I still have me.* The lifetime companion that never left. The one that could be your best friend, your advocate, your truest helpmeet.

He had covered her hand, and their fingers had twined, hers tightening on his. Too much. She eased the grip, though he didn't seem to mind the hold as he stared at her.

At length, his gaze shifted to the largest thing in the room with them. When he blinked again, as if doubting his whereabouts, his lips curved in a slow smile, as if he'd found what he was looking at a familiar and welcome sight.

The back rooms of her shop were divided between storage, a full bathroom, and a weaving room. Her cot was in the weaving room. She had several types of looms in here, the largest one an eight by ten Navajo frame loom made of maple and big enough to do carpets. Ruby had once asked why Ramona didn't put it somewhere on the farm, where she could have windows. With how deep she went in her head when she used it, she didn't need them. The pattern she created was a world coming together.

Same for the thread she spun from a variety of materials. Silk, wools, cotton. His attention had moved to that section now. While like the looms, she had several different spinning devices, like a drop spindle and a Charkha, her favorite was her spinning wheel. Polished wood, and over a century old, it held the vibrations of its past users. Whenever she laid her hands on it, she felt like she was reconnecting to souls who knew her, fingertips meeting through the windowpanes of time.

"You make your own thread," he said.

"Some. I also buy or barter from others."

The intent to leave that was keeping his body upright seemed to reluctantly ease. "I came to the right place to reconnect to this world. A weaver, a spinner." He sent her a look. "You asked who my boss is. It's the Fates, technically."

"When did this happen?" The suspicion forming in her heart made it an effort to push out the words. She admitted she wanted it confirmed, though. Even if it was pointless pride, it would be a balm on the hurt she'd nursed and turned into other even more painful possibilities.

His eyes held hers. Despite whatever else he was dealing with, he was noting her reactions, logging them. "Same day we met. Though don't let me off the hook just because I was trapped in a pit of interdimensional evil."

"Wouldn't dream of it." Her heart thudded painfully. Their hands were still linked, and she'd shifted her chair closer between his knees. "You're not the first jerk to use that excuse for bailing on me. When did you get free?"

That furrowed brow again. "Not long before I came here. I had to get Cal to The Gate first. After that, my mind wasn't clear on a lot of things, but the need to get here was."

It made sense. An unconscious choice, fixating on his last good memory. *You're trying to protect yourself, and there are bigger issues right now*, she told herself. "Cal?"

"The soul I was supposed to shepherd that day."

"Shepherd does sound a little less scary," she noted. "Is that why you prefer it?"

He reached out, tapped her ring. "Lot of propaganda out there. Making us something to fear. Big, bad and scary."

She'd seen the flash of dangerous heat in his eyes, felt its energy when he'd brought that scythe into the equation. He could be something to fear. She wasn't going to remind him of that, since he seemed to have decided to stay. But the big, bad and scary was probably also why he'd gotten a soul where it was supposed to be, despite what had tried to interfere with that.

Her gaze rose. Seeing his fully restored face, including those distracting lips and deep-set eyes, the gleam of his brows and hint of his hair growing back to feather against his forehead, brought a rush of other feelings. When they'd met, she'd thought the prominence of his bone structure had added to his captivating looks. Now she could almost see the shimmer of his true form beneath the firm skin. It didn't change her desire to stroke his skin, touch his mouth. It might actually increase it, knowing that, like her, he was something most would consider overwhelming. Or dreadful.

She looked down at the cucumber, turning it in her hands. "You heal fast."

"Faster when I'm trying to impress a beautiful witch."

She frowned. "Don't do that. I'm glad to see you. But even if I wasn't, you don't have to be charming when you feel like shit. Let the healing take the time it needs."

He deliberately touched her face, her jaw. She stubbornly kept her gaze on the vegetable, scraping at the bumps with her nail. "Ramona, I want to know if there's more I need to apologize for. I want to know why you thought I didn't come back sooner."

"There are plenty other things to deal with—"

"This is the matter I want to deal with right now. It's important." He dropped his touch back to her wrist, loosely holding it, stroking the words branded there.

"It doesn't matter. It wasn't true. It has no relevance."

"Tell me." He took the cucumber away and set it aside. Lifted her face to look at him. Even in a weakened state, he had a gaze that could laser right through a woman's defenses. Damn it all.

She sighed. "I figured you didn't come back for the same reason most men do, after they feel the shape of my magic. They realize it's too...unpredictable."

"Tell me who left you for that reason," he said with deceptive mildness. "Their current life will expire far sooner than they expect."

She chuckled, she couldn't help it, though other emotions were going to strangle her. "You sound like a mob guy. Can you do that? Expire someone's contract?"

"I can do lots of things. It's not my most impressive talent, though." That light smile was back, though she could tell it was on a close-to-snapping thread. He was an excellent masker, but she wasn't fooled. He was in pain.

She put her hands on his upper arms, applied pressure to ease him back to the cot. "Seriously, stop flirting. You're suffering."

When he laid back down, a breath escaped him. She noted the easing of his muscles as fatigue made itself known again. But when he lifted a hand to her face, his expression made her swallow every word she could have said.

"Flirting with you is the nicest thing I've done...in a while." It was the second time he'd paused over the issue of time. "How long have I been gone?"

Sixteen months, two weeks and twelve days. But what she said aloud was, "About a year and a half."

"Lord and Lady," he muttered. "Damn it all."

"How long did you think it had been?"

"In the translation of time there, it was a couple weeks."

Shock coursed through her. She'd thought about time distortions like in the Fae world, to justify his prolonged absence. But still... "Why weren't your own people, the ones in this time zone, looking for you?"

"They very well may have. But what we do...it's not unusual for a Reaper to take a few months to recharge, or disappear altogether when they can handle no more of it. Or their time to do it is simply done."

So guiding a soul from its body wasn't easy on the Reaper. She wondered if he meant physically or emotionally. Possibly both.

"While the ranks of a Wake are mind-connected," he continued, "and our Cast leadership can likewise speak to the commanders of those divisions, we are also solitary. When one of us vanishes from our collective minds, the Reaping schedule realigns. Because of that, we rarely question it. The Reaper may eventually reappear, or never return."

"But would that realignment happen if you were taken?"

"I'm not sure. I've never been completely out of contact with my Wake commander like this, and the connection has not yet reestablished itself, despite my return." His tone suggested that was unexpected. "I don't believe any of my kind have ever done what I did, and that may have affected the usual course of things."

"What did you do?"

His mouth tightened. "A Soul Collector tried to seize the soul and pull him into the demon realm of the Underworld. I followed. We're supposed to obliterate the soul rather than let it be taken. We're not ever supposed to cross that threshold. But I thought I could protect the soul, get us out of there, with him intact."

"Which you did. But the Soul Collector got there first because of me, didn't it?"

His gaze locked on hers. "I made an error in judgment that day, but spending time with you was not part of that error. You were not aware I had somewhere to be. The responsibility was mine. Understand?"

"If you understand how sorry I am it happened." She laid a hand on his arm. "There might be another reason you can't communicate with your Wake. I think you've been cursed with Dark Soul magic."

He didn't immediately react as she explained what had happened. But as she finished, he had his hand on his chest. When he concentrated, she saw him detect it.

And it realized it had been detected.

Silas became rigid again, his jaw set. As he probed deeper, the ash soot symbol came forth, and he dipped his head to look at it. The vein in his neck pulsed black, worrying her. She bit back her protest. She didn't know his capabilities, couldn't say that whatever he was doing to dislodge it wouldn't work.

But when a foreign body planted itself, capable of vast harm, even destroying its host, she expected that host would experience a primal desire to knock it loose, dig it out. Like using a blow torch to blast a leech off the skin, the revulsion a form of hysteria.

Silas didn't reach that point. Still, when he left off whatever he was attempting, too many moments later, the skin over the mark was weeping blood, and he was bent forward, breath shuddering out of him in a way that told her he was in agony.

"Damn it." His curse reassured her that what he was experiencing was the ebbing aftermath. As the mark faded to a dull impression and disappeared again, he stared at the spot. Put his hand over it, despite the blood. "It seems my pride may have caused far bigger problems."

"I doubt it was pride. The soul was yours to protect."

Silas pressed his lips together. "It's perhaps a good idea to ask your friend to send her beautiful Dark Guardian over."

"Already did. He's away right now, but due back soon."

He digested that. "You have good instincts."

"I have no interest in facing something coughed up from the demon world without serious backup."

He nodded, though his expression was brooding. After a brief hesitation, she retrieved the basin of water to clean the blood off his chest, since it was slipping down his abdomen toward the waistband of his trousers. Afterward, she'd offer him her shower, if he felt up to cleaning himself.

She pushed the chair out of the way and knelt between his spread knees, putting her hand on his leg to adjust herself on her heels. She brushed her hair back over one shoulder to keep it out of the way and wrung out the cloth. Then she looked up at him, and froze.

His brooding expression had altered, become something different. Though her trepidation and worries ran deep, she offered him a nervous smile. "It's funny how our bodies sometimes distract us with better things when it all gets to be too much."

He traced the side of her face with his fingertips. "It's one of the Lord and Lady's nicest miracles," he said. "Another is that there's more than one way a Reaper can restore his energy."

Which explained why he looked like he could be thinking what she was surprised he might be thinking, after all he'd been through. She also saw him tone it down, recognize the weight of what remained unresolved between them.

But as he moved his touch to her hair, winding a lock around his fingers, she had to admit a lot of things could be resolved without words. Particularly when a man's touch had just enough weight to it to tell her what kind of male rested behind those eyes, what he wanted from a woman.

The kind of woman who needed that exact thing from him.

I'd say he picked up that option and marked you as his.

She pressed her lips together, conscious of the position of her hand, poised at his chest and abdomen, and what held her in place.

"May I tend to you, my lord?"

Green fire sparked. "You may."

Yes, it was a miracle. A very welcome, heated one that sent electricity through her. She cleared her throat, put the cloth to his flesh. Sought a distraction for them both.

"You said Cal. Did you mean Cal Horscht?"

"Yes."

She didn't know much about Cal, but she recalled his obituary, people assembling for the funeral. "Will you tell me about him?" She noted Silas's abdomen was every bit as firm as it looked, muscle curving under the palm of her hand, separated by damp cloth. The arrow of hair above and below his navel gleamed with the moisture.

"He lived a colorful first life, though relatively sheltered, usual for a first incarnation. He was a young soul, so this was his first body," he added for her clarification. "Ideally, a soul is more protected on the first round, a sampler of possibilities. He played baseball as a teen, dreamed of making it to the minor leagues. Became a business owner instead, a pizza restaurant up north. Retired down here."

Her hand stilled as he spoke. The matter-of-fact glimpse of his job held the mysteries of life and death to most people, including her.

"Yes. He liked to fish. When his grandchildren came to visit, he'd take them out on his boat." She remembered that much, through the conversations of others. Few degrees of separation in a small town. "Do you get all that information when he's put...on your schedule?"

"I get the basics, but I usually gather more. Observe the soul a few times before their Reaping, to know what reaction I might expect when the death happens. Helps me know how best to prepare, to guide and care for them."

Silas paused. "During our time together in the Underworld, I learned far more."

"While you were going through this?" Her gaze slid over the bloodstained trousers.

"They were trying to force me to give him up, so I'd surrounded his soul energy. He could speak in my mind." His jaw set. "Cal was brave. He helped me persevere, tried to assist me however he could. For a new soul, he showed remarkable courage and resourcefulness."

He subsided, staring into space. She'd sought to distract him. Instead, regrettably, she saw her questions had taken him back to what he had endured.

In the company of the soul he'd been trying to save.

～

To make it end, all Silas needed to do was let go, expel the miniscule but treasured spark that Cal had become, hidden where nothing but Silas's own will could allow it to be reached.

Silas wouldn't consider it, would never consider it. The alternative was unacceptable; living with the knowledge he'd failed the soul he'd been charged to protect and shepherd to The Gate. But having Cal help him with the resolve had been immeasurably helpful. He would never forget the surprisingly intrepid soul, and hoped their paths would cross again.

He jerked, realizing the witch had spoken to him. A soft, "hey," before she leaned in, standing up on her knees to brush her lips against his shoulder. As she recognized his awareness, she laid her hands on him and slipped them around to his bare back. A loose hold, not restrictive, but a reminder of another body. Bringing him back to the present.

He shuddered at the feel of her mouth, and cupped her skull, stroking fingers through her blond locks. "I have dreamed of this hair. Touched with fire."

He thought of her wrists. The way the words had embedded themselves in her flesh, telling him the depth of her feeling, even months later. The bond between them...it had to be what he believed it to be.

But he wouldn't speak of it. His mind was soup, and he needed to go into a Deep Sleep, recharge, finish the full restoration of his body and spirit. But his need to be conscious and in this moment with her felt as important to his healing as the dormant regeneration period.

Plus he needed to reestablish ties with other Reapers and talk to the Dark Guardian about the Dark Soul marker embedded inside him. Its roots were buried deep. Not like a parasite. It wasn't drawing anything from him. Truth, he couldn't feel it when it was dormant. But that only made its potential purpose all the more dangerous.

Since the thought made him unwisely want to try to dig it out again, he gave her more of Cal's story when she settled back on her heels. The emotional blank spaces Cal had filled in as they endured hell together.

"His first wife cheated on him with his partner in the restaurant, and the two of them moved to Florida. That happened after the kids were in college or out in the world, saving ugly custody battles."

But the pain of betrayal remained. Learning that love could be a rose bush with more thorns than petals, and the heart's blood accounted for the deep red color in them, had been the first important imprint lesson for Cal's soul. As it was carried forward into different lives, those imprints would form foundation blocks. Depending on how he made peace with them, it guided his future choices. It didn't necessarily determine how bumpy the road ahead would be, though, since life had far more than one difficult lesson to teach a soul.

Silas had done everything he could to make Cal insensible of the things happening to him and around them in The Pit, the name they called the demon's Underworld realm. That horror wasn't intended to be part of those lessons. But Cal had realized enough to know Silas was fighting to protect him, and done what he could to help.

Silas's gaze went back to Ramona. She seemed to be mulling his words, possibly thinking about the vagaries of love and loyalty. Though he'd corrected her impression, he didn't like why she thought he'd left. He would take his first opportunity to prove she never should have believed that.

"Cal's heart attack happened while winding up the garden hose in the backyard. His youngest daughter was living with him to help out, but she was at work. He had a great dog. A chihuahua with a warrior's heart."

"Zed. I see his daughter walk him by the shop some days." She rested on her hip, leaning against his leg. "Cal's journey was more harrowing than most, but are they usually scared?"

The question would have meaning for her, as it did for anyone who asked. Everyone had lost someone. Or was facing their own mortality and what lay beyond it. He focused on answering her question, though his gaze lingered on her face, the curve of cheek, shape of her jaw and lips.

"It depends on the soul. There was a girl I escorted—she was not a new soul, but she died as a child and, depending on the maturity of the soul, that can be more jarring for some than others. Sometimes they don't let the wall fall between that life and the past ones as quickly, so they don't necessarily realize what lies ahead. She held onto her child's form and asked me a lot of questions on the way to The Gate. Held my hand the whole time."

It gave him a slight smile, remembering. He turned his hand over on his knee, looked at his palm. "Occasionally, her fingers would tighten on mine, when she felt the waves of fear that came from being separated from her mother, her family, and all she had known in life."

Ramona slipped her hand into his, and his fingers closed over hers as he shifted his gaze to her face. "She had blonde hair, too," he murmured. "Only whitish gold, like you see on the young, like swan feathers."

When they'd finally approached The Gate, she'd stopped, staring at it. He'd told her Reapers didn't cross The Gate, and she'd latched onto that. *How can you be sure what's on the other side of that is something okay? That it's not something to be afraid of?"*

Silas had dropped to his heels. She had seen him in his human form, much as Ramona was seeing him now. Despite the young soul's fear, she hadn't changed him into anything else, like a familiar relative. Which meant she saw him as a trusted authority figure.

He touched the outline of light around her energy, an affectionate reassurance. *"Fear is just the gateway to wonder. It's merely a matter of finding the courage to step through it. Besides, why would they send someone like me to guide you if it was scary?"*

He'd made a comic scary face, lifting his free hand to act like a monster's claw. She'd giggled. When he'd gently shepherded her through The Gate's light, she held onto his hand until the last moment, the rest of her disappearing, her fingers suddenly loosening and then sliding away, peaceful as a toy boat released into a pond's current.

"Silas?"

Another voice, just as gentle, bringing him back to the present. To the hand linked with his on his knee. He didn't know if he'd told her the full story or drifted off. He really needed that Deep Sleep. He was not acting like himself. He should be more concerned about that.

Gazing at him with a healer's insight, Ramona separated their hands, but only to rest her palms on his knees. "I'd like to give you some additional healing energy. I think it would help."

The Deep Sleep would be sufficient to restore him, but he was reluctant to give himself to unconsciousness so soon after being in her presence again. Though perhaps he should. When she glanced down, he realized he'd gripped her wrist again, was holding her tightly.

He hadn't been jesting about other methods of restoring himself. Being around her, inhaling her scent, touching her flesh, reminded him of all the comfort that could be found from a woman's body. The deep, rejuvenating pleasure of bringing her to the brink of surrender and well beyond it, made the thought of doing so almost irresistible.

Especially after what he had just experienced. He could still smell the stench of sulfur. Feel the agony of the poison fire, the cut of the flail, talons ripping...

He wanted to bury his nose in her hair, her soft bodice, her flesh. Between her legs, inhale the earthy scent of her arousal, reminding him how generosity, beauty, love and pleasure could purge the plagues of hate, pain and cruelty from his blood, his mind.

A Reaper had many job stresses, but he'd received a concentrated shot of all the worst aspects of them. He shouldn't have come here first. He had regenerated his form, but his mind, heart and soul were shredded.

Deep Sleep. He needed the Deep Sleep. But what he wanted was something very different from that. Wanted it strongly enough to call it a need.

She'd risen to her knees again, hands moving from his knees to his shoulders. Yet when she moved one hand to his nape, to stroke his hair, he gripped the other wrist and pulled them both in front of him to stop her from touching him.

Her hurt expression turned to something else as he put his forehead on her captured knuckles. Pressed it there and held. He couldn't hold back the words, the emotions surging dangerously behind them.

"You can't touch me like that, witch. I won't be able to control myself, and there is too much in me now. I will pin you to a wall and possess you completely, with no regard for the things we need to say to one another first. You will feel I used you, rather than wanted you. No one is allowed to treat you like that, including myself."

A tremor went through her that tightened his grip. While she wisely remained silent and very, very still, he took several breaths. Thought of her kneeling at his feet, tending him with her warm cloth and gentle hands. Ironically, the submissive nature that so tempted him helped him regain control. She deserved the best from him.

Time and courtship, what every Dominant male owed a strong woman who craved submission.

At last, he lifted his head. "Yes," he said formally, "I would be honored and grateful for your healing skills."

While her expression appeared calm, the little pulse in her throat was jumping, and he could feel the tension in her slim body. That Chaos energy that could turn her hair to fire was close, snapping in the air, electricity on his skin.

She might think she wanted him to take her over, but the fantasy of having a male rut on her with mindless need was far from the reality. Submission wasn't always sensible. Which meant he had to be the Master she needed.

Steadying the explosive edge of her response wasn't difficult, but it was a relief to find his ability to do so well within his range. He also had other tools in that arsenal, ones connected to a different, more earthy energy.

"Ramona," he said with quiet firmness. A reminder that she was making him wait for an answer.

She snapped out of her racing, erotic thoughts, which meant he could relax his jaw, stop gritting his teeth to restrain himself. The tendrils of desire from her had been playing up the columns of his thighs as noticeably as her fingers on his nape.

"Yes, sorry. If you could lie back, my lord."

When he did, he realized he might not have helped his control much. An accomplished witch wielding power was a sensual, moving exercise. Fortunately the academic side of him was curious, since he hadn't yet had the pleasure of watching her purposefully exercise her magic.

She prepped herself by tilting her head left to right once, a stretching of neck muscles. She gave him an absent smile, a surprisingly effective attempt to ease the intensity of the past few moments.

"Do you offer your healing talents to many in the community?"

"Sometimes. They tend to work out differently than expected. Almost always in the ways they're supposed to, but it's difficult for people to accept that. Some spontaneity is fun, but people like to be able to predict most things. I guess that's why so many people fear death, right? They don't know what to expect, can't predict how it will happen, or where they go afterward. I like what you said to the girl."

She had spread her palms out over him as she spoke. He saw the energy gather to her, as if eager to come to her hands, wind around them. He understood the feeling keenly. "Do you remember her name?" she asked.

"I remember all their names," he said. "Birdie. It was Brittany, but her baby brother called her Birdie. It stuck."

She smiled. The magic was spinning out, becoming a web of light drifting down over his bare chest, hips, arms and legs like a blanket. At its first touch, he felt things that brought relief and comfort from unexpected places. The touch of a snowflake on a brow. Sunlight on a car hood, felt through the palm. The wildness of a storm.

Dance with me in the storm.

I'll never bring you harm.

He kept his gaze upon her as the words danced through his mind. When his hand had been crushed, he'd held onto those two lines. Two partners dancing who couldn't be torn apart, as long as he could keep reciting them together. Just as Cal couldn't be torn from him.

She twisted her fingers around one another, separating the energy into threads she wove into his body, like stitches for a wound. While the pattern seemed random, the raw edges that had been ripped open were being brought together. With astounding strength of purpose, she was retrieving his shredded mind and spirit from that terrible, desolate place. That trauma was the biggest wound that needed healing, to clear his head and deal with that mark, what it meant.

Her eyes had fallen shut. She was focusing, intensifying the healing. Her Chaos magic unfurled fully. It had its own will and intent, not consciously guided by her, but still her.

Which was when he recognized the danger. Something he would have seen right off if his mind wasn't so scrambled.

As a witch, she would know to skirt the edges of the mark and leave it untouched. But Chaos and Dark Soul magic existed hip to hip with one another, and the healer in her came too close. What lived in that mark grabbed hold.

The veins in his regenerated flesh turned black as the invader used those routes to seize her glittering strands of magic. It reached for the fuel that Chaos magic could provide it. Even more importantly, it reached for *her*.

His current physical state be damned, he was off the bed, his scythe called back to hand. As he swung it, he shoved her away. A twisted marriage of golden and black energy arced in the air between them. He sliced through it and lit it up, torching the poison down to the smallest molecule. Ashes fell like rain.

Since the severing snapped the mark back into its unwilling host—him—his chest cavity burned like a son of a bitch.

When he'd shoved her, she'd landed on her pretty ass by the wall, but she'd sprung back up. She threw out what looked like...cupcake sprinkles. Each one speared a piece of toxic ash, spinning it down to the floor and dissolving it into a multi-colored mist that smelled like candy.

He was sure there was a reason it had taken that form. He'd have to ask her.

Unfortunately, the Deep Sleep had a way of coming for a Reaper, when the Reaper took too long to come to it. For one more moment he stood tall, the scythe grasped firmly. Then he swayed and she was lunging for him.

"I won't keep fainting in your arms," he promised her. "Do *not* do anything further until the Dark Guardian arrives."

Then he promptly lost consciousness again.

CHAPTER FIVE

For a male passing out, he'd delivered that last order with a pretty forceful look. He'd also been courteous enough to collapse on the cot.

After she wove shielding around herself, the storeroom and him, in case anything else unexpected tried to spout from that disturbing curse he carried, she made him as comfortable as she could.

When he started to shiver and mutter, she tucked more of her blankets around him. Then she fetched one of her essential oils and touched it to his forehead, palms and heart, a calming concoction that fortunately helped him subside into restfulness again. There was no room on the cot to lie alongside him, though the thought occurred to her.

She pulled out a selection of arcane titles from her library, but soon confirmed what she'd feared. She needed access to materials that pertained to his world uniquely. Souls, the afterlife, threats to that crossing. Dark Soul magic, Underworld doings.

She needed a Guardian. She hoped Mikhael hadn't run into that shitshow, or that Derek had come home earlier than expected. She didn't know much about Silas's kind, but everything she'd learned thus far said an attack on a Reaper wasn't a random thing. The mark's leap to suck in her magic was a hunger for an intent that required limitless fuel.

Setting her books to the side, she leaned back in her chair, studying him. She had her bare feet propped on the edge of the cot, her toes tucked under his thigh. His flesh was warm, and the contact told her how easily he was resting, giving her information on his heartbeat, the flow of blood and energy through him.

While doing the healing on him, she'd felt the shocking depth of the trauma he'd endured. She thought of what he'd said to her earlier. *There is more than one way a Reaper can restore his energy.*

When she'd attempted the more intimate touch of his shoulders, his nape, the sudden seizure of her hands, his forehead pressed to them, had been a supplication, but pure demand and need had been in his unshakable grip.

He'd told her he wouldn't take that route, not when things were not balanced between them. Very considerate, but some primal part of her had thought, *Yes. That's exactly what he needs.* There were few magics as potent for cleansing the psyche as a good, thorough coupling, leaving the mind empty and the body completely spent.

But he was protecting her, and she needed that protection. That he was honorable enough to offer it to her made her perversely want to offer that solution to him anyway.

She was a strong witch who could be extremely fragile—and destructive—when it came to sex. Which was also why she craved the surrender of submission so much.

She put her hand on his foot. He had a beautifully shaped sole, the arch coaxing the trail of her fingertips up to his ankle, his calf where the ragged trousers revealed them.

When he was ready for that shower, she'd offer to help him with the hard-to-reach places. Even Reapers probably needed that. She shook her head at herself, but it was as she'd said. The body didn't care that the fate of the world was at stake. All hers knew was the male it had desired for sixteen months was within reach of her fingertips, her mouth and her whole throbbing body.

It was also a coping mechanism, because she was worried as hell about him and that damn mark.

Thank Goddess, she got a ping on that Link she shared with Ruby and Raina. Raina, sending her a formless "push" that Mikhael was on his way.

When she heard the knock on the store's back entrance minutes later, it told her he had portaled to get to her, rather than using the Ferrari. That worried her more. An attack on a Reaper had implications grave enough to provoke a 911 response from a Dark Guardian.

When she let him in, the look on his face, even more intent and serious than usual, confirmed it.

Mikhael Roman was not a warm and cuddly male. *If Hell put out brochures recruiting Dark Guardians, he'd be their top poster boy.*

Raina's droll observation, and Ramona didn't disagree with it. As a sorcerer serving Lucifer and the Underworld's needs for over thirteen hundred years, Mikhael looked the part. Intimidating, powerful, with eyes of dark hellfire. He was also a sharp dresser, preferring bespoke suits that fit his broad shoulders perfectly. He chose colors drawn from the shadows of cemeteries, blacks and grays. With a single glance, he reminded anyone of all the powers and pleasures of darkness. And the consequences of getting on the wrong side of it.

The hotness must be a Guardian thing, because Derek had his own unique brand of it. The Light Guardian preferred jeans that he filled out just right, worn with his favorite pair of dragonskin boots. Outdoors, he usually wore a cowboy hat pulled low over his serious brow and get-lost-in-the-depths blue eyes. He and Mikhael had a friendship that wasn't always easy, as they represented opposite sides of the spectrum.

As a witch, Ramona understood the interdependent and mirrored relationship between light and dark. Light could burn away flesh, or heat it against the cold. Darkness could cocoon and comfort with its cloak, or take away a compass, plunging the heart into a void of despair.

While she took him to her weaving area, she gave Mikhael the latest details. "He's been unconscious for a while now. I know nothing of Reapers, but I sense his body has put him in the optimal state for healing."

"Are you all right?"

"Yes, my lord. Thank you." His penetrating gaze usually flustered her, since he radiated to the tenth power what the sexual Dominants who came to Raina's establishment did. Once, when he'd looked in her direction, she'd conjured a riding crop in his grasp.

In all fairness, the sex demons had been having an animated

discussion in Raina's parlor about pony play. Smoothly, so no one else had noticed, he'd laid the crop on a side table without reaction. It reduced her mortification, though Raina had tossed Ramona an amused comment.

"If a woman doesn't think about whips, chains and being naughty enough to earn a spanking around Mikhael, she's beyond dead."

With her mind on Silas, Ramona had far greater worries than her magic generating inappropriate reactions to Mikhael. "The mark is like a curse, but with a broader purpose. He tried to extract it, but it appears effectively weaponized to resist those attempts. When dormant, it's mostly undetectable, though I had a sense something was off when I first discovered it."

Mikhael reached out to brush his fingers along the cut on her neck, his sharpened eyes demanding an explanation.

"When I was tending him, I didn't shield myself as I should have. He's recuperating from a terrible trauma, and thought he was under attack," she said. "My injury was unintentional."

"I'll give her the opportunity to pay me back when she doesn't feel like she's kicking a puppy," said a weary voice.

They'd rounded the corner. Silas was sitting up on the cot, blinking sleepily, the blanket loosely held around his waist. The curve of his back showed the protrusions of his spine against smooth, muscled flesh.

Though he appeared stronger, his gaze composed, more like the male she remembered from months ago, he didn't rise at Mikhael's approach. He nodded in a formal manner. "Guardian. Thank you for coming."

"You do me honor," Mikhael returned. He pulled an extra chair closer to the cot and sat down, his gaze sweeping over Silas. "Do you know how or when the mark was inflicted? Or who did it?"

"That would certainly make things easier." Silas shook his head. "I expect it happened during my imprisonment in the demon realm. There were ample opportunities to insert it, since torture can be distracting."

He had the British gift for understatement. Come to think of it, the preciseness of his language sometimes reminded her of Colin Firth's character in *Kingsman*. An observation she thought might make him smile, in other circumstances.

"Can you attempt to determine its nature?" Silas was asking Mikhael. "As she indicated, it has reacted badly when poked, so I'd advise you protect yourself and her."

Mikhael's dark eyes glinted with his version of humor. "No one can shield her but her. Her magic disrupts regular spellwork, unless it's in the mood to be cooperative."

"I'll take care of my own protection." Ramona shot Silas a look. "Before you say it, I'm not leaving. Mikhael can provide backup so your scythe doesn't end up at my throat again."

Mikhael's gaze flickered. "She owes you more than one kick."

"No disagreement." Silas grimaced. "I shouldn't have come here and put her in the middle of this."

"The 17th century wants its stupid ideas about women's ability to speak for themselves back," she informed them. "For those of you who want to stay in this century, 'her' has the ability to level this building with you in it."

She didn't restrain the strength of the emotions she felt. "I missed you, for sixteen long months. Thought about you." She lifted her wrists. "Obviously. But all that aside, I think there's a reason you brought yourself back to the door of three powerful witches and two Guardians, don't you?"

Silas's eyes held that quality that made her want to look away, offer an apology for her tone, but she resisted it. She wasn't going to be cut out of helping him.

"Very well," he said at last. "Show me your shielding capabilities. If I'm satisfied, you may remain."

"I'm going to kick you now," she grated, but she cast the shield.

Silas raised a hand to Mikhael, a mute request to wait on the examination. The Reaper's eyes followed the shape of the shield she'd conjured. The pressure of his energy leaned against it, testing. It held, though Ramona did have to augment the barrier to do it. Just as she grew concerned he would push through, he apparently satisfied himself that it would hold against whatever might happen in this controlled environment. He nodded to Mikhael. "Whenever you're ready. Thank you for your patience."

Mikhael's brow quirked. "I'm familiar with the challenge of matching wills with a determined woman."

The Dark Guardian stood and slid out of his jacket. Ramona took it to her coat rack to hang it up. Mikhael's nod might have been simple thanks for the courtesy, but she thought she caught a reassurance as well. Probably because her response to Silas showed she wasn't as calm as she wanted to appear about this.

Mikhael resettled in the chair, legs braced as he leaned forward. When he reached toward Silas's chest, he had his long fingers splayed out and crooked to pull what information they could from the symbol.

Ramona had spent her life learning about the many ways that energy could be channeled, woven, and bound to other energies. While she knew how extensive Guardian training was, Mikhael had over a millennium of experience on top of it. He didn't appear to be using complicated spellcraft. He worked with only the amount of energy needed, wielding it with a precision so fine he could paint masterpieces with it.

Watching a Guardian do their shared craft was a rare and coveted privilege. But then her gaze shifted to Silas, and concern eclipsed her admiration.

The Reaper was still, but the effort was costing him. His fingers were clamped on the edge of the cot, a sign of pain or stress. But as he bore down, she held her tongue, because sometimes pain was preferable to uncertainty, doubt. Fear of the unknown.

Unexpectedly, his gaze shifted to her. "I was brought to *your* door," he managed. "That is what I like to consider fated. The other witches and their Guardians are just happy coincidence."

She swallowed. "Nice charm, but I'm not forgiving you yet. You still could have called. Cell phones are weapons of total evil, so they would have had baskets of them lying around the demon world."

He tried to smile, didn't manage it, but his eyes warmed on her. A man who could make her toes curl while he was in acute distress was definitely trouble. To her heart and sanity.

Despite their banter, she stayed watchful, ready to counter if the mark reacted against Mikhael or Silas. She kept her shielding shifting, a moving target. Trying to anchor it could irritate her magic, make it react in the wrong way.

Mikhael's face remained a passive mask, but tension grew across the broad line of his shoulders. The thigh of one braced leg bunched, the buttock against the seat of the chair flexed. Slowly, as if dealing with a complicated incendiary device, he drew his hand away from Silas.

He hadn't touched him, only hovered over the mark, but the symbol was fully visible, the ash color gone to dull silver. The quivering of Silas's shoulder muscles and biceps confirmed it was punishing its host for the exploration. Fortunately, as Mikhael withdrew, the mark faded, returning to its hidden state. Silas's body eased, even if his expression didn't.

"I believe it is a possession mark," Mikhael said. "Though it's a make I've never seen before. Put there to call you to its service when its owner is ready, for a purpose too deeply embedded to identify. It will only be removed when it is served, or you are dead. Even then, I expect the magic will implode, evading close inspection."

Silas's gaze flashed, a muscle twitching in his jaw. Ramona shifted uneasily. What vibrated from him suggested a storm. But when Silas spoke, his voice was controlled.

"Why a make you've never seen before?"

"It is as if she created it," the Dark Guardian said, dipping his head toward Ramona, "The Chaos element, that is. But her craft is graceful, skilled, imbued with her understanding of the power, what creates it, how it connects and binds itself to other strands. This is garbage magic. Someone with tremendous skill threw it into a pot and kept adding ingredients until it worked."

Mikhael paused. "They are a magic user, but not a crafter. I felt no desire or patience for that. There is no pride of making in this. Getting it to work, no matter the cost, was everything. Unfortunately, their determination was enough to achieve something astoundingly effective for the destructive purpose I suspect is its ultimate end."

"They were lucky, rather than good," Silas said grimly. "And destruction is far easier than creation."

Mikhael pushed the chair back so he could put an ankle on his opposite knee. "Yes and no. This is the luck that evil seeks, so I believe it was reinforced by someone closely watching the conjurer's work."

"A magic user tapping into Dark Soul magic, his purpose getting co-opted by demons he was sure he could control." Silas shook his head. "Like that happens."

"Only every single fucking time," Mikhael agreed. "If you can give me the details of everything, before, during and since this happened, then I will do all I can to track and find more information."

Silas pressed his lips together. "Good. I'll also need your assistance reaching my Wake. I believe the mark is preventing my communication with them."

"I'll get the message to the Reaper Cast leadership so your Wake commander will be aware of your situation. Where can they find you?"

"Here," Ramona said. "With me."

She flushed at Silas's sharp look. It was getting harder to pit her will against his. Even in tattered trousers and at less than his full strength, he was a being who gave orders, versus taking them. "You need a place to recuperate," she hedged. "You said so yourself. You'll have additional shielding and a second set of eyes on the mark."

"It's a sound decision," Mikhael noted.

Silas's steady look stayed on her. She would *not* squirm.

"As long as I am not putting her...*you* at an unacceptable level of risk, I will be here." He glanced at Mikhael. "Unless I earn her ire and she kicks me out."

"Pissing women off is what men do," Mikhael said. "My mate says as long as I provide sufficient compensation to balance it, I am welcome in her home, and her bed."

Since Silas had returned his attention to Ramona, the glint in his eyes deepened her flush. "Good point," she managed, salvaging her dignity. "I have some new inventory to unpack. Lots of shelves to dust."

That trace of a smile, but then Silas focused on Mikhael again. "I'll tell you all I remember."

The moment of sexual promise was the last levity the next half hour offered. Ramona adjusted her chair so she was still near, but took herself out of direct line of sight. She wanted the clarity being a silent observer afforded her, so she could absorb information while gauging reactions. Monitor with a healer's eye how Silas was doing.

As he excavated everything that had happened since she saw him last, he recited it dispassionately, like a police or military report. Mikhael listened with the same neutrality. Yet the more she heard about what he'd endured, the harder self-condemnation pummeled her.

She'd decided not to ask Mikhael or Derek to dig deeper. Told herself whatever his reasons for not coming back, she needed to respect them. What total bullshit. She'd been protecting herself, not wanting to be hurt with what she'd imagined the truth to be, bogged down in a history based on males who had nothing to do with this one.

Was there anything more pointless than one's baggage? Never had she seen a single case where the energy spent on it couldn't be put to far greater use. Like saving one's insta-crush from an interdimensional hell pit.

Yet guilt over it was an equally selfish act, unless she transformed it into a resolve to take him on his own merit going forward. Banish the cauldron of hurts, past history and painful memories that had made the destructive and distracting toxic brew in the first place.

"So that's it," Silas concluded. "From what we know about the mark now, I suspect I was allowed to 'escape,' though only when they realized I wouldn't abandon the soul. If I had let them have Cal, I expect they would have conducted that farce much sooner."

"It also supports our theory that there are two forces at work. This mark is far beyond a Soul Collector's skill, but perhaps the soul was intended as payment for trapping you where it could be inflicted. Yet you said no Reaper would have followed the soul into The Pit, so they could not have anticipated that. Or that you would be late. Which suggests putting the mark on you in The Pit was simply an opportunity they took advantage of."

A shadow crossed Silas's face. "While that made my act all the more foolish, I can't say I would have done differently."

"I'm not in a position to pass judgment on you, Reaper." Mikhael rose as Ramona brought him his jacket. As he shrugged into it, his gaze traveled to Ramona's Navajo loom. He cocked his head at Silas. "Being faithful to our priorities is the fabric we weave. Evil takes advantage of our decisions when they see that chance, but they can only stain that fabric. Our choices alone break the threads of who we are."

$\sim$

She pointed Silas to her full bathroom, because he expressed his desire for a shower. When he disappeared in that direction, his expression pensive, she walked Mikhael to the back door. "Is there anything I should do for him that I might be missing?"

Mikhael also appeared preoccupied, but his answer told her he'd given her question the proper weight. "Reapers are a critical part of the cycles of life and death. They execute the will of the Fates' Loom. If one has been compromised, that is a sobering thing." He offered her a serious look. "Silas belongs to the most experienced Wake of the Reaper Cast, so that makes the situation even graver. If he thinks of anything else, let Raina know. Until then, do what you can to encourage him to rest and fully recuperate. I see you watching him with a healer's eye, so I know you sense what I do, that he needs more time."

At her faintly irritated look, he shook his head. "I am not keeping you from the thick of things. Helping him find the best response to what was done to him is more important than you realize. Reapers are the only ones who do what they do. A death angel may be called in to help with a particularly troubled soul, but only a Reaper can connect with and deliver a soul to The Gate. Imagine if the millions of souls that die every day in the universe had no way to pass through it? If something has a plan to fuck with that, it can cause unimaginable chaos. Not the right kind."

He touched her face. The light caress stilled her, his dark eyes holding her. It was the touch of a Master to a sub. Not his own, but conveying a guidance she understood on levels as deep as the currents where her magic ran.

"You know what you are and what he is," Mikhael said quietly. "He needs that. I am not telling you to do anything you do not wish for yourself, but I am saying your instincts are correct. The pull between you is strong and can be useful. Good night. Call Raina if you need anything." A tip of his head. "And tell that Reaper he will not like what will happen if he puts his blade to your throat again. There are two witches who will make what he endured seem trivial."

She managed a smile. "You and Derek will just stand back and watch?"

"As dutiful and devoted mates, our task will be disposing of the body."

She let him out the back, but before she closed the door fully, she re-opened it, just a tiny crack, hoping it might go unnoticed. And that he'd depart the way he'd arrived, rather than calling his car to him.

The Dark Guardian moved into the center of the alleyway. A wash of cold air, and his wings emerged, making her draw in a delighted breath. They were shaped like a bat's wings, with wicked talons at the joints and a leathery look that moved the wind over them in a substantial rush as he used them to take flight, so swiftly he was gone in a blink.

He'd likely known she was watching, but she was glad Mikhael had indulged her wish. It left her with a nice adrenaline rush, since those he wasn't hunting rarely saw a Dark Guardian's wings.

The hunted ones didn't live to savor or share the experience.

Enjoying the little things was important. Particularly when there might be a demon slash sorcerer plot afoot to disrupt the order of life and death.

Returning to the weaving area, she was surprised to see Silas had already finished his shower. If she'd been him, she would have stood under the cleansing spray for a month. But his sense of duty apparently wouldn't allow him that indulgence. So much for her offer to scrub his back.

She should find him something in her clothing inventory, but she had no objection to the towel, tucked low around his waist. He leaned back in Mikhael's vacated chair, one leg bent so his heel was braced against a chair leg, the other leg extended. The towel parted to show a length of thigh. Not a deliberate tease. He was lost in thought, unaware he was displaying a lot of appealing firm male flesh. The charnel house smell was gone. Her soap fragrance mixed with the vividly remembered scent of him in her shop months ago. As she inhaled it, she sat down on the cot.

"The Reaping schedule has not reappeared in my mind," he told her. "Which means the Fates are being blocked from awareness of my return as well. Or this filth inside me has made me unfit to shepherd souls."

When Mikhael was here, he'd presented a calm, disciplined demeanor. Hearing the roiling emotions told her how much was going on below the surface. "I hope he's able to get the message to Honora quickly," he added. "My Wake commander."

"Too bad she's not in the phone book. Or accessible by carrier pigeon."

That dry smile, tinged with regret. "Yes. Though when she comes, I will have to summon extra courage to face her."

"After hearing what happened to you, I think you used up your reserves." Stabbed, boiled, the skin peeled from his flesh, his hand crushed, all to keep a soul's precious spark protected. She leaned forward to rest her hand on his tense one on his thigh. "Seriously, Silas. Courage is the one thing you don't lack."

"If I hadn't been late that day..." He shook his head.

She studied him. "You know, I've been flagellating myself for acting like a girl, thinking your absence had something to do with me. But it hasn't stopped my brain, and I don't think your guilt has yours, either. Whatever chain of events resulted in this, that mark took a lot of time to create. Random opportunity or not, this is a plan that has been in the works for a while."

He straightened, though he didn't remove his hand from her touch. "Which means it may not have been specific at all. I may not be the only Reaper targeted." Frustration. "Damn it, I wish there was a way to contact her directly. The Guardian has enough responsibilities of his own to pursue, without adding mine to them."

"Can you do it the old school way? Use a protected circle with a strong enough energy raising to send out a broadcast, without anyone else intercepting?"

Thoughtful, he gazed at her hand, the exposed wrist and lettering there. *For only she that has my soul...* His attention moved to her other hand, gripping her knee. *Can engage my sword.* Fitting, since she saw the warrior in his face.

"If needed, we could call Ruby and Raina," she added. "As a trinity, we can channel enough energy to reach Mars."

The green eyes twinkled. One moment a warrior, the next a sexy librarian. She really needed to get him some metal spectacles. "It's worth a try," he acknowledged. "I'm accomplished at channeling and focusing energy flow. For a message, just the two of us might be sufficient. If our intent isn't directed toward the mark, it should remain dormant, but that's not a certainty."

"I can cast a containment around it that will flag us if it wakes up," she said. "You really do need rest before you do anything else, though. You're continuing to squeeze a mustard bottle that's almost empty."

"I won't delay if others might be at risk."

"Thought you might say that." She summoned her own courage. If self-protection only meant she was denying herself, well, she'd been denied sixteen months already. She met his gaze.

"Nothing better than a Great Rite for a strong energy raising. And you said it yourself. Sex is one of the ways you could restore yourself. Two birds, one net."

CHAPTER SIX

*A*lmost before she finished making the offer, refusal was in his expression. Before he could voice it, she'd slipped off the cot to kneel between his thighs. Her hands rested on his knees as she gazed up at him. Under his suddenly intent look, her words came out a whisper. "I know what you said, but I'm okay. Tell me what you need, my lord."

He caressed her cheek, twining a lock of hair around his fingers. Her magic was quiet, despite her strong emotions that could scatter in all directions like the escaped gargoyle balls had at their first meeting. Maybe he was doing that steadying thing he did, or her magic was just behaving, as it sometimes did when its distraction really wouldn't help in any way.

When doing something else would help more.

His fingers held the strength and surety she remembered. Though his expression reflected the hardness his experience had put him through, she felt what lay behind it, all the things that had drawn her to him from his first touch. Compassion, resolve, character. A man's need, but tied up with it was his regard for her needs, his care for her well-being. Which he proved with his next words.

"I'm sorry that I gave you a moment of doubt over my motives. The reasons for my absence."

"No." She shook her head. "That wasn't your doing. I was being an idiot."

"Your experiences have given you doubt of the men who express interest in you. Experience doesn't make you an idiot," he said. "I won't tolerate you speaking about yourself that way. Do you understand?"

Did he know that how he framed his words could tighten her body, make it reach for its desires? His next statement told her he did.

"I require you to acknowledge it, Ramona."

She wet her lips. "Understood."

Watching the Doms and subs at Sweet Dreams act like this had mesmerized her. Because under the formality was an intimacy so deep it allowed those properly structured exchanges to go hand in hand with straight-out raw emotion.

"I hate that you were in pain and I didn't know," she said. "It leaves me a lot of feelings and nowhere to put them."

"You are to blame for none of it. Our desire to spare one another pain makes me hope we were destined to be back together. Let's let go of anything else and move forward with that thought. Agreed?"

She nodded against his touch, closed her eyes to press her lips and cheek to his palm.

"Conjure the circle around us and set your containment." His voice got rougher, and his other hand cupped her throat, gripped her shoulder. "I'll reinforce it."

In the mundane world, this might be seen as either one of them taking advantage, using sex as an excuse. But in this instance, the decision had a strong purpose. Their equally strong, matching desire didn't make it less so.

Under his touch, the power of it, her mind took her down the path where this could go. That was when her courage faltered, the past warring with the present. Something mere words couldn't fix. Silas detected it, and his touch altered, reassuring rather than commanding. "Or we can call your friends to help and use a different form of magic," he said. "Your choice."

Her heart plummeted, stomach twisting into a knot. He wanted and needed the sex magic. It would bring him restoration on several levels. Things would open up that might help him see a wider range of solutions to the mark problem. He could call his Wake commander.

It would also connect him even more deeply to her. The bindings he'd put on her wrists would take a step closer to becoming a true binding, a Master who could command her desires, who she'd yearn even more to serve. To care for.

That was the kind of thing she'd allowed herself to imagine when the idea of him had been a fantasy. Then he'd walked into her shop and become a potential reality. She stood at the threshold of finding out if the reality could answer her craving, or if it would fall short. Be obliterated entirely by what she was or the vagaries and intentions of Fate itself.

In the end, it boiled down to one decision. Be a coward or not. Live life or hide. Risk the pain. But every creature learned to avoid pain.

Except him. He'd just gone through hell for a soul, and then pushed through the aftermath to be back with her.

Trembling, she rose on her knees, pressing against his touch, bringing her close to his face. She put her hand on his cheek, stroked the skin that etched out the strong bones beneath. As she looked into his eyes, she could still see the emerald sparks that had existed in those empty sockets. The Reaper face was as much his as this one. It was all him, all the layers and facets of his experiences, the responsibilities he carried.

The primary charge of his life was the fabric of his very soul.

"I want to," she whispered. "But sex can get out of control for me. It's problematic, for what you're needing."

"What I need has far deeper levels." He thankfully interpreted her words the way she'd intended. "I won't let it get out of control. I won't let you get out of my control, Ramona. Will you trust me, when I've given you no reason to trust me?"

"No reason?" She stared at him. "You came to me first. You weren't gone because you were being the dick guy who didn't call the girl who was interested in him. I think you've earned some of my trust. A little bit at least," she allowed with a small smile. "Enough to send a message."

"Enough to join with my body," he said. "That's more than sending a message." He sighed. "As I warned you earlier, it's been a long road since last I saw you. A lot of imaginings. For you...it's been life. You've changed your shop around. Added new sections."

"Reaper merchandise sells very well," she defended. "Meeting you was just a coincidence. Don't let it go to your head."

"I was actually talking about the puzzle table at the entrance, and the coffee corner." His hands fell to her waist, squeezed. "I like your Reaper section, though."

He sobered. "I also saw the pictures pinned up behind your counter. Your friend had a baby with the Light Guardian. And the succubus and Mikhael mated. My reappearance is much like that 'dick guy' showing up on the second date and expecting what he has no right to expect."

He'd laid out everything that had happened to him without holding back, knowing she was listening. She owed him the same. Though to tell him required an in-depth study of his bare shoulder, her eyes fixed on it as she ran one finger in a short track back and forth along his collar bone.

"I've imagined myself with you almost every night since I saw you last. You know that."

She drew back, showed him her wrists. Then, deliberately, she lifted them as if offering herself to be bound again. With rope, cuffs, or magical bindings of all kinds.

Or the best kind. His own hands, rising to close over them as his gaze showed honed male awareness. "Whatever this journey," she said, "I'm not wasting a minute of it."

He mattered to her, enough to give her pause, to make her fear, but the enduring lesson of her life held the gift she could give them both. She followed the magic where it swirled, even if it went in more than one direction, to places that didn't initially make sense or could cause heartache and unbearable loss.

An overused term, since the worst things possible were bearable. Resilience could be a curse.

"All right." His grip tightened. When her lips parted, he increased that hold upon her. "I'm doing this for the magic, but not only the magic. I want you to understand that. I want you, Ramona. In ways that might be frightening, if you don't have a lot of experience, so tell me your experience."

"I've had sex, but only once," she said. When she flinched at his surprise, he released a wrist to cup her face.

"You need have no shame. I don't know much about Chaos witches, but I know it is a born gift, and not one easily managed, let alone during intimacy."

She nodded against his touch, shifted her gaze to his jaw. He had a nice one. She wondered if the light sandpaper of it she'd felt under her hands was conjured as part of his human form, or if he did actually have to shave. "I couldn't reach climax during it," she said. "Probably because I brought the house down around us right before. Surviving the hail of building materials became more important than completion. I'm telling you this, not particularly because I want to be mortified, but in case it changes things. If it says we really should bring in Ruby and Raina to help."

"How old were you?"

"Seventeen."

He considered. "Let's give it a try. If I suspect any problems, we can always stop and call them. Or call them afterward. I see no significant time advantage in stopping what demands...completion."

The trace of erotic wickedness in his gaze took her by surprise. He traced her cheek with those distracting fingers, the side of her nose, her lips. The curve of her chin as she lifted it for him, to give him access to whatever he wished.

His green eyes watched her the way he had that first time, as if she were the most remarkable thing he'd ever seen. Some men recognized how much that meant to a woman, used it as a seduction tool. But when a man did it because it came from him, that wonder and fascination, something deep in a woman responded.

She looked at him the same way, closing that circle, so they could get lost in one another. There were a lot of things happening in the world—there always were—but this never stopped being important, this kind of moment. It helped and healed a lot of things.

He thought he would frighten her, but she knew when in control of himself, Silas would never let her truly be afraid. She thought of Cal Horscht. He had certainly been afraid, knowing what might happen if Silas was overcome, but she expected as long as Silas's protection held, Cal had learned what being truly safe meant.

Silas bent, his lips finding hers. That first kiss, after such a long separation. A quiet whimper caught in her throat. She lifted her hand to cover his, where it rested against her face. When he stroked her throat with his thumb, that sound of need vibrated against his touch.

She'd dropped her other hand to his thigh, holding, feeling the shift of muscle as he slid forward. The towel parted further, his thigh against her side as his arm went around her to pull her closer. He held her between his spread knees, his fingers kneading her back, tracing her bare skin beneath the thin cloth of her top.

He had a heated mouth, firm lips, a tongue that lazily seduced and played with hers. His scent filled her senses, that sandpaper jaw grazing her tender skin. All of it felt so good. She was already portioning it, though, knowing how to space it out in the necessary manner. It was far more challenging doing it with him, but she'd had a lot of practice when she self-pleasured, building to a careful climax that stayed within certain limits.

Unlike when she was self-pleasuring, though, she was with an intuitive Master. Silas lifted his lips from hers. "You're tense, trying to control your reactions. You don't have to do that."

"My magic...you heard what Mikhael said. I'm the only one who can fully shield myself. Please...I want this."

If he didn't believe her, thought she didn't, her heart might just crack open. He brushed her wrists with his fingers, his eyes piercing as a falcon's. "This says you want to give me everything."

"I don't allow my wants to make my choices." Trying to lighten things, she added, "I don't want to demolish my store. Do you know how long it took to get those top hats in a pyramid?"

He stroked his knuckles along her face. "I'll help you put it back together. Of all people, you know exactly what wondrous things Chaos can bring."

She stared into his green eyes, deep as a tunnel of spring grass. She smelled the scent of it. She'd probably have a lawn instead of wood floor any minute now.

Though her hands rested on his chest, fingers curling against the hair and feeling the thud of his heart, a chasm was opening up between them. If she couldn't find the right words, get him to hear and understand them, it would become so wide they wouldn't be able to cross it.

"I've spent my life learning who I am, what my magic is. Protecting others is important to me, Silas. It's a responsibility I don't relinquish. I can't do it, even for something as wonderful as I know losing myself in your touch would be. Yes, you've proven that you can help steady it, and because of that, I will give you everything I can, up to that line. I can promise you'll have that."

But the truth she wouldn't speak, because she wouldn't kick him while he was down, was that they didn't know the full capabilities of that mark. Plus, his normal command of his abilities might still be temporarily reduced.

Chaos magic wasn't kitchen magic. She literally could level a building with it. Every building on this street.

He was listening to her, thinking through what she was telling him. A flicker of darkness, a tightening of his mouth, suggested he intuited the things she didn't say, because he was an intelligent male and experienced magic user.

She steeled herself for his withdrawal, but he didn't take his hands away. They rested at her waist, stroking the top of her buttocks, the small of her back. His fingers were beneath the waistband of her thin skirt, finding flesh.

"Did you know, a Reaper has no knowledge of his lives before?" he told her. "The moral structure is there, and experiences come forth when needed, but never enough to make a full picture. You just know, deep in your bones, you chose this. Committed to being a Reaper, with everything you ever were and ever intended to be, no matter how short you fell of the goal."

He brushed a kiss along her temple, her cheekbone, her jaw, moving like a drifting feather to breathe on her lips, touch them with his, swallow her trembling breath. His palms glided over her arms, back to her waist, gripped hard. "I just spent an eternity protecting one soul. There is nothing more important to me. I understand what you are telling me, Ramona. Which is why I'm telling you this, as the male who wants to command you, possess you, and the male who wants to reassure you that you can trust him with that ultimate gift. You will cause no harm by letting me have everything."

She'd closed her eyes, absorbing all the potent things he was doing to her, with words as much as his touch. "You're asking a lot for a guy I just met."

A smile against her flesh. "I tend to be demanding. In a lot of ways. That's what you should be most terrified of."

"'Fear is just the gateway to wonder. It's just a matter of stepping through it.'"

He lifted his head, met her eyes. "Exactly."

"I will try. I promise." Then, slowly, she reached up, gripped his shoulders, and gave herself to it again. The heat of his kiss, the demand of it, the strength of his arms. They circled her, a rumble of approval low in his throat. He teased her tongue with his own, played with her mouth like he was tasting an unforgettable meal. Filled with textures and flavors to savor, making one marvel at how the cook had brought together the ingredients to taste just that way.

"Cast a circle around us." He spoke against her mouth.

His arms kept holding her as she did it, giving her his strength and reassurance, even as his hands moved, awakening other senses. Sliding over her back, her shoulder blades, down her sides, over her rib cage. His fingertips teased the swell of her breasts before moving back to her hips. He hadn't even removed her clothes and she was already...

On fire.

He took care of it with a wash of coolness like the mist billowing away from the striking power of a waterfall. Her eyes opened, and he was stroking her cheek, his gaze filled with the power of what he'd promised her. He'd balanced her magic before she had to do it herself.

She'd had a taste of it when they met, but she'd told herself she'd exaggerated it in her memory. Even if she hadn't, it had been fifteen minutes, one kiss. Yet he'd just demonstrated the same level of skill that Mikhael had, anticipating the twists and turns of that mark and countering them, keep them from becoming too agitated.

Only in this case, Silas wanted her agitation. He wanted her wild and restless like that waterfall, roaring for more.

More was something she definitely wanted. As she cast the circle, he lifted her from the cot. If he did have reduced strength, he was still far stronger than a normal human. He had no difficulty pressing her up against the pillar that braced the roof, and fortunately fell inside the cast circle.

She'd plastered the pillar with old music sheets, giving it an antique look. Sometimes when she put her hand on it, music would play, notes on the papers randomly rising and falling along the pillar's length, like a piano keyboard.

Now she heard a discordant sound, as if he'd pushed her against one, a la Pretty Woman, Richard Gere setting Julia Roberts down on the baby grand.

His towel had loosened, so when Silas guided her legs around his hips, her heels pushed it away and her calves crossed over his very firm ass. It brought her dampening core against his abdomen, and his erect cock brushed her ass. It had been so long since she'd held a naked man against her, all the textures and differences.

"Show me your desire," he growled against her mouth. "Let it loose, Ramona."

He put one hand back against her throat, dipped his head and bit. She arched, dug her nails into his shoulders, legs tightening over his hips. She was unable to deny herself the waves of pleasure as she undulated against him like those notes along the pillar.

Her energy swirled forth and blew through her shop, strumming the warp threads on her looms, making the wheel on the spinning wheel creak. She was able to draw that power to her, and he helped, pulling it in, inviting it inside the circle, turning it into a vortex that pressed them even closer together. Everything outside the few square feet of space around them vanished, walled off by whatever protection he'd just added to her circle casting, keeping her and her energy contained within his hold.

Under other circumstances and maybe later, she'd want to explore and understand how he did it, but other things rose up in her. Desires that had not been let this loose in far too long, and never with another. Never where she didn't control all the variables.

He pulled her shirt off her shoulder, put his mouth over her collar bone and suckled, his tongue exploring the tiny pocket. With her back arched, her small breast pressed against his jaw. His hand came up to capture the soft curve before he adjusted to put his mouth over the nipple, the way he'd done that first day, with the shirt in the way. She pleaded, an unintelligible noise, as the thick hair feathered over his brow caressed the base of her throat.

When he lifted his head to take in her reaction, the ruthless set to his mouth thrilled her. He intended to break her into pieces and set all those pieces on fire.

He helped her pull the shirt over her head to get rid of it. She moaned as he gave her the full wet heat of his mouth. He suckled gently at first, exploring and shaping her nipple, taunting it into an aching hardness until she was bucking. It didn't make him move any faster.

He gave her that look of fiery satisfaction again, his claim on her reactions driving everything. He relished her wildness, and doubled it when he moved to the other breast and gave it the same treatment. She was throbbing, her cunt wet and slick as she worked it against his muscled torso.

He had his arms under hers, so she couldn't reach down, pull at his hips, bring his cock in contact with the part of her that knew he was meant to be there.

No, he would take his time, underscoring the point.

She could be savage and powerful, and she was. Without his hold on it, her energy might have crushed them like a giant's fist, but it kept whirling around them, a silent rush of heat and vibration, containing all the thrill of life lived at its most free, a full gallop.

They balanced the pleasure with the ability to experience every detail. They were a God and Goddess, at the center of their creation, lost in one another, because that was the hub. There was nothing they could harm in the universe, because they *were* the universe.

Chaos and focus could expand awareness to encompass far more than the norm. She could do it when she was fully absorbed in her magic, but it was something she'd never been able to share with another. Even in mindless passion, she realized it was a momentous thing. One that had her gripping his hair, damp and thick under her touch, before he claimed her mouth for another triumphant kiss, a demanding, passionate message. He was rewarding her trust and acknowledging she was giving him something just as special with it as he was giving to her.

"Please," she said into his mouth. "Please."

His hands were under her skirt, finding only her, sliding over her thighs, then probing with gentle thumbs. He muttered a reverent oath as he found how slick she still was, no matter that she'd painted his abdomen with her juices in patterns as chaotic as her energy.

She wanted to touch him, and he let her get a hand between them, close it around his thick length. A Reaper yes, but also blessedly male, a word with simple power and primeval meaning.

Then he took control, gripping her hand, so they both guided him to her ready sex. When the ridged head fitted into that opening, his hand came back to her face, lifting her chin, his gaze locking with hers.

"My witch," he said softly.

The words made her tremble and shudder. He was certain of

them, of himself, but what gave her a heartbeat of fear was she was equally as certain. Which meant the way forward could be fraught with peril, because the world loved to fuck with that kind of certainty, do its best to tear it apart and take it away.

She wanted to throw an impenetrable protection spell over them, but the spellcraft that could hide them from those kinds of avaricious, seeking powers didn't exist.

He was waiting for her response. Wouldn't enter her body until he had it.

"Yes," she whispered. *I am yours.*

He came into her slow, with a restrained power. She felt every inch, but she also felt his care. She'd told him how long it had been, and he wanted to make sure he didn't hurt her. That broke her apart in ways as devastating as his demanding side could do it, integrating and driving into her heart and soul, claiming both.

He let out a soft groan, his eyes alive with that fire. "Everything," he murmured. "I want to give you everything."

She wrapped her arms around his shoulders, pressed her face into his neck. In this moment, he was doing just that.

"You told me you imagined being with me every day. I'll demand those details, and make every one of them a reality."

As he spoke the hoarse words, he began to move, at first slow and easy, driving her body up a steep, excruciating track toward release. He made sure she felt the full sensation of every stroke, every dragging, pleasurable inch of movement. Her muscles contracted on him in need, but also purposefully. As she kept doing it, she earned a feral sound of pleasure. He braced a hand against the pillar, the other holding her securely as the power of his thrusts increased. The crashing sounds of piano notes increased, a jazz piece, discordant, triumphant, bittersweet.

She tilted her hips to take him deeper, as her hands clawed, tried to pull him even closer. She kept squeezing him inside, muscle groups that Raina's demons had taught her how to use. Inside and outside she gripped, stroked, told him *yes* and *more*, in every way.

Her body spasmed, the climax so close. The little leap of panic in her chest told her she hadn't held back enough. The circle was holding, her energy swirling around them in this second, but that didn't mean anything.

"I've got you, witch." His breath in her ear was hot as the tempera-ture between them. "Let it go and trust me. Dance with me in the storm...I won't let you...cause harm."

Her attention snapped to him. It was a rhyme she used for balance, to calm herself. She must have been murmuring it to herself that day. Now he gave it back to her, amended.

She couldn't completely abandon herself to the slide, but she honored her promise to him. She offered up more control to another than she ever had before, leaving behind the trepidation as she leaped and found herself securely in his hold, her magic a fireworks around them that could incinerate, destroy, remake, create...

It did all of those things.

As she cried out her release, body writhing in his hold, she couldn't see beyond the circle. They were caught inside a prism flooded with colored lights, her energy churning around them, but they held onto it together, rode that storm, and it did no harm.

He was deep and full inside her, the friction making her gasp and shudder, and then cry out again as he released just behind her. Even in the midst of that, even as she sensed he got his own full measure of satisfaction, he didn't fail her, didn't abandon it all to her. His care of her was part of his pleasure, and knowing it, seeing it, did things to unmake her, unmake decades of pain.

She *was* his witch. Gladly.

And then she discovered what he meant about being demanding. He wasn't done.

She'd forgotten there was another reason for doing this, for raising the energy. He needed to send a message to his fellow Reapers.

As she shuddered through the aftershocks of her climax, he deftly used the currents stored in the circle to send it, murmuring in a language she didn't know. He did it with enough ease she wondered if he'd really needed her help to do it at all, but even a person skilled in cooking needed the ingredients and fire to make the dish, right?

His gaze cleared and he brushed her mouth with his own, arms still securely around her. "Open the circle," he murmured. When she silently dispelled the Quarters and opened the boundary, he slid from her body. At her quiet moan, his hands tightened on her, his own answer to the vibration that the separation sent through them. He also didn't release her, not letting her feet touch the ground.

"Now that we've taken care of our chores, time to give you the attention you truly deserve."

Holy cow. She slid her arms further around his shoulders as he hefted her higher on his body. She adjusted her legs for a more secure hold over his hips, and was gratified when he tightened his arm across her back. He brushed his mouth against her ear again. "You're so thin. Do you ever eat?"

"Says the man whose true form is nothing but bones. Literally." She made a face at him. "Chaos magic burns a lot of calories. Raina threatened to have a bumper sticker made that said, 'this is my stick family,' and put me on it. Sorry. I don't really have curves."

"You have more than enough for me." He molded a palm to her buttock and stroked, sending a wash of sensation through her. "More than enough to spank."

The sensual—and purposeful—menace in his chuckle made her quiver. And he noticed.

Apparently, he'd familiarized himself with the contents of the storeroom she had across from the full bath. Particularly an old scarred antique dresser she'd bought as a scratch-and-dent sale item from Cordelia. She kept brochures and other small items in the drawers, but had future plans to make it into a creative display for her linens.

A mirror was bolted to it, so when he put her down, she was facing it. She was naked from the waist up, her skirt somewhat falling back into place. He stood behind her, off center enough she could see his thigh, the way his chest tapered to his hip. When he kept his arm around her waist and pressed closer, her eyes widened, because he was fully erect again. Her sex, still slippery from his release and her own, contracted. He'd been thick and full, and she'd liked having him stretch her, fill her up inside.

"I told you I was demanding," he said, meeting her gaze in the mirror. "There's only one thing that will stop me, witch. Do you know what it is?"

He slid a hand around to brush her clitoris. She jolted at the vibration through his fingers, the electrical energy, and saw the wicked intent in his green gaze.

She'd given her magic to him, and he was playing with it, exploring it. Using it. Channeling it through them both, mixing it with his own energy, twining it over his fingers.

He tangled his other hand in her hair, the blond locks wrapping around his fingers. "Maybe I'll keep you on the edge of orgasm, denying you until you let that last wall drop, fully trust me. Place your palms on the dresser."

With the pressure of that hold and the weight of his body, he canted her forward, helped her obey. She let out a moan as he adjusted his stance, fitted himself to her still wet opening and eased back in, inch by inch. The movement pushed her against his fingers, onto the electrical pulses he was sending through her, through both of them.

"But I won't do that," he said, his gaze lifting to pin hers in the mirror. "I know trust must be earned, and you said you would try. You did. We'll get there together. But when we finally do," that wicked glint came back, "That's when I'll punish you. A reward for your trust."

She would laugh at all the contrasts in that statement if she wasn't so overwhelmed. He'd just given her an orgasm, and he was barely giving her a breather before he was driving her up again. Not asking for a response from her—demanding it. She was giving it to him, as if her body knew its sole purpose in life was to obey his commands.

When he was fully seated inside her, he stilled, tilted her head back. He took her mouth in a kiss she met with a needy whimper. He ignored it, holding her there and plundering her mouth with slow, leisurely strokes of his tongue, nips of her lips, giving her the edge of his teeth. The more she made those tiny sounds, the hotter the lust in his gaze grew. Her need was feeding his Dominance as surely as the energy they were raising was restoring his strength. Maybe they were one and the same. She wasn't sure she could think clearly about it right now.

"Look at your wrists."

She did. The script burned into her flesh was alive, twisting, tingling. She could see the golden brass glow of the ribbons spiraling up her arms, crisscrossing over her body, binding her spread legs, just like the night she'd awakened his parting gift. He gripped her left wrist, brought it back against the small of her back, his fingers tangled with hers as he kept the other hand at her hip. He held her fast as he pushed into her slow, drew out the same way, watching the way her body arched, her left breast jutting forward.

"That thing you were doing. Milking my cock. Do it again, while I try to destroy your concentration."

She would have laughed in a joyous kind of despair if her whole body, all her energy, wasn't spiraling so madly only gravity told her she was on the ground, not spinning through the universe. That tingling was all over her skin, in between her legs, bringing everything to life, so much energy, and she realized that was what he'd done. Turned it all toward her, toward her pleasure, giving it a place to go, rather than dismantling anything outside of them. Instead, it was dismantling everything *inside* of her.

She gripped him, watched his eyes glow, mouth tighten as he reacted to the pleasure of it. He played over her clit with those magical fingertips, bent his head to suckle and nip at her throat and collar bone. Then he guided her hand back to the dresser so he could take a hard, bruising grip on her ass, kneading it, thumb working between the crevice, against her rim, bringing her onto her toes.

"Silas," she gasped. How long could he do this? Could she keep up? Did she care about the answers to those questions? His vast need was only deepening her desire to satisfy it. Whose magic that was, she didn't know, but maybe they were creating it together.

"When you can take no more, we stop...just past that point. You know why."

She did. It was why those bindings were on her wrist. To tell her she was his. That she served him.

He'd told her she'd tell him every detail of her fantasies about him. But long before she'd met him, she'd had a night where she was working on pieces of new spellcraft, playing with words. Her mind had drifted to a wish, for the man who could be everything she needed him to be. Her feelings had overwhelmed her and spilled onto the pages of her spell book. Those words rose in her mind now, that call she'd put out into the universe.

I try to speak your name, the one given you by your mother, the Goddess, the name known by all others. It shapes itself in my mouth, but I can't speak it.

I can't call you anything but who you are to me. Like an endearment between only us, but so much more. A true name for my heart. Calling it out, I will find you in the darkness, because it is the name that binds us together. That bound me to you and you to me.

To me you are Master.

"Come for me, witch," he told her, and they released together, that magic once again spiraling tight against them, vibrating against their damp flesh. She held onto it, once again not fully able to let it go, but this time, with his hold overlapping hers, he left no doubt he had it, and her, securely in his grasp.

CHAPTER SEVEN

 *H*e did it all one more time. Power of three, and all that. She was proud of how long she lasted, but she'd had a lot of desire for him stored up. Maybe almost as much as he had. Even so, when they were done, he had to carry her back to the cot. Raina often referred to "being fucked until your legs no longer worked," but Ramona now understood why her friend spoke so highly of the experience.

When he lay on the narrow mattress, Silas tugged her down so her lower body was between his spread legs, her stomach pressed against his finally somewhat resting cock, her cheek on his chest.

She hoped to take him home when they both woke. She had a much bigger bed there. But despite Mikhael's recommendation that Silas take a couple days, it was likely wishful thinking. Sending the message had apparently worked, so she assumed they would eventually be getting an answer. All the things she'd imagined for their reunion, spending time together...well, so much for that. They had a threat from the demon world to counter and a possession mark that needed to be removed.

Even semi-conscious, he responded to her uneasiness. His arms tightened around her, hand moving to her hair to stroke. It gave her a quiet wash of hope. This was what they had, and she would take it. With that thought in mind, she drifted off to sleep.

When she woke, it was nighttime, which meant she'd slept several hours. She was alone.

He'd left. She sat up, a jagged ache in her lower belly. Then she viciously quashed the feeling of abandonment. *You spent sixteen months believing he didn't come back because of who you are, and you were entirely wrong.* Goddess, how quickly the fragile ego could drag one down the same tiresome roads. Maybe he'd received that message response and had to leave. Maybe he'd left her a note.

As she folded her arms over herself, her thumb rubbed against her right wrist. The ribbons were gone, but the ink remained. He *had* left her a message. His own energy coursed much more strongly through the bands, because she'd opened herself to what the bands meant, invited him in to take full possession of them. Her feelings for him were still fueling them, but now so were his for her.

The thought thankfully took her past her freakout moment. Nevertheless, she detected an unsettling vibration through her shop. Plus Silas. He hadn't left. Rising, she slipped her clothes back on and went to find him.

He was standing to the right of her front display window, out of direct view. Most the shops closed at dark, so Main Street was populated primarily by people coming or going from the handful of restaurants. He looked like he was staring into space. Thoughtful.

He was also dressed. He wore snug cargo trousers, plus an open button-down shirt whose cotton fabric lay against him as his robe did, a flowing remark on the beauty of the form beneath. Mikhael and Derek had a cache of possessions they could call upon when needed, a cosmic storage locker of sorts. She supposed Reapers had the same.

His head was dipped down, his thick, unruly hair falling over his brow. With the resilient leanness to him, it made his silhouette almost look young. The shirt was open and he had his palm on his chest, was rubbing the marked spot with an odd repetition, as if unconsciously trying to remove a stain, even though it wasn't currently visible.

The disruptive energy waves were coming from that, messing with the shield she kept on her shop to ease her clients and occupy her Chaos energies. Which was why her toy train changed routes, and her inventory routinely rearranged itself or transformed into other things.

As she drew closer, she saw his eyes were unfocused. Slowly, she brought her hand to hover over his rubbing one, listening with all her senses, feeling for it...

His head jerked her way. For a flash, she saw the skull beneath the skin, the empty eye sockets with green flame. Then the image was gone. His hand dropped from beneath hers before they could touch and he stepped back, giving himself the room for the energy to dissipate.

"All right?" she ventured.

"Yeah. Sorry, I was trying to probe deeper into it again. Thinking it might be more accessible now that I have most of my strength back." He gave her a half-smile, the heat of which rippled over her skin. "Thank you for that."

Her cheeks warmed as he took her hand and pressed his mouth to her palm. "Does it hurt?" she asked. "Having it there?"

"No. When I think about it too much, it just feels like something is clinging to me. A leech, without the useful bloodsucking properties." Though he spoke matter-of-factly, she sensed the storm crashing against the wall of his self-discipline. If she wanted to rip that marker out of him forcibly, burn it to ash, she could only imagine how he felt, having to suffer its presence, its unknown but surely malevolent purpose.

Looking more closely, she was also certain he hadn't slept well. Was it due to his revulsion over having it within him, or because the thing itself wasn't allowing him the respite, with the intent of wearing him down, weakening him?

Sensing any talk related to the mark wouldn't be helpful to him at the moment, she chose distraction. It often widened the perspective on a problem, giving the puzzler more options to solve it. Gina's question about celebrities came to mind, so she gave that her own spin.

"So you said you were meant to be a Reaper. But do you ever want to do something else, just for a while? Rock star, short order cook?"

He chuckled at her expectant look, rubbed a hand over his face. "I've spent the day with both of those. Reapers get a lot of vicarious experiences. It's enough. So, no. I've never known a Reaper who didn't feel the same as I do, that this was their chosen destiny. When they can do it no longer, they simply fade away. Usually into moving water. Underground springs, rivers, creeks. Oceans. Why are you smiling?"

"When I was little," she said, "I would conjure origins for myself like the old stories. Pegasus and Chrysaor, spawned out of Medusa's neck when Perseus cuts off her head. Or the trickster who became a seed to escape the sorceress Cerridwen's wrath, so she turns herself into a chicken, swallows him, and that seed became the famous bard-wizard Taliesin."

"So what was your favorite?"

The question sent a shadow across her heart, a vision of her mother's face, but she gave him an honest answer. "That I came from a river, formed from the tears of a goddess. I thought of bodies of water as places to be born, so it makes sense that a life like a Reaper's goes there to end, completing the cycle."

He stared down at their joined hands, then drew her to him again. He put his mouth to her throat, just under her jaw. She made a soft sigh of pleasure at the pressure of his lips. "Is this insatiability an immortal thing?"

"Afraid so. I'm restraining myself. I want to have you until you're too weak to walk again. In my very impractical fantasies, all you'd do is wait in bed for me, all the time."

"Unless I hire more staff, that's a very impractical plan, my lord," she agreed. "Have I mentioned I have a very big bed at my home?"

Smiling, he lifted his head to kiss her mouth again. When she leaned full into him, she threaded her fingers through the light mat of curling hair on his chest. It was a shade darker than the strands scattered across his lined brow.

When she glanced up at him, she saw the smile had died away. He touched her face. It wasn't just the limitations of her more fragile mortal body holding him back.

"I have to go soon," he said. "I heard from Honora."

She was in a peculiar position, suddenly intimate and involved with a Reaper, but having no sense of her standing with him, or enough information about his kind to assert anything of what he should or shouldn't be doing. But she could express her feelings. "I wish you had more time to rest and recuperate."

"I'd like nothing better than to lie in bed with you all day." He gave her a speculative look. "Dedicate myself to earning your trust, see what happens when you fully offer it to me."

"The climax was beautiful. The first I've experienced at the hands of another." She didn't like thinking she'd fallen short of what he'd desired from her.

He frowned, but spoke with a tender firmness. "If there is any failing here, it is mine. Either in my understanding, or in my greed to have every corner of you too quickly. Forgive me if I made you think otherwise."

He clasped the hand she had on his chest, stroked her fingers. "It isn't merely what happened to you at seventeen that holds you back," he added. "That story of your origins, there was pain there."

He was too good at discerning her thoughts, but she wasn't going there. "Yes and no. That inspired me to learn as much as I could about my abilities. That knowledge, the places it's taken me, have made me cautious. You've given me a happiness, Silas, more than I can express."

"I plan to give you more, if time is kind."

Which it rarely was. But before they could feel the weight of that obvious cloud, she took them back to lighter footing. "If I'd known you had to work, I'd have packed you a lunch."

"Ah." The corner of his mouth tipped up. "In creating my identity, what did you decide I like for lunch?"

"A peanut butter and jelly sandwich. Potato chips. A cookie for dessert."

"You know all my favorites." He cocked a brow. "What flavor jelly?"

She rolled her eyes. "Grape. It's the only kind you like. You're such a man-child."

Sobering, she shifted her grip to either side of his open shirt. Her thumb brushed his nipple, not intentionally, but it captured his attention, his hand rising to rest over hers again, his gaze stilling on her. "Take me with you," she said. "It's not been long enough. Last time you left, I didn't see you for eighteen months."

As soon as she spoke the words, she knew they were right. While they came from her heart, everything else be damned, it wasn't just that which prompted the request. She was as certain she needed to stay close to him as she was that the mark was keeping him awake.

"Ramona..." He framed her face with his hands. "You said it had been sixteen months."

"It felt like eighteen."

When he caressed her mouth, she kissed his fingers, her lips parting to tease them with her tongue. "You are misbehaving," he admonished gently.

"I'm a witch. It's in our DNA." But she couldn't smile, could only grip him tighter. He sighed.

"I am meeting Honora and others of my Wake at a Reaping. It was a skirmish, in a region at war."

"I can handle death. I've seen death."

Her voice faltered, as the images came to her and were just as quickly pushed away, because they would take over. Their talk of rivers and his intuition had brought those memories too close to the surface.

He studied her. "I'm sorry for that. Yet have you stood passively and watched people kill one another? Seen the looks on their faces, witnessed that violence grip and control them? It is different."

"No, but I know what lies in people's hearts. I know how close to the surface darkness lies."

His gaze flickered, acknowledging that truth. "I am still learning what you are, but immersing a Chaos witch in such despair doesn't seem like a good idea."

"No more than a Reaper being there who's operating on too little sleep with a crazy symbol of evil pulsing inside him." When he didn't say anything, she tapped his chest. "You remembered what I said about storms."

"I remembered everything about that meeting. Every second of it." He met her gaze. "Holding onto those words helped me. I spoke them to Cal, and they helped him as well. Like Taliesin, who could weave words that spoke to the heart and inspired great magic."

She grimaced. "Trauma has given you an inflated sense of my literary strengths. Rhymes help with spell work, focusing intent. Some witches really are poets, but it doesn't have to be that way, thank Goddess. It can be simple, practical stuff. *This is the path I will choose today. Laugh and play, true to my heart, soul and way.* I shamelessly stole that from two girls I heard playing hopscotch."

He gazed down at her. With about six inches difference in their heights, when she tipped her chin down, she was staring at his chest. She felt like that hateful mark was glaring balefully at her.

Good. Maybe that meant her compulsion to go with him to the Reaping didn't serve its purpose. "The other Reapers will be busy, right? As I said, it's a good idea for you to have a set of eyes on the mark. It's a possession magic; it could compromise your judgment or observation skills, right?"

"There is some sense to what you're saying."

"Why, thank you." She scowled. "Derek and Mikhael have the patronizing immortal thing, too. It still seems to shock them when us mere witches come up with something they haven't thought about."

He held up both hands in surrender. "I plead recent trauma for my insensitivity."

"Smooth talker." She curled her fingers inside his grasp. "I wish I'd been your backup with Cal. After you took him to The Gate, we could have gotten lunch at that café I told you about."

His brow pulled low, his lips firming. "The last thing I'd allow near you is a Soul Collector."

"I have a way of turning scary things into less scary things," she told him stoutly. "Like kittens. Or kitchen utensils. A potato masher. An ice cream scoop." She returned to the main point, determined. "I want to go with you. I can handle it. Please."

Apart from her real concerns about the mark, she was back to her original motive. She'd missed him. She wasn't a clingy person, but she couldn't handle being apart so soon after seeing him again.

He released her hand to brush his fingers along her cheek. She could see him weighing the pros and cons with the same thoroughness he'd tested her shielding ability. But from the tightness around his mouth, she knew her logic was sound. Even if they both wished it wasn't.

"When we get there, follow my direction," he said at last. "If it gets to be too much, turn away, shield yourself to shut it all out. I will transport you back as soon as I can."

"I'll be fine," she repeated.

"The deaths you will see are fated," he said. "We are only watchers, unseen by the living. You'll be able to see what I am seeing. Do not stray from where I tell you to be."

"All right."

He gave her a hard look. "I mean it. I know you are more than capable, but this is unfamiliar territory."

"Yes, sir."

She tagged it with a smile, but his look kindled a ball of the same in her lower belly. "I don't entirely dislike the sound of that," he said.

She arched a brow. "I didn't entirely dislike the way you said 'you're misbehaving.' Almost as if you were encouraging it."

He chuckled, shook his head. Then gazed up and around him as he was showered with white and gold daisy petals. Several landed on their clasped hands. At his quizzical look, she explained.

"Your laughter," she said. "That's how it makes me feel."

The sexy smile he answered her with told her she might "Sir" him a hundred times over, if the promises behind it were her reward.

Then the humor died from his face. She could tell he was considering if he should rescind his permission for her to accompany him, though it pleased and reassured her to recognize he was also weighing her points.

While Raina and Ruby teased about it, the truth was, no matter how much Derek and Mikhael loved and respected their mates, at the end of the day they wouldn't be overruled if they didn't agree. On certain things, their authority as Guardians, as immortals—and yes, as Dominants—was absolute. Silas had the same manner to him. Frustrating and titillating both.

At last he gave her a serious nod. "The living, their weapons and physical matter, can't affect you, but the elements, the earth they fight upon, will be as real as what you stand upon here. Wear something you don't mind getting bloody."

~

She changed into old jeans and a dye-spattered T-shirt she kept at the shop for dirty work. She also pulled the thick mass of her hair back and braided it.

When she rejoined him, he'd donned a cowled robe with wide sleeves over his clothes, what she assumed was the standard Reaper uniform. "Do souls see you like this, or in your Ghost Rider form?"

He got the reference, his eyes sparking with a more serious humor. "It depends. Sometimes neither. They see us in the form they need to see, to ease their transition, cut the link to their body." He curled an arm around her waist, positioning them for portal travel. "I've appeared as a boy's dog before. His pet had passed a couple years before his own death, so Bruno was the perfect guide to The Gate."

"Ah." She put her hands on his shoulders, spreading out her fingers to maximize the contact, for the transport and her own enjoyment. "How was that?"

"I received a very thorough ear rub and belly scratching. And many hugs. It was a good day. Hold onto me, witch. And remember what I said."

She'd done portal travel before, though never on her own. Those channels weren't used except by those who had regular need of them, and doing it properly was a highly developed skill, learned under the tutelage of the more experienced. No surprise that a Reaper could do it as intuitively as a fish could swim.

An apt comparison, because it was like being plunged into a strong ocean current, no obvious control or anything to hold onto. For Silas, that is, since under her clutching hands he was a solid anchor. He'd drawn her even closer when he'd stepped through the portal, so she had both arms wrapped over his shoulders, body full against his. It quelled any anxiety she might feel, any stray horror stories she'd heard about catastrophic portal jumps.

If there'd been time, she would have made an inappropriate joke about the mile-high club equivalent for those plastered together during portal travel, but they reached their destination. Then all the air around her seemed to be sucked away, because where he'd brought her, there was no room for laughter, sex or anything of joy.

Only screaming. Smoke and blood, human waste. The staccato pops of guns, more screams, a roar beneath it all.

The roar of negative Chaos. *Shit.*

She'd told him she could handle it. She could, but he was right—she'd never stood on the sidelines of wartime violence. In the space of an indrawn breath, her Chaos magic was threatening to go off like fireworks tossed on a bonfire.

His concern about Chaos witches and despair was also apt. Though losing hope could cripple any person, when one commanded the kind of magic she did, losing hope could have far wider ramifications.

That observation raised an abrupt flag in her mind, a question about his mark's nature, who had created it. But she put that aside and dropped to her heels, a physical posture representing her mental one, getting low to make a smaller target. She was already speaking the words to seal herself in a bubble of quiet, where the negative forces couldn't get through and pull her magic to the surface, co-opting it for its own uses.

Cast a bubble, do it right now. Nothing gets through but what we allow. All is heard and seen, all through a screen.

Silas was over her, hand gripping her shoulder. He was within a breath of sending her back.

She shook her head, her hand landing over his to tell him she had this. In a matter of seconds, the shielding was stabilizing. She'd intentionally cast it opaque, with a gradual move toward transparency that would filter in the sensory impacts. She used that momentary respite to use his hand and her own propulsion to draw herself back to her feet, stand at his side. When she rose on her toes to speak into his ear, his arm slipped around her, his green eyes close and intent.

"Just needed the right shielding. I'm okay. Do what you need to do."

If he overrode her, there'd be no time for rebuttal. She'd be in her shop again. But after a lengthy moment, he inclined his head, though he kept her close, pressed against his hip. She noted he had his scythe in the other hand, was leaning on it as he hooked his thumb in her waistband, his fingers passing over the sensitive skin of her lower back.

"We don't step in until the fight is done. There's too much of that negative energy you wisely shielded yourself against. At first, a rising soul believes it's still fighting. They can't make sense of their reality until it dies back. That's when most will release their tie to their fallen mortal form."

The shield was beginning to let in sight, sounds and smells. She modulated it to keep the sounds recognizable but muffled, because the overwhelming noise of battle had the strongest impact on her magic.

They were in a rocky field, just off a road with a wooden fence running along it, fields beyond that, forest at her back.

The clash between rival factions involved over three dozen people. Mostly male adults and teens, a scattering of women. Some firing guns, others in hand-to-hand combat, with blades, rocks, fists. Some wore uniforms, others wore street clothes. Beyond that, she didn't recognize anything about them. A small fight in a small corner of the globe that wouldn't make the news in her part of the world. Yet here, this fight, whatever had driven it, was everything. Particularly for those who fell and didn't get up again.

Silas had said she'd be able to see the souls, but even so, the first one was a shock. A teenager fell, bullet wounds in his face and chest. He was gone with a blood-laced cough, a jerk. Staring eyes. After five heartbeats, the soul erupted from him. Still looking like the boy, but up on its feet, continuing to fight.

Leaping away from his fallen corpse, he went after the opponent who had shot him. He was using his fists, so frenzied in his attack he didn't realize they were passing through his enemy. The violence of the energy carrying him did have an effect, seeming to disorient the older man. The shooter stumbled, pivoted back into the soul, so the kid kept hitting. Then the living enemy shook off the feeling and dashed forward to engage another opponent.

The boy came to a confused halt, trembling. He seemed to have no awareness that he stood up to his calves in the chest of his sprawled body. Instead, he saw a dropped gun and dove for it. Ramona swallowed, her hands rising in a tight knot against her heart. His awareness of the battle seemed to die away as he couldn't make sense of it, why he kept scraping at the weapon and couldn't grasp it. Like a child on a playground, trying to pick up a worm as it writhed from his touch.

It was an insidious skill of negative Chaos, translating the small pleasures of life into a horror like this. The crash of how life had been into what it had become, for reasons that seemed impossible to unmangle and reverse, brought despair. Robbed a body of hope.

Countering it required a different kind of spellwork, one available to anyone with the will, not just a magic user. She pulled the image of the toy train in her store into her mind. Broke it down by the details of each car and worked it into her shielding. The gaily clacking noise, the way it would suddenly spiral around the track, upside down and back upright again, delighting children and adults alike as they tried to figure how it did that. In her shop, she could get away with telling the plain truth. *"It's magic."*

Unpredictable, fun, hopeful. It existed, and when needed, could hold the line against this. Even as it shredded her own heart and made tears roll down her face.

The boy was stumbling toward the perimeter of the fighting, still trying to pick things up, as if choosing something different would work. It was then she saw a Reaper waiting near him. And behind him, there were more. All in cowled robes, a mix of males and females, standing along the perimeter of the field.

Ramona's gaze was drawn to a female who stood at the highest point of the battlefield. The flame that sparked along the edge of her silver scythe was a glittering blue, like liquid topaz. Her lowered cowl revealed silk platinum-colored hair, just past her shoulder blades whenever the wind settled.

That had to be Honora. The mantle of leadership rested as obviously on her shoulders as the crown on a queen's head. Plus her attention was fixed on Silas. Until it shifted, that regard falling on Ramona for a weighted moment before it returned to the field again.

The boy was next to the Reaper. As Ramona watched, a lump grew in her throat. She hadn't expected to see the Reaper as the soul would see him. The cowled male's tall frame altered into a much shorter, thick-waisted, broad-hipped woman, wearing a colorful print dress and embroidered slippers. On the wind, Ramona inhaled a scent of tomatoes, basil. Lamb and figs. She looked like the boy, only older. When he fell to his knees, gripping her skirts, and sobbed, she bent to put her arms around him, hold him.

The tether between the soul and his fallen body broke. The end attached to the body whipped into the air like an untied ribbon, a good-bye.

The Reaper was himself again. Without the cowl, she could see the smooth skull, his skeletal fingers wrapping over the boy's back. Then two of them were gone, melted away. The cord continued to flap. In the boy's absence, there was something desolate about it, unnerving. As if it was looking for something it needed, but was no longer there. Or was calling for it to come back.

It felt...wrong. Not the way it was supposed to happen.

At the moment she had the thought, Silas stiffened. His attention locked on where the Reaper and boy had vanished, and Ramona saw them rematerializing. It wasn't part of the plan. The Reaper's demeanor had gone battle-ready. He had his scythe turned toward the body. Ramona drew in a breath. The cord was no longer an inanimate thing, carried by the breeze. It was coiled and stiffly arched, like a serpent preparing to strike.

The boy had lost the peace he'd seemed to acquire from the Reaper's touch. Terror was taking over. He was being pulled away from the Reaper, dragged back to his body.

"Stay here," Silas said tersely. Two other Reapers were closing in on the same location, and he headed down the slope to join them. But as he left her side, Ramona's attention snapped to him. An outline of darkness was thickening around his shoulders, growing in size and height, a hunching predator hovering over him. A horrible wrongness to it, just like the behavior of that cord. The feeling rippled outward.

Honora was moving with swift grace toward the same point as Silas and the others. All of them coming to aid the soul and his assigned Reaper.

Under no circumstances should that specter get any closer to the boy's struggling soul. She was sure of it. Silas's scythe was gleaming, not with that pure gold and blue firelight, but a sickly greenish yellow. Infection.

He didn't seem to notice. None of them seemed to notice. Which meant no one else could see it.

As Silas passed through battling, struggling humans, that damned poisonous thing cared about none of that. It wanted that soul, and it was going to use Silas to get it.

Ramona cast off her protective shield. She didn't brace for the onslaught of violent energy she'd been protecting herself from; she surged through it, visualizing a mermaid figurehead cutting through crashing waves. In her element and determined on her course.

Through the cacophony of battle, she reached out to the poisoned wisps coming off of that specter. Chaos and Dark Soul magic had been twins in the womb, so she wouldn't be ignored. When the wisps responded to her caressing whisper, she began to play with them, twisting, turning, winding them over her fingers. Keeping the right mix of tension on the line so it wouldn't know she had it hooked.

Come to me, dear fish,
I will grant your dearest wish.
To find the nourishment you desire
Give you a resting place when you tire.

A siren's song, calculated to be irresistible to something wanting to suck life out of a soul. Silas kept moving forward, but the specter's attention slowly flowed toward her. As it came deeper into her hold, she entranced it with a sky of souls, like shooting stars leaving sparkling trails for it to chase, obscuring the path it had turned from.

A quick glance told her Silas and the others had reached the soul. The ripple of flame along the arc of Silas's scythe was the pure blue-gold it should be.

That was when her quarry realized it had been tricked. Part of it had been a magical binding, but way too much of it was illusion, because she hadn't had time to cast something stronger. What was it Raina had said?

"If we're not building the track an ass hair's width ahead of the roller coaster wheels, I feel spoiled."

Pretty much. She had another precious second to throw all she could into the binding while the thwarted and disoriented thing tried to figure out what had happened. It shrieked and thrashed, trying to figure its way out of her trap. Goddess, it was strong. Then it realized what had it. Its stench, the desolate energy, tried to invade her.

If it couldn't have that soul, it would take hers.

She charged her intent and spoke the words, using their power to thrust it away from her.

Now you go back where you belong,
Your intent here malevolent and wrong.
Wrong, wrong...wrong!

The recoil that came on the final syllable was an arcane cannon. She let it hit her, no time to block. She expected to sail through the air, land against something unyielding and painful.

She got the unyielding part, only it wasn't painful.

"Ramona." Silas was holding her in his arms, kneeling next to where she lay, a grassy area populated with a lot of jagged, speckled rocks, tufts of dandelions thrusting up between them. From the peaceful surroundings and the silence, she wondered if they had left the battlefield.

She sat up, helped and steadied by his touch. They were still here, but it was over, the battleground strewn with the fallen. She must have blacked out for a few minutes.

"The boy..."

She looked, and saw his fallen body, but not his soul. Other souls were in the process of being claimed by the Reapers. Some of those spirits were on their knees by their corpses, staring, while the Reapers stood at their sides, in various forms. They spoke to the soul, or just silently waited for the cord between past and future to be severed.

"He was taken to The Gate. He is fine. We felt a Soul Collector's hand in what happened, but never saw it. What were you doing?"

She wished she didn't have to answer him, and not just because he looked pretty intimidating, like he was planning to give her total hell for engaging whatever it was. She could handle that. Telling him the truth was harder.

"It was coming from you, Silas."

His gaze flashed. "The mark was commanding the soul back to its body?"

"No. And yes. The mark called what I assume was some version of a Soul Collector, but it cloaked it. Taking the soul was its intent, but the mark was using you to make it happen." When his brow creased, she knew she wasn't stating it clearly enough. "The mark was using your power to call a soul. Your blade changed colors."

She suspected it had been testing its intent, its hold on Silas. She expressed that to him, adding, "I distracted the Collector, broke the summoning."

Silas's expression was wooden as Honora arrived to kneel beside them. Her face was grooved and gray as the bark of the live oaks that lined the road to Raina's plantation house. Close up, her hair had the mix of colors and crinkled waves of the Spanish moss that dripped from them. Her eye color matched. A Reaper that looked like a tree spirit. The fingers she wrapped around her staff were gnarled, but not with age. Her spirit was ancient, but her body was straight and strong, bosom firm.

"Sylvanus," she said. "You have been corrupted."

CHAPTER EIGHT

"Yes," Silas said. His grip on his scythe was tight. "I assume that was why I was removed from the Reaping schedule."

Honora frowned. "I reviewed that possibility when you sent me your message. The Fates do not seem aware of your return. It is as if...you are not visible to them."

His expression flickered, but he helped Ramona to her feet. She noticed he made certain she was stable. While he stayed close enough to help if that changed, he turned to face his Wake commander. "The Dark Guardian, Mikhael Roman, is seeking more information," he said.

"I did not direct you to bring in a Dark Guardian."

"I called him when Silas showed up at my place," Ramona supplied. When Honora's gaze turned in her direction, the prolonged silence made Ramona uncertain if she was expecting more information. "He's kind of my brother-in-law," she added.

Honora blinked once, then returned her attention to Silas. "Come speak to me alone." Then she walked away.

"I'll send you back first," Silas said to Ramona. Granite was in his voice, the set of his jaw.

"No need. I'll stay right here and wait for you. It's a nice spot. Dandelions and everything." Plus a panoramic view of human carnage. When he gave her the same Sphinx stare, she shook her head. "She didn't see it. None of them saw it, Silas. Not even you. She might need more information from me when you two talk."

Though she could sense his desire to override her and send her back to her shop before dealing with Miss Stick Up Her Ass—if anyone could have a stick up their ass, it would be a tree spirit—he at last nodded. "Stay here. I mean it. I'm already wanting to wear your ass out for the danger you put yourself in."

"Because only you're allowed to risk yourself?" Though his penetrating look made it difficult, she held his gaze.

"Stay. Here." He pivoted and followed his commander.

"Though I'm not opposed to spankings in general," Ramona called after him. "If it will make you feel better."

Three Reapers looked her way. Silas came to a stop, his shoulders tightening. He sent her a glare over one, but she also saw a slight easing of that stonelike expression, a firming of his lips as if suppressing a faint smile.

Chaos magic could do that, too. Know when an off-the-wall or seemingly ill-timed comment was actually spot-on, sticking a spoke in the wheel of a mind going in a bad direction. For her part, it told her he had a durable sense of humor. Kind of a miracle, given not only the situation, but what he did for a living. Maybe that was why he had one. She knew it was why she did. Battlefield humor couldn't save a body, but it could salvage a soul struggling against bad odds.

Surrounded by death, souls in peril of something unnatural after them, Silas being "corrupted." That was when Chaos gamely stepped in and refused to let it become overwhelming.

If she could give him that gift, even at her own expense, she would. Honora had her worried. Ramona didn't know if the female Reaper was in Silas's corner or not, so she wasn't letting Silas out of her sight.

Honora had returned to the knoll that offered the best vantage point of the field. When Silas joined her, she inclined her head toward the fallen. "I sense your strong compulsion to help, but it is best not to attempt a Reaping until this is resolved."

"I know." She wasn't dictating to him. As the leader of their Wake, she had the right to do so, but it was rarely necessary. Protecting and guiding souls held sway over ego, pride or individual desires.

Even so, it was hard to tell her what Ramona had just shared. But he did. "While it called the Soul Collector, I don't sense that is the mark's ultimate purpose," he added. "As she suggested, it seemed more of a test, of how easily it could command my ability to call a soul." Ramona had disrupted it before it could find out.

"We should have been able to see it, sense it, and we did not. But the Chaos witch saw it clearly."

"I believe so, yes."

Her gaze slid to Ramona, back to him. "Tell me what you did not include in your message. I will share all of it with the others as you tell me."

Through a mind link not currently available to him. He put that aside and made his report. He felt tension increase on the field as the information was relayed, a warrior reaction to a threat they didn't yet know how to fight.

Even so, many turned his way, meeting his gaze, giving him a slight bow. He had their support, their loyalty. Their aid, in whatever way he needed it. Reapers were mostly solitary, for personal and professional reasons, but the ties between them were strong.

The knowledge helped. He was angry in several different directions. A cold block of rage was lodged against the mark within him, and what it had tried to do to the boy's soul had only increased its density. He was also angry with himself, because he still carried pointless guilt about how it had gotten there.

On top of that, a lethal fury was ready to take over if he gave any more thought to how Ramona had risked herself. She'd tangled with a Soul Collector all on her own.

And handled herself damn well.

He didn't enjoy feeling helpless, but he wasn't going to deny it merely because his manhood was getting kicked like a rosin bag by his current state. He had underestimated her abilities.

Because Reapers *were* his family, when he concluded the report, he made the rare decision to pose a personal question. "Honora, can you see the witch's death?"

Surprise flickered in her gray-green gaze, but she moved her attention to Ramona.

Ramona kept looking toward him, so at the Wake commander's regard, she shifted her gaze to Honora. In intimate moments, or when he was imposing his will upon her, Ramona responded to the Master in him, sometimes averting or lowering her gaze. But now Silas saw an obvious challenge in the witch's eyes, one that Honora registered with a faint smile.

"She is protective of you."

Then the smile died away as Honora's regard intensified. Her grip constricted on her scythe handle as she probed for the information Silas sought.

Ramona looked at Silas, a question in her eyes. He held up his hand, a silent reinforcement that he needed her to remain where she was. He combined it with a reassuring look, though the sadness in his chest was like a wet towel being twisted to drip water on a barren concrete floor.

The strength of the reaction surprised him, but he turned toward Honora and spoke calmly, before she offered the obvious. "You can't see it."

"No. I cannot. I assume you asked because you cannot, either. I have sent out a request to the others on the field to confirm if it is the same for them."

He appreciated her thoroughness, but knew the results would be the same, since he and Honora were the strongest Reapers present.

"What explanation do you have for this?" she asked.

"I believe it's because she is a Chaos witch. What's predictable for others is not for her. The Dark Guardian warned me of it."

No surprise, Honora had picked up on his mixed reaction to the news. "You thought she might be your soulmate." She studied him. "It is a rare occurrence. Many Reapers never cross a soulmate's path, or feel its lack. Our lives are full."

"They are."

Regardless of the reason, he acknowledged it was a comfort not to see the information about Ramona's mortality. His connection to her, whatever its root, made his feelings too strong to easily bear the knowledge.

She'd taken a seat against a large tree on the flanking forest's edge. Its leaves were scorched from homemade firebombs, the bark patterned by missing chunks, dislodged by gunfire. She'd drawn her knees up, was gripping the faded denim covering her legs, narrow backside pressed to the ground among the roots.

He wanted her to move to the other side of the tree, where she would face the woods instead of the battlefield. He knew the damage viewing such a scene could do to anyone, let alone someone with her heart.

"You are very drawn to this woman. As she is not a soulmate, we should perhaps question the timing. You met her right before the encounter with the Soul Collector. Could she be connected to its arrival?"

Honora's cool tone and fixed expression drew his attention back to her. "I haven't sensed that from her. If she is part of this, I believe it is to help, not harm."

"After you escaped The Pit and delivered the soul, you went to her first. Can you be sure your judgment is not impaired by the Dark Soul mark?"

He controlled a spark of temper. As Wake commander, Honora had the right to ask the difficult questions.

"No, I can't." Even though he believed he could, he couldn't deny the possibility of compromised judgment. "I will escort her home and then go into seclusion."

Honora had been regarding him closely when he answered. Now her expression cleared, and she made a noncommittal noise. He frowned. "You disagree?"

"I'm inclined to trust your instincts about her. You are a strong Reaper, Silas. It is why you will take over this Wake when I ascend higher in our Cast."

"Though I wish for your leadership skills to be honored, I am in no hurry for that to happen."

Honora made a dismissive gesture. "Your witch is detecting activity from the mark we cannot, and has provided you healing and opportunities to acquire a deeper understanding of its nature. I would advise remaining in her company while we investigate other avenues. The two of you may make further discoveries."

His witch. Whether true or not, it only strengthened the responsibility he felt toward her. Some of those "opportunities" had put her at risk.

Correctly reading his expression, Honora met his gaze with an unflinching one of her own. "She has proven she is a power in her own right. We are protectors, Silas, but it is best to know when that is useful and when it is a hindrance. Particularly when you are subject to stronger emotions than most Reapers experience at your age."

No censure in her tone, though he knew she found it both a puzzling and a worrisome thing. Yet he knew her worry was driven by her personal regard for him, not a doubt of his abilities. As she'd said, all Reapers were protectors. Every person he met, he knew their soul might at some point be under his care. He didn't relinquish that responsibility until they stepped through The Gate and into the keeping of a different power.

"She may not wish to put up with my company for much longer." A statement much along the same lines as what he'd told Mikhael, and intended to protect Ramona's options. He wouldn't impose himself upon her.

Honora's gaze swept over him. "I'm sure you can offer pleasures that make it worthwhile. Witches are sensual creatures, connected to primal energies."

The frank comment was also startlingly similar to Mikhael's response, but it was the grimly teasing tone that surprised Silas the most. It was rare Honora showed that side of herself anymore, though having been with her Wake for some time, he knew it existed.

Then she returned to her usual impassive self. "I will seek out the Dark Guardian and we will work together to research what is happening. Would you recommend anything else?"

"Talk to Reapers who've run into trouble lately. An encounter with a Soul Collector, or anything unusual. Since I don't remember the mark being inflicted upon me, others may have suffered the same."

"Agreed. I'll spread the word to other Wake commanders, and the Cast leadership. I will find you when I learn anything new." She paused. "The others on the field confirm they cannot see the witch's death. As you said, it must be her unique make-up. Chaos witches are rare. She is only the third I have met in my life span."

As she turned away, the silver blue light on her scythe flickered from the sunlight. A beautiful day, even as the heat had started baking the field of corpses.

She glanced back at him. "It has saddened you, knowing she is not your soulmate. I'm sorry. I did not anticipate that you desired that bonding."

"I don't think I did. Until I thought I'd found it." And then a bitter poignancy had gripped him at learning he hadn't.

"Perhaps it is best. Chaos witches rarely have long life spans." At his sharpened gaze, Honora added, "Managing their magic is difficult and isolating, and often expands beyond their ability to manage it. Though she seems to have a far better relationship with it than the other two I met."

No surprise to him. Since the moment he'd met her, the woman had proven herself extraordinary. Unfortunately, his inability to see her death was not.

"All is as the Fates will it," he said. Falling back on a Reaper mantra seemed his best option to deal with everything going on inside him. Truth, they had enough on their plate right now.

Plus, soulmate or not, Ramona needed him. Now.

Just as he feared, things were escalating. Sometimes the worst thing about a battle of any size was what happened in the aftermath. The fighting force that had prevailed had brought reinforcements to the field to retrieve their own dead and wounded. Plus make sure their enemies were dispatched. He was halfway across the field when one such combatant found a fallen man who was still alive, and aimed her rifle at his face.

Silas quickened his pace as Ramona bolted to her feet, her power gathering to intervene. He blocked the attempt, and was in front of her by the time the rifle discharged. He had his hands on her when she flinched.

"They can't see you," he reminded her. She clutched his arms, pushing against him, but it was an act of frustration, not trying to get away. As he kept a firm hold on her, Silas turned his head to see the shot man's assigned Reaper, Ishaaq, standing beside the body. The soul struggled from its mortal coil, falling forward on its hands and knees as the woman who'd killed him knelt to rummage through the corpse's pockets. The Reaper dropped to a knee next to the soul and spoke, drawing his attention.

Silas had kept himself planted in front of Ramona, blocking her view. When he turned his attention back to her, her hands were flexing against his biceps. She was bringing her reaction under control, but he could feel her body revolting against what was bludgeoning her senses here.

"The soul, he can't touch the person who shot him. His hands pass right through their body," she said tonelessly. "And yet, when he drops to his hands and knees, the earth holds him. Doesn't make sense, does it?"

"It makes a lot of sense," he told her. He knew he needed to get her out of here. But even if he couldn't help the others, he couldn't bring himself to quit the field, not when such a labor-intensive Reaping was taking place. So he guided her away, a few steps into the forest. He pulled her down with him into a sitting position against another mature tree. He angled himself so he could still glance over his shoulder and see what was happening, but the wide trunk would mostly screen her view of it.

"Remember what I said about changing clothes? To the earth, the elements, there's no real difference between a living person or a soul," he explained. "The earth exists on multiple planes of existence, whereas a mortal form exists only on the one."

He touched her face, stroked the troubled expression. Tending her held his attention better than he'd expected.

"Oh." Her gaze rested on the scythe. Unless he gave it specific guidance, it chose the most needed form. Right now it was the shepherd's crook. It rested against his bent knee. "Is it okay to touch it?"

"It is."

Her fingertips slid over the smooth wood. "It's ash."

"In this form, yes."

"A tree considered a bridge between earth and the heavens." An attempt at a smile quivered on her lips, then died. "How do you...I mean, this is bad enough. What about major wars? There must be a lot of Reapers."

"There's a goodly number of us. But when you visit a place where a large number of people died at once, and you feel that lingering sense of it, it's because there weren't enough of us to take every soul on time. We had to keep coming back, gathering up more. Plus there will always be stragglers."

He slid a hand along her upper arm, thumb rubbing over the freckled skin. "The confusion of those delayed souls, it's an imprint that can remain on a place. Sometimes we do have to be more like shepherds, taking a group of souls, rather than one at a time. Reapers who handle slaughterhouses deal with souls more used to operating as a flock or herd. Human souls are harder to keep together."

She swallowed. "Thanks for making me glad I'm a vegetarian. Are you okay?"

Her face was pale, her eyes big, but she asked it of him from that calm center that he'd not yet felt falter in her. "Yes, thanks to you. You kept the mark from causing harm."

His power might eclipse hers in many ways, but Honora was right. She'd covered a vital blind spot for him and his fellow Reapers.

"No...I mean...you looked a little sad, leaving your boss."

"My boss?" A grim flit of humor at the modern characterization for Honora. "Yes, I guess I am. I'm relieved of duty for now. A wise decision. But not being able to do my work is difficult. I'm connected to the souls to be Reaped, particularly the ones that are my specific responsibility. To see another step in to take over for me is difficult."

Mentally conjuring from the cache where he kept his belongings, he produced his journal, lifted it for her inspection. The flicker of interest he saw would hopefully dilute the horror trying to drag her down.

"The Reaping schedule is something embedded in my mind, updated without conscious act. We are connected to the Fates' Loom. I know who I will be Reaping several full moon cycles in advance, though it's a fluid schedule. Like now. The names I would have been Reaping have been removed from my mind."

Though he couldn't keep himself from grimacing at the words, he lifted the book. "But they are still here. I like transcribing the names into a book, adding notes. How I anticipate they'll react to their deaths, how I can ease that transition and the journey to The Gate."

She flinched at another shot. He put his hand to her face. "Ramona, you suffer needlessly."

"No. You feel like you still need to be here, and I want to understand. Your talking helps. That boy, his Reaper appeared as his mother. Does your research help with that?"

"Yes. The choice of our form is driven by the soul. But behind her body and voice, Etienne is still himself, so it helps if he knows more of her personality, to help the soul let go of memory to grasp truth."

She reached toward the journal. He assumed she wanted to hold it, but she touched his wrist instead, slipped her hand down to rest on top of his. "I expect it's hard to let someone else Reap a soul you've gotten to know."

"I have confidence in my brethren." Yet there was an undeniable sense of connection, of loss.

The tree they rested against was close enough to the edge of the wood that the sun could penetrate its canopy, grow dandelions and long grasses. Those plants were weaving together, as if trying to create an organic buffer wall between them and the battlefield. He'd been aware of the creaking of the tree, and now several branches had bent low enough to enter his field of vision. They were doming over them, touching the tops of the grasses.

He didn't know if she did it consciously or not. She'd shifted so she sat against his bent knee, their bodies canted toward one another, another cocoon. She kept her gaze on him as if the earth would crumble if she looked away.

He would honor her strength of will, but he added to her natural cocoon weaving, reinforcing it so their spot was further buffered from the bloodshed. When her shoulders eased, he could tell the additional screening helped.

"Do a lot of your souls ask the same kinds of things? 'Where are we going? Is it nice? Will I see loved ones? Is there chocolate?'"

Her hand still rested on his on the journal, fingers between his, so he squeezed them. "Yes. They also talk about the life they have left behind, thoughts they have had. What they were doing on that last day, what they regret or are happy about. It's a library of information on the nature of a soul, what it feels, thinks, accomplishes. It's a part of my job I enjoy very much. I like my conversations with them."

"You'll get back to it soon, I know it," she said staunchly. "Mikhael is one of the best trackers in the Guardian world." She paused. "So did your boss say what you should do while you were off duty?"

"She said I should...spend time with you."

Ramona gave him a shrewd look. "Her advice is to fuck like rabbits until they figure out something?" The corner of her lip curled in an almost impish way, making him think of her blatant offer to be spanked. Just like then, her comment startled a smile out of him, when he would have thought nothing could.

"Simply being with you, having a conversation, is such a pleasure, it would be greedy to ask for more."

With the battle scene so close, she couldn't hold a smile for long, either, but his words did make her lips soften, her fingers curving under his to create a full lock.

"You have a very old world way about you sometimes. I like it." She moistened her lips. "But I also like it when you...want more."

"You were about to say something else." He met her gaze. "Tell me."

"I like it when you...demand more." She drew in a breath.

"It seemed so much a part of you, even in that brief time we were together, I think it made it impossible for me to imagine it any other way between us. For a while, I thought I...exaggerated it in my memory, but then you came back."

"And you confirmed it?" He caressed her wrist, the script rippling under his touch, making her draw in a breath.

"Yes. The reality confirmed my imaginings. And made me want more."

That message went straight to his groin, pulling his mind away from its obsessive litany of *you have a demon force inside you trying to destroy souls*. It dampened the near agonizing desire to cut the damn mark out of him, even if he had to dig a hole to his spine.

"While Honora didn't phrase things the same way you did, she did remind me of the earthy side of witches, your matter-of-fact attitude about things of the flesh."

Gripping her braid, he pulled it forward over her shoulder. "It is in my mind right now, a desire to put you on your hands and knees under a tree like this. Remove all your clothes. Unbraid your hair." He slid his finger in between the twisted strands, tugged. "I'd spread it over your shoulders, and kiss my way down your spine to your lovely buttocks. Mark them with my teeth."

He'd leaned in to whisper the last comments, and she turned her face toward him. He wanted to pull in her desires, use them to draw her away from the darkness he hadn't wanted her to see here. But even as he felt her body answer his, something shifted, her eyes getting a pained look, cloaked by shadows.

"Silas, what I feel from your mark is...a waiting. That thing on your shoulders was something different. Like a hungry leopard in a cage, watching a herd of antelope. There's a master of the leopard, wanting to release it to some purpose."

"The leopard only desires to hunt and kill its prey." He nodded. "That's an accurate description of a Soul Collector."

She shivered. "A leopard hunts as a natural part of things. There's nothing natural about this." Her gaze strayed back to the field. "Or maybe we just tell ourselves that."

Mikhael had warned him.

Wild energy surged outward from her, as unexpected as that leopard leaping out from a camouflaged lair. A swipe of its talons shredded their combined buffer screen. The full weight of the hatred, death and grief on the field rolled in, an avalanche that covered them in the space of a breath.

She had scrambled to her feet, and stumbled from the impact. Though he was up in time to catch her, he saw her eyes become stark as she absorbed the shock of it. The tree groaned, the branches snapping upward to their original positions. The trunk shuddered.

Drops of blood struck her face. It was raining blood through the tree limbs. He pulled her close, shedding his robe to wrap it around her. His crook became a staff as he projected a shield from it like an umbrella.

"I'm sorry," she said again. Chagrin and panic were in her voice. She gripped his shirt, her pupils large and dark. "You were right. Doing nothing while it's happening is terrible. After is even worse." Her gaze flitted over his shoulder, then pulled back to him again. "Though I guess the ones who shot the wounded were better than those who preferred throat slitting or stabbing. Oh, Goddess, I need to get out of here. I can't do it anymore, Silas. I'm sorry."

He'd sensed her reaction all along, but he'd woefully misjudged how deeply it ran. She'd effectively locked it down, until they started being playful. He suspected the sexual teasing had loosened her lock on whatever she'd been doing to hold it together.

It was a mistake he wouldn't make again. He had so much to learn of her. Perhaps his ability to channel her magic during intimacy, keep it intertwined with his, was because it was what the unpredictable and wild magic within her wanted, too. One focus, one intent. When other things were happening, his ability to shield her was just as susceptible to disruption as the Guardians' magic.

He should have gone with his gut instinct, not brought her here. But what would have happened to the soul the darkness within him had been hellbent on letting the Collector take? That no one but her had been able to see.

He didn't have good answers to any of it, but there was one thing he could do, better late than never. He needed to care for her more than he needed to be here. There was a bitterness to the thought, but the day had possessed enough kicks in the teeth.

Keeping the other arm around her, he guided her hand to his chest. When he laid her palm there, he felt an anchoring feeling, a centering. "We're going," he said.

She should be relieved her reaction had been confined to a light shower, versus a full deluge that would make them look like they'd attended a prom in a Stephen King book. Ramona was also glad Silas had recovered swiftly enough to provide an umbrella-style shield for them.

Even so, she still wanted a shower. She wanted to scour away the oily coating of despair that battlefield had layered over her soul.

After she wiped away the few droplets that had stained her face, she decided on a calming tea blend instead. They'd come back to her store, and she'd directed Silas to the spot by the side alley window where she provided refreshments for her customers. The coffee corner he'd noted.

He'd had a crappy day himself, and she knew he felt he should have brought her back far sooner. Yet instead of brooding over it and requiring her to expend emotional energy to reassure him, he offered to make the tea for her. When she shook her head, he stood by her as she made it, his hand on her lower back, letting her lean against him as they watched the brew steep.

It was a unique experience, to be with a male mature enough to offer a quiet, encouraging presence as she found her balance. What she really needed, rather than trying to impose his idea of how to fix it.

You've always been with boys, Ramona. You've never had the pleasure of a grown-up man.

She hadn't understood what Raina meant. But she was getting a promising hint of it.

She still wore his robe. It was too long for her, the sleeves covering her hands, but she held it close. The threads were a resilient fiber she didn't recognize, but the fabric was soft, smelled like him, and lay upon her with the same reassurance the shelter of his body had provided.

"May I ask another question?"

"You can ask me anything," he replied.

She nodded to one of the two small table and chair sets she kept in this corner, and he moved to take a chair there. The cargo trousers stretched over his thighs as he sat down. His black shirt made the most of his jeweled green eyes. While the way he moved made her think of a wolf, the eyes made her imagine a dragon. How he'd swirled the cloak off his body to cover hers had added to it, the folds rippling like a dragon's wings.

Being fanciful helped. So did looking at him. But she couldn't help needing to know the answer to her question, even if it raised darker issues again.

"Does it make it easier to watch, knowing you're about to take the soul away from whatever has happened?"

"Watching someone suffer is never easy," he said. "But yes, it helps to know that it's a moment in time, even if some moments are far longer than we could wish."

She thought of the way the Reapers had stood there. Honoring what was happening, silent witnesses. She hadn't sensed detachment. They didn't stand apart from it.

When she made that observation, he nodded. "The soul senses our presence, and finds a comfort in that connection, but they can lose that awareness during great stress. However, if our grip on it is steady, it will be there, ready when they let go of their life."

She brought the tea to the table. After she put a mug in front of him, she slid her palm along his and gripped. "Now I know why your hands are so strong."

She stared at their linked fingers. "Not everyone goes to good places, do they?"

"Redemption is a necessary path for most souls to strengthen and heal themselves for the next life. But the degrees of it are different." He shrugged. "Mikhael would be the best source for that information. My role ends at The Gate."

"Do you ever wonder about the day you'll cross it, what you'll find?"

His gaze didn't falter. "Reapers don't cross The Gate. When our time is over, we are like the angels. The knowledge we carry, what we are, it makes more sense to disperse that to the energy of All rather than keep it contained in one body, one soul. It serves future Reapers, Guardians, others who serve the Lord and Lady. The energy finds its way to those who need it."

She looked back down at their hands. "So after you're gone, I would never see you again."

He touched her face, drew her gaze to him. "I would be the breath you draw into your lungs, the sun on your face, a deep sleep with good dreams. If you were a bird, I'd be the endless sky, the wind that carries you, the tree that beckons you to take a moment of rest in its arms."

He captured a lock of her hair, let it slide through his roughened knuckles. "See? Here are your feathers."

He tipped her chin up with the other hand, closing the distance between their bodies to put his lips on hers. She tasted the heat of the water, the flavorful tea. As her eyes fluttered closed, relief and pleasure spilled from her heart, into the waiting pool of strength he offered.

When he eased back, she slid out of the chair. She sank down between his knees, laid her head on his thigh. The thick carpet in this section cushioned her knees, but so did the folds of his robe beneath her.

In the weighted silence, his hand settled on her shoulder, the exposed point of her neck where her hair parted and fell forward. More things eased inside her. Through his touch, he communicated his awareness of how fragile she was, that he would give her what she needed.

In her fantasies, submission to a Master was about more than sex; it was also about trust and care, hence the involved aftercare imaginings.

With a little sigh, she closed her eyes, willed her vibrating body to settle.

"You know what I think?" she said at length. "Gina said they were doing a role-playing fashion show at Raina's. We need to go. They did it yesterday, but they'll have zero problem doing it again and coming up with new ideas."

At his quizzical look, she added, "Raina runs the local bordello. Her employees are all succubi and incubi."

He appeared to take that in stride. "Bordello is an old term. Not an escort service?"

She shook her head. "Because of their energy, they have to offer their services in a place where she can protect the clients from a lethal dose of it." She managed a smile. "Raina also sometimes uses the term bawdy house. She likes that one."

"I'm sorry I kept you from attending the fashion show."

"Yeah, well. It was a bummer, but at the time I felt tending the Reaper who'd had his skin tortured off of him took priority."

He'd lifted a lock of her hair, long enough to press his lips to it, brush it against his cheek to feel the texture. The kindness, the simple pleasure, choked a sob from her. When she would have drawn away, he brought her up into his lap, cradling her in arms as strong as his hands.

"It's okay," she told him. She kept her face pressed to his chest, her tears wetting his shirt. "I have to cry after seeing something like that. I think everyone does, even if it's only inside. I can tell you feel it that deeply, too. But it's your job, so you have to keep it tamped down."

"I would have spared you the pain." His voice rumbled against her cheek, his knuckles curving to trace her cheek, take away the tears.

"Little good ever comes from that, if the pain leads to where we're meant to go. That said, we both could use a distraction. Are you good with the fashion show idea? How about, when we head that way, we stop at Boris's and get that grilled cheese I told you about, back on the day we met. Do you remember?"

Before he could answer, she shook her head, drew back enough to knuckle at her eyes. "'Of course. While the skin was peeled from my hot body and I was dedicating every ounce of my considerable strength to protecting a soul, Ramona, I was thinking about what I'd choose off the menu of that fabulous café you recommended.'"

She loved his smile. It was a gift, because though he might be the calmest person she'd ever met, she felt so much from him. As he proved with his next words.

"Do you remember what *I* told you, witch?" Silas met her gaze. "I recall every word of that conversation. The smell of your hair, your expressions, the way you moved, how your clothes lay upon *your* hot body. The taste of your lips. Nothing keeps a man company in dire times like a memorable woman."

His words made her still, a hand curling into the neckline of his shirt. He covered that hand, squeezed it before he passed his fingertips over the tracks of new tears. He cupped her skull, fingertips kneading her nape. "You let your emotions show so easily."

"Emotions are the root of Chaos energy." It took her a moment to recover and answer him, but he waited for her, seeming to register everything she was doing to pull herself together. She also wasn't used to a man paying such close attention to her. She didn't hate it.

"If I try to hide the stronger ones, it interprets it as a form of deception and gets riled. The only time it seems to be okay with that is if I'm doing it to spare someone's feelings." She took a breath. "Okay, then. We'll do it as a to-go order, bring some for everyone. Matilda, Raina's cook, will give me the stink-eye, but that's just for form's sake. They have pizza party nights all the time because they like to flirt with the pizza delivery folks."

Before he could respond to her nervous prattling, the copper bell chime over her front door went off, its haunting note echoing through the store. Ramona twisted around to see a young woman had opened the door a small crack.

"Oh, sorry. Hi. Are you open?"

A young man stood with her, their hands linked. Even as she asked the question, the girl was peering around the store with avid shopper eyes.

She should have locked the door. Regardless, Ramona rose from Silas's lap and gestured them in. "Not technically, but we're here, so come on in and look around."

As they complied, attention already captured by the display

nearest them, she turned back to Silas. "Sorry," she murmured. "We can go as soon as they've looked."

"No." He rose, laying a brief hand on her shoulder before going to turn the sign to *Open*, surprising her. "Doing what you might normally do this time of day would be helpful, wouldn't it? I'd like to watch you run your store."

He was right. It would help restore balance to her fractured psyche. She felt a different, better kind of imbalance when he leaned down to brush his lips over her mouth. He lingered there, his green eyes close.

"But I better still get fabulous grilled cheese and a sex demon fashion show," he said.

Silas shifted to a stool behind one of the display cases. There were some boxes stored there, but enough room for him to brace his legs, lean his back against a shelf. He was out of the way, but still where he could watch her.

He wanted to learn small things about her as well as larger ones. Or more intimate ones. And observing her run her store kept his impatience for news from Mikhael and Honora manageable. He'd already noted that dwelling on the mark like a damn bomb ticking down to some unknown catastrophe made it feel even more embedded inside him. If positive emotions and experiences ended up loosening its hold, it would be one more thing he'd know about it. And be one step closer to getting it the fuck out of his body.

Another set of customers came in behind the young couple, a group of women who showed every sign of being there for a while. No surprise, due to her extensive inventory, the artfully arranged clutter.

She was speaking to them, telling them about her store offerings. Lord and Lady, her voice. It held everything that made life a painting, one held forever in the mind, even when death's curtain was drawn over its window.

She sent his mind in a different direction when she mentioned a discount on her Grim Reaper collection. As she sent him a sultry wink, he remembered her voice when she was gasping her pleasure or pleading with a thready undercurrent, wanting more of what he could give her.

He'd known what she needed when she'd knelt at his feet, her hands on his thigh, her head resting there, the nape of her neck exposed to him. Being offered a submissive's gift of trust in his care had restored a vital part of him that felt battered by all the other things the day had revealed.

But watching her send him secret smiles and move around her shop, win over every customer with her open spirit and soul-deep beauty, it was impossible to quell the urge to move from giving to taking. She'd shed his robe, carefully folded it over a chair. The fit of the T-shirt and jeans she wore innocently molded every curve. He was fascinated by the triangle of flesh revealed by the neckline of her shirt, the freckles scattered over her arms.

When she'd knelt at his feet, he'd inhaled every nuance of her scent, including the faint perspiration from the stress of the field, the arousal of her body that his kiss had invoked.

One of the women looked his way, and he offered a courteous nod. *Cancer. Four hundred forty-two million, seven hundred sixteen thousand heartbeats...*

Or fourteen years, two weeks, three days, five hours, twelve minutes and sixteen seconds. Fifteen seconds, fourteen seconds...

He shifted his attention away from her. He could cloak himself, become invisible to mortals, but often preferred to blend among them. However, because he knew his direct gaze was unsettling to them, even if they didn't understand why, he didn't hold it longer than necessary.

The woman gave him a female appraisal, then a knowing smile. She said something low to one of her fellow shoppers, nodding toward Ramona. They chuckled as they moved toward the top hat display.

"He looks ready to devour her. Let's clear the path."

Ramona had picked up on the comment, her startled gaze shifting to him. He didn't bother to disguise where his thoughts had gone, interested in her reaction. She didn't disappoint. Her lavender gaze got deeper, her lips parting. She absently pushed back her hair, gave him a little smile.

His bird. He wanted to send her soaring again.

One of the women emerged from Ramona's potions and spellcraft aisle, a wax heart in the palm of her hand. "Melt to soften the heart of a loved one," she read the card to her friends. She cocked a dubious though amiable look at Ramona. "So that's all you need to do?"

Ramona chuckled. "Your intent matters as well. You're committing to an act that softens your own, opens your eyes to what might be keeping the other person's heart hard and closed."

Her gaze slid to Silas. "It's rarely a straight line, what we need and desire."

Truer words.

CHAPTER NINE

*S*weet Dreams was the name of Raina's establishment. The tall, rambling Queen Anne structure had a first level wraparound porch and several balconies on the second and third levels. The complicated roofline of cross gables and a block tower had a seemingly random design Silas knew helped channel and contain energy flow in the areas that most needed it. He wondered if Ramona had helped with that spell craft. The top tower was where Raina had her private rooms. A weathervane shaped like a witch riding a broom crowned its roof, the broom's bristles curled like the witch's long streaming hair.

The house possessed delicate arches, decorative brackets, stained glass windows. The winding drive had been almost a mile long, through thick woods and marsh, and lined with ancient oaks draped with Spanish moss.

Ramona had asked him to portal them to the mid-point, so they could walk from there, and she could tell him about the place, show him the grounds. He didn't oppose the plan. He liked looking at her, her hand gestures, the way her body moved and eyes flickered, everything going on with her.

She was aware of it, a brightness to her eyes. Every time their bodies brushed or her hand fell on his arm, the erotic awareness between them intensified.

Sweet Dreams was presented as a bed and breakfast, but no guest came seeking a room for the night. Unless they had deep enough pockets and wanted the services they could find here for that length of time. Law enforcement was managed with distraction magic and Raina's savvy community outreach. Apparently, the way for a bordello to be accepted was by winning over women in the community.

"Raina hosts monthly tea parties," Ramona informed him. "Grand, lovely things. The succubi and incubi are the waitstaff. I told you about Matilda, the cook? She's also an excellent baker, and she's got a couple of apprentices. Li is the leader of the pack, after Raina. He's interested in cooking. A couple of his clients have a food fetish. They want it prepared, served or eaten on their bodies. Some of them like being the centerpiece at group dinners..."

He'd picked up her hand as she spoke, put his mouth on her fingers to nibble at them. The teasing touch of tongue he added had her trailing off. "They also have a romance book club that meets in the parlor," she added faintly.

"You seem to know a great deal about the operations."

"I'm one of the voyeurs. Ruby and I have an open invitation any night we want to watch in the public rooms."

"You've never participated? Or been a client?"

She glanced at him, then away. "No. Not really."

Being open about sexual matters wasn't the same as being open about vulnerabilities, past disappointments. He felt the closing of a door which held things she didn't want to discuss right now. It wasn't the time to push it, but he filed it away for later. He pressed a kiss to the center of her palm, released her as they mounted the stairs to the front door. It opened as they reached it.

"Gina," Ramona said warmly, an indirect introduction for Silas to the female standing in the doorway.

The young succubus was not yet in full control of her powerful erotic miasma, but the house's protections helped neutralize and tone it down. Her red hair framing sparkling dark eyes was even more riotous than Ramona's blond locks. Drawing Ramona over the threshold, she hugged her. Hands with painted golden nails wandered over Ramona's back and hips with easy familiarity.

"I'm so glad you decided to come. Ruby's upstairs with Raina, gathering things to bring down. They have plenty of help, so Raina said to give your guest the house and garden tour, and they'd be down shortly."

Gina was appraising him with great curiosity, her nostrils flaring, head cocking. Just like any other wild creature, she assessed him first as food. At least with these particular sex demons, that wasn't a lethal proposition for humans, though without Raina's spell work, it might be.

When he kept his natural offensive skills close to the surface, making it clear he wasn't prey, she took a deferential step back, acknowledging it. To fully reinforce the message, he had to meet her gaze and hold it, but he absorbed the impact of what he found there and refocused without a change in expression. A learned trait, developed over centuries.

"You're welcome here, sir," she said courteously. "Or is it 'my lord?' Can I bring you anything?"

"I'm fine. *Sir* works. Or Silas. I have all I need right here. Thank you."

He clasped Ramona's hand when he said it. Gina shot a look of female appreciation and a secretive smile at Ramona. Then she left them, bounding up the wide main hall staircase like a graceful deer.

"I thought you only wanted me to call you *sir*." Though Ramona's tone was light, he heard the question in it.

"There's *sir*, and there's *Sir* with a capital letter."

"Hmm." She cocked her head. "There's this really subtle shift in your gaze when you first look at someone. That's when you know how and when they'll die, isn't it?"

"Yes."

She nodded. "You register it, but then you move past it. It's a road you've traveled down so many times you know exactly how to keep the car on the road. But when you looked at Gina, I could feel how you feel it. It's difficult, every time. Isn't it?"

Even the souls he Reaped rarely thought of how their mortality impacted him. Which was how it should be, but having someone interested in his well-being as a lover was unexpected. And not unpleasant.

"There are many questions Reapers don't answer, because it wouldn't make sense to others," he said honestly. "When I see a death that will come too soon, or be ugly, it's like being stabbed by a knife.

And yet I will do nothing to change it, which makes me sound like a cold bastard with no compassion."

"Except for where you said it feels like you're being stabbed." She put her hand on his chest, drew a pattern over his heart. While it was an unfocused movement, merely exercising a desire to touch him, she was tracing an infinity symbol. "Did you ever try to stop one?"

"Yes. Once. Every inexperienced Reaper does. It changed things for the worse, for that soul. I was responsible for putting it through that." He grimaced. "Lyra was my mentor during my first years. She told me to focus on what happens when we bring them to The Gate. How, when they cross that threshold, there will be a respite from whatever suffering they experienced."

"Do you know that for certain?"

"When The Gate opens for the soul, the energy that is emitted... you know it is a welcome home."

She mulled that. "The one you interfered with. Was it a male or female soul?"

"Unless it's their first incarnation, souls come from multiple lives, where their body home has been different genders, races, species. So we simply say 'the soul,' unless they are holding onto a particular incarnation and have a preference, or it's useful for clarification. Like Cal."

"Body home. I like that. If you turn it around, it becomes home-body. You're avoiding the question." A teasing spark entered her gaze. "The one where you tried to interfere. Was the 'body home' male or female? Adult or child?"

"Female. Pretty, young, and sad. A suicide."

"So, testosterone influences Reapers as well."

"I do not believe I have given you cause to doubt my testosterone." Smiling at her chuckle, he admitted, "Lyra said as much. Though she wasn't too harsh. We all have certain souls that affect us. Honora thinks it's because of lives we don't remember, before we became Reapers."

He rubbed at his chest, which was itching. Ramona gestured toward a wide hallway. "Raina said to give you the full tour. We'll start with the path to the parlor. It's how Raina displays client options, so it's pretty distracting."

"Is there anything in this place that isn't?"

She twinkled at him. "Absolutely nothing. It's like concentrated teenage hormones multiplied by a million here. I don't know how they manage to do anything but think about sex. Matilda acted like a scalded cat the only time I asked her how she deals with it. She says she has nothing to do with the 'shenanigans' that go on in this 'den of sin.'"

Ramona rolled her eyes. "But while she'll whack them with a spoon when they step out of line, she loves them like a momma badger. The only one she treats anywhere near an equal is Raina, and even that depends on the day and Matilda's mood. She's a hundred percent mortal, but Raina has decided it's an act. She thinks Matilda is an ancient mother goddess slumming as a cook. She could kick all of our asses with sheer disapproval alone."

The wide hallway had a Persian rug, the colors highlighted by the diamond-drop chandeliers that lit their way. The sensual delights available at Sweet Dreams were foreshadowed by artwork mounted against the floral wallpaper. Each of the gilt-framed original oil paintings, done in classical Romantic style, displayed an erotic act. Scattered among them were whimsical pencil drawings or watercolors that somehow didn't clash. The mix reminded the viewer of all the things sex could be. Sacred, fun, intense, loving, a treasure of shared emotions and possibilities.

Silas had tucked Ramona's fingers into the crook of his elbow, but now he slid his arm around her waist, drawing her closer to him. Her eyes rose to meet his as he molded his palm over her buttock, bare under the skirt of the dress she'd worn. He wanted to seek her heat, increase the arousal he could scent.

Fuck it. He wasn't a human, but he was all male.

He bent his head, met her lips, already parted, and she was leaning into him, her body pressed close as he took two handfuls of very nice female ass. Underneath the dress, he knew her buttocks were smooth and silky to the touch. When he'd teased her between them at her shop, she'd become even more wildly aroused.

While he suspected decorum wasn't a big priority in a bordello, he also knew the pleasures of anticipation. He moved them to the wall, put her against it but then eased back. "So you like the idea of calling me 'Sir?' Being more formal with me, under certain circumstances? Circumstances I control?"

"Maybe," she admitted. "Yes. The desire is there, Silas. It's strong."

He braced a hand by her head, combed a lock of her hair over her breast, offering a deliberate caress. "But?"

She lowered her eyes to watch his hand. "Surrender has a lot of faces. I've experienced some of the bad ones. So outside of fantasizing, what I want is new territory, which makes me nervous. I know a lot about the gap between what we wish for and what we can have." She paused. Lifted her face to his as she spoke carefully. "Would you like it if I called you that? Sir?"

Her breath, thready, was a touch of silk against his mouth. The script on her wrists was glowing with heat.

"Under the right circumstances, I like the idea very much." His hand slid over the curve of her buttock, bringing her lower body in contact with his, the pressure of his erection reinforcing the answer.

"When she saw the gift you'd left me, Raina said you had a 'kink flair.'" Her grip on his shirt told him she was rolling over a lot of things about that, needing deeper into his mind on it.

"Being given control of a woman's passion, her trust in what I'll do with it...it's been a skill I've developed, plundered and explored for a very long time."

The pulse in her throat throbbed. "It never gets old?"

"It's never failed to fascinate and remain unpredictable in the right ways, just as its predictable side is a nectar I've never tired of."

"Unlike the women themselves."

He'd known he was dipping into perilous waters with that one, things that came close to her past heartbreaks. It was clear she hadn't had a relationship that hadn't fallen short of her hopes, which meant males who hadn't been able to handle who or what she was, let alone fulfill her needs beyond the short term.

"It was a pleasure with a natural beginning and end. Reapers know nothing is permanent until...it is."

Knowing she wasn't his soulmate brought that inexplicable tinge of disappointment again. He put it away. It shouldn't change anything about how strongly he was drawn to her, or her to him.

When he cupped her face, she nipped at his fingers, her eyes full of what she needed and wanted. "This hallway is like being dropped in a vat of pheromones without a life jacket," she sighed, with a half-smile.

"No fire analogies?"

"Raina would try to turn me into a frog if I burned one of her rugs."

"Try? But not succeed?"

"Unless we catch one another by surprise, we're pretty well matched," she said.

He stepped back, offering her his arm in a way he expected she'd call 'old world,' but she'd said she liked that. With her hand in the crook of his elbow again, they resumed their stroll along the montage of paintings. At the end of the hallway, they entered the parlor.

In the early evening, clients were entertained there and matched up with Raina's stable of beautiful male and female demons. From there they'd go to a room outfitted for their desires. He was shown those rooms, plus the big dining room sometimes used for the food fetishes. She took him past a bank of windows with a view of the extensive gardens, where exhibitionist play could happen. Guest houses were available for those who paid to stay the night.

As the last stop on the tour, Ramona took him into Raina's impressive library, which included many ancient arcane texts glassed in on the top shelves.

He arched a brow at several of the titles he knew had been reported stolen in the past couple decades, but figured that was Mikhael's area to handle with his succubus-witch mate.

Sometimes *not my job* was a term to be thankful for.

"Do any of those she employs ever move on?"

"None so far. They're family, and act like a pack. It's not unusual for three or four to share the same bed." She sobered. "When they're out in the world, sex demons have to be solitary, hunting and operating alone. It's not easy for incubi or succubi on their own, because most of them can't *not* kill their prey, and that attracts attention. A kill here or there can be covered, as long as they're smart about it, but they're very much creatures of impulse. As full-blooded sex demons mature toward thirty, it gets worse, and they lose control. Raina's concerned about Li, because he's getting close to that age."

She gestured around her. "While I freely admit there's a personal pleasure to watching things unfold between the demons and the guests, their joy toward it has a bittersweet side to it. There's none of the ugly edge of hunger, and you can see how much that means to every one of them. There's a huge difference between anticipating what's for dinner, and wondering if there will be dinner at all. Or if you'll be hunted when you can't stop killing, because your hunger has become an addiction you can't stop."

She drew a steadying breath. "Here they're safe. They can be a family."

"You understand the value of that," he noted. "Chaos witches must live solitary lives as well. You are fortunate to have your coven sisters."

"I'm thankful for them every day." She reached up to touch his jaw, fingers grazing his cheek. "You know what loneliness is, too, but you've turned it into simply being alone. There's a lot of good things waiting once that threshold is crossed. But you never forget what you leave behind. Or stop wishing for it."

"No," he said. "You don't."

He lifted his head at a stray wisp of energy. The French doors behind them opened, bringing in the scents of the ornamental gardens. He could hear a fountain gurgling, the buzzing of bees and chirping of birds. Ramona's eyes sparkled. "The house likes to suggest things. Apparently it thinks we could do with a walk in the gardens."

Many homes were infused with the energy of those who'd lived within its walls, but it was rare that the structure itself took that energy and used it to manifest its own will so directly. But he guessed with a powerful witch in residence and a dozen sex demons, it wasn't surprising.

"Luke, another incubus, complains that it's like having a house mother, literally. He calls it Nanny McPhee. If one of them is running late at night, taking too long in the shower, it will turn the water ice cold. Or if Raina needs to be up early, she'll wake up with her bed moved in front of an east-facing window."

"Convenient." Gesturing her courteously ahead of him, he rested his hand on her hip as they stepped outside. She tipped her head back to the sun, hair whispering over his arm. He enjoyed its silken softness before he took her hand, so they could wander the paths together like that. As he studied the arrangement of vegetation, flowers, statuary and benches, she pointed out storage places stocked daily for the anticipated evening needs of the clients.

Snacks, water. Vibrators, harnesses, rope to bind a playmate to a bench, perhaps while they were blindfolded. The sex demon might use a thorny stem or the silken touch of a flower to stimulate, alternating things of the natural world with the more unforgiving touch of a whip.

He noted the flick of her lashes when she explained that, how her hand tightened on his. Reaching out to a flowering bush, he removed a white bloom. "Close your eyes," he said.

Her eyes widened when he issued the command, taking control. As her lids lowered, he brushed the flower bloom over her eyes, her nose and lips. "I would press this between your legs, decorate you with flowers, draw lines upon your back with the thorns of a rose stem. Then flick all of the blooms off with the touch of a crop, and give those lines an extra sting. I'd save the bloom between your legs for last. When I struck it away, I would put my fingers inside you, with the crop's handle. Would you like that?"

Her lips were pressed together. She gave a quick nod. He threaded the bloom into her hair behind her ear. "Good. Open your eyes."

Surprised, she put her hand up to the flower. Her dazed expression said the romantic gesture pleased her. "I'm not sure we're going to make it through the fashion show," she said in a throaty voice.

"If I can run the hallway gauntlet without taking you on the parlor sofa, I can handle a cornucopia of role-playing outfits presented by a nubile group of sex demons."

She laughed, eyes clearing. "I hope so. Because Raina is as rabid about her parlor sofa as she is her carpets. But maybe we should run that gauntlet again, just to test your fortitude. You know, there's a bathroom along the hallway. Very Raina-approved tile floors."

"I would not take you on cold tile. But if you keep tempting me..."

She stepped back to the full extent of their arms and then moved forward to duck under his, executing a twirl.

He'd teased her to make her smile, and also to help him pull back. Being around her was like resisting the desire to taste a cake just out of the oven, that tempting aroma begging for it to be consumed with both hands.

But as far as challenges to his self-control went, it was one he could handle and enjoy. Learning how people would meet their end was as he'd described it. He did it every day, but that knife-in-the-gut feeling when he discovered the demise would be ugly or too soon—it never went away. It was why many of his kind preferred not being among people. He'd learned to push past it, see the person as more than their death.

The research he did beforehand on the souls he Reaped? It was to help with their transition, but it also helped him remember what he knew was more important.

How they lived.

~

Raina leaned on her balcony railing, outside her tower bedroom. Cathair, her crow familiar, hopped along the rail, traipsed over her hand, giving it a light peck to get a stroke of his feathers, before he fluttered up to the eaves.

She'd watched the erotic tension between Silas and Ramona grow, had sensed with interest Ramona's energy tangling with his, which contained and channeled the Chaos elements back into whatever they were sharing. Then she saw Silas place the flower behind Ramona's ear, his hand lingering. Whatever he said made her smile. She stepped back, holding their hands together and then lifting them to do a twirl beneath, close enough her hips and shoulder blades brushed his body. Her golden hair gleamed.

"Have you ever seen her like this with anyone?" she asked Ruby, standing beside her. "In all the years we've known her, and ever this fast?"

"There was that surfer, the Marine," Ruby noted thoughtfully. "He lasted a couple weeks."

"Yes. Until he mentioned how he'd always wanted to see a whale close up while surfing. He nearly drowned when one came up under him. And broke the surfboard."

"I think it all thrilled him. It was Ramona who freaked out. She ended it right after. That was the last mortal she ever considered being with."

"Well, she was on a losing streak." Raina sighed. "The one before that was the gamer. He woke up inside his first-person shooter game without a weapon."

"He'd rolled off of her and picked up his phone to resume play, like he'd just finished takeout pizza. We should have left him there long enough to cure him of being an inconsiderate dick."

Ruby leaned her elbows on the top rail and propped her foot on the bottom. In her faded, ripped jeans and tank T-shirt, she looked like the sexy badass Raina knew she was. Her dark ponytail slid over her tanned shoulder, the wind fluttering it against the sleeve of Raina's black velvet dress. "She's had it rough," Ruby added. "She has the same problem you do, just a different shape."

Had that increased Ramona's isolation, knowing Raina no longer had that challenge? Laced liberally in the house's spellcraft now was a Dark Guardian's touch. Raina could go to town like a normal person. Visit Ruby at her gun shop and shamelessly flirt to help increase her sales. The unsolicited help annoyed Ruby and guaranteed sensual punishments from her Dark Guardian—two reasons that totally justified doing it, in Raina's opinion.

"You had your own challenges," she noted. But not wanting to send Ruby to that dark place, she chose a more lighthearted interpretation. "Your monumental mommy issues, plus Derek's overbearing ass was in your life practically from birth. Cradle robber."

Ruby rolled her eyes. "He's centuries old. He doesn't have much of an age-appropriate dating pool. Plus, he's my soulmate. We both always knew that."

Raina elbowed her, but then returned her attention to the two below, strolling through the garden again. Silas was a handsome male, made even more appealing by his obvious attentiveness to their coven sister.

Over the years, Ramona hadn't risked romance often. The Marine and the hapless gamer had been part of a sparse group. Yet knowing how important love was to the heart and soul, Ramona had turned her capacity for it to her friends, her passion to her shop. But her longing for a romantic bond had never abated. And from the way she concentrated on the BDSM play at Sweet Dreams, sitting still and silent on the sidelines, seeming to forget to breathe as she watched the interplay between Doms and subs, Raina knew her desire for a Master hadn't abated, either.

Silas seemed cognizant of what Ramona was, on both levels. By now, he'd experienced her Chaos energy first-hand, and given Ramona a real-life submissive sexual experience. He wasn't running. Ruby had rightly pointed out Ramona might be the bigger obstacle to their relationship, but the male was immortal. Plus, even from up here it looked like you could bounce a cauldron off his ass.

There was such a thing as setting your standards too high.

"Do you think that's what this is?" Raina asked. "A soul mating?" At one time, she would have scoffed at the idea. Then Mikhael Roman had become her entire universe. Not that she would tell him that. Well, maybe on his birthday, and for *very* special events. Like the hundred-year anniversary of some kind of comet flying over the Earth.

"I don't know," Ruby responded. "But whatever this is, she deserves an actual relationship. Even if it's not forever, just please Goddess let it not turn into a cosmic train wreck."

"Well, she's a Chaos witch interested in a Reaper. What could go wrong cosmically with that?"

Ruby shot Raina a look. "There goes that fluent sarcasm."

"Derek finds it arousing."

"Yeah, right." Ruby snorted. "That's why he fantasizes about strangling you so often."

"Breath play is an expensive service. He can't afford it on his salary. Remind me again how Light Guardians are paid?"

"The universe provides him what he needs."

"Which means he conjures money when he needs it. If he had celebrity tastes, he'd drive up inflation rates."

"Says the woman whose male loves bespoke suits and Ferraris." Ruby smiled fondly. "I think Derek's last major expense was a new pair of jeans. Only because off the rack doesn't fit him right."

"I think all governments everywhere should ensure men have jeans that fit right. Particularly Derek."

"Keep your eyes off my man, bitch."

Raina chuckled, then cast her gaze back down to the gardens. "He's claimed her. Even if I hadn't seen that spellcraft on her wrists, it's obvious."

"Does she know that?" Ruby's countenance became thoughtful. "There's a gate to that part of the soul. He has to find the key to unlock it, or be invited in."

"Or he kicks it down, then politely asks if he can come inside." Raina arched a brow at Ruby's look. "Tell me that isn't what Derek did. I know Mikhael sure as hell did."

She glanced back down at the subject of their conversation. "That said, if he fucks her over, I'm going to figure out how to annihilate a Reaper. She does deserve some happiness."

"Yeah. But when it comes to Fate, *deserve* is a tricky and complicated word."

Hearing the echoes of pain in Ruby's voice, Raina brushed her shoulder against hers, a reminder that the past was in the past. "We need to go do a fashion show. And see how my demons have been spoiling that son of yours."

"You did tell them not to let him chew on the rubber sex toys? Derek had a conniption last time."

"Which is exactly why I encouraged them to let Jem do it again. Only the new ones right out of the package, of course. Properly sterilized with baby-safe soap."

"One day, Derek really is going to choke you with that chain you like to yank."

When it came to role playing, the sex demons were enthusiastic and creative. A female pirate taking a British captain as her captive, a maid coyly drawing the attention of her female employer. A prince seducing a fire-breathing male dragon into shifting to his human form. A dance of seven veils, done with provocative grace by one of the male demons, for a client who liked men who dressed and behaved as women.

Those were past scenarios for clients with specific fantasies. Raina and the demons had developed the scenes, stocked the session space with everything needed and, Silas suspected, had taken them far beyond their expectations.

After they showed off those costumes and pranced through highlights, they performed and dressed for standard tropes. Cop/traffic stop, boss/secretary, or princess kissed awake. The classics never fell out of favor with the clientele who wanted roleplay.

Ramona sat at the end of the embroidered sofa, and he'd pulled a chair up next to it, his arm behind her. Her hand rested on the sofa arm between them, within reach of Silas's grasp.

Several of the demons had piled up on the sofa next to her. Li, a slim Asian male wearing an open white linen shirt and belted, faded jeans, sat closest, backside on the sturdy sofa back, Raina-verified clean feet braced on the seat cushion next to Ramona. Two female demons, Ana and Sharone, twined in one another's arms on the other side of Li, indulging in tongue kisses or stroking Li's leg, coaxing his fond smiles. They and Raina served as directors, throwing out additional suggestions to the demons acting out their roles with impressive dramatic talents.

During Ramona's tour of the playrooms, she'd explained how they could be modified with minor changes to become the perfect settings for such fantasies. If, as she'd originally suggested, her intent was to turn his mind to things other than that mark, give him breathing space to work the problem in his subconscious, he gave her props for the brilliance of suggesting this.

But what interested him was her behavior now. As the young demons improvised, laughed, smoldered, caressed and played, showing off toys, restraints and props, she was very quiet, almost unnaturally still. He became intrigued by the way her fingers flexed against the sofa arm, the subtle movements of her lips as particular fantasies came to life.

She was in her head, feeling those scenes, being a part of them. There was often an absentmindedness to her gestures, how she responded to the conversations around her. He suspected she was channeling her stronger reactions. But not suppressing them; she'd made it clear that wasn't the way her Chaos magic worked.

Testing, he covered her hand with his and stroked her palm, making tiny lines. She became even more still, and the power of that reaction rolled over him.

Watching her behavior alter from scene to scene had confirmed what held the most appeal to her. Any scenario involving a male Dominant and female submissive, where the Dominant fully took over her care and owned her pleasure. She wasn't much into pain, like the pinching of nipple clamps or higher-level impact play, but spanking definitely grabbed her.

Which made sense. At its deeper levels, spanking was connected to an act of care and protection, a lesson imposed for the sub's own good. He liked doing it for exactly that reinforcement, as well as the serious pleasure having a sub squirming on his lap gave him. He'd been tempted to do it when she risked herself on the battlefield. It didn't matter how capably she'd handled herself, because the reaction didn't have to do with that.

He wasn't affected by the sex demon energy in the way a mortal was, not fatally caught in its web, but sexual energy worked on him the way it did any male. He might have had centuries to learn how not to let it rule him, but he'd never contended with it around a female who affected him like Ramona did.

So he observed, responded in the right ways, smiled, but eventually he was done waiting. He leaned over, spoke with his lips against her ear, capturing the shell with his mouth, teasing it with a hint of tongue. "Need some air?"

She shivered, fingers twitching in his grasp. She turned those large eyes to him. A strand of her hair was caught on her bottom lip, and he guided it back to its place alongside her soft cheek. "Yes, my lord." Their faces were so close her mouth grazed his jaw. Her voice dropped lower. "Yes, Sir. Capital S."

His instincts to take and possess surged forward. She was going to kill him.

He was aware of chuckles and knowing glances as he rose, drawing her up and pulling her out of the room. Raina and Ruby's measured attention had been on him more than once, and he knew they intended him to recognize Ramona had people looking out for her. He was glad for it, but right now he had no time for anyone's claim on her but his own.

In the hallway, he opened one of the doors leading to the gardens. He kept his hand on Ramona as he gestured her to precede him out, but then she surged ahead of him, moving along one of the paths swiftly.

He was willing to let her lead, since she knew the grounds better and he wanted to see what level of privacy made her feel the most secure. But the early evening breeze kicked up around her, a warm wind that hit him strongly enough to tell him she was in a tornado of emotion, a whirlwind of response. It almost knocked him off his feet before he countered and steadied it. By that time, she'd cut through the gardens and was headed for the woods behind them.

When he caught up with her, she was physically spinning along one of the forest paths. Dancing. The leaping movements took her into a clearing, and that seemed to be where she wanted to stay, because she started to move in concentric circles. Putting his back against a tree, he watched her, her hair whipping around her, the grasses cutting back and forth, pressing down and then releasing, leaving a moving pattern, like viewing crop circles through a kaleidoscope. She was channeling, letting the Chaos energy choose its expression within a framework she was providing.

She was burning off the more volatile edge of her need, afraid to let it be part of what was between them. She'd told him trusting anyone with responsibility for her magic was difficult for her. He respected that. He'd be patient with it. But ultimately, when it came to this, he wouldn't tolerate her holding anything back. As a Master, his job was to give her the ability to completely let go. Trust him to care for her. Because she needed that, just as strongly as he needed to take control and provide it for her.

He'd also learned an important lesson. Controlling her magic with his own had a specific sexual framework where it worked. From the heat being generated between them in the parlor, he'd say they were well within that zone.

He left the tree, walking forward through the patterns. The grasses wound around his legs but fell away when he commanded them to release him, to let him pass. When she spun toward him, he felt the energy press against him, mental hands pushing him back. He came through it, took her hands, and let the wind hold him, spin him with her. Wrapping his arm around her waist, he put his mouth on hers, letting her energy carry them off their feet like a kite caught in a whirlwind. He slowed the movement, took them to the center of the vortex.

"Bring us down, witch. Hold fast to me and my command. Use it to bring us down."

Slowly, slowly, the surplus energy spilled off. When they were together on the ground again, the normal night sounds returned, the rush of wind and grass receding. Her gaze held his, uncertain, but hopeful. Then her attention dropped, and he felt her panic surge. He shifted swiftly, had her hands in an unshakable grasp, opening her balled-up fingers to place her palms against the slashes in his shirt, letting her find his unmarked flesh.

"Even if it had gotten past and marked me, when I hold you in my arms, the pain feels like nothing."

Ramona's gaze came back to his face. "There are so many times I thought I could control it, could change its intent. Or it was okay at first, and then... how do I know it won't be the same?"

"How does anyone know a relationship is going to work out?" The debris of the past was there in her delicate face, compelling him to frame it with his hands, thumbs moving over her skin. "I want to be on this journey with you, not because it's perfect or not fraught with peril, but because it's with you. Everything you are. It's the unpredictability, the unknown ahead, that can add to its joy. Not knowing how long you'll have it." He paused. "Ramona, I can't see your death."

She stared at him a long moment, then she let out a relieved breath. "Oh, thank goodness. There's been this part of me itching to ask, like poison ivy you know not to scratch, but you just can't help it. And I thought, if you do care for me, enough that we're together and what's between us grows stronger, that would be a terrible burden for you to carry."

Her kindness and passion for life matched the strength of her magic. She was also intuitive enough to see more than he'd intended. "That bothers you. Is it because you think the mark is preventing it?"

"No. None of the other Reapers can see it, either. I asked."

"I'm not surprised. My magic messes with everyone's." She kept gazing at him. Waiting.

He'd never contemplated how to present the information, because how did one plan for it? It wasn't like it appeared on his mental calendar like the souls did.

10:03 Morris Smith, car wreck.

2:21pm Sheila Grissom, stroke.

3:58pm Incorrectly believe you ran into your soulmate.

4:30, Cal Horscht, heart attack.

"If a Reaper can't see when a soul will give up its present body, it means he's met his soulmate. So that's what I thought, at first."

While he could anticipate certain things from her, he wasn't sure what was happening in her mind now. He did note the wind had disappeared, but the grass seemed to be vibrating from a force in the soil.

"So you're telling me this to help me understand why you'll be moving on soon?"

"No. Hell no." When she started to draw back, he dropped his hands to her shoulders. "The connection I feel for you is so strong, when I couldn't see your death, I immediately believed you were my soulmate. I wanted it to be true. Even now, my desire to be with you only seems to be getting stronger. Whatever our bond is, my power and skills seem to mesh with yours, at least when we are intimate. Which is why I stand by what I have said from the beginning." He eased his grip so he could touch her face, a firmer caress, with a hint of admonishment. "You won't harm me."

"You don't know that," she said stubbornly. "And...you don't even know my favorite color. Or if I have any really terrible habits. Though I guess that's not the kind of thing that would be a dealbreaker to a Reaper. You're not proposing we set up house together. You can't really do that anyway, can you? You're traveling everywhere, here today, gone tomorrow for a year and a half, so why does it matter if I trust you, really. It doesn't change—"

Her voice rose. The wind abruptly gusted in force around them. Several large branches in the swaying trees snapped. They fell like crooked spears, piercing the earth. Leaves spun down upon them while dirt churned at their feet. The sky above had darkened, clouds scudding.

He didn't immediately react. He could feel the full amazing breadth of her power, the edges held in her hands like a swirling cloak. Perhaps he'd pushed too hard. But he also might have prompted a scenario where he could prove his point.

She bolted, ran again. This time he followed, stayed with her, and not just physically. He caught her arm, pulled her around to face him.

"Stop. I can't control..."

"Ramona, in your fantasies, what did you want to call me? Tell me what you called me."

Her attention snapped to him at the unexpected segue, the one he sensed might knock her off her axis. Her lavender eyes sparkled with white light.

"Sir," she whispered. "Master."

He locked down the surge of triumph. "Then obey me in this one moment. Look around you. Really look."

He threw one hand out, and his scythe appeared in it. He brought it to the ground like a lightning rod, bolts of energy crackling from it. When her gaze traveled from it outward, he saw her finally register what he was trying to tell her.

Despite the power of the maelstrom, he'd woven his power with hers as he'd done in her shop. In the same way their combined desires kept those marks on her wrists, so too, did their yearning for one another keep the energy weaving around them, going nowhere but where they wanted it. Like a dance with a partner who knew how to anticipate your steps, it was a glorious meeting of what was meant to be joined.

Yes, there was dangerous debris spinning through the air, but in a controlled spiraling pattern, like the rise of a vase on a potter's wheel, grooved with the objects that had been caught in that wind.

"Oh." She cried out as she saw a pair of raccoons, twisting over and under, but his hand flexed on her upper arm.

"Look."

He'd modulated it, so the animals were not being harmed, merely tumbled as if wrestling together in meadow grass. The debris spinning with them was contained, causing no harm to the animals. Her energy had a fascinating stitching rhythm to it, the power sliding in and out of the grasp of his. But always coming back to join with it again.

The witch in her became intrigued and fascinated by this new development, wanting to examine it. As that helped her calm down, she took control back from him, bit by bit, as he gave it to her. The magic was hers, the power was hers. He'd merely steadied it, helped the reaction balance before the negative Chaos caused by her fears could take over.

Slowly the winds once more died back, the branches settling to the ground. The raccoons, looking a little dazed and dizzy but other-wise all right, came to a safe landing.

She was leaning against him, his arm tight about her waist, her hand on his beating heart. He disappeared his scythe and met her gaze.

"You *are* the magic. You feel it in ways no one else might be able to understand. That's the way I feel this truth, that when you are aroused with me, you will cause no harm. The only obstacle is earning your trust in my judgment. I know you need time for that, but while you seek it, you will not run from me." He shot her a firm look. "You are cautious, and you care for me and others. I respect that, but I will push on that caution until you know you can truly let go with me. No apologies. If I have to fuck you senseless a hundred times to prove it, I will."

She moistened her lips. "That may just be the *best* pick up line a man has ever used to get a woman to have sex with him. And only him."

"If the truth serves more than one purpose, who am I to argue with it?" Sobering, he touched her face. "Tell me how your magic works, witch. I want to hear you describe it, because I think there's a truth in there, waiting for both of us."

Her gaze grew thoughtful at the question, and then she inclined her head. "Chaos isn't chaotic at all. Not on its face, because there are forces guiding everything, even chaos. Chaos is just the child that the Fates allow to run amok and see where it ends up, with faith that it will end where it's needed."

He smiled at that, and she gave him an absentminded one in return. "It's the grenade that doesn't detonate after the pin pulls," she continued. "Luck, stroke of fate, whatever you call it. It's what doesn't make sense, but might eventually. It's the manifestation of what we don't understand, what's beyond our understanding, that we have to believe may elude our understanding but is still what's intended. It took me a long time to get confidence in it, and I made a lot of mistakes along the way. That's part of Chaos too, but when it's your magic, harder to accept."

He saw her make the connection, and her gaze lifted to his, locked. He covered her hand, squeezed it. "So tell me what it is you fear."

"You." She drew a breath. "You make me feel wild and uncontrolled, like I did at the beginning, when I wasn't sure of anything. But I want to feel you inside me, Silas, and all that energy spiraling around us and within us. I want to trust."

That impish smile returned, a little tremulous on the edges. "And as you said, the only way to get there is lots of practice."

~

"If the truth serves more than one purpose, who am I to argue with it?"
When he'd said that, he'd given her a dangerous smile, one that

raised gooseflesh on her arms. No man had ever been possessive with her.

Or taken such care. He brought her to a creek that ran through Raina's property, a border place that could augment and sharpen energy use, including the erotic kind. Despite the knee-weakening thought, he let the arousal between them simmer. They sat together, him leaning back on his braced hands, her against his side. He was quiet, letting her have her thoughts.

While he'd warned her he wouldn't let her back away from his challenge to take her over, he was also showing her he'd give her the space within that framework to adjust to the idea. Her whole life, Chaos had taught her to follow its lead. She'd learned to have faith in everything but this, because this had been a hurt that struck at her most vulnerable core.

"You know, it's like the death thing. It's better not to know."

She was resting her cheek against his shoulder, so he put his chin on the crown of her head. "What's that?"

"The soulmate thing. Giving it the whole, 'if you can't see her death, she's your soulmate' absolute, puts a lot of pressure on both parties. What if one of them isn't ready for that? Or if they're already married?"

His lips tugged in a smile. "Nothing guarantees a Reaper's soulmate will be ready for that bond the first time or life their paths cross. So it obligates that person to nothing."

"But the Reaper can tell that's their soulmate right off, regardless of which lifetime it is? That would suck."

"It would be difficult." He feathered his knuckles along her cheek, caressing the hollow of her throat before curling that hand over her thigh, holding her. She was resting on her hip, legs folded to the side. "Tell me which role you most enjoyed watching. I want to see if I am right."

She was amenable to the subject change. She didn't want to dwell on what it could mean, that a Reaper was given an eventual soulmate and she wasn't it. She'd just met him, after all. Talk about getting overly clingy, way too fast.

So she thought about pleasurable things, like the intensity of his regard during the fashion show. It had kept her warm, her body tingling. It made her feel the same way now. "Do I have to choose one?"

"You have more than one favorite?"

"Oh yeah. But Viking pillager and demure nun is at the top of the list. I waffle over fantasies of who's in charge. I don't have any Domme to me, but I have an equal opportunity imagination. I see the nun putting the Viking on his knees. She opens her robe, makes him kiss the cross between her breasts. Shows him the benefits of reverence, worshipping at the altar between a woman's thighs."

She paused. He was drawing his finger up and down her thigh. Slow, but the line was getting longer, going higher, making wider turns for the return trip. "Tell me another."

Her heart pounded a little harder. "Naughty bratty girl stopped for speeding by serious Daddy Dom cop."

His thumb passed over her cheek, tipping her face up to meet his serious green eyes. "These are stories you enjoy playing out in your head. What is *your* fantasy, Ramona? What do you imagine when your body hungers?"

She rose, moved to the water's edge. He didn't follow, instead leaning back to brace himself on his elbows. A Master, watching. Waiting for Scheherazade to tell her story, knowing he held her life in his hands. That he could have her whenever he wished.

She could tell him that, but there was another story, an imagining closer to the truth. She let it grow in her as the wind moved her dress against her. She was thin, but he'd given her a new appreciation for how female her body was. He would see the fabric outlining her hips, her thighs, her hair fluttering over her shoulders.

"I'm in a mist. It has that leafy, post-rain smell. I sense there's someone coming, for me specifically. Close by my ear, I hear a voice. The heat of his breath ripples over my skin, and I realize I'm naked. Around him...I'm always naked."

"What does he say?" His deep voice vibrated inside her.

"Run." She tilted her chin to her shoulder, holding him in her peripheral vision. "I don't obey right away, because how he says it...I can't seem to move my feet, take myself away from him."

She pushed her dress off one shoulder and cupped the bare curve of her shoulder, imagining his hand. Silas's attention was sharp as his scythe. Her thumb passed over that healing scratch on her throat. She'd been marked by him.

"I ask him, 'Why do you want me to run?' The mist gets thicker, and he goes silent. I usually wake up or stop imagining right then, because it's a question that can only be answered by the right male."

She pivoted. "Do you know what the answer is?"

Silas rose. She felt like he saw everything that mattered about her. "I do," he said. "Ask me again."

"Why do you want me to run?"

"So I can chase you." That same dangerous smile, holding all the promises she'd ever hoped to be given by a man. With an answering smile, just as dangerous, she was gone. She made sure the mist she left swirling around him was steeped with her scent. The echoes of a laughing, breathless whisper.

"Let the hunt begin, my lord."

As she'd already known, the mild-mannered librarian Reaper could be replaced by the relentless hunter-warrior whenever he called it.

Because it was a game, she delighted in what her magic devised. Roots rose up to try to trip him, clouds of leaves plumed to obscure his way and her path. A deer crashed through the woods before him as a distraction. The rain shower that soaked only him wasn't intended, but by then his tenacity was unsettling her, how little she managed to reduce her lead. As he was closing in, the game became less about play, and more about the reason she'd initiated it.

When her magic knew a pursuer was benign, it didn't throw hazardous things in his path. So as her edginess started to grow, along with the temptation to test him further, she recognized the warning and changed tactics.

Choosing a live oak with a trunk far wider than herself, she put her back against the solid base and became part of it, its shape changed to accommodate her profile. Trees, their trunks, the reach and curves of their branches, often looked like people.

As he entered the clearing, air currents rippled around him, sending him a confusing mix of odors. She thrillingly suspected he could track her by scent alone and didn't want to give him that advantage.

He'd stripped the shirt off when it became soaked. His hair was still wet, but he'd raked it with his fingers, sending more drops to his shoulders, adding to the gleam of the brown hair on his chest and arms. She tried not to notice how appealing he looked in only damp jeans, because her magic might respond to her spike of lust by thrusting her from the tree like the prize from a gumball machine.

"A riddle for you, witch. What's the one thing you can't deny, refuse or escape?"

Her heartbeat quickened, and his head turned her way. He studied the tree, and then he was prowling toward it.

She could swirl to mist, drift away on the wind again. Become a toad, crouched on the forest floor. Or a rabbit, ready to bound away.

She laid out the options, but her magic would choose. When she became the mist, wisps of fragrant smoke, Silas reached out and wrapped the tendrils around his forearms, countering her magic with his own.

It felt like it did when he pulled her into his arms. His ability to hold her that way in this form startled her enough she materialized in his grasp. She'd left her shoes behind, so one bare foot curled into the forest floor, the other over the top of his shoe.

"You didn't answer my question." That penetrating gaze, the rough voice, was equally capable of holding her to him. "What can't be refused or denied?"

"Death," she whispered.

She saw the glimmer of his Reaper side, always there behind his more human features. He put her back against the tree, lifted her hands in his. As he did, slender branches dropped from the tree's leaders, wound around their clasped fingers, their wrists, holding them to one another. He glanced at them, then back down at her. "Does the magic answer to the witch, or does the magic provide the witch with answers?"

"Both."

When he brought their bound hands down, the vinelike branches extended, giving him the slack to do it. His magic or hers? She didn't know. It didn't seem to matter.

He cupped the outside of her thighs, fingertips on the lower curve of her buttocks, as hers rested on top of his wrists. "I'm intrigued by this Viking and nun idea," he said, dropping to one knee. She wanted to touch his wet hair, stroke it, but the branches didn't allow her to do that. Which told her she wanted him to restrain her. Keep control. And he wanted that, too.

"He comes in, intending to pillage, to defile her body, and instead finds an altar to worship at, with touch and tongue and cock..." He gathered up her skirt as he spoke, her hand on top of his seeming to help as he used their combined pressure to bring the cloth to her hips. He leaned in, licking at her exposed bare sex, an experimental taste that had her jerking. His grip over her wrists tightened.

"She may have brought him to his knees, but he will have her under him, plowing her folds, feeling her arms and legs clasp around him, needing more, pulling him in deeper."

"Ah..." She could only manage sounds.

"Tell me you want my mouth on your cunt."

She found a word she could speak. The only one that mattered. "Please."

He dipped his head, another slow lick that had her shuddering, her body arching. "Oh...please."

"More, little nun? What if I want you to worship *my* cock? Put you on your knees, make you pay homage it?"

She could only manage a whimper for that, because he didn't wait for her response. He was licking her again, tongue dipping into her folds, exploring. Her noises of need were answered by a growl of appreciation. The wolf again.

Wolf, dragon, Reaper. All things that could come for someone, hunt them down. One of them could safeguard her, guide her. Become her shepherd.

My lord is my shepherd, and with him I will do nothing but want. Yes, please.

Her hands clawed at his, hips lifting and falling back against the rough tree bark, the scratch of it against her flesh a welcome discomfort. Leaves fell around them. It was raining again, only a warm rain, like what was between her legs. Drops rolled down his curved back. She noticed a brand highlighted by the glistening light. A curved shape like his scythe, crossed with a shepherd's crook. Had it been placed there when he'd become a Reaper?

Her body was rising toward that pinnacle. She did her best to modulate it, let the energy spill into channeled directions, but her desire to believe him, to trust that he had her, had increased even since the time he'd had her body last. It scared her.

Silas rose, shedding his clothes and tossing them aside. His mouth brought her scent to her lips. The branches binding them fell away with a flicker of hot male energy, telling her he'd done it. "Don't pull back," he demanded, and his hand was on her upper thigh, the other around her waist as he lifted her.

When he lowered her down upon him, fitting his cock to the mouth of her sex, it was with a controlled strength that broke another tether on her resolve. He brought them together, executing the downward move and shoving her against the tree in one forceful impact. The impalement felt as deeply rooted as the tree's anchor point. She'd wondered why one of Raina's sex demons liked to call the male sex organ a "root." Now she knew.

"Don't box it in, sweet witch," Silas muttered. "Let it loose. Let me see that glorious power."

He was learning too much about her and her magic, enough to know how to plant a suggestion it could seize and run away with. The tree pressed into her back and then was gone as the mist swirled around them, took them up, twenty feet over the forest floor.

She grabbed his shoulders and waist, afraid he would fall, but her magic had him, and he had her, securely in his hands, driving into her body, her legs clamped around his waist as they spiraled. A shower of acorns from the tree pelted their flesh like hail, but all he did was cover her with a shift of his arm around her skull, bending his head over her face to protect it.

The shock still brought her back to earth, but while she was the one who put their feet on the ground, he took them down upon it, her on her back, him still buried between her legs, a slow thrust and retreat.

Retreat seemed the wrong word, for nothing in his expression suggested it. Nor his words.

"So the Viking ends up just where he intended to be." He moved his mouth to her throat. "Due to her willing surrender, not the forced coupling that would have fractured his soul and shattered hers. I love the taste of your cunt. Every cry that comes from you when my tongue is inside it."

She held onto him, gasping with every thrust. Tears rolled down her face. She worried what he would think of that, but he only kissed them and kept moving.

Happiness was complicated for a Chaos witch. He understood that. Happiness was probably pretty complicated for a Reaper, too. Perhaps that was part of the draw between them, the overlap. Death had an inescapable element of Chaos, too. During the battle Reaping, it had reached out, recognizing her. Light and dark were inseparable. Joy and despair, danger and exultation, horror and wonder, were the most macabre but enduring of friends.

Or lovers.

She was whispering the words, putting them in rhymes, singing them, holding him. His arms tightened around her.

"You think and explore, imagine and theorize, to keep your mind from coming completely untethered," he said in a husky voice. "When I make you mindless, I'll bind you with something you can rely upon, just as strongly. But for now..."

He bit her throat as he curved a hand over her buttock to tilt her up, take more of his substantial thickness, increase the friction against her clit. Her nerve endings sparked with electrical response.

Keeping control over her own self-pleasuring was a far different thing from keeping control with a lover with this kind of skill and raw determination. He intended to possess her every reaction—and command them. Maybe she hadn't completely let go, but he had her considering what it would be like, to release one rope to strain for the one he offered.

Rain came as the climax crashed over her. Her nails dragged over that brand as she screamed, arched against the earth. Her hands dropped, scrabbled at his hips, digging into his buttocks to pull him deeper. It hurt a little, but she didn't care. Without his clothes it was all Silas under her calves, his hips pressing against the tender skin of her inner thighs, shoving them wider. The ribbons of sensation spiraled over her limbs from her wrists, waking up all her nerve endings.

He released, his shoulders flexing above her, his face intent on hers until the very last possible moment, when his eyes fell shut, making the sharp planes of his face, the determined jaw, more pronounced.

It was a long, pleasurable ride. As it eventually slowed and came to a halt, the energy soaked into the earth like the rain that had left everything damp in its wake, rolling drops over quivering flesh.

A few flakes of snow feathered in his hair, too. To help them cool off. She raised a trembling hand to touch one, and he clasped her marked wrist, kissing it.

The letters were pulsing a deep red, like blood. As time evolved, people became new things, additional things. The change suggested she was becoming not just a Chaos witch, but perhaps also his Chaos witch. A Chaos witch willingly bound to a Grim Reaper.

She assumed the "grim" came from human attitudes toward death, because it didn't fit him. Determined and just, but not grim. She shared that, her hands wandering over his chest and shoulders. "People might have viewed you differently if you were called the Gay Reaper. Original usage. Perky. Cheerful."

"You and your lovely mind." Lips curved, he kissed her throat some more, giving her lazy touches with his tongue. She liked feeling him on her, surrounding her like this, his body still locked with hers, her flesh pulsing around him. Her fingers slipped over the brand.

"You said you don't really remember the lives you had before you were a Reaper. Does that bother you, not remembering your parents, or where you came from?"

Before answering, he lifted his head, followed the tracks of her tears with his mouth. She closed her eyes, trembling at the tenderness. He brushed his nose against hers.

"There is a tale about the origins of Reapers. It is said the Lord and Lady cut their palms, clasp hands, and the drops that fall become our kind. A reminder that even the gods bleed. And we all have endings and beginnings."

He paused. "But to answer your question, no. Whatever I was, where I came from, those questions feel as if they were answered to my satisfaction before I became this. I do not know if that's the same for all Reapers, though. But for me, the Lord and Lady are my father and mother. The other Reapers are my siblings. And where I came from was a starting point for the rest of the journey. Like a birth."

He adjusted, making her bite her lip to absorb the pleasurable aftershock. "Which today has led me here."

She moved her hand to his chest, and when he laid his hand on it, something in his face made her bring up the one thing she'd rather not. "Does the possession mark change in any way when we do this?"

"I feel it even less. That may simply be the strength of the distraction," he gave her an appraising look, "or its hold may lessen during our joining. All the more reason to do this as often as possible. Though I typically do not wish for anything attached to me to fall off during sex, this is the exception."

She smiled. "Raina claims a man can't fuck his dick off. I'm sure she's tested the theory."

"Good. My worry over that was keeping me up at night. No entendre intended." He seated himself more deeply, braced himself on his elbows to put his mouth to her neck. "Let's start all over again."

She quivered through her smile, because she knew he was serious. But who was she to complain?

Then he lifted his head, eyes sharpening. "What is it?" she asked.

"Mikhael is here. And Honora."

CHAPTER TEN

They were waiting on the road to Raina's house. Once they emerged from the woods, Honora didn't waste time on greetings.

"Your instincts were correct. Fifty-seven other Reapers have been marked," she said. "That we've identified thus far. There may be more."

Silas stiffened. "How?"

"Differently from you. Most did not engage in a battle with a Soul Collector. They remember lying down to sleep, or a period of blackness, but did not know of the mark until we probed for it. A small handful did engage in battle, but they were notably our more powerful and experienced Reapers, like yourself, whose minds could not have been overtaken in such a way. It has happened to them within the past week. They had reported the incident to their commanders, but until now did not realize it was happening wider than their own Wake."

"How many of the more experienced ones?"

"About twelve, so far."

The look the three exchanged told Ramona things were bad. It gave her a thought, an idea she suspected Silas wasn't going to like, but this was escalating too fast.

"We know the mark isn't the Collector's magic," Ramona interjected. "So it bears the maker's signature."

On the battlefield, Honora had barely acknowledged her existence, but now the Reaper leader's attention shifted to her. Paused that speculative beat. Ramona supposed it was probably strange for all of them, not to see her death.

"Without exception, every marker is too bonded with darkness," the commander said. "Trying to untangle or separate it ends in an abyss. It also risks the Reaper." Her gaze met Silas's. "We lost two. The agony drove them mad. They took their own lives before we could stop them."

His mouth had tightened. "Who?"

"Samaira and Hrolf."

Ramona closed her hand on Silas's rigid arm, offering silent condolences. *Lord and Lady.*

"What happened to the mark when they succumbed?" Mikhael asked, his voice hard.

Honora's expression was flat, containing her emotions. "We put them in a protected circle before we made our attempt, to prevent the Dark Soul magic from escaping. But all trace of it self-destructed when the Reaper died, just as you predicted."

The Wake commander looked at Ramona. "What are you thinking, Chaos witch?"

She was thinking she should have kept her mouth shut. Learning that a serious attempt to do what she was considering had caused two immortals to kill themselves... She couldn't subject Silas to that risk.

But whoever was trying to control Reapers with Dark Soul magic wasn't planning to open a Hallmark store. Their intent would likely claim far more lives. And everything she sensed about that mark said when that plan was executed, destroying the Reapers carrying out its will wouldn't be a problem for it. Obviously. They had two bodies to prove it.

"There's a pattern, even in an abyss." Ramona dropped her pointed attention to Silas's chest. "To figure it out, you use the right tracker, one who knows how to navigate the terrain and the risks. Set the right conditions, and I can follow it into that abyss. Profile the creator of the mark, what's driving this."

"Absolutely not," Silas said. "If it has claimed two lives, under the supervision of Reapers with centuries of experience, I will not risk a mortal human."

The tender and humorous lover had vanished. She was facing three ancients, all of whom had plenty more experience and power than her —in their field of expertise.

Mikhael's expression didn't hold the same resolve as Silas's, though, because the Dark Guardian knew more about her capabilities. Plus he knew her backup. Honora's face didn't reveal her opinion, though she'd likely back Silas's judgment, because that was who *she* knew. So Silas was the key.

Ramona faced him squarely. "With respect to those who attempted to unravel the mark," she nodded to Honora, "a Chaos witch is one of the few magic users born with the tools to interact with Dark Soul magic, keep it contained, and not be pulled into its web. With the right experience and training, that is, and I have those skills."

"I do not doubt your skills." Silas's green eyes were hard. "But you are pitting yourself against something powerful enough to impose its designs on over five dozen Reapers."

She let her lips tip up. "I'm not going to pit myself against it at all. I'm going to invite it to dance. In a protected circle," she added.

"If you are in the circle, you are not protected."

Having to resist a man opposing her solely due to his desire to protect her was a new experience for her. It might warm her, but it also strengthened her resolve. She had a vested interest in doing it right, and that interest was standing in front of her.

"Something is trying to harm you. If the shoe was on the other foot, would you stand down because of the risk?"

His jaw set. "I chose to let our paths intersect, and it has brought you into harm's way."

"Living a life worth living brings us into harm's way. Labor would be a pointless torture for mothers, if all we did was live inside another kind of womb."

She wondered if it was respect for Silas, or her, or both, that kept Honora and Mikhael silent through the exchange. Regardless, it reinforced that Silas was the only thing standing against her. "Are you worried about me screwing up and getting you killed?"

His gaze narrowed. "Don't try to manipulate me, witch."

She crossed her arms. "Don't deny me the chance to help you when I know I can. You asked for my trust. Is that only a one-way street?"

Their gazes held. Then frustration swept his face, and he muttered an oath. "Tell me your plan for protection."

"I do it in a closed circle, with Raina and possibly Ruby's help."

"Why not automatically include Ruby?"

"Because Ruby nearly lost herself to Dark Soul magic." She glanced at Mikhael, then back to Silas. "There's risk to her opening herself to it again. She has a baby now. I can likely do it with just Raina, if she doesn't want to chance it."

"If she does, Derek will wish to know, which means he will come if he can. The two of us can offer additional protection." Mikhael tipped his head toward Honora. "I expect you will be present."

"For certain." Her gaze was on Ramona, assessing, but Ramona's attention didn't move from Silas. He continued to stare at her, that set expression on his face, the request she'd made for his trust hanging in the air between them. Then Mikhael spoke, drawing Silas's gaze.

"With Raina involved, my heart is also at risk in that circle, Reaper. Derek will feel the same." He glanced at Ramona. "Because you know Ruby will help."

The Dark Guardian directed his next words to Silas and Honora. "Their trinity is a powerful one. Ramona's point is sound. Whatever is doing this has a bad purpose. We must do what is necessary not only to protect those closest to us, but those we are charged to protect."

Seeing Silas's conflicted expression, Ramona took another step closer to him. "You know why I asked if you were worried about me screwing up? Because I'm worried about it. I don't want to lose you. But everything tells me if we don't figure out what's going on, that's a real possibility anyway. If we're not...what you thought we were, then it really can't be a coincidence our paths crossed when you might have need of a Chaos witch. Right?"

He closed his eyes, and she put her hands on his forearm. He was holding his scythe, wearing his robe. He'd conjured them as he came out of the forest. Respect for his commander, who wore and carried the same, an indication the meet was official Reaper business.

His gaze flickered to his scythe. A half dozen bees crawled across the blade, wings flickering copper gold. She grimaced, knowing they'd arrived because all the thoughts she wanted to use to convince him had been buzzing through her mind like...well. She really needed to be less analogous in her head.

He kept staring at them, though. "What?" she asked.

"I like bees," he said unexpectedly. "It is a...hobby."

She blinked. "You have hives somewhere? Like with honey?"

At his nod, she smiled. "You'll have to show me sometime."

Two of the bees moved to her hair. He watched them, then dipped his gaze to her. "I do trust you," he said. "But you remember what *I* said, about being brought to your door. I don't want to lose you when I have just found you."

He'd said that, right in front of his boss. She was blushing. "I get that. And I love hearing it. But I think we still have to let me try."

He gripped the scythe's handle, thumb worrying a worn spot, evidence it was a habit, a meditative gesture. Finally, he nodded to Honora and Mikhael. "We will do the circle and let the witches determine what they can. I thank you for your willingness to be there and lend them your additional protection."

Perversely, knowing she'd won his agreement brought apprehension, a doubt of her own temerity. But she did as she always did. She trusted that Chaos would take her where it needed to go.

"Let's return to the house and get what we need," she said.

While Ramona met with Raina and Ruby to discuss the plan, Silas stayed in the gardens, receiving the full, sobering account from Honora of Samaira and Hrolf's ordeal, as well as the details of the experiences from those who'd been found with the mark.

It brought home like a sledgehammer that he couldn't forbid Ramona to use her power to help. The overwhelming desire to do so didn't abate, however.

He thought of what she'd said, that knowing someone was a soulmate could be a lot of pressure, almost a burden. While it might not be a soul mating, what he felt for her seemed like it had been waiting a long time. Waiting for her.

Mikhael had left to inform Derek of the situation. When Honora finished speaking to Silas, and the two of them had shared a prolonged silence, a brief mourning, she, too, left him to attend to other matters. She would return when they were ready to begin. She'd linked with Mikhael's mind so he could communicate with her.

Silas had always had the feeling of his brethren in his head, his heart. Without the Chaos witch, her way of occupying those parts of him, plus his strong physical desire for her, he realized his loss of that connection might have driven him closer to Samaira and Hrolf's madness faster than it already seemed to be doing.

He needed to clear his mind, center himself for what was ahead. But as he attempted a meditation, the mark was a disruptive influence, seeming to dislike such activity. He pushed harder, turning it into a fight, which was the wrong tactic. He became more unsettled, his mind full of doubts he recognized as not his own. With an oath, he rose. Fine, he'd go through combat stances, shadow sparring. What his mind couldn't do, he'd achieve with exertion.

He was in the middle of his third full cycle of offensive and defensive practices with his scythe when he heard feet crunching along one of the gravel paths near him. It was Ruby. She'd circled around from the front, where she'd left her van parked in the drive, a battered but solid-looking older model. She had a diaper bag on one shoulder, and was carrying a gun wrapped up in the straps of its holster and harness. An elderly mastiff trotted along next to her and immediately approached Silas, giving him an olfactory once over before allowing Silas to stroke his giant head.

Soon. Too soon. His loss will hit her hard, but he has loved her well. And she him.

"Diaper changing can be a dangerous business," she said, noting his glance at the gun.

"I see that. Do you carry such weapons into a cast circle?"

"Sometimes. There's the risk of it being turned against me, but most magical opponents I've faced have little control over mundane weapons, if I put the right charm on them. Sometimes a key shot at the right moment can disrupt them enough to give you an advantage. But that's not why I have this. It's Raina's. She needed it repaired, so I'm bringing it back to her." She gave the scythe an interested look. "I would have thought it was a cumbersome weapon, but your technique suggests otherwise."

"Long practice."

She nodded, hesitated. "I know you have reservations about what we're going to do, but if it makes you feel better, Ramona is the only one of the three of us who could interact with Dark Soul magic without unacceptable repercussions."

"So she said, but it's not been my experience that any magic user is safe tangling with Dark Soul energy. She said you have firsthand knowledge of that."

Shadows crossed Ruby's expressive gaze, making it bleak enough he almost regretted bringing it up. But she squared her shoulders. "Which is why I hope hearing those words from me is even more reassuring. It's hard for any of us to understand how Chaos magic works. Its very nature defies boundaries and description. Even after so many years as her friend, it can still mystify."

At his dubious expression, she set the diaper bag down and unwrapped the gun so he could see it. With its pearl handle and fancy etchings on the metal, it looked like it belonged in an old western movie. As did much of the first floor of Raina's bordello.

Fishing a bullet out of the belt, Raina put it in one chamber of the revolver, showing him the others were empty. Then she spun the barrel and snapped it into place with a deft movement of her wrist. With a hand and eye fixed as a surgeon's, she pointed the weapon at the forest line beyond the garden.

"Imagine a game of Russian roulette," she said. "To the person facing the barrel, it's chaos. Not knowing when the bullet will fire. Some of that chaos belongs to the person who holds the gun, because they spun the barrel and took away the choice of when it would happen. But the gun knows."

Her gaze came back to him. "Somewhere, there's always the gun. Someone who knows there is order behind what others see as chaos. A person who has absolute faith in that, not just from experiencing it all her life, but from knowing it deep inside her soul, because that's how her soul is made."

She lowered the gun. "A Chaos witch is the only one who understands the mapping of her power. Even for her, it took time, and a hell of a lot of courage, to look into that abyss and find her way. Most of them live pretty lonely lives."

It was an echo of what she had told him, her struggles and worries. But he thought of her warmth with her customers, the generous love she showed Ruby and Raina. "Why lonely?"

"If you're with a Chaos witch, most things aren't going to go as planned when you're around her." As Ruby spoke the words, he could feel her measuring his reaction. "Imagine she runs into a friend at a restaurant. He's there to interview for an important job, worried about making a good impression. Now Ramona will want him to do well, get the job, but that may not be what the Chaos magic decides."

Ruby took a breath. "It might splatter his nice suit with salad dressing, tangle up his words so he seems like he isn't qualified for the position. Later, he might find out it was the wrong job for him, or the boss was a slavedriver, and the interview getting messed up helped spare him all that. But who appreciates that kind of meddling? No one.

"Ramona has told us time and again, 'control' is the wrong word when it comes to her magic. She doesn't control it. She rides it. She understands it, embraces it, even when it breaks her heart, stresses her out or drives her batshit. The salad dressing story is a really innocuous example. Chaos magic travels down plenty of darker roads than that, especially if the witch resists learning what it took Ramona years and a very painful childhood to do."

Ruby unloaded the gun, put the bullet back in the belt and re-wrapped the gun in it. "Dark Soul magic isn't safe. But then, neither is Chaos magic. It's why she can 'tangle' with the Dark Soul shit and not be tainted by its darkness."

She gave him an even look. "The kind of man worthy of Ramona will understand what it took for her to become what she is. She deserves a man who'll love every single thing about her, and consider himself damn lucky if she loves him back. Even if he has to wait a while for her to open that door."

"I agree." He was patient. Ruby and Raina loved her. But he also had his limits, and how he felt for Ramona, what they were to one another, exploring that, defining and discovering all its facets, also existed inside a circle that belonged to the two of them, its questions and answers.

However that door was opened, whether by Ramona's hand or his will, or a combination of both, she would find him on the other side of it. To guard it, to come inside, to do whatever she needed.

He said none of that, but as Ruby held his gaze, she nodded, satisfied. "I'm going to handle Jem's diaper crisis, then get back to helping Raina and Ramona finish up our prep."

She tilted her head toward the windows. "You look like you could use a distraction. While you're waiting, wander in and let the sex demons corner you. They've been plotting to get you alone."

"For what purpose?"

She chuckled. "I didn't know a Reaper could turn pale. If you were talking to Raina, she'd string you out, torment you a bit, but you've had a rocky enough day. They just want to ask you a bunch of questions. Raina told them what you are, so they'd know they don't have to worry about their sex demon vibes draining you like a juice box. They do some of their own shielding to give Raina a break, and to keep in practice for when they travel or go into town, but it's always a welcome respite when they're around someone that doesn't need that."

Silas glimpsed a hint of movement at one of the large picture windows. "You think I need a distraction?" he asked.

"Yes. Your fighting skills are terrifyingly impressive, but you're soaked through." She added to the frank assessment with a gesture at his shirt, dark with perspiration. "You're pushing yourself hard, but it's not working. If I was about to willingly step into the ritual equivalent of open-heart surgery, the kind that's already taken two of my family, I'd be looking for a way to decompress, too."

He saw kindness in her hazel eyes. "I'm sorry for that, by the way. From what Ramona has told us of Reapers, they didn't deserve that kind of end."

"No, they didn't." The anger over it had been one of the more prominent emotions driving his physical exertions. Hrolf and Samaira were newer Reapers. Samaira had come to Silas several times to get his advice on handling her reactions to more difficult Reapings.

He appreciated the sincerity to Ruby's condolences. Leaning forward, he plucked an item from the thick ponytail that fell over her left breast. She tracked the gesture with wary curiosity, but when he handed her what he'd found, her straight mouth tipped into a bow shape.

"Cheerio," she said. "It's a multi-purpose food. Good for projectile games as well as consumption."

"Projectile games?"

She tossed the Cheerio up. Before its light weight could send it off on the wind, she had it suspended, with a mere flicker of her gaze. She made it do a lazy spiral. "I can put two dozen of these in the air and do the 'here comes the plane' thing to get Jem to eat." She hummed a zooming noise. With a twinkle in her gaze, she let the Cheerio fall and roll away. "I keep hoping it will make him smile like it just made you do. He's a little too serious."

During the fashion show, her son had been in the kitchen with Matilda, so he'd not yet had the pleasure of meeting the child. However, the sadness he detected in the mother said her son's somber nature was not a little thing to her. "Sometimes a soul carries things forward it must work through," he offered. "But the new life means they are striving for that resolution. You and your mate are formidable allies to have as loving parents. That in itself is a mark in his favor."

She gazed at him. "Thank you for that. Um...this is going to come out the wrong way, but I'd rather not see you two meet. Or know that you have. When you look at him, I know you can tell... I just can't bear to see that knowledge in your eyes, crazy as that sounds. Okay?"

She shook her head. "Crap. Sorry, that was rude and entirely disrespectful. My apologies, my lord. I'll leave you to your thoughts."

"Ruby."

When she halted her retreat toward the house, he gave her a bow. "You are not the first mother I've met who suffered the loss of a child. I will do my best to respect your wishes. You have given no offense."

She blinked back the emotional reaction. "Thank you."

By the time she'd reached the back patio, she'd recovered enough to toss him a humorous look. "When they're not trying to suck out a person's life force through their libido, sex demons are kind of like kids. Curious about everything, like a first-grade class on a field trip to an insectarium. Raina threatened to tie Li's dick in a square knot if he didn't keep them from pestering you, but if you show them the least encouragement, all bets are off. They're very good-hearted, though. If they get to be too much, just shoo them away and they'll mostly listen."

She moved into the house, her heeled boots crisp and decisive across the patio bricks.

Silas returned to his shadow sparring with the scythe, but she was right. He went through one more rotation just to prove to himself he could, but then he transformed the scythe back into a shepherd's crook. When he turned to study the reflection of the day's dying light against the parlor windows, he could feel those multiple sets of curious eyes.

Preparing the mind for an ordeal often required a perspective shift, and a horde of curious sex demons certainly qualified as that. Wanting to choose the room where he'd be most comfortable, he used the library entrance. He took a seat in one of the chairs, putting an ankle over his knee, hands resting on the arms, and waited.

It didn't take long. His guess at who they'd send as their emissary was correct. His near-smile pulled some of the weight off his heart as Gina peered in, all wide doe eyes and soft pink lips. Her red hair fell in silken waves over her shoulder and arm, the hand resting on the door latch.

"May we keep you company?" She had a surprisingly throaty voice. "Bring you something to eat or drink? Oh, sorry. Raina said you're going to be doing a ritual circle with them, so they usually fast before that. We can give you a massage or a bath. We have a wonderful bath house."

"I don't require anything," he said. "As for the other, thank you, but I'm...my affections are bound to another."

"Oh..." A little giggle escaped Gina. Her fingertips, nails painted glossy purple with silver sparkles, went to her lips. "I didn't mean to imply we meant more than a bath or massage. We know you're Ramona's. We're glad."

A surprising statement. "Did Ramona say that?"

Gina's girlishness gave way to sly female wisdom. "It's obvious. And just in case we missed it—*as if*—Raina told us, too. Why? Do you not consider yourself hers?"

At his look, she got busy scraping a fleck of paint on the door jamb. "If it's okay to ask you questions like that. If not, I beg your pardon. Sir."

He could be deliberately intimidating when asserting his authority as a Reaper. Or topping a very intriguing submissive Chaos witch. Neither was called for right now, but the tension inside him kept surfacing in more or less strong waves. He expected it could be off-putting.

The hell with it. "Your company would be welcome."

The light that flooded her features told him he might be diving headfirst into a pool of cheerful piranha. In a matter of seconds, a full dozen sex demons had slipped into the room. While they entered with graceful, sensual movements and a deferential posture, their shy smiles didn't mask the bright curiosity in their oddly intense eyes.

Li gave him a nod. His serious demeanor confirmed Ramona's comment that he was the pack leader, after Raina, and Ruby's comment that he was there to keep order. When they sank down on cushions and chairs around Silas, they left Silas a buffer of space. If Li wasn't present, he wondered if they would have piled in his lap.

Curiosity must fuel the sexual energy. Though it seemed at maximum non-lethal volume, a hapless mortal would have been mindless with violent lust.

Raina's magic shielding was as strong as the house itself, though. She'd infused it into its sentient structure, so it reached every corner. It told him what a strong witch she was, even without Mikhael's power, which he felt intertwined with and reinforcing it.

While Silas adjusted his shields so it wouldn't affect him adversely, he let enough of it through as an aid to distraction. It turned his thoughts to Ramona, holding her against the tree, driving into her. Her arms and legs gripping him, her soft gasps, all the pleasurable things they'd done, all the things he still wanted to do with her and to her.

The gentle waves of erotic energy made him imagine lying on a beach somewhere together, the warm, wet surf lapping at their feet.

They were respectfully waiting for him. Fervently hoping his Chaos witch would rescue him if he was opening a flood gate, he cleared his throat. "So...you have questions for me?"

Many of the abundant questions had to do with how he became a Reaper, whether it chose him or he chose it. But given the age of his audience, one of the earliest inquiries was no surprise.

"Have you ever reaped anyone famous?"

"Are we talking popular culture famous, like Amy Winehouse, or historically famous, like Ben Franklin?"

Ana, who'd asked the question, beamed at him. "You just answered what Isabella wanted to know. She wondered if you watch TV or movies, or read *People* magazine."

Isabella, the curvy brunette Ana had mentioned, was leaning against her. A close friend or bedmate. Possibly no true distinction on that for succubi or incubi, either option possible depending on the day.

"You haven't let him answer your first question," Li sent Ana a gentle reproof. He had a thick shock of dark hair up top while shorn close at the neck. The style revealed two Chinese characters on his nape. They meant *Strong*.

"I have Reaped those who were considered people of note during their lifetimes," Silas said. "But it didn't signify. Are any of you trained as healers?"

"A couple of us know the basics, but Ramona comes when we need more," Li provided.

"When she puts her hands on you, it always helps," Saul said. Sex demons were not large, but he was the biggest member of their group, his chest and shoulders noticeably wider than the others.

"I've found that myself." He didn't sense disrespect in the suppressed laughter. All he saw was affection for his witch. Gladness that she was finding pleasure with another.

"Reaping a soul is like that," he continued. "When Ramona is healing, what she sees is your pain and what you need. That's the only way a soul's identity in their mortal form figures into it, how it contributes or takes away from the Reaping." He paused. "You might also think about it this way. No one enters The Gate wanting to meet famous people who died. They hope to see loved ones who've preceded them."

A quiet pause, then a question, spoken hesitantly from the back. "Are there Reapers for beings like us?"

Gina stood at the doorway, perhaps in case the ornate phone in the main hallway rang, or Raina called down the wide staircase for assistance. But when Silas raised his gaze to hers, he wondered if she'd hung back because she'd been struggling with whether to ask the question or not.

He'd seen her playful and giggling, but what he saw now was reflected in most the faces gathered around him. Were their souls valued like others, or were they thrown away at the end of their physical lives? It reminded him of what Ramona had said, how hard the lives of most sex demons were, how often they were hunted, even by

Guardians like Derek or Mikhael. The incubi and succubi's eventual inability to control the lethal side of their natures as they matured, the increasing hunger to take more and more energy, could transform them from hunters seeking nourishment, into indiscriminate and insatiable killers.

Her expression, the need he felt from her, reminded him of what he was, what he served. It balanced his disquiet better than a million combat exercises. He swept his gaze over all of them, so they could see the truth in his expression. "There are Reapers for all souls," he said. "At the end of your mortal life, there is always a Reaper there, to remind you that a soul has value. And we will initially appear in the form you most need to see for your transition. This life is a journey your soul chose to take, and there will be others, to teach you many things."

He shifted his gaze back to her. "You will not be alone at the end of this life. Or at the end of any other."

A sudden wetness came to Gina's eyes, but she nodded quickly. "Thank you, sir. I think...Marisa had a question."

He hadn't missed how her gaze had strayed to Li, though, and not just hers. Saul bumped the Asian male's shoulder, a silent communication. Silas recalled there were some concerns about his maturing age, and maybe that added to some of Li's seriousness, a slight tension the others didn't have. Perhaps he was already demonstrating behavior suggesting that slide, though it wasn't evident right now.

Li's sculpted jaw had tightened, and though his expression remained neutral, Silas thought he was holding back a strong emotional response, similar to Gina's, at his family's support.

Souls were all different. They were also all the same.

"So you said a Reaper appears in the form I want to see," Marisa was asking. "So a movie star could be my Reaper?"

That set off a chorus of choices, shifting the mood back toward the tone of a playful slumber party. He'd had to do a Reaping at one of those. A nine-year-old girl had choked on a bite of hot dog and her best friend, underweight for her age, had wrapped her arms around the taller, heavier girl and found the strength to get her to hurl it forth. When the hero of the moment excused herself to go to the bathroom, the adrenaline-fueled excitement had given her a dizzy spell. She passed out, hitting her head on the edge of the sink in the right spot to kill her instantly.

"It's how your soul needs the Reaper to appear. Not how you want him to appear," he corrected. "We are seen the way your heart needs to see us. A mother, a pet, a trusted teacher. Some don't need that, and see us as we are."

Gauging the temperament of the room, he willed the transformation to show itself, just a flash of the skeletal visage, his hand on the chair arm gone to bleached bone, draped in the folds of his cloak. The scythe appeared in the other hand, the weapon glittering with its flourish of blue and gold flame.

Several shrieked, scrambling back from where they sat at his feet, but as all of it was gone in a blink, leaving him sitting there in casual clothes and human form, they recovered as quickly, laughing at each other, though he saw their surprise and speculation.

"Scary things aren't always truly scary," he said. "Though they can be."

A reminder of the fears attached to their own species. Those at his feet scooted closer again. "Would you maybe do that again, so I can feel the robe?" Constance asked. When he brought back the robe, she fingered the hem. "Like velvet, burlap and silk, all together," she told the others.

Silas patiently allowed the others to touch it. He noted every one of them asked permission first, and still looked to Li to be sure it was okay. Like curious children yes, but very polite ones. Likely another tool Raina used to help them reinforce the vitally important impulse control.

"Why are you called Grim Reapers?" Luke asked when they settled again. He sat next to Saul and seemed to look to the other demon like an older brother.

Silas half-smiled, remembering his post-coital discussion with Ramona. "We don't call ourselves that. Reap simply means to gather. To receive or harvest, like one plucks an apple when it's ready."

"Can you change your mind?" That came from Callista, a Mediterranean-looking female with short curly hair and eyes brown as wet stone. "Decide the soul isn't ready to go?"

He shook his head. "While I may feel sorrow over their ending, it is destined by the Fates, and their wisdom is far greater than mine. To disrupt Fate's destiny for a soul is a far greater crime against it, even if the soul doesn't feel that way at the time, or we wish it wasn't so."

"And animals have souls, right?" Ana prompted. In her lap, a purring brown tabby cat looked at Silas with slitted eyes that said, *Of course we do*. It almost made him smile.

"Only someone refusing to see the connections between all life would think otherwise."

She bent to kiss the top of the cat's head. He batted at her long hair with unsheathed claws. "Have you ever spent extra time with a soul?" Saul asked. "Like an afternoon playing soccer with Gerd Müller?"

"One soul spent three hours teaching me how to prepare an exceptional soufflé. If the soul needs to linger, take extra time, we can. To a point. Three days is the limit."

After that, depending on the difficulty of getting the soul to The Gate, other Reapers might join in to help. In rare instances, a death angel was called in, but he'd only seen that happen once or twice, when complicated magics and circumstances were involved that impacted the angelic realm of influence.

"What's the weirdest death you've ever witnessed?"

"That seems a mean question," Sharone objected before he could answer. "Making light of something that's serious."

He thought of the girl at the slumber party. "Ironic comes to mind quicker than 'weird,'" he said. "I had a soul who was accidentally stabbed with a nail file. But she was wearing a corset and didn't realize it until it was loosened."

"Keep nail files away from me next time I'm laced up," Marisa commanded Ana. "You like to tie me tight."

"Another of my brethren Reaped the soul of a teenager who caught on fire and died of his injuries after hiding a cigarette in his coat." That had been one of Honora's. "He didn't want his mother to see."

"The moral of that one," Li informed them all, "is don't try to hide anything from Raina."

Luke snorted. "She'd set you on fire herself if you did. Screw the cigarette." Luke's blond hair and blue-green eyes called to mind the colors of sand and water Silas had once enjoyed at Al Mamzar Beach in Dubai.

"Do you have a work schedule? A routine, vacation days? Are you ever 'after work,' sharing a beer with other Reapers, exchanging stories about the souls you've Reaped that day?"

He recalled a night Brenner had split a truly exceptional Blanton's Single Barrel bourbon with him. A soul Brenner had Reaped had told him where to find it. He'd intended to share it with a friend he ended up losing during the Vietnam War, so he'd kept it in a memorabilia chest for years.

"The only one I'm leaving behind is my daughter, and she's an alcoholic. Five years sober, and I don't want her finding it in my stuff and thinking she needs to toast her dear old dad. If you don't drink it...could you at least take it away where she won't find it?"

It was an infraction of the rules, but when Brenner had come to him with it, Silas had felt it was all right. They'd intended to dump it into a river, but instead, he and the Scottish Reaper decided to sit on the bank and give it a taste. The soul had made an impression on Brenner, and he'd wanted to toast him.

"Socially, we rarely get together in groups of more than two or three. The power we hold to tether and guide a soul is a strong energy. Unless we are in a different plane beyond their reach, it draws souls to us before their time, like the Pied Piper. And once we connect to their lifeline, they cannot leave us."

It was for the benefit of the soul, giving the Reaper time to calm a disoriented one, guide them safely to The Gate when it was time. The thought gave him pause. Almost seventy Reapers affected. If they could be called and commanded by that mark, brought together...

His grip on the chair arm tightened, and he had to make a conscious effort to keep the polished wood under his touch from splintering. Damn it, the information was there, but there were too many missing puzzle pieces.

If you knew what was being kept from you, you would revel in the oblivion that pain provides. Just as I did.

The rasping voice was an echo, buried in that mark. As soon as he heard it, he was chasing it, right into the heart of the damned thing. He knew he was pushing it, going too deep, but it had taunted him, rousing that parasitic feeling, clamping down on his insides, on the carefully constructed wall of calm he'd been maintaining against it. He was close, he could *feel* the bastard, almost see his face...

The darkness exploded like he'd stepped onto a landmine, filling his head with a disembodied smoke, made up of negative emotions, fear, pain, despair. Hatred.

It matched what Silas had heard in that voice.

As his sight cleared, he saw the curtains rolling against the windows like an angry sea, books falling from the shelves. The detonation had filled the room with that smoke, clawed hands reaching through it to grab, infect. Suck life out of whoever was nearest.

He had his scythe in hand and threw out a containment spell, simultaneously carving a shield between that energy and the young demons, except he was the one causing the danger.

"Go," he snarled. "Get out of here."

Li and Gina were already doing that, Li directing half out the garden exit, Gina waving the others through the doors that led into the rest of the house. After Isabella and Ana ran past her, the young female spun to check the room had emptied. The darkness was shooting for the doorway, and Silas saw her make the same calculation he did. She'd have time to run or close the doors, but not both.

Gina grabbed the solid oak doors, brought them together and secured them, a blink before she was slammed against them. As the hungry foulness coiled around her throat and limbs, she screeched, and clawed, trying to fight. But a sex demon only had one magic. It was a lethal one, yet against this, she was helpless.

Since it was coming from him, the quickest way to protect her was obvious. He uttered the words, turned their power against that source in his chest, and let it go.

He was flung against the bookshelves, sending more books raining upon him, bruising his shoulders. The recoil scorched the carpet, the walls, shattered the glass in the garden doors. But the blackness was yanked away from Gina. She fell to the ground.

Dazed, Silas nevertheless noted Li swiftly picking her up, taking her back out into the garden. He sent Silas a questioning look, but Silas managed to shake his head, make a fierce gesture, the meaning unmistakable. *Go.*

He struggled to one knee, kept muttering, his scythe cutting through the air, sketching the necessary motions to slam a field down around him. He'd throw away the damn key if needed, take away everything the mark used for oxygen, starve them both if necessary.

He wasn't going to become a harmer of innocents. Never.

Don't you mean never again? Nothing in this world is pure, Reaper. We know this.

The thought burrowed deeper, trying to dismantle things buried at his core that instincts told him weren't ever supposed to be unearthed. They were gone, dead and buried.

Something new entered the fray. Rain. Sheets of it, like a summer thunderstorm, the drops coming down hard enough they stung when struck.

Ramona's energy was in the rain. It gave him the space to plunge the magic of his scythe into the solid ground of his will. Its fiery light illuminated the darkness closing around him, trying to drag him down...somewhere he'd once been. A place he shouldn't go.

A beast like a harpy reared up in the barren landscape of his mind. Neither male nor female, it possessed vast staring eyes and a tumorous body. The corporeal form of what had embedded itself in him, vibrating with hate, with that hunger.

A cloud of color descended upon it. Butterflies with wings like knives that cut into its energy, dicing it into pieces. It shrieked, taken by surprise.

He reached out, clasping his magic to Ramona's like joined hands. He was already exposed, so he knew he shouldn't try to press the advantage and cut out the mark. But he had to make the attempt.

Once again, the reaction to its excising was swift and brutal. Agony erupted in his chest, rendering him vulnerable enough for the mark to seize even more control of him. The harpy screeched, mouth opening impossibly wide. He struck at it with Light energy, ripped the flesh from one side of its hideous countenance, but it kept coming.

Before he could do it again, brace himself for it to overtake even more of his mind, it was yanked back. Ramona had clamped down on a corner of the darkness and was dragging it back.

Hated creature, back in your cage. You have no power away from your mage.

Back in your cage. Back in your cage.

There's no place here for your rage.

It lost form. The process reversed, the energy becoming billowing dark smoke again. He couldn't see Ramona, but he could feel what she was doing as if she stood inside him. She was like a laundress, catching a wind-tossed sheet up against her, working it into a smaller and smaller ball of cloth. Then, with a sharp snap like a lid slamming down, it was re-sealed inside the mark.

His heart was pounding painfully against it. That sense of claws digging in was there, trying to drive him to tear at it, start this all over again. He summoned all his discipline to pull back, find his center. The struggle felt endless, his mind and body fighting a fatigue he shouldn't have, a cavern now seeming to exist inside himself that was far too deep and wide. Somewhere in all that, Ramona was with him, fighting as hard as he was, which helped him find a reserve from an even deeper well. If his witch was fighting his battles, he sure as hell wasn't going to let her do it on her own.

Just as he thought it wouldn't be enough, abruptly the Dark Soul energy gave up, the mark doing its monster-back-in-the-closet impression again.

He fell forward, catching himself before he landed on his face. The scythe was next to him, the point sunk through the carpet, into the wood beneath. Someone had hands on him. Familiar, female hands.

"Don't..."

"Be easy, Reaper. We're here. We're all here. We're not going to let it harm anyone."

He was hearing his Chaos witch's firm voice, the voice of the healer. Raina and Ruby were with her, but it was all blurry, as if his senses had been affected.

"Don't touch the scythe. Not safe."

She helped him back into the chair, touching his face, his shoulder. "We're all right. All of us. Pick a focus. A memory with good feelings, lots of details. Focus on those."

"Raisins. Soft, moist, poured in my hands. Sweet on my tongue. Smelling of the sun, soaked into them. A woman's laugh. Tired, sad, but true. Right before steel...a blade, cutting my hand, then... clasped in another man's hand. A blood oath, taken...to connect us..."

Startled, he trailed off, came back to himself. Ramona was gazing at him. Seeing deep into him, searching, her eyes gone a swirling color. Their hands were clasped, her grip sure.

"Gina," he said.

"Raina's checking on her now. Did you learn anything new?"

"That memory...the raisins, a woman's laugh. I think that's from my childhood. But we have a clean slate."

"Pardon?" She freed one hand to brush a lock of hair across his brow, though her gaze stayed alert, probing.

He was hearing Lyra in his head, explaining how it worked. He spoke her words. "A family, a childhood. That's when you build your moral foundation. Determine what's right and wrong, have painful experiences that give you baggage. Reapers...you keep the foundation, but let go of the baggage. Something wipes all that clean for a reason."

He blinked, focused on Ramona again. "What created the mark, it wants me to remember. I don't know why. Maybe it thinks it will help it gain more control over me."

"It's made a serious error in judgment, then. Your moral grounding is real and strong. I felt it." She cocked her head. "Otherwise, you'd rob the dead after you Reap their souls. Go live on your own private island."

"I did drink some expensive bourbon recently. But the soul offered it freely. I also thought about lying on a beach with you."

Her tense smile got a tinge of softness. "I like that idea."

He had regained enough control to grip her hand. "You did well." It was the second time her abilities had kept that mark from doing harm. Or third? It didn't sit well with his pride, but he wouldn't deny her what was due. "I was impressed."

"You didn't do so bad yourself. You should have seen that thing's head snap back when you used Light energy. I liked fighting at your side."

Ruby was leaning against the wall, backup for Ramona if she needed it. As Raina came into the room, his attention immediately went to her. "How is the girl?"

"She's all right," Raina responded. "Dark Soul magic has to expend some energy to compete with the nightmares sex demons already have. It didn't have time to do that, thanks to you." She glanced at his hand, which was still absently rubbing at the lingering throb in his chest. Her expression told him of her gratitude, though since the threat had come from him, he felt less than deserving of it. He'd known the mark was dangerous if provoked, and he'd succumbed to an almost primal drive to combat it.

Raina's gaze had shifted to the rest of the room. She put her hands on her hips. "Do you think you two could have avoided destroying my library?"

"Because that's what's important," Ruby said dryly.

"He said himself there are plenty of Reapers. This rug was one of a kind, created by master artisans."

Silas shifted his attention back to Ramona. "You were listening to the questions?"

"Raina has an intercom upstairs." She put her hand over his. She'd learned the lesson better than he had. Her healing energy drifted over the area, leaving the mark untouched but drawing that throbbing pain away, lessening the clawing feeling. "I'd like to hear how to make that soufflé."

He drew her down to put his forehead against hers. "Before I jumped into The Pit, I had thoughts of coming back and taking you on a picnic to one of my favorite places. As our first date, so to speak."

"So this isn't your usual way of showing a girl a good time?" She arched a brow, glancing around the library.

"I apologize," he told Raina. "I will help put it to rights."

Raina shook her head. "That's why I have an army of sex demons." She glanced at the carpet. "And a Dark Guardian who always needs ideas for my birthday. Despite some people's doubts of my under-standing of priorities," she tossed Ruby a look, "I think this makes pretty clear that we need to take that closer look at this thing you're carrying around. Before it does any more property damage."

"Or worse," Ruby put in.

Ramona's fingers slid along his wrist, a gentle stroke. Her gaze met his. "Do you feel ready to do that?"

"Yes," he said. "I'm ready."

CHAPTER ELEVEN

*T*hey'd chosen a spot on Raina's property where the women did their full moon rituals. Once there, Silas noted that Ramona separated herself from the others. She stood alone, head tipped back, eyes closed as the other two women prepped the space with a circle of salt, and items representing the elements at the four quarters. All three wore ritual garb, calf-length black dresses with symbols embroidered in silver thread. Matching silver triquetra pendants were their only jewelry, and they were barefoot, hair loose. Ruby's dark brown locks, Ramona's blond tresses and Raina's sable mane with one dyed red streak.

Mikhael leaned against one of the old trees that surrounded the glade, watching. Directly across the circle from him, at the northern point, Derek did the same. They'd had nothing new to report, but several leads pending. Honora, also standing outside the circle, had conveyed much the same status. Silas expected they were all hoping what happened here would offer better direction.

For his part, he kept thinking of the echoes that had come from the mark. *Nothing in this world is pure, Reaper. We know this.*

As he watched Ramona and her coven sisters, Silas realized he'd made certain assumptions about them. All were powerful in their own right, yes. Ruby's focused intensity and serious nature, and the leashed succubus energy that twined around Raina, the power of the shields over her home, said either one could take the lead when circumstances fit their respective talents.

The disorganized nature of Chaos magic, how Ramona had to work with it, likely made her abilities take a second seat to theirs when that application wasn't needed. But it didn't change what her actions on the battlefield and in the library had revealed.

She was the most powerful of the three.

Experienced witches channeled the nebulous creation energy in their souls in different ways. Ramona was a composer. She talked to herself, lips moving as she swayed, tapping into patterns with the singsong rhythms.

She'd asked him to remain in the center of the circle, handing him four oblong-shaped creek rocks, two to hold in either hand. Their smooth, cool weights seemed to draw heat away from the mark pulsing in his chest. It was agitated, as if it knew something was up. A feeling that increased as Ruby and Ramona cast the circle.

He focused on keeping the thing settled down and worked to steady himself. This kind of magic required effort and vigilance from all involved, even the one at the center of it. She would need for him to hold that center.

His gaze slid back to Mikhael. He and Derek were here to gather information, to be ready for what might be reached, but also to back up the women who held their hearts.

Behind Honora's gaze, he saw her worry, the terrible memory of what had happened to Samaira and Hrolf. After he'd updated her, before she left him in the circle, she'd pressed a brief hand to his shoulder, given him a steady look.

"What do you need?" Ruby had approached Ramona. She spoke the words low, a gentle prompt. If she received no response, she'd likely back off until Ramona surfaced from her own meditations.

But her timing was on target. Ramona's eyes opened to survey the area. "You gave me space to dance," she said. "That's all I need."

Ruby stroked a hand down her back, then stepped out of her path as Ramona pivoted and came to Silas. "Should Honora hold your scythe?"

It was not in evidence, but she well knew it could be brought to his grasp in a blink.

"It's linked biologically to me. No matter who holds it, it will come to me when called."

"Like Thor's Hammer," she said.

His lips tugged. "I expect the principles are similar. Yes."

He felt the power emanating from her, energy she had primed to use for the ritual. Even so, when she met his gaze, he saw something else, a different but no less potent magic.

"May I remove your robe, my lord?"

He brushed a fingertip along her temple, her jaw. He wanted to say things to her. Give her things. But first they needed to do this. At his nod, she loosened the rough rope, her fingers light at his waist. They moved up so she could spread open the fabric.

"You have a nice chest," she noted. "I like touching it."

"I will enjoy your touch even more when I know nothing resides beneath my skin to do harm to you or anyone else."

A poignant smile touched her lips. "Other than your heart itself. Because nothing can do quite as much damage to another as a change of heart."

"My heart's only desire is to give you joy," he told her.

"Chaos magic doesn't make that easy."

"When it comes to love, easy offers little of value."

Her eyes became luminous, that power she'd raised within herself, ready to call, even more vibrant. He wanted to kiss her, no matter the seemingly inappropriateness of the timing, and followed the desire, leaning in and pressing his mouth to hers. Held there a long moment before easing back. The energy thrummed between them, providing a different kind of centering.

"Thank you for not going all male on us," she said.

At his raised brow, she clarified. "Deciding that you need to go hide in a cave due to some misguided idea that you're protecting us. Thank you for staying with us, letting us help you protect those who need our protection. That was the right thing."

He gripped her hand. "If we had not planned to do this, I might have done that very thing." His gaze shifted to Raina. "I would prefer to be excessively male if the alternative is harming innocents."

"While excessive maleness has its uses," the half-succubus observed, "let's figure this out so neither choice is necessary." Ruby nodded in agreement.

Ramona drew his attention back to her. "Raisins, sunshine, a woman's laugh, the cut of a blade," she said. "Remember those things when you need them. Those are things that belong to you, not to it. Treasure what can't be taken."

She took the creek rocks from his hand, caressing his palms and briefly linking with his fingers before she placed them at the four points around him. A circle within a circle. Markers for her, he assumed. Then she stepped back, but her words and the kiss kept the energy between them humming. "We are beginning."

The message was for everyone else, not just him. Though he kept his senses tuned to her, he sensed Raina and Ruby positioning themselves.

Her hands began to move. They danced in the air, her arms sweeping before and around her, enhancing their graceful movements. She started to hum. There were words behind the music, but she didn't speak them aloud. Despite her attention seeming to be everywhere else, the sky, the trees, the attending elements, he felt a pull inside his chest, a shifting.

He tensed, worried for her, but she'd told him she intended to invite it to dance. Remarkably, he saw her doing just that. She was murmuring her storm mantra, telling the energy it would come to no harm. She wasn't talking to that beast they'd come face-to-face with in his subconscious. She targeted the energy itself. It possessed no good or evil, and it was that essence she was calling, not whatever had driven it into him or was using it to serve its purposes.

"There you are," she crooned. "There are lullabies to sing us to sleep, there are lullabies to bring us to waking. Come show yourself to me. Come dance with me."

Black mist, unfurling from him. But as it drifted outward, it narrowed, gained solidity, became rope. She extended her arms, let it twine over them. It covered the script he'd placed over her wrists, that her desires for his Mastery had reinforced, branded into her skin.

No.

What surged up inside him wasn't the mark's darkness, but his own. Despite that, he didn't prevent it, didn't stop his will from making its demands known. It yanked those tendrils from her before they could get a good grip.

Shit. Despite her gentle coaxing, him pulling the magic back resulted in a recoil almost as bad as what he'd felt in the library. No, worse, because those ropes were wrapping around his chest, squeezing so that he couldn't talk. The drumbeat roar of pain was what he suspected Cal's heart attack had felt like.

He'd dropped to his ass, and she was down next to him, her hand pressed against his chest, other hands on his back. The women were chanting, working to loosen that vise, without much success, because he was giving them an additional opponent to fight. Himself.

"Let it go," Ramona was exhorting him. "You're increasing its hold, Silas. Turning it against yourself to protect me. Trust me, damn it."

He overcame his primal reluctance with vicious determination, until he won enough breathing room to focus on her intent expression. Among her trepidation was a great deal of annoyance with him. Oddly, he found that reassuring. The hold loosened further.

"It was starting to bind you," he gritted out. "Couldn't permit it to hurt you. Take you."

Her knuckles slid along his face, her gaze flickering as his hand rose to grip her wrist, hold tight. "A dance is a joining," she said softly. "Clasping hands, holding onto one another's bodies. That's what I was doing. When you Reap a soul, it's a dance, right? The soul has to trust you enough to follow your lead."

"I'm not much of a follower."

"Me, either. Until just recently, I haven't found someone I trust enough to do that."

Their eyes met. "Now you've put me on the spot," he said.

"Intentionally. Male pride has its uses. You know my capabilities, Reaper. Do you doubt my understanding of my own magic? I've spent my life earning it."

"I am unwilling to risk it harming you." He was alive because it needed him alive, but it could kill her. No matter her abilities, he felt that, knew it.

She rested her fingertips on his chest. "I'm unwilling to allow anything to *keep* harming you. So let's work together. These women understand my magic better than anyone other than myself. Trust them, and the Guardians watching my back. Plus your boss."

"If you come to harm, I will be angry with you."

"You're pretty sexy when you say stuff like that. I imagine all sorts of things."

Her humor never discounted the seriousness of a moment. But it had a unique way of helping all those involved ease back, see things differently. An important power in its own right.

"My reaction...it was deeper, visceral. It touched the marks I put on you, and I felt an irrational possessiveness." Admitting that had compromised him was uncomfortable, but this was no time for concealing information due to pride.

"It can't take anything about those marks from me." Her mouth firmed, and he saw the glint of that Viking *völva*. "They exist because I want them. I want you. I want what they mean. That means even if the Dark Soul magic covers them, they're not touching them."

They held gazes. She'd extended her wrists to him, together, a gesture she'd done more than once, a symbolic and literal offering of herself to his binding. It had a steadying effect. He clasped them again, felt the beat of her pulse. He shut out everything else. Everyone watching.

"All right, then. I'm at your disposal, witch. I'll do better."

She pressed another brief kiss to his mouth, but he gripped her nape before she could draw back and deepened it. He let her feel how much he wanted to protect her, wanted to keep her safe. But that he would trust her.

As she rose and took two steps back, he returned to his feet, his attention on her eyes, the parted lips.

She began to dance again.

The coaxing forth took longer this time, because he'd spooked it. But he kept his mind centered, his energy calm, willed himself to trust and remain open.

He was a vessel for energy, and he let it pour into him, a heated, fragrant shower of his witch's magic that sought every corner of him, understanding, mapping, learning, working its way toward that dangerous center.

He had to keep that out of his mind, keep himself relaxed. Trust. Dance. *It's a dance...*

~

The power behind that mark was a minefield that could be triggered to reject her. Fortunately, though his reaction had startled what she was calling forth, Silas's response had been a hundred percent from him. While as a woman, she found his possessive and protective instincts thrilling, her focus returned to the goal. She rode the currents of pure energy she raised in the circle in that peripheral, upside-down way she did. She used them to coax forth the pure energy within him, like attracted to like.

An invitation to play. The whole world was made up of curves and angles, an infinity symbol that twisted back on itself, forming a flower with layers of petals.

Come and dance, come and dance...

Ruby and Raina held the circle's integrity, their attention following what she was doing, anticipating and ready to counter, weaving additional power toward that if needed. She reached for clarity, for an open heart. She had to make herself vulnerable, show it her throat so it would trust her. The problem was, what was behind it, holding the reins, didn't deserve that trust. It was why dancing made more sense than anything else. It was easier to dance along an edge than to walk it.

The dark smoke wound over her fingers, her legs and arms. She turned with it, wrapping it around her. She clasped it, seeking the vibrations.

Rage. Arctic cold, the kind that came from helplessness, and a grief grown so strong it became madness, cutting ties away from everything, such that nothing and no one else mattered. It wasn't about alleviating that pain. It was about making everyone else feel it... No, that was wrong.

It had a mission. A mission that had taken twenty long years to come forth, a crooked path as chaotic as any map she'd draw.

Ironic, carrying a torch for a witch... Strangulation was a mercy, the garrote around the throat as she was tied to the stake, strong hands tightening the rod.

The ribbons around her wrists constricted, activating the dormant spirals around her arms and legs. No, not them. This was the darkness pretending to be them, wanting to choke off blood flow. What Silas had feared was coming to pass. The energy twisted into a solid rope around her throat.

She'd been found out. She'd drawn the attention of what controlled her dance partner. But she'd had that dance. She'd succeeded.

She opened her eyes and started. Silas's eyes were fixed on hers in a haze of fiery hatred, his mouth set. That stern regard she found so arousing was now terrifying. His hands were up and clutched in the air as if he held the rope on her throat. Teardrops of soot and fire rolled down her face.

His face was hers. Hers was his.

"Stop it..." she rasped. "Stop... It's not...him."

It is him. You would have stopped him as I am doing. We know one another, witch. You would have stopped all of them. I am doing the same. Free will.

She was losing consciousness, life. But she couldn't move.

Silas's eyes had become twin pits of hell. The flesh burned away from his skull, his twisting hands long finger bones, oddly elegant in their movements. Then they clenched into fists. The Dark Soul magic wasn't burning off his flesh. It was Silas, shoving his power against it, transforming to his full Reaper form to come to her aid.

His flame went from blue gold to white hot rage. He reached for her.

She cried out in sudden fear and pain. Though his hands were on her, the flame engulfed her. She couldn't move, tied to that stake, helpless as the life was choked out of her.

The scythe flashed before her eyes, came down within a hair's breadth of her skin, slicing the garrote free, the blade twisting aside before it could embed itself into her shoulder. He severed the bindings on her legs next. The rush of blood back through the life-giving arteries was so painful she cried out and would have fallen, except he had her, was easing her to the ground, standing over her.

The blackness of a storm surrounded and towered over them. Ruby, Raina, the forest, the Guardians, Honora, all of it was gone. It was as if they'd been sucked into a different place, like when she and Silas had joined hearts and bodies. But that was where the similarity ended.

At least the realm they inhabited was still contained inside the circle. She could feel its boundary, even as this seemed a daunting place, far away from anything. Her hand rested on one of the creek rocks, felt its smooth hardness. She tipped her head back, her hand on her throbbing throat, and saw a sky, miles above. The tiny circle of it was getting ever smaller.

The abyss closing in.

"If you are using me for your own purposes, then fight me," Silas snarled at that blackness, his voice holding a warrior's resolve. "You will leave her out of it, or I will destroy you. You will not fuck with the truths in her soul."

She felt those soulless eyes, whatever lay behind the façade. "Whatever I once was, I will reclaim it," Silas told it. "I will find that darkness and use it against you to end you, no matter what I destroy to do it. Look into the depths of my soul and know it is there."

Counting on it. Abso-fucking-lutely counting on it...

That whisper through her head again, but this time Silas heard it. He bared his teeth as the darkness took form, several creatures with talons, wings, ready to dive in. "You've danced with her. Dance with me instead."

She screamed as the dark creatures came rushing down that tunnel toward them. Not three, but three hundred, intending to bury him, tear him to pieces. She could see blood running off that mark from his chest. It was no longer a mark, but a dozen sets of claws, trying to dig into him, trying to tear his heart out because he'd thrown down the gauntlet, refusing to bow as he stood between it and her.

She was between his braced feet. When his Reaper form had come forth, so too had a long, dark cloak with tattered edges. In the whipping wind, it seemed like a dark dragon at his back, the snap of the cloth the snap of its teeth instead. She pushed herself up, bracing herself on his taut thigh to slap her hand against the throbbing ash-colored mark on his chest. In the same breath, she shoved her amalgamation of gathered power into it.

The power in Silas's scythe culminated in a blinding flash. The heat of it wrested a hoarse scream from her throat. Her flesh was coming off her bones, her hair on fire. The garrote had not taken her life. She'd come back to consciousness as the fire took her, and she screamed and screamed, staring into his eyes, reaching out with the Chaos, forcing her judge, her Inquisitor, to face it, thrusting him into it, so he would know just how lost his soul really was.

Only it wasn't him. It was her.

She was him, he was her... The nature of Chaos, turning every-thing on its head, making them face what no one wanted to face.

There was ever only one face in the mirror.

Silas let out a battle yell. The creatures shrieked, the scythe cutting through and turning them into confetti that sizzled into a snowfall of ash and embers.

He dropped to one knee over her, protecting her from it. The snapping of his cloak added to the roar of the wind and fire. She was protected. She was not burned.

With a roar of her own, a she-lioness standing with her mate, she gripped his shoulder and thrust her hand toward the sky, next to the scythe. Fire shot from her fingertips, using the runway of the scythe's curved blade to launch and spread it out, fan-shaped.

Their powers joined to meet another mob of the dark creatures, taking one last desperate dive. Like giant vultures, with snapping wings, sharp beaks and glittering eyes.

Duck.

She dropped at the thunderous command in her head. The scythe spun over her. A scream, a rush of noise, the darkness falling on them like the weight of a suffocating blanket. Silas's arm went around her, holding tight. She pressed her face to his throat, clung to him, letting him know she was here, they were together, as they were supposed to be, no matter what happened next.

Another kind of roar, sharp, decisive. The beings outside that protective covering howled, burning up from the fire she and Silas had generated. Any reinforcements behind them were under attack, telling her Raina and Ruby were out there, Derek, Honora and Mikhael helping.

Aiming high, to avoid the two of them. Which meant maybe they could be seen, even though she and Silas couldn't see anything.

Who reaped a Reaper? Did anyone? He said they didn't go to The Gate, but surely when they dissolved...was no one there? Were they alone? No. She was with him.

As he'd told Gina, no one went to The Gate alone. That had to include Reapers, no matter where they went.

Things cleared, the darkness slowly receding.

Ruby held her Desert Eagle, muzzle still misted with the power she'd charged into the bullets. Raina's aura had the glitter of sword edges. The Guardians and Honora had held the circle's boundary, containing everything within it while the two witches came to their direct aid.

She couldn't lift her head, but she didn't know if that was because Silas was holding her so fiercely or because she had no strength left. But she had to see him, so she did it.

His Reaper form was receding back behind flesh and muscle, the rugged and handsome face. But there was a terrifying truth between them now.

It wasn't a soul mating that bound them. She didn't know who was who.

We began this journey together. We will take it, over and over again, as the Loom wills, until we are at peace with it, and with each other.

He'd spoken in her head, a binding effect of the circle. It would disappear when it was opened. He traced her face, the tears she felt there. She glanced down at herself, expecting charred flesh, but he'd taken the brunt of it, when he'd put himself over her. Just like with Cal.

Was he atoning for others he hadn't protected, had thrown onto the fire himself? Or was that her? Had the Chaos magic given to her in this life been punishment? Or a method of redemption?

"Ramona." Ruby and Raina were crouching next to her. The circle was still in place, would be until they were sure what was happening, until everything had settled. She put her hand on his chest, and Silas's rose to cover it.

The mark was back to that sullen pulse. Gone back to its lair. Her fingers curled, nails pressing in.

I will get you out of him. No matter what.

"Whatever started this, is human but not," she said. "His core feels human. Like a person who fell into a vat of radioactive waste and became a supervillain."

At Silas's curious look, she offered a wan smile. "Comic book metaphors are easy to follow."

"Like rhymes. A child's way to understand Chaos, complexity," he said. "A simple, powerful method."

When a man put things together without a woman having to draw him a map, it said he was paying close attention to the route he was taking with her. Paying attention to her.

A simple, powerful reminder to help her swim toward the surface of the turmoil she was feeling.

"Wielding this level of power, with that range, it's unlikely he would be totally human," Derek commented.

"I couldn't see his end objective," she said, "but it's to turn everything to what he imagines Chaos is. People think there's no pattern to Chaos. But there is, and it connects to the Lord and Lady's design, Fate's will, what have you. The Big Picture. He plans to use the Reapers, their ability to call souls, to knock everything off kilter. He has a catalyst event. That was the part...it was almost there, but I couldn't get to it. I can go back in."

"No. I forbid it." Silas set his jaw. "And it's not necessary. Focus on that. Focus on him. Who is he?"

She was set to argue, but everyone looked a bit ragged out. What she'd unleashed hadn't been easy to contain. Even Honora didn't look like she disagreed. They'd gotten all they could from this strategy.

"If I had to guess, I'd say he's a sorcerer. One who lost more than he can bear. It's broken his mind, but not in the way that makes him inert. Just the opposite. He has one goal, one he won't stray from for anything but death."

"We can help him with that," Raina said grimly.

"Witch means of the people who are 'set apart,'" Ramona said. "The one who did this has set himself apart. He's meddled in a world not naturally his own, but he's acquired great skill at manipulating it. He's learned how to warp it to fit the warping of his own soul."

Silas's gaze sparked, and he looked at Honora. "He said something to me, through the mark. *Nothing in this world is pure, Reaper. We know this. We.*"

Shock flitted through the Wake commander's expression. "A Reaper. One of the vanished."

Silas nodded. "One we assumed gave himself back up to the natural world, the collective energy. It fits. His knowledge of our kind, what we can do. How it works with the souls. Very few have that information."

Silas turned his attention back to Ramona. "You said he had an incomprehensible pain, rage. Greater than even grief could create?"

"That's an interesting way to put it, but yes," she said. "It's pretty all-consuming."

"What are you thinking?" Mikhael asked.

Silas glanced toward Honora. "Reapers are separated from their original lives, blocked from them," she said. "We speculate that it is because we bore unimaginable pain or created it, inflicted it on others. The wisdom gained from that pain is the foundation of what we are, supporting the rest, but not disturbed by the inflammatory nature of memory that can undermine it."

"So being a Reaper is penance?" Ruby asked. "Or a desire to give back because of your blessings?"

"It could be both," Honora acknowledged. "Lives are long. Most of us believe Reapers are drawn from the ranks of those who have a special relationship with death. They understand what it is and isn't. It doesn't hold sway over us, so we can help others to cross The Gate."

Silas sat back on his heels. Ramona's hand slipped off his chest, but he took it in a light grasp. "Remember what I told you. When we have had enough of Reaping, we return to energy. However, like any transitioning soul, the knowledge of who we were in past lives is revealed to us, to guide us in our next existence. If someone came face to face with that knowledge and couldn't bear it, or it broke their mind..."

His eyes darkened, looking toward Honora. "Instead of dissolving into the collective energy, he developed another objective."

"That fits. It's not just about burning down the world to ease his pain," Ramona said. "He's...cold. The emotions I sensed are being very deliberately channeled into his purpose. He's not allowing a single emotion to go to waste, everything fed into the compost fertilizing the end game."

The danger past, Raina and Ruby had quietly begun to open the circle. As the information Ramona had offered was digested, her gaze went to Silas, still sitting on his heels. He held his shepherd's crook, but traces of silver through the staff hinted at its deadly primary form. Shepherd or Reaper. Light and dark, existing together.

She felt the garrote, the flame, and her heart squeezed in on itself. His gaze turned to her. Every time she experienced strong emotion, it sent a ripple through her magic. From the beginning, he'd promised he could help her balance that, but now she wondered if he meshed so well with her magic, was so aware of its currents, because he knew it far more intimately than he realized?

"You need to recuperate," Raina said. "Use one of my guest houses."

"No," Ramona said. "I need to go home."

She pushed herself to her feet, resolute, and her knees buckled. Silas caught her at the same time Raina did. Raina gave her a tender look, but let her arms slide free to relinquish her to Silas.

She could tell her coven sisters didn't want her to leave. But she was fine. Plus she expected Silas wanted to get away from what was inside him, even if he could only do it symbolically. They needed to move, needed solitude to figure things out. She had understood that need all her life. From what she could tell about him, it was key and core to what he was as well.

"We'll reinforce the Linking," she told the two women. "It makes sense anyway, in case the worst happens.

"We're connected, as coven sisters," she explained to Honora and Silas. "If one of us is in danger, we know it. Enhancing the Linking means we'll have better locating abilities. It heightens the noise in our heads, which is why we don't normally keep it on that volume, but we can, if needed." She glanced at Raina and Ruby. "If we all consent to it, we could also do a Confluence."

A merging of consciousness. If they needed to see something through Ramona's eyes, or Ramona needed to draw on their power to boost her own, or call them to her side, she could. It required massive trust, since it allowed them to overstep and dig into the subconscious. Look at the things a person didn't care to reveal to anyone.

Silas and Honora had moved a few steps away to confer. Though she sensed some anger in the low words Silas exchanged with his commander, Honora merely met his gaze, nodded, then disappeared into the forest. Silas then asked Derek a question in the same low tone. When it was answered, Ramona knew Silas had asked about the Confluence, because her Reaper immediately came back to her, his gaze concerned.

A Confluence was more than being able to dig up skeletons. As powerful witches, they could take that shovel and dig one another's graves. Which Ramona would actually prefer, if either of her coven sisters found out how lonely she'd been since they'd mated with Guardians. Enough to consume and throw up a whole dozen vegan cupcakes the night after Derek and Ruby got married.

"Ramona, you don't have to—"

"It's not for you," she assured him. "I mean yes, you're part of the reason for it, but bigger things are happening. This is for more than their desire to babysit us."

Ruby made a face. "I wouldn't have called it that."

"I would," Raina said bluntly. "I prefer you to be right where we can see you, but I get it. You're about to jump out of your aura. Enough analysis. Some things you just follow your gut and do it."

The ritual was straightforward. A linking of arms, a pressing of knees and feet together in a tight circle. Ruby knew the technical aspects the best, so she took the lead on it, doing the chant. When the Confluence connected them, the flood of energy was strong enough to rock Ramona, hence the reason for linking arms instead of just handholding or standing in a closed circle together. She felt Raina's fiery heat, Ruby's cool ice water, and her own mixture of earth and wind, all woven together. The existing connection between them was suddenly embedded deep, a root system with all three of them in it.

Adjusting that awareness down so the volume wasn't overwhelming took more time and some complicated spellcraft. They coordinated their magical imprints so the energies aligned and settled, quiet guests resting in the deeper layers of their consciousness.

As swiftly as it was done, when they finally finished, Ruby and Raina were sweating and brain-weary. Ramona was depleted, done. But she found something solid was immediately there to lean again. She looked up at Silas.

"Hi there. I figured you and the Guardians went back to Raina's to have a beer."

He gestured to where Mikhael and Derek were closely watching, waiting. "It has been the kind of night where no one wants to be out of sight of those they care most about."

Ramona's fingers curled around his nape. "Your eyes are fully, really green now," she said. "Like pictures of Ireland."

She made a surprised noise as he lifted her. "I'll take her home," he said to the others. "She'll be safe with me."

"You have no way of knowing that," Mikhael said quietly. Raina stood at his side, her eyes worried.

"No," Ramona answered for him. "But we both need it to be true. At least for tonight."

Raina reached over Silas's arm to touch Ramona's face. "We'll be close, and we're here. We love you."

Ruby, with Derek at her back, nodded. Though Ramona had had some trepidation about her suggestion, the upside to a Confluence was the flood of affirmation. She felt even more strongly how much they loved her and each other, beyond any shit or problems they'd given each other over the years. The potholes were just part of what made the road theirs.

Raina brushed a kiss against her cheek, spoke against her ear. "Next time don't keep those cupcakes to yourself. Invite us over. We'll share them, so you get less sick. That's what sisters are for."

CHAPTER TWELVE

*S*he told him where her home was, and that she couldn't wait to take a shower. When he portaled her there, they emerged in her gravel driveway.

"So Reapers must have a factory-installed internal GPS, just like Guardians do," she observed, arms still locked around his shoulders. Despite the light tone, Silas could tell how much was weighing on her mind. He was also pretty sure what topped the list. It was bothering her, what she'd seen during that ritual about her previous lives. And his.

"We have an intuitive sense of direction," he confirmed. "Otherwise, no telling how many times I'd be late for a Reaping because I went to the wrong Smith Street in the wrong Washington. There are about ninety towns called Washington in your country." He gazed at her. "Ramona..."

"Raina has a spell on her driveway. Whenever someone who believes Sweet Dreams is an actual B&B tries to find it, they end up at one of the other three actual B&Bs in the area. She says they should give her a commission." Ramona dipped her head forward. "It's far easier to find my place."

It looked like many of the ramshackle farmhouses he'd seen in rural Southern areas, a mix of wood and stone put together at the early part of the twentieth centry. The creativity that came from a lack of cash meant that repairs and maintenance over the decades had been done with mismatched materials, function over aesthetics.

Though it looked disordered, inconsistent, the end result was sturdy. Patches to the tin roof made a lightning pattern. Ivy covered two outside walls. She had raised bed vegetable gardens, wind chimes and fluttering garden flags holding court among them. Statuary, much of it headless, one armed or halfway crumbling, existed amid a thicket of wildflowers and vines surrounding the house.

A thicket infused with protective magics, which gave the place a welcome feeling, the sense that safety existed here. Respite. Telling him why she'd wanted to come home.

She looked up at him with haunted eyes. He put her down, but kept his hand on her. He wanted to touch her more than that, but the ache he felt from her was too much.

He'd wrestled with whether he should leave her after he took her home. Honora had nixed that, ordering him to stay with Ramona. Nothing had changed. The bulk of what they knew about the mark thus far had come through its interaction with her magic.

"So I honor a brave woman by putting her at greater risk."

"There are bigger things at stake, Sylvanus."

He'd said something he'd never thought he'd say to his Wake commander. But she'd simply given him an even look and portaled off to update the others.

Protecting the woman engaging his desires had always aligned with who he was. The way she held him when he carried her, conveying that need to be vulnerable under his control, only reinforced it. Resolving that conflict was shredding him worse than the mark.

After that meet with Honora, he recalled how the Guardians had flanked him, during the Confluence. The three stood together, watching their women. "I know where your head is," Derek said. "Shit isn't right inside you, and you're doubting your instincts. Which makes you all the more determined not to pull her any deeper into this."

He crossed his arms over his chest, dragonskin boots braced so he could rock on his heels in a contemplative pose. "Mikhael and I are going to track this son of a bitch down. Honora's right. You're her second-in-command. Having your headspace right for when and if the shit really hits the fan, taking time to get that balance, is important."

Derek nodded toward Ramona. "So's she. She waited a long time for your return. Give her a day."

Mikhael shot him a sidelong glance. "He has selfish motives. If you don't take that time, we'll have to listen to our mates verbally eviscerate you for taking off on her again. And blame us, because we're male."

Derek's blue eyes glinted in agreement. "A woman's disappointment can make a man's life miserable. Death doesn't offer an immortal male the same escape hatch as men with far shorter lives."

Yes, it was possible being here with her now would serve a purpose as important as any other effort. Their reinforcement of that helped. However, he doubted either Mikhael or Derek would have found the decision any easier to make than he did, if it were their women in the crossfire.

But all of it be damned, he would still ask the woman in question her mind on it. "Do you wish me to go, Ramona?"

She turned to gaze at him. There were crickets chirping in her garden, several loud frogs warbling. The night had a warmth to it. She stepped close to him. He'd changed into street clothes, and she slipped the buttons of the shirt, spreading it open to place her palms on his chest, on the light layer of coarse hair. He studied her, not sure of her intent.

Then her fingers curved in, pressed down with a sudden, stabbing violence, nails embedding themselves in his flesh, letting him feel the rough pain. He didn't stop her, his hands gripping her waist.

As the throbbing increased, she rose on her toes, leaning her weight into him, increasing that penetration. He cupped the back of her skull, fingers diving into the thickness of her loose hair, wrapping it over his grip as their mouths met. Her lips were already parted, her hips pressing up against his, a seeking. He growled into her mouth, and she responded with an urgent noise.

When she drew back, her lips wet, eyes hot, he was clear on her message. She didn't want space.

Her gaze dropped to his chest, to what lurked beneath his skin. "Fuck you," she said clearly, a threat, a challenge to that symbol and whoever was behind it. Then her eyes became slumberous, a siren's, and she was back on her toes, brushing her mouth over his.

"Fuck you..." she whispered. She kissed the corner of his mouth, his jaw. He had a tight grip on her hair, her waist. Her mouth curved, an invitation. "Language is a lovely piece of Chaos. It can mean entirely different things, with just a change of tone."

She slipped from his grasp, moved to her front door. When she reached it, she turned around, looked at him. "Will you come into my house, my lord?"

Her choice of when to use the formal address was effective. He came to her, braced his hand against the doorframe and brushed his fingers along her face. When he did, the siren's attitude dissolved and he saw the starkness in her gaze again, felt the tremor in her body under his touch. "We will need to talk about what happened in the darkness," he said quietly. "Not what we're fighting out there. But what happened between you and me."

"Does it need to be now?"

Her gaze lowered to his throat, his shoulder. She waited for him, telling him she would honor his decision. Her choice of when to defer to him was powerful as well, drawing on the desires between them, how they wanted to shape and declare themselves.

A woman's submission was something he'd explored in a thousand ways, but she'd just given him a gift he'd never experienced before. When a Master was struggling with powerlessness, she could hand him back power with her trust, her faith in his control.

Remind him to live up to it.

"Show me your home."

She pushed the door inward. No lock. A foyer opened into her living room. It had mismatched furniture, the sofa and easy chairs upholstered in multiple colors that seemed to harmonize, rather than creating a dizzying clash. No glass knickknacks or glassware of any kind.

A shoebox-sized lion made of concrete, more garden statuary, slept in a pet bed by the door to a hallway. A bag of yarn and unfinished knitting project were tucked next to his silver-gray body. In the center of her living room, a dancing nymph fountain gurgled and splashed. No electronics. The house had much of its original wood flooring and trim, giving it the aroma of long past history.

"When was your first Reaping?" she asked, an unexpected segue. She'd gone to her kitchen, and he followed her there. She gestured him to a metal-framed ice cream parlor chair with a red vinyl seat. It was next to a rectangular table surfaced with white tile. The tiles were covered with doodles, magical symbols, as if she'd been transcribing spellcraft inspiration on the closest thing to hand. The erasable crayons she'd used were stacked there; a rhyme scribbled next to them.

How silly to use all the colors in the box,
Merely to find one pair of missing socks.

As she moved to a tea kettle, he answered her. "My first solo Reaping was in the mid-1600s. New Reapers train with an existing one. Mostly it's learning how to manage the emotions, your reactions and understanding, letting go to trust the Fates."

She turned. "How specific is the information the Fates send you?"

"They provide us the when and where part." He nodded. "My mind is where yours is. Somehow, the intent of the mark connects to the whole process. The Fates, the marking to influence Reapers, the rage at something he couldn't change, a loss he can't get over."

"Stating a problem is usually simple." She polished a spot on the tea kettle with a washcloth. "Handling it is the complicated part. I can grow food to eat. Simple. Now put it into practice, and see just how 'simple' it is to prepare soil, deal with bugs and blight, make sure your plants have the right conditions to grow..."

She shook her head. "He's put together something that perhaps has never been done before. He's taken it one careful step at a time, spent twenty years building it. It's not going to be easy to derail it, because he's considered it from all angles."

She stared at the tea kettle. Its heat was starting to build, telling him she was using her own abilities rather than lighting the wood-stove. The lid began to quiver, a prelude to the steam whistling from it. She put her hand over that opening, cupped it.

"What are you doing?"

He was up out of the chair and to her, pulling her hand away as the steam emitted its first curling blast, a faint train whistle sound.

"Do you know what else I can do, my lord?" She freed her hand to stroke her fingers down his chest. He'd left the shirt open, so her hands passed over the hidden mark, moved out wide, stroking along his pectorals, then down to his abdomen. Her hand was hot, as if she'd drawn the temperature of the water into it before he pulled it away. A tingling sensation followed her touch. He sensed that not-entirely-centered focus when she was channeling her magic.

Her gaze slid up to his, then flicked away, a teasing shyness as her fingers descended. She played over his length, hard against the jeans, and his hands flexed on her as whatever magic she had in those fingers jolted through him, but not with pain.

Pleasure rocketed right to his root, to his balls, his upper thighs, even between his buttocks. If she kept those waves going, he would release in no time. Except the way her fingers twisted over him, the lavender of her eyes becoming deeper as that in a predawn sky, told him she had ways of prolonging that feeling indefinitely. She could hold back the final denouement until she'd given a male the most unforgettable sexual experience of his life.

The sensation spiraled up his arm, tingling through his throat, nipples, every nerve ending or erogenous zone he'd never even realized he had.

A solitary experience, because she was showing him something. Not sharing it with him. His gaze snapped back to her face. She took pleasure in his reaction, but she didn't feel a part of it. Pleasure could be a one-way trip to the destruction of the soul.

"Ramona. Stop it. Now."

Delivered with force, it was nevertheless a controlled command. It brought her up short. She dialed back the energy, though the lingering vibrations through him were strong enough to let him know what he was missing.

"Do you not like it?" Her voice was a throaty purr, but her eyes were uncertain. "The males I've been with found it—"

She sucked in a breath as his grip on her wrist tightened. He made sure she felt the cool ripple cut through the electricity, ground it as surely as the earth itself.

"Ramona," he said with deliberate care, "did they give you pleasure in return? Did you take that journey together?"

His reaction yanked her out of her head. She knew she'd gone to the wrong place with him, but she was drowning, and she'd reached for the familiar.

"Not their fault. I couldn't. Not and be sure they'd be safe. I learned how to do this, became skilled enough they would never..."

Suddenly, under his passive regard, she was blinking back tears. He finished the thought for her.

"So they would feel so much pleasure from it they would never realize they'd left you out in the cold while you were doing it. They did nothing for you."

"They would hold me afterward." Sometimes, she'd have to pick up a limp arm, the man overcome from the force of the climax she'd given him. She'd wrap it around herself, hold it there until he found the strength, and remember he had an obligation to care for her. "It was all right. I was never left uncomforted. I figured out other ways."

He muttered an oath. She crossed her arms over herself. "Maybe... you were right. Maybe you should go and do..."

"Which hand?"

"What?"

"Which hand do you most often use to...comfort yourself? You don't appear to have a dominant one."

He'd noticed she was ambidextrous. He noticed so much, it made things hurt worse. She'd started this. Why was she deliberately challenging him, pushing him? She'd never relied on a male to pull her out of such a dark place in her head. Maybe she was testing him, seeing if he could meet the challenge. Which was wrong, too.

None of this should matter when they were facing so many more important things, but she'd done it to herself. She'd come back to the quiet haven she'd built here, and it was mocking her, an undeserved gift. Not so many years ago, she'd believed her magic and isolation were a punishment. She'd gotten beyond that. Now she was facing that mirror again, and breaking it didn't make it go away. It multiplied the image, taunting her for trying to look at it any other way.

When she'd said she found other ways to comfort herself, self-pleasuring wasn't what she'd meant. However, under the unsettling directness of his gaze, she raised her left hand. Just the gesture brought the act to mind, making her body quiver. He closed his hand on her wrist. Brought himself closer, so her backside was pressed against the stove as he put her fingers to his mouth.

"Ramona, I was there with you," he said. "I saw what you saw. So if you believe who I was in those memories, hear what I'm saying now and believe it. It's too close. There's too much. Leave it for now, what's in your mind. Let it go, so you can look at it later, with an easier heart, a clearer mind. Trust who you are *now*. What I am *now*. What you want me to be to you. What I demand to be to you."

He paused. "Not because you owe me that, or it changes anything. But because everything is what it is at a soul's birth, before it chooses its first life, as well as what it grows to be through all of them. You can't live backwards without tying yourself into knots that harden with the salt of your tears, and stop you from living your life as it was meant to be lived."

She was trembling harder. His gaze held hers, relentless, until she managed a little nod. Then his tone changed, smooth. A command. "Good. Stroke me the way you would stroke yourself."

He drew two of her fingers into his mouth, played his tongue over them, until she figured out his meaning and began to move them.

She'd never imagined it could be sexy, having her fingers in a man's mouth and pretending the heated, wet strength of his tongue was her clit, but as she did, it ignited fire down her center. She lost her focus and coordination.

He took over, his tongue working in between her fingers, summoning the idea of that same part of him stroking between and around her labia. Slightly sucking, nipping lightly with his teeth. Her dampening cunt and the heated wetness of his mouth became the same, making her sway into his embrace, her knees weak again.

When he let her hand slide free, she arched against him, a cry breaking from her as he dropped his hand and pressed it between her legs. She still wore her ritual dress, the embroidered fabric a thin barrier that absorbed her response. He manipulated his fingers, a firm pressure that showed how different his touch from hers, demanding so much more.

He stopped, keeping his hand there. She was clinging to him. He gripped her hair, tipping her head back to look up into his eyes. "You said you wanted a shower. Go do that. Right now. Keep your mind clear." He pressed his fingers against her core, bent and brought his lips to her neck. She gasped as he bit her, held her firmly by those two clamps. "Do you understand me?"

She answered him the only way her aching need would allow. "Yes, sir."

Green flame bathed her in heat. Her body was humming like a neon sign that said *fuck me now*, but she moved toward the stairs in the hallway. At the bottom one, she looked back. There was too much knowledge in his gaze. While she knew there was no joy in escaping a truth that was going to face her eventually, he'd told her it could wait. She'd choose to believe him.

"Um...help yourself to anything in the kitchen. There's a guest bathroom if you want to clean up, too."

"Go, Ramona."

Her second-floor bedroom had been built around a large tree at the corner of the house. The trunk twisted up through the floor and disappeared through another hole in the upper right corner of the adjacent wall. Vines wound around the trunk, some of them trained into the slats of her picket fence headboard. Among the white fragrant flowers that bloomed, she'd hung ornaments.

As she shed her clothes, her gaze passed over her pictures, covering almost every available inch of space on the walls. Magazine shots, framed art, photographs. A montage of the world. None of the photographs were of her or her friends, her sisters. She had a half dozen of those on a table by the bed. Her, Raina and Ruby standing by a body of water. They were watching something offshore, their hands linked. She'd been in the center.

Ruby and Derek's wedding picture, Ruby lovely in a blue lace dress, wearing a topaz and pearl necklace Derek had given her as a wedding gift. Next to that were the two of them holding Jem, just after he was born in a room at Sweet Dreams, Isabella and Matilda serving as co-midwives.

She lingered on it, closed her eyes. The word *uncomforted* came back to her mind and made her fists clench. But then she followed his direction. She thought of his possessive hand between her legs, his mouth on her throat. He was entirely aware of her. Present. Here for her and with her.

There was a comfort to that, and she grabbed for it. *Trust what you want me to be. What I demand to be.*

She went to the shower. She did need one, if they were going to be intimate, and she wanted that. No matter the aftermath, she wasn't strong enough to resist her desire. And if both of them were wrong, the shower was where she found her 'comfort.' Letting him believe the word related to masturbation was less embarrassing to her than the truth.

She stepped into the heat of the spray. The pressurized water closed around her.

Every woman knew not to bring up other lovers, even indirectly, in the presence of the current one. What had she been thinking? But Silas was different. She couldn't find her usual impulse control.

She let out a little sigh, turned. Once, twice, and she felt the water start sculpting itself to fit her need, getting more solid. That shape became an embrace, a strong male she leaned into, his head bent over hers, arms around her as she cuddled against him, was cuddled by him, held close. As if she mattered, as if they could become truly intimate, not just the false or temporary state found through sex.

Her magic gave this to her, a comforting, translucent illusion made of an element, the heat and pressure providing a form for it. But she wanted it to be Silas. She'd never felt such a strong pull toward a male, a need to be with him, bond with him, surrender to him.

She agreed with him. There was no payoff for protecting yourself from living the journey you were given, from living it fully. Death was not a payoff for that. It was simply the end of any chances for that life. But the more complicated revelations in the circle called that into question. How could she draw any comfort from the things she'd thought mattered the most?

She squeezed her eyes shut, pressed into that watery embrace. *Let it go.* The steam swirled around her, enclosing her further. She could stand here until she pruned, but a small noise came out of her throat as he touched her, as the arms grew stronger, more encompassing. As the head that bent over hers became even more substantive. Real.

Silas pressed his lips to her temple, his bare body firmly against the side of hers, from shoulder to hip to thigh.

It wasn't fantasy. It was him. One arm slid under her breasts, the other around her back, his mouth against the drops rolling over her face, sipping at them, at her.

"Forgive me," he murmured. "I misunderstood, though I shouldn't have. For a woman, comfort is a well that sex alone cannot fill. Without it, the aftermath will strip the pleasure away, leave you at the bottom of that empty well by yourself."

When she swallowed a sob, his arms tightened around her. "I'll take my pleasure with you, but I'll never take without giving you that. I'll never leave you alone."

"Silas." She pressed her face to his shoulder, her forehead against his chest as he held her even closer.

"There is no obligation to this. It's a gift. You're a gift. And now, Chaos witch, let me show you everything a Reaper can do for you."

Turning her to face him, he lifted her up against the wall of the shower, her back against the slick, heated tile. As he held her with strong hands, he lifted her even higher, guiding her legs over his shoulders, holding her where her head rested against the painted sheet rock above the shower.

Sensation roared through her. The lights flickered and the water sprayed in an arc that painted the ceiling, splashing against her breasts and throat. She grasped at the energy, and he helped. Their energy tangled the same as their laced hands, pressed against her thighs.

"Oh..." She jumped at the tingling electricity, remembered how she'd channeled that through her hands, letting him feel what she could do with it. Same as he'd done to her before, and now it was back under his control, his magic, delivered from his mouth to her tender flesh.

"Silas..." She gasped his name again. He pinned her wrists to her thighs. Those inked bands came to life, only this time they didn't offer only heat. They acted like actual bonds, locking her wrists to her thighs, pulling them wide and holding her open. She remembered the way his mouth had felt on her fingers as his tongue now slid over the petals of her sex, leisurely stroked and thrust into her. When he closed his mouth over her clit and suckled, she arched and groaned out a deeper need.

He shifted her legs off his shoulders, controlling her descent to adjust her thighs high on his torso, crossed heels resting on the upper rise of his ass. He cradled her breasts, nuzzling them, teasing them. Treating them gently until he suckled her nipples with that electric-infused pressure that had her writhing, body lifting and falling back against tile.

He was unleashing a level of power he hadn't shown her before, overwhelming her. When his gaze moved to her face, gauging her reaction, she saw a man in control of every cell of her body. In control of her life, her breath, her pleasure. Her comfort. He would care for her, not allowing her responsibility for anything until he was damn well ready.

She hadn't really understood what the word Master meant until this very second. It was far more than a fantasy with him. It could become as much her reality as the heartbeat that kept her alive.

"Silas." It was a plea, a fear, and a need.

"I'm here," he told her, sliding her down so that now her hips were locked over his. His erection pressed against her, her body shaking so hard he cradled her face, pushed the rest of his body against her to steady her.

"I'm not afraid to dance in the storm with you. Let's dance. When it's done, I'll still be with you, Ramona. Holding you. Your pleasure is what will drive my every act. Don't ever do what you tried to do downstairs again. I will never settle for giving you less than you deserve."

She wasn't dealing with the ancient Reaper, the immortal. She was dealing with a man who had very decided views on treating her like a woman. "If you fail to remember that," he added, his expression becoming something that made her quake, "I'll think of ways to ram the ill-advised nature of that strategy entirely from your thinking."

He punctuated the verb with a meaningful push of his hips against her core that had her sucking on her bottom lip. His eyes went to it, and then his mouth did, replacing her teeth with his own, biting, scraping, making her moan and wrap her arms around his wet shoulders.

"I'm afraid of wanting this so much," she whispered. "That something terrible will happen. I'm so afraid it will all be the same. And now I'm afraid there's a reason for that, a truth I've never had to face. I know you told me not to think about it now, but everything is open inside of me, so I can't help not thinking about it."

He touched her face, turned her head so their noses brushed. He tasted the water on her lips. "Have you ever had a Reaper in your bed?" When she shook her head, he nodded. "Then you already know one thing is different."

He paused. "Did you know I can take a soul from a body, even before its time?"

The rush of the shower water didn't blur the words, their meaning, and the hardness of his green eyes told her he wanted her to hear him, isolate the words, their significance. "It's less difficult than having the thought. Think about the power of that, what it requires in terms of discipline, of knowing my own soul and the shape of my powers, down to the very last cell of my being. The confidence and faith vested in me, in my judgment."

He caressed the side of her throat. "Your magic may be able to change mine at other times, but when they tangle together for joining our bodies, I can feel the shape of it. I can wrap it around me, like the ribbons of power around your wrists. You're safe, bound to me, able to surrender whatever you wish. It's a shelter with a wide-open sky and endless worlds to explore. A haven. All right?"

She closed her eyes. "Okay." She was too afraid to say anything more, and hoped he understood.

He did. But apparently it wasn't going to change how much he would demand from her, to ensure *she* understood.

Her tiny, terrified act of trust intensified what he felt for her. She was courageous, strong. He wouldn't tolerate anything taking that from her. That included present fears or past sins.

Unclothed, he saw inked symbols over her breasts, her upper thighs and above her mons. Preparation for the ritual they'd just done. The henna had an earthy flavor to it, and he'd sucked on those symbols the same as he had the sensitive flesh below them.

He put his hand back between her legs, let her feel the strength, the pressure of his fingers against her cunt again, the lips of her sex. "What does that feel like?"

"The touch of the man I belong to. The one I want to belong to. The one I want to belong to me." It was a monumental admission, reinforced by the shudder that rocked through her, the desire to flee her feelings and the vulnerability it placed upon her.

"The one you do belong to. The one that belongs to you."

Her gaze flickered, that vivid silver hue reflecting her feelings. Satisfied, he went back to what he was doing—proving they weren't exchanging lust-fueled empty promises. He'd just demanded her faith in an oath he was offering to her. He didn't give a damn about soulmates, what defined them. He knew what he would be giving this woman.

He kept her pressed to the wall as he returned to enjoying her breasts, exploring and taunting them with mouth and fingers. Small but perfect, like milky pearls. When she rocked against his touch, her response building past anything that she could make sense of, he kept driving her.

When she was begging for mercy, he finally put her back on her feet. But only to turn her around and bring his erection against the seam of her buttocks. Gripping her wrists, he pushed her forward and guided her palms so they were flat against the tile. "Don't you move," he whispered into her ear, the water adding to the rushing sound. "Or I'll give your cunt a spanking with my hand."

She jolted, a little mewl coming from her. He dropped to a knee and put his mouth between her legs again, this time from behind. She had a sweet taste, mixed with the earth-rich scent of the water drawn from the well on her property. Each time he bit her, she'd jump, but she'd immediately still, trying so hard to obey him. What more could a Master want?

Everything. Her body surrendered, her heart handed over. He would break her open down to the darkest corners of her soul, and it would come into his hands, belong to him forever. A soul he'd never have to let go.

When he gripped her slim buttocks and used his thumbs to play with her rim, she went to her toes. Her fingers scraped the wet surface of the tile wall as she pleaded, driving him to greater savagery.

"Silas, please...need you..."

He understood the raw note in her voice, because he felt it, too. Everything they'd dealt with, the mark, the uncertainty of the future, that moment in the circle when her arm had aligned with his scythe and their power drove back the night...they had to defy it this way, too.

Rising, he turned her to face him. She was shaking so hard, his beautiful Chaos witch. She didn't seem to realize how much of her magic he was channeling, feeding back into this moment. It was a tornado in the room, but he had it wrapped, locked to him, directed into the power he was putting into her pleasure, into their coming together, into the earth beneath them and the sky above.

It was the first time he'd succeeded in getting her to let go. To trust him fully, not even aware she was doing it. He smoothed her wet flaxen hair back, clearing water from her eyes, her face. Her hands hooked over his forearms as she watched him commit the tender act among his more ruthless ones.

He put the lightest of kisses on her mouth. His cock was aching, her body was wet and ready for him, but he took the moment. A male who reached this point, breaking open a woman so she was giving him everything, who didn't acknowledge it as a sacred gift, was a fool.

He shut off the shower, leaning past her. Her arms went around him, holding on. It made it easy to adjust, bend and scoop her up. So small and light. She was his bird. "In your bed," he told her. "I want to be inside you, you under me, your arms and legs locked around me. Close as we can get."

She pressed her face to his wet throat, and then they were there, lying amid a nest of blankets, the haunting scent of the white flowers twined in the headboard cloaking them.

When the rumble of thunder shook the house, her eyes went wide, her hands clutching his shoulders. He smiled, a painful, fierce joy to it. "It's a thunderstorm," he told her. "A normal one. Smell the rain coming."

She had her windows open, so he saw her nostrils flare. He tightened his grip on her. "You stay with me, Ramona. Focus on me."

She was used to protecting everyone from her magic. He'd told her he needed her trust, and she understood just how hard relinquishing that control was. She'd known it when she'd asked for it from him, during the ritual. He saw that memory there, as he made the same request of her now, only he made it a demand, because that was what he would be to her. The Master she could trust to understand who she was, what she was. And demand more from her than she was used to being able to give.

He slid into her, and she rose to him, deepening the lock. She wrapped her limbs around him, and as he thrust into her, her body rising and falling with his, going toward that edge together, the magic of it twined with what was swirling around them, passing through them, holding them.

When it was over, he would hold her in his arms, give her that, too, so she didn't have to find it with a water mirage in her shower. He wouldn't soon forget that, seeing her seek comfort through the manipulation of her own magic, because she didn't believe she could ask for that from him.

The savagery increased, a male's need to prove to a female she could count on him for the things that mattered.

When she climaxed, the victory was equal to any gift from heaven. But in the way that love did, the nature of her cry tore a jagged wound in his heart. A release from yearning pain, a million lonely nights, fearful moments, a yell into the darkness that had curtained despair, arousal, crazed desperation. A declaration.

I am no longer alone.

No, you're not. Never again.

He'd taken them straight from the shower, so the sheets were wet. He withdrew slowly, pressing a kiss to her mouth, her chest, abdomen, mons, thighs. Her hands drifted over his back, the Reaper brand, to his shoulders, his damp hair. He found several towels in the bathroom and returned, setting them aside to shift her to the far side of the bed.

She curled on her side, watching him as he spread the towels out over the wet areas and moved her back into place. Her fingers had been opening and closing on the mattress. When he wrapped himself around her, putting a leg over hers, bringing her fully into the cocoon of his embrace, they went to his chest, did that movement there.

A little sigh. "It's really just raining?"

He nodded against her hair. The rain was falling more gently now, a soak her vegetable gardens would appreciate. He looked at the pictures by her bed. "Derek married Ruby according to mortal ritual. Is that what she wanted?"

"She said he insisted. Derek wanted her to know he saw himself as hers as long as they both should live. She always adds 'well, as long as I live,' but he corrects her. He says, 'For as long as *I* live. I'll find you, lifetime after lifetime.'"

A smile against his throat. "It's surprisingly sexy to see him wear the ring. That evidence that he belongs to a woman, gives himself to her."

He stroked her bare back. "You said he insisted. Did she not want marriage?"

Ramona paused, suggesting she was choosing her words to respect her friend's privacy. "Her life was very difficult growing up. Plus she suffered a terrible loss."

"A child."

"Yes. Even now, she has a hard time with too much seriousness, what it makes her feel. So when he says things like that, she usually says something like, 'Nope. I'm only putting up with you for one lifetime. Then I'm done.' Even though we all know the truth. They've been fated for one another since the beginning of time. True soulmates."

In the shower, he'd said to hell with it and meant it, so the word shouldn't be able to punch him in the chest the way it did. When her breath hitched over the word, he thought she'd realized the word might be troublesome to them both, but then he realized her distress wasn't that. What had plagued her since the circle finally refused to be ignored.

"It's all right," he said quietly. "It's time to talk about it, Ramona."

Her fingers constricted in his chest hair. "What we saw, that previous life, where our paths crossed. At first...I thought it was you who had done the awful things...to me. To others. Which makes me feel even worse, because that's some fucked-up denial crap, putting it off on others. But..."

"It's all right. The mind deals with trauma in strange ways." He stroked her hair, but she took her hand away from him, closing it into a fist against her breast, her knuckles pressing into his side.

"No, it's not all right. Because it *was* me. Wasn't it?"

"I don't have the power to see what former lives held, not for a soul whose body is still living. I can feel its age, how many lives it has lived, but not the specifics."

"Don't." She sat up, her long hair draped over her breasts, her eyes troubled. "That may be generally true for souls, but this is about *our* souls. You saw what I saw, Silas. Always be honest with me. Even if it hurts me. Promise."

"Hurting you isn't something I would ever do easily."

She drew back as he reached for her. "It's a gateway drug. You lie to be kind. Then for other reasons. To protect yourself, to keep things okay between us, to..."

"Stop." He rose, came around the side of the bed and sat next to her. He pinned her with a firm gaze. "Do not confuse me with past lovers. Remember?"

When her shoulders slumped, her spine's curve was prominent against her pale skin. He skimmed a hand down the scattering of freckles. "Yes," he said. "I saw it, that life that's troubling you. But Ramona, I do not know how many lives I had before becoming a Reaper. Before that, I may have been a groom to a Templar knight, a child soldier in Nigeria. A guard at a concentration camp." He met her gaze. "Or a witch strangled and burned. You know as I do that enlightenment is a road with many experiences, good and bad, awful and miraculous. Mundane and exquisite."

"Nothing exquisite about being an Inquisitor who sentenced a witch to burn." She rubbed her arms, the hairs that raised there. "I watched them draw the garrote around your throat, felt my sureness of how *right* I was... That was the most terrifying thing. Because I felt it so strongly, I knew I was reliving one of my own lives, not watching someone else's. To have no doubt when doing something like that... I hated being in my own skin, couldn't bear the feeling—"

Revulsion captured her expression. The wardrobe doors burst open, their quick rattle his only warning. He saw the flash of silver as energy lashed around her like rope, jerking her to her feet. Her eyes had slammed closed, her face rigid, arms thrown open by a force inside her taking control.

He shoved them both to the bed, himself over her. He grunted as the athame struck, but didn't let it stop him from balancing the volatile energy trying to get to her.

"No." The sharp one-word command was directed to the magic, to what took control of her, her flailing conscience, her sickened soul. He drew a line in the sand and drove it back behind it, settling it, pushing it out to every corner. "No."

She was fighting him, so the second admonition was for her. She had her arms wrapped around her head, her body hunched in against itself and rocking, even lying beneath him. "No, I can't bear it. I can't."

"Stop. Ramona, stop." He pulled her arms from her face, made her look at him. "Healer, cease. I'm bleeding."

"What do...what?" As he'd intended, she snapped out of it. Rising up slightly so he didn't lose full contact with her, he twisted so he could gesture to her athame, buried in the left side of his back, just below his rib cage. "I'm going to pull it out, but you might want to grab that towel so I can keep from bleeding on your bed linens."

"Holy Goddess." She scrambled up as he gingerly moved to his knees, putting one foot on the floor. She grabbed the towel. "I'm so sorry. What was going on inside me, I couldn't..." Her expression cleared. "It would have been aiming for me. Why did you..."

"Do you really want to finish that statement?" He gave her an even look. "It's a good thing you said you don't oppose spankings. Though I expect when you experience the kind I want to give you at this moment, you may feel differently."

"If you can make my toes curl with that look and tone, it must not have hit anything immortal-life-threatening."

He was glad she was sounding more like herself. Though she looked shaky, the energy in the room stayed settled like fallen snow, leaving a weighted silence. She wrapped the towel around the blade and drew it out herself, then had him grasp the terry cloth to put pressure on the wound.

"It requires nothing further," he told her. "You've seen how I heal."

"If I'd given you time, you could have gone full Ghost Rider and it would have just scraped a rib bone. You'd look really sexy riding a motorcycle in the cloak, by the way."

"Until it caught in the engine and wheels and I became a heap of shattered bones." He made her set the ritual knife aside, sit next to him. "Does that happen often? Your magic harming you when you are upset with yourself?"

"Not since I was a teenager. I learned to deal with self-destructive mood swings early." She shook her head. "It's been a long time since it's broken free like that. But it's not every day I face historical verification that I'm a monster."

"You are not a monster. No more than any of us." He touched her jaw, made her meet his gaze. "None of us escape it. We all have to commit crimes against one another, cause pain, to understand who and what we are. To love one another fully. All our darkness and light."

"Easy to say. But to feel the weight of something you did like that... Even thinking about it... You go along, thinking you're trying to be the best person possible, then find out you did something heinous in previous lives." A shudder went through her. "Now it makes sense that the Reaper saw what he was in previous lives and went batshit."

"Possible. Though there are intelligent reasons we are blocked from our previous lives, typically it is assumed a Reaper's nature can handle it."

"But every rule has an exception," she pointed out. "And maybe that's why the mark was able to unlock the former life we shared during our circle. Maybe it's designed to create mayhem like that. It could have driven us apart." She stared at the wardrobe, the athame, her expression stark. "How is anything like that forgivable?"

"For the reasons I just said." Silas gripped her hand. "You wish proof? I was your victim and yet I am here, in this lifetime, hundreds of years later, other lives lived, and we are together again. Wanting to be together. Perhaps I had to endure being burned at the stake because of lives I harmed in another cycle. Perhaps one of them was you."

She sighed, rubbed her forehead. "I know this crap. Everything we know spiritually is a spiral. But to actually see its truths...it's terrible, Silas."

"Yes, it is. But you live a life where there is day and night. Those two parts make the whole. No matter how horrifying that might seem close to it, from the heavens it makes sense."

"Maybe the heavens need better eyeglasses."

He let a smile cross his face. Not because he felt like smiling, but because she needed to see it, to be reminded that she was not in that terrible past life. *Past* being the important point.

"I think there's a reason Chaos magic users walk so much closer to the Loom, to the Underworld and Dark Soul magic. Because you *know*." He wrapped her hair around his knuckles, gently tugged. "It showed itself to you, thinking to knock you off your axis, but you understand it. Find your balance, Chaos witch. It is there, waiting for you."

She dipped her head again, staring at the floor. He could sense when she started to pull away from the turmoil that had gripped her. As she gathered her energies, separated them out, wove them into a balance again, he drew back enough to give her the space to do it. While he didn't touch her physically, he watched, felt the marvelous shape of that process on the periphery, learning more about her. About how she did what she did.

He wasn't going to let his mind dwell on what would have happened if the blade had found her. She seemed far more upset by stabbing his immortal flesh than a threat against her own life, which suggested how often she'd dealt with a teenager's self-directed volatile mood swings.

At length, she sighed. "Well, this has shattered my notion that I was the queen of a Polynesian tribe during the Dark Ages in Europe."

"The bulk of lives never make the history books. But all that matters is they are a strand on the Fates' Loom."

Her gaze rose. "When I die and my soul rises, my Reaper might see the Inquisitor that burned you as a witch. Especially if you're my Reaper."

He didn't like the thought of her death, no matter who was in charge of taking her to The Gate. He tapped her wrist, giving her an appraising look. "I doubt that would be the incarnation you feel closest to. I think this one is. You've had hundreds of years to go through redemption, heal, forgive, find a better path. Some of those you helped may be the souls of those you've harmed."

"Like how I'm trying to help you now," she said slowly. "That makes me feel better, but I'm not sure I deserve to feel better."

"You have committed no such crime in this life. And if you want proof that your soul has evolved, you have it. Your horror over what you might have done in the past life was so great you tried to stab yourself."

"I wouldn't have died," she assured him. "It was seeking to inflict pain, not death. If there'd been time, and I hadn't been half out of my mind, I would have told you that."

"And you think that means I would have stepped out of the way?" He shot a glance at her open wardrobe. "There's a belt hanging in there I am about to put to good use."

On one side were her ritual supplies. Crystals, candles, a goblet, a flame douser. A folded velvet cloth, which was where the athame had rested. On the other side were clothes and useful accessories. Like the belt.

Her uncertain look said she wasn't sure if he was serious. He was, especially when he noted reluctant intrigue behind her reaction. He'd follow up on that when strapping her with the belt was for their mutual pleasure, rather than his desire to give her hell for scaring him.

She sobered, squared her shoulders. Her gaze was full of emotions, a witch's knowledge, as she faced what was in her mind, made herself recognize and accept what was past, what was present, and all that might link the two.

"All right. Okay. But since I don't know if my soul has ever said it to your soul, I'll say it now. I'm so sorry, Silas. To the very depths of my heart. And I am going to help you figure this mark out. Help you in whatever way I can." She lifted her fingers to his mouth. "And before you do the stern, 'Don't help me because you feel you owe it to me,' I'm doing it because I want to."

He gave her a look. "Because you find me insanely attractive and can't get enough of me."

"That goes without saying." But then she bit her lip. Her eyes brimmed with the emotions of the witch he knew.

And was falling in love with.

"I need to cry about it a little while, though," she said. "Cry for you, cry for all of us."

"I need to hold you while you do that."

"Okay."

CHAPTER THIRTEEN

*H*e didn't stop holding her, not once during the several hours that she cried. They took their rest together. When she roused, it was before dawn. As she left his arms to visit the bathroom, she caressed the firmness of his chest, tugging at the hair there, a habit that was becoming pleasantly familiar. His green eyes showed themselves, and he kissed her hand, letting her go with a lingering grip that told her he expected her swift return.

Yet when she came back to the bedroom, Silas wasn't there. She found him on her screened back porch, facing the rising sun in the east, the scythe-now-crook in his left hand. He wore just a pair of jeans. Honora was striding away across the back field. As Ramona watched, she disappeared through the quick flash of a portal opening.

Ramona came to his side. "Everything okay?"

"My brethren have dug deeper and found that the Reaper markings are more widespread than we discussed earlier. The younger, less experienced Reapers were not even aware it had happened. It appears this has been going on for some time. Our Wake is the strongest of the Cast. Whatever is doing this therefore chose to target us last, because they knew it would not escape notice."

Uneasiness gripped her. "So whatever the plan, it's about to happen."

"It is likely." Silas's expression was tight. "All souls Reaped by the less experienced Reapers have gone to The Gate without a problem. She has checked."

"Is it possible your being taken off the Reaping schedule may have come from you? An unconscious block to protect the souls?"

"It is the conclusion we've reached, because the twelve who are comparable to me in experience and power reported the same silence from the Fates."

"I'll bring Raina and Ruby into the loop so they can let Mikhael and Derek know."

"That would be wise."

She moved back into the house, but paused to give him a more intent look. He had his eyes closed, but from the rigid line of his shoulders, she expected he was attempting some meditative exercise to keep from losing his mind. For someone like him, the waiting was the hardest part. He was obviously used to doing, fixing. Leading.

The phone in her kitchen had a long cord. She pulled it out to the porch so he could hear her pass the information to Raina, in case he wanted to add anything. When it was ringing, he opened his eyes. "Ask how the young one is doing. Gina."

"I will." She reached out, touched his hand on the crook. When Raina answered, she made it her first question.

"Tell Silas she's doing just fine. She was more worried about him. She also said to tell him she hopes he'll come back soon. Matilda is going to make him some of her world-famous croissants. Which is a pure bribe, since Gina knows it's the only thing in the world worth getting endlessly interrogated by a bunch of sex demons again."

Silas didn't smile. Ramona kept her attention on him as she relayed Honora's update. Raina's thinking on it matched hers. "I think the stronger the Reaper, the harder it is for the mark to stay dormant and unnoticed, because something in them is fighting it, rejecting it. It's like a monster in a cage, and that resistance is poking it like a stick. So even though my library doesn't thank him, I think it's a good sign that it keeps fighting with him. Keep that bitch stirred up, Silas."

Ramona was holding the receiver away from her ear so Silas could hear. His jaw eased a fraction. "What news from the Guardians?" he asked.

"Mikhael reached out to Derek about an hour ago," Raina said. "He's got a solid lead, so Derek's gone to join him."

"Do they need any assistance?"

"Last word Ruby got was for you and Ramona to sit tight, and if your people find anything, to pass it along through one of us like you just did."

"Honora also wishes me to continue to stay here." Silas's expression became stone once again. With a curt nod, he exited the porch, the screen door slamming behind him.

"Ramona?" Raina said. "Everything okay?"

"I think...oh." The word escaped her like an exclamation point. The crook became an axe, so quickly she didn't see the transition. Picking up a log from her pile of wood waiting to be split for firewood, he slammed it down on the stump and then swung the blade. It went through it like a guillotine. More logs followed, Silas splitting them faster than a chef could dice carrots, back and shoulder muscles flexing.

"Ramona?"

"It's okay. I think. He's angry, and frustrated, and taking it out on my firewood. His scythe can apparently be an axe."

"I appreciate a man who puts his testosterone to productive use." Yet Raina's grim tone told Ramona they all shared some of what Silas was feeling. And she echoed her earlier thought. "Waiting is the worst kind of torment. I wish you two would come here."

"Between the Link and Confluence, we're as good as right in front of you," Ramona said. "You'll know if I'm in any trouble, and I'll be able to call you as easily as I did on this phone. Easier, actually," she added as the crackle of static told her that even her ancient phone was protesting prolonged exposure.

"Except in the face of an immediate threat, you'll be dead long before we arrive."

"My place is just as reinforced as yours. I need to be here, with him, like this. It's just something I feel, and I've learned to trust what I feel."

"Doesn't make it less frustrating. You don't have that much uncut firewood. Go see if you can distract him. If your distraction tools aren't too sore from frequent use, that is. I have a great restorative spell, if you need it."

"Go away," Ramona told her. Raina tossed her the reassurance of a sultry laugh before she cut the connection.

Silas paused. The jeans rode low on his hips and his back and shoulders gleamed with the perspiration. He disappeared his own axe slash scythe slash crook et al, and picked up her axe instead. Maybe because the stump where she usually cut the wood had a big crack in it now.

Choosing to split the wood with a mundane tool and more proportional strength told her he'd settled some. Leaving the phone sitting on the porch boards, she sat down on her back stoop to watch him.

His hair feathered over his brow, while the short hairs at his nape were damp. She wanted to put her lips there, taste the salt of him, run her hands along his back, his sides, rest them on his hips. She'd curve her fingers over his visible hip bones, press her pelvis up against his taut backside, though she might have to rise on her toes to accommodate the difference in their heights. She could use a log from the woodpile for that.

She *was* sore this morning, but in a nice way. When Silas had that need again, she would accommodate him however he desired, because she knew he would be gentle if needed. The desire to have her wouldn't overwhelm the desire to care for her. He'd proven that to her already, and it was the most potent of a Dom's weapons to win a woman's surrender. The ones who knew it were damn near irresistible.

Yesterday's revelation about past lives kept coming back to her, the terrible images, the helpless feeling of guilt. It would take her a while to deal with that. But with Silas's help and her own lifetime of control, she would manage. For this morning, she simply wished they could resolve the evil bad guy issue. Not to beat a dead horse—what a sick saying—but waiting for the worst to happen seriously interfered with savoring what would ease the wait.

Buford came to her hand for an ear scratching, eying their visitor. When Silas surfaced from his thoughts, he met the gaze of her familiar and acknowledged him as such with a respectful nod. Buford bleated and moved to the fence to nibble at clover growing around a post. Several of her chickens scattered at his passing, though one pecked at his cloven hoof, earning a brush of his horns. Buford hopped up onto a stump and went over the fence to see what her other animals were doing. He liked to stand on top of Esmerelda's broad backside while the elderly horse grazed. It helped him survey his domain.

"Are you hungry?"

She brought her attention back to Silas, whose gaze was covering the thin robe she wore, the way it split away from her thighs. "For what?" she asked.

His gaze glinted. "We'll hold that thought until after I've gotten a meal into you. I want to take you on that picnic. We can pull a breakfast together here if you prefer, or pick something up on the way."

"Where are we going?" Though she didn't want to discourage him, Raina's observation about the ineffectiveness of backup that was too far out of reach crossed her mind.

"That favorite place of mine. I want to share it with you." He didn't smile.

She came to him, stepping on the log to give her those few inches of extra height. It let her slide her arms around his shoulders, hold herself to him, without him having to bend down so far. His hands went to her waist, and she felt their tension, as if he might not let her press herself to his chest. With it so heavily on his mind, she knew he didn't want the mark near her. But it wasn't part of him. She pushed against that tension and won the point.

When she let out a little sigh of contentment, he nuzzled her cheek bone, then dipped his head to put his lips beneath her ear, against her throat. She pressed harder against his body, and he muttered, gripping her ass and lifting her up against him, earning a soft breath of pleasure when his wakening arousal pressed against her core.

"We'll pick something up," he said.

"I think you just did," she teased him.

She'd been right about his gentleness, but he was also thorough and demanding. Once they were done, they showered together. He held her against him like he had when he'd replaced her water visualization, hand threading through her thick hair, helping her rinse the shampoo. He liked touching her and did it a great deal. She wasn't sure she'd ever want to bring herself pleasure again, because he was so much better at it.

He'd said casual wear would be fine for where he was taking her, so she donned a V-necked thin T-shirt and coupled it with a knee-length knit skirt and sneakers. Her tender tissues wouldn't handle jeans well. Plus—the real reason—if he wanted her again, she wanted him to have easy access.

When she emerged from the bedroom and he turned to look at her from head to toe, he extended a hand. He drew her to him, his touch on her hips firm, possessive. As he gathered the skirt fabric under his palms, she felt the touch of air high on her thighs.

"Want me to be able to take you where and when I want, don't you?" He kissed her parted lips, offered a distracting touch of his tongue, his fingers flexing on her hips.

"Yes," she said.

"I'd tell you to stop being such a damn temptation, but I don't think you can." He gave her a censorious look. "Those gorgeous eyes and sweet mouth. Put your arms around me, witch. We're going for a ride."

"If you prefer me to drive, we can take my broom."

A flash of teeth, his heated chuckle, reminded her that laughter was a good distraction, too.

When they'd arrived via portal at his chosen picnic spot, it was a reminder that she was with a male connected to death in intimate ways. Like dating a funeral director.

When she shared that with him, Silas accepted the comparison with a thoughtful, faintly amused air. As he led her through the rolling hills of the wooded grounds of Arlington National Cemetery, with its sobering views of lines of crosses, the sun's silver morning light touched the ancient ivory of the monuments they passed.

She'd been to DC's tourist spots when she, Raina and Ruby had visited fellow witches in the area. At that time, they'd had to stick with the rest of the tourists. This time, it was early enough the park wasn't yet open to visitors, though she saw an occasional maintenance worker at a distance.

"No one can see or hear us," Silas reassured her. "I have us cloaked."

A few minutes later, they reached the Tomb of the Unknown Soldier. A soldier on duty was doing a precise walk along the dark runner before the Tomb marker. Despite bird song and the rustle of the wind, Ramona heard the click of his heels as he executed the steps. At the end of the runner, he stopped, faced the Tomb for a measured set of beats. He changed his weapon to the opposite shoulder, the one closest to the roped barricade separating the pedestrian walkway from the Tomb. Then he faced back down the mat and started in that direction at the same measured pace.

Silas squeezed her hand, drawing her up the steps, past the soldier to a corner of lawn shaded by a cluster of trees. Taking the picnic blanket she'd brought, he spread it out, his long arms making it easy work. It was one she'd woven herself, with a wash of sunrise colors. Silas offered her a hand to sink down on it before sitting next to her.

It made sense that this was a favored spot for him, a place where warriors watched over the bodily remains of the fallen and the spirits that lingered. Being here also seemed to ease the tension he was carrying.

"Hungry?"

She nodded. They'd changed their mind about picking something up after she'd found enough to quickly throw together a meal. Though it was early morning, she'd chosen what she thought they'd like, regardless of the time of day. She set out the two containers of stew, made with her garden vegetables and herbs, plus bread with a chive-flavored goat cheese spread. "It's good," he noted, taking a bite and chewing. "From a goat farm in the area?"

"Yes. What I don't make and grow myself, I get locally when I can. Though I buy lunch from the town restaurants during shop hours. Support local business, keep in touch with what's happening, networking, that kind of thing."

"Raina isn't the only businesswoman."

She grimaced. "Raina is a shark, I'm a minnow. Compared to her, I'm like a flea market booth."

"I've Reaped plenty of souls from flea market bartering gone bad. It's brutal."

Though he was teasing her, and he'd told her they couldn't be heard, she noted he kept his deep voice low. She determined it was out of respect for their surroundings, the sentinel's purpose. The energy that hovered here.

"Isn't this sort of like a busman's holiday? Did you take any of the three souls here to The Gate?"

"No, but I like the inscription, about their identities being 'Known But to God.'"

"And Reapers," she added.

"And Reapers." He gestured to the soldier. "This place says no death goes truly unwitnessed, no name unknown. They aren't forgotten. No one is forgotten. Like I told Gina."

Several times, when she'd been putting together their lunch, she'd seen him take out his journal, hold it, fingers passing over the cover. "Wherever you came from, however you were chosen," she said, "this is a calling. You love what you do. You know why it's important."

He sent her a sidelong glance, nodded. "Death is what people fear most. We can't tell them there's nothing to fear, because the transition can be unsettling, and there's almost always some redemption owed, but beyond that...there's an order to it, indescribable in its peacefulness."

She saw him recognize how she might interpret that, but before she could reassure him she wasn't offended, he added, "Order doesn't always look like one expects. It's a lot of different things, depending on the death."

"How so?"

He considered. "You've witnessed birth. Ruby's son."

"Yes." Ramona remembered the wonder in Derek's eyes, a male who'd seen over a thousand years in his current life, but never the birth of his own child. Ruby's tenderness had eased her usual sharp edges. The emotions emanating from her had tangled and integrated with Derek's, settling around the sharing of responsibility for this new life, the celebration of Jem's arrival.

"The rising of a soul from the flesh, its coming to The Gate, to see what's next...it's a birth, too," Silas said. "And while a babe comes with newness, the imprint of its past lives not obvious, in death, that imprint is there. I witness what has been, who the soul is becoming, where they might go next. They handle their body's parting, those they must leave behind, for now, in many ways. It's a library that never fails to fascinate. Or inspire."

"Unexpected?"

"Often. And also reassuringly the same."

"Hmm." Her gaze moved to the soldier as he pivoted, followed the same measured pace again. He took twenty-one steps in each direction, she realized. The pause to face the Tomb was also twenty-one seconds. Ritual could provide the foundation to potent magics. And resolves.

"Tell me more about this. How long does a shift last?"

"Thirty minutes to an hour, depending on the seasons. If we're here long enough, you'll see the changing of the guard." Something difficult seemed to grip him. "Would you like to hear the Creed they follow?"

"Of course." Following an instinct, she put her hand over his, braced on the blanket.

Silas's gaze never left the soldier, the rhythm to the words seeming to follow the cadence of his steps, the click of his heels. "*My dedication to this sacred duty is total and whole-hearted. In the responsibility bestowed on me never will I falter. And with dignity and perseverance my standard will remain perfection.*

Through the years of diligence and praise and the discomfort of the elements, I will walk my tour in humble reverence to the best of my ability. It is he who commands the respect I protect, his bravery that made us so proud. Surrounded by well-meaning crowds by day, alone in the thoughtful peace of night, this soldier will in honored glory rest under my eternal vigilance."

She gazed at Silas's profile. Yes, she could understand what he found here. And why he had refused to destroy or abandon Cal.

"It's said that every man or woman who patrols here has to be a certain size." The lighter note in his voice told her he'd stepped back from the solemnity that had gripped him. "Women have to be between five-eight and six-two."

"So I have no chance."

His attention slid over her. "Somehow I doubt your height would be the main reason."

She made a face. "Just because the words regulation and structure are like flags to the charging bull of Chaos magic doesn't mean I should be discriminated against. Sheesh."

When she bumped his side with her shoulder, he pressed a smile and a kiss against her hair. He'd finished his stew, put it back in the basket she'd used, so she scooted into the shelter his braced arm provided. "Why does he change the gun to the other shoulder when he turns?"

"The sentinel always keeps the weapon between the viewers and the Tomb. Because he's guarding the remains." A pause, then Silas spoke carefully. "Will you tell me, Ramona?"

"Tell you what?" His tone made her wary.

"You told me you never relinquish responsibility for your magic. You hinted that was about more than what happened when you were a teenager. About more than the sex." He held her gaze. "I want all the way inside, Ramona."

"Have you earned that?"

She didn't mean for it to come out defensively, and the second she said the words, she flashed to that past life. Of course he'd earned it. He'd earned the right to her life if he no more than asked for it.

"Hey." He touched her face, a firm admonishment, drawing her gaze to his steady one. "Don't do that. The past doesn't impact the present. Not for this. If it's important for me to earn the knowledge, then tell me how I might. But I also know for some things there is no earning. They're offered as a gift or not at all. A gift because the giver wants the pleasure of the giving."

"There's no pleasure in what you're asking." This was a peaceful place. They'd enjoyed one another. There might be a shitstorm ahead. She resented having to kick one up.

"Is it something too painful to open? Or does it just need time between us?" He pressed onward, though his tone stayed gentle. "Does anyone else know?"

"Yes. Raina and Ruby." She tried not to twitch away from his touch, but she was unsuccessful. He let her shift so she could fuss with putting away her finished lunch containers. She tossed an apple core to a squirrel, remembering when the squirrel seemed to ignore it that they were invisible. Silas leaned over, picked it up and tossed it even further away. It appeared outside the cloaking field and two squirrels raced each other to snatch it up.

"Ruby understands certain parts better than Raina and vice versa." Because of that, they didn't require her to discuss it. Sometimes silence was the best gift to offer someone's truth. A response required another response, and some stories took up all the room inside when shared, leaving nothing, no energy to give after the telling.

She tipped her head up to the sky. "You've witnessed so much, so many things. My story won't be unique. Only to me. Do your souls treat you like a confessor? Do they ask you to absolve them?"

"No. But they tell me things, and the telling is often enough. If it isn't, sometimes they refuse to go through The Gate. They wander a while first. That is permitted if it's part of what they need, part of their transition."

"How many stay behind to be restless spirits?"

"As a Reaper gains experience, not as many. You learn how to help with the letting go."

"Do you seek to be my lover or my confessor?"

He grasped her hand, drawing her attention to the tense fist it had become, and caressed her white knuckles. "I've never heard mockery in your voice before. It's an angry, bitter thing you carry." Before she could marshal a response, he pressed on. "From the moment I saw you, I wanted...this. The ability to be near you, marvel at your complexity, how unexpected you are."

His lips curved, humorless. "Your beauty, your life. You make no sense, nothing I can predict or anticipate. It's wondrous, strange. Unsettling. And yet, at the center, there's something like this." He nodded to the soldier. "An order aligned with honor, and all that is supposed to mean."

When he met her gaze again, she saw the emotions behind the words. "I want to do and be whatever brings you happiness, Ramona. Joy, peace, pleasure. I want to be the reason you smile, that you sleep easy, that you are able to find hope when all else seems lost. I seek to love you, by whatever path that takes."

Words deserted her, the bitter anger draining away. It didn't have anything to do with him, and he'd ably reminded her of it. "That's a gift," she said at last. "Love. But the why is important."

At his curious look, she gave him an even one in return. "Every soul is remarkable, which means none of us are. Yet you find something quiet and still when you look at me." Humor tugged her lips. "Words no one has ever used to describe me."

"Yet it's your essential core," he said. "You hold the center of that whirling, chaotic energy. The sun at the center of a galaxy. It warms me."

"You can't see my death." A last-ditch attempt at defensiveness. "That's why you feel all that around me."

"No. That was the threshold to my interest. It's not why I stay."

She cursed herself for needing him to say it. She'd learned to let men go, never expect much from them except brief, limited pleasures, some basic companionship. And here was one who not only wanted to hang around, he wanted to move in and explore all the rooms. Even the scary basement with the padlock on the door, crime scene tape and *danger* written across the panel in blood.

Though it was important for their spellcraft, she thought the divine forces of creation had been doing a *hey, y'all watch this* moment when they gave Chaos witches such creative skills, because her powers could trigger and conjure with the prompting of the slightest bit of mental imagery.

Was it a cue in her face, or could he tap into the outer realms of her thoughts? Perhaps he was just that intuitive, due to his vast experience in reading body language. His cocoon of shielding tightened around them, so whatever crazy thing had been about to happen from her horror movie visualization didn't. A good thing, because she didn't want to put that vigilant sentinel on hyperalert due to blood raining from the sky, or the appearance of a tourist in a ski mask with a big ass knife. Et cetera.

She took a breath. "It's not a room I'd ever invite anyone into, no more than I'd invite you into a nightmare."

"You do not have to tell me now," he said, surprising her. "I'd like to know, but I demand nothing from you that strips armor from your soul and subjects it to such obvious pain. I don't want you to remove it just to satisfy my curiosity."

It was a relief, but coming in behind that surge was the surprising realization that maybe she did want him to know. She just didn't want to go there herself. Maybe she could have Raina or Ruby tell him.

Or maybe she could suck it up and just do it. "I know curiosity isn't why you want to know. You said it. You want behind the armor. You want all that I am."

"You said I hadn't earned that."

"I questioned if you felt you had." She looked down at her hands, now twisted in her lap. "Earning is a separate act and choice. The telling is an offering of trust. An offer I have to believe you will earn, but should put no obligation on. Love is constant steps of faith. And failed expectations."

"Expectations are a spiral. The failure today becomes the foundation for success tomorrow. I'm pretty sure that's on a corporate poster somewhere." A tinge of a smile, and he squeezed her hand again. Waiting for her decision.

Maybe that was the problem. Underneath his mild tone, no matter how gentle or patient, was the male who had claimed her. To give him everything he wanted from her, she needed that part of him.

"Sometimes," she said slowly, "it's better if you demand."

An intrigued light kindled. "Is that so?" he asked softly.

Leaning in, he took her lips in a thorough kiss, one that held through all twenty-one steps of the sentinel in one direction, then the other. One full rotation, during which Silas's hand rose to clasp the side of her throat, letting her pulse beat against his rough palm. When he met her gaze again, his held the steadiness that made things inside her not steady at all. "You asked if I seek to be your lover or confessor. I seek neither. I want to be your Master, Ramona."

The words rose, an ocean wave ready to crest, but then it kept building. Panic joined the mix, emotions rising too high.

"Ramona." He had his hands on her. "You're inviting me behind the armor, not removing it. Start with the easier part. A corner of the tapestry, the first threads."

～

Silas wanted to pull her into his arms, onto his lap, cradle her there, but memories as painful as these obviously were often didn't permit touch. Not until they were shared, the sharpest pain of their telling purged. She had his full attention, but he split it between her emotions, what he could do for those, for her heart, and what she needed if they stirred up the world around them.

He considered taking them away from the Tomb, since having her tell the story a rock's throw from a soldier with a loaded rifle might not be the wisest choice.

But she cupped her hands before her, slow and stiff, like she was balancing something fragile but with substantial weight in her palms. He felt the swirling energies pause, re-channel, slowly fade away, though the effort cost her. It was a reminder that she knew how to do this without him. That she would not fully rely on anyone for it. And she was about to share with him how she'd learned that painful lesson.

"I was raised by pixies. The Spiraling Wind clan. My mother...I

235

have a few memories. Pieces. She liked cereal for dinner and drove a car with a faded rainbow sticker on the back." She lowered her hands. Beside the blanket, she drew patterns in the grass. The patterns changed, like a snake writhing at her prodding.

"I was relatively normal until I was five. Then I changed. On a playground, I turned a swing into a bird and launched it fifty feet into the air. The spiral slide started moving, twisting, becoming a circle, letting the fun go on forever. The merry-go-round spun like a top, and the sand in the sandbox became figures. Dinosaurs. Snakes." Her gaze went to the grass, and longer strands climbed on top of one another, arched in a braided strike pose. "No one was hurt, luckily. The children liked it."

"But not the parents."

"When it was understood I was the source, people came to my mother. Pretended what had happened was something else, said I had special needs. They would pay for me to go to a top hospital, care for me. My mother played dumb, acted like it was a relief, and said okay. Set up a day for them to come get me. Then she packed us up and ran."

Ramona's eyes were sad. "She recognized a threat against her child and responded accordingly. It didn't matter that she had a daughter she didn't understand, that she had no idea how to help or protect me. She tried. She bought an old camper with cash and she moved us from campground to campground, each one more remote than the last. Wild places where I wasn't around other people."

Ramona's right hand lifted, sketched a scene before her, a miniature diorama, her intent face the Goddess of its creation, hovering above it. He saw a river flanked by forest, a blue sky above. She expanded the river so she could put both hands in it, watch the water pass over her fingers. Then it dissipated, though she kept her hands there, as if reaching for something long gone.

"My mother, she prayed. She knelt by a river and prayed what to do, for she was running out of resources, and they had plenty more. They were getting closer."

Some of that urgency, the desperation, came into her voice. Silas held his place. Watched and listened, as he'd done for so many other souls. Though in this case, just like the strength of his impatience to remove that mark, *do* something to help Honora and the Guardians, he was nearly overwhelmed by the wish to go back in time to help protect Ramona's mother, help her feel not so alone.

The way he wanted to do for her daughter.

"A log floated by, bumped up against the shore. She'd read me a story about sailing away into a rose-colored horizon, so the log became a boat filled with flowers, blooms growing out of the wood. The boat was small, only big enough for a child. She saw it and wept. Great, heaving sobs. I'd unwittingly given her an answer, but it broke her heart."

Ramona's voice hitched. "She picked me up, hugged me so tight. Told me how much she loved me, and that everything would be fine. 'Use your magic, find your way.' That was what she whispered to me.

"She put me in the boat. Her tears were on my face, my shirt. I clung to her hands, tried to get her to come with me, not let go. She pulled free, had to do it with a hard jerk, because I was frightened, crying, but she blew me kisses, told me it would be okay, that Momma wasn't mad, Momma loved me, it was all okay...Momma..."

She closed her eyes, spoke the name in a whisper. The energy around her was dense. Reaching out to her was like putting his hands through a swift current. He did it slow, shifted her so she was between his bent thighs.

When he did, everything around them changed. As if they'd been transported into that diorama, they were on the riverbank, deep in a forest. He knew they were still on the blanket, at the Tomb, but their surroundings said otherwise.

Her shoulders eased some, telling him the illusion had been deliberate, channeling the surge of magic expanding with her emotions. He rested his hand at her waist, his other stroking her hair. A woman's laughter was in his head, that elusive scent of raisins. Origins were a connecting thread in the tapestry of souls, whether Reaper or Chaos witch.

"Tapestry. Threads. It always goes back to weaving. Connection and patterns hold all the answers."

He didn't interrupt her, point out their energies were so inter-woven—another weaving reference—that she'd pulled that right from his surface thoughts, as he sometimes did with her. It was just there, offered for those with the skill to detect it. Or the strength of the binding between them.

"There are thousands more maternal chromosomes in your DNA than paternal ones," she said. "Did you know that? Makes sense. We start as an egg in our mother, grow there, whereas our fathers provide that single ambitious sperm. Not to say a father is any less loved or important," she added. "Just an explanation for why it's so hard to let go of that cord to the mother. Like the soul to its body, right? It's biological. Guess that's why we think of the Earth as Mother, Fates as women."

She moved her hands in a wheel motion around one another, as if weaving energy over and under her fingertips. "I floated, fell asleep in the flowers filling the boat. When I woke, I'd bumped up under a tree that had fallen into the water. It had been lightning-struck, forming a child-sized alcove, hollowed out by the elements. The branches still had leaves, providing shade, coolness. A screen. I crept in, let the boat go, spin away, become a log again. I was there a couple days, I think. I lost track of time. Dehydration. Hunger."

He lifted his gaze as the tree appeared close to them, hanging into the water, a new element in the scene. As was the pixie, wearing a yellow dress in a fabric that flowed over her slim figure. Her long hair was piled up on her head, fastened with sparkling combs and decorated with tiny blue flowers. Her four wings, overlapped like a dragonfly's, were glistening green with traces of blue.

"I heard this fluttering, like a bird, only the wings had a papery sound to them. The tree was Crescent's favorite place to sit and do her spinning. She was the Clan's weaver. She made most of the fabric for their clothing."

He pressed a kiss to her crown. "She found you."

"Yes." Ramona paused, and darkness moved in her, gave her magic an ominous vibration. He surrounded it, let her know his was there to lean upon. Count on.

"For a long time, I wished I'd drowned in that boat. Or died before my powers came to me. I wished I'd been a changeling, given to the Fae as an infant, so my mother didn't have to suffer."

"Is she still alive?"

She shook her head. "Crescent took me to see her months later, when the flowers were growing over her body. She lay down in a meadow, and simply...died. She lost the will to live when she put me in the boat."

She swallowed. "When you said you remember your mother's scent, I have that, too. Coffee with a lot of creamer, vanilla. Cigarettes. Butterscotch. She had a sweater with those scents. She wore it a lot."

"Your father?"

"A boy who died in a car wreck. She had me at seventeen, while she was still mourning him. He was a bard, a Renaissance Faire player. A poet. When I come up with my rhymes, I imagine him wincing, for she would sing his songs to me, and they were true poetry, songs of nature."

"I like your rhymes."

"Men like everything about a woman when they're first having sex with her. Raina says so. You can't help it."

Though the barbed humor was an attempt to ease some of what was going on inside her, it was the wrong path, one he wouldn't let her go down. "Ramona."

She glanced at him, and the image wavered. "Sorry."

He helped her steady it, put both of his arms around her to hold her closer. She tucked her head under his chin, her gaze on the river, on the image of Crescent.

"Another clan told Crescent where to find my mother, what had happened. They'd seen her stumbling through the forest, weeping and talking to herself. She laid down and died in a meadow on a full moon night. The clan covered her with flower petals and pine branches."

The meadow appeared to their left, amid a swirl of white flower petals. Daisies. "Probably due to the trauma, the memory of my mother vanished from my mind for a while. As a cushion for that, Crescent told me a dozen different origin stories."

"That was when you came up with the story of being born from the tears of a Goddess."

"Yes. Crescent's favorite was the wind played with fall leaves on the forest floor, and after they swirled away, there I sat, crusted with moist earth, like the birth of a new plant."

She absently fingered her blonde hair. "I had brown hair, dark as that soil. Same color as my mother's. The memory of her returned when I was twelve."

He stroked her hair. "Tell me of the pixies. I know little of them."

"Their language...it's thought and feeling, gestures, flight. So much

239

communication in the movement of their wings, how they dance through the air. There were about fifty members of the clan, spanning four generations. I couldn't fly with them. At first, they always had someone stay with me, keeping me company, so I wouldn't be afraid when they crossed the threshold to the Fae world, a place they couldn't take me. Predators were only a danger if I was left completely alone, an opportunity. Nothing attacks a human when it has a better option. My magic proved far more dangerous."

She curled her fingers into his forearm. "I told you my memory of my mother returned at twelve. I became a confusion of emotions. Anger, impatience, sadness. Nothing I did was intentional, but negative Chaos took the upper hand. Hormones played havoc with any benevolent intent.

"I would send the pixies spinning on erratic air currents, dash them into trees. Drop them into the river. Food stores turned to rocks and feathers. As soon as I had a thought, a fear, some manifestation of it would come to pass. It drove me into a cave, and I made it collapse, lock me in. Crescent and the others unburied me, one rock at a time, coaxed me out."

Her voice had dropped in volume, become emotionless, but he heard the loneliness, the struggle. She hesitated before speaking the next words.

"When my mother held me, I felt a joy. Like birds. As I said, my magic started manifesting regularly at five, but I remembered one earlier instance, inspired by the intensity of that feeling. I had a bird mobile over my crib, so I spread out my arms like wings while my mother held me...and flew. We were floating, at the ceiling. She got frightened, and I dropped us. Because she cushioned me, she was knocked unconscious. I sat next to her crying, joy gone. When she woke, she rationalized her memory of it as a dream. Nothing else happened until I was five."

The images died away, leaving them on the picnic blanket. The park had opened, because a trickle of visitors passed by the velvet rope, watching the sentinel perform his duty. As the day waxed, the numbers would grow, especially when it was time for changing of the guard.

Ramona didn't seem to notice. She tipped her head up from his shoulder, apparently listening to the birds in the trees around them.

Her hands rested in her lap, the fingers still knotted. "If you believe in an order to things, it's hard not to blame the gods, to see things as a mistake, where there's fault to place," she said. "But instead, the whole world and everyone in it are a big mash between order and chaos, joy and fear. It's when you know nothing, really realize that, that you can let go and be part of everything. It's not just flying and joy all the time. It's also crashing, and accepting that as part of it, too."

The light around them dimmed, the volatile cauldron of emotions he'd sensed on simmer suddenly increasing in heat. He adjusted his protections accordingly, but kept his hands light on her. Though her mother's end was bad enough, he expected they were getting to what made her most not want to tell this story.

"Pixies can be mischievous, but they're not clandestine or duplicitous. They saw no reason to conceal their care of me. A High Fae discovered they'd taken me in. He said they needed to turn me out. Leave me in a hospital or church if they wished, or abandon me to the coyotes. He didn't care which option they chose, but he called their compassion a betrayal of their people."

"Sounds like he had a massive chip on his shoulder against humans."

"Understandable, since we mostly drove them out of this world."

"Not understandable if his hatred would cause him to harm a child."

She made a noncommittal noise. "I would shut down around him, become as non-magical as a beer can. Though he didn't doubt it when the pixies said I was magic born, that I was safer among their people than with my own, he didn't see the scope of it. Not that that should have mattered."

"They refused him."

"Yes." She went silent for another few minutes. "In the Fae world, time is different. When he issued his ultimatum, I was eight. He returned when I was fifteen. He was an authority figure of some kind, had the right to impose penalties for violations of laws. He cared nothing for the pixies' arguments. Their beliefs. He was going to take me, end me himself, handle my execution."

Another pause. "They piled on me. The clan had increased in numbers over the years, to sixty-three. I'd been present for the new births, helped care for their young. All of them, the whole clan, every age, covered me like your bees, cloaking every spare inch of me they could."

He drew her closer as she spoke the words in a trembling voice. "I heard him say, 'so be it.' Just three words, stated without any real emotion, which only added to the awfulness. Then there was fire."

She clasped his forearm, drew his hand down to her lap, played with it on her thigh as she stared at the ground. "Like that battle you took me into. A corner of the world removed from everything else, one clan among many. Some Fae treat pixies the way humans treat insects. Knowing that, I've never been able to do the same. Ants have communities, they care for their young, build them nurseries, have warrior clans and a queen. We think we're so different, we think our lives are somehow more precious to us than an ant's is to him, or a butterfly's is to her. Or a tree's."

The deep breath she took held a shudder. The curve of her back against his side was rigid. "I'd been learning about my magic, how to work with it, encouraged by Crescent and the others. Any stumble I had, they took in stride. They understood learning magic the way my mother would have understood me learning to walk. But I hadn't yet found that center you talked about."

Her raw emotions spilled into her voice. "I lost control. No, that's wrong. I didn't lose control at all. It was when I found it. I became the pin holding the wheel in place, no matter how fast it spins. I learned how to find the focus in the storm, the target of the tornado that seems random but isn't. I took that fire he'd used, its wrongness, and turned it on him. He died where he stood, a pillar of ash."

Silas didn't speak, but shock went through him. Killing a High Fae was almost an impossibility for a mortal. And she'd been an untried teenager. He was right, what he'd thought about her power level. It also told him the Fae had never learned who'd killed the male, because they would have come after her with a vengeance.

"My scream of anguish created a blast of wind that scattered him. Whatever Reaper was in charge of his soul, I have no idea where it landed, where it found him." Her expression hardened. "Nor, to this day, do I care. He treated them as nothing. So to me, he will forever be nothing."

Her hands passed over herself, an absent stroke, then rubbing into her skin. "I was coated in their ash. I didn't bathe for days, wandering, crying, the coyotes singing with me. Woodland creatures, even the predators, are mostly friends to pixies, so as I'd grown older, they were no longer a threat to me."

She held her arms out before her. "Eventually, I bathed, watched the ash flow away. But I was left with these." She touched the scattering of freckles on her arms, a light cinnamon gray color, flames and ash mixed. "There are far more now, but that day, I counted. Sixty-five." At his look, she managed a tremulous smile. "One of the clan was pregnant with twins."

"Ah, gods." When she folded back against him, pressing her face to his shoulder, he stroked her back. "I'm sorry, Ramona. I'm glad they gave you so much love that you carry the proof of it, but I'm sorry you had to lose them that way."

Her arms slipped under his, and they held one another for a while without saying anything else. The river scene reappeared, the current carrying its message of change and movement. She was cleansing the emotions, giving herself the strength to restore herself to her usual calm.

"When you hold a power no one else can control, then there is no full surrender," she said at last. "There can't be. Not until death." She lifted her head and their gazes locked. "But I do understand that we all choose our path, make our decisions. We have to allow one another that." Her voice became harsh with pain. "Crescent's last words were, 'We do not regret loving you. Not one of us. We're your family.'

"Knowing what I am, what it attracts, can endanger those I care about, I have to remind myself that if someone who cares for me understands the risks, it's not my place to push them away out of fear. Or guilt over the past." She bit her lip, that recent revelation in the gesture. "But I *will* protect those who matter to me. Including you."

The dangerous resolve he suspected that long dead Fae had seen flashed through her gaze. "Can you accept that, and not stand in my way?"

He met the challenge with his own. "Everything I do will be in my capacity as your lover. Your Master. I have my own desire to protect those who matter to me."

He wanted to say soulmate. But Master was enough.

He could tell she was tucking her past back into that room, the curtain drawn again. But it was done. He knew what was there.

At one point or another, they all fought for something they were willing to die for. He looked toward the soldier, then touched her face. "Would you like some ice cream? I believe you like the place near your store."

"You offer me ice cream for one of the worst memories of my life." A ghostlike smile crossed her lovely features. "Perhaps you do understand the nature of Chaos, how complicated *and* simple it can be."

She looked toward the sentinel, noticing the gathering of people. "It's almost time for the changing of the guard?"

"Yes."

"Let's watch that. Then we can go."

Her chocolate-dipped waffle cone contained vegan vanilla fudge swirl. They sat at an outside table, saying little. Though she greeted a few familiar faces, she noted Silas rarely made direct eye contact with anyone who passed.

A couple with a stroller went by. Though tired-looking, they appeared happy, his arm around her waist, their hands overlapped on the stroller as they pushed it together. It reminded her of Derek and Ruby.

"It's a nice picture," she said.

He nodded, but his gaze was on her as she put a spoonful of ice cream between her lips. Taking pleasure in her enjoyment of the sweet was all he'd said he desired, not wanting one for himself. Just in case he'd changed his mind, she offered him the next bite, but he shook his head. On a partly playful, partly serious thought, she extended the spoon. "Would you like to give me some?"

She'd anticipated him correctly. He took the utensil from her, fingers brushing hers. A handful of semi-sweet chips was precariously perched in the thick chocolate syrup she'd had them drizzle on top. As she parted her lips to take the bite he offered, he held the spoon just out of reach, so she had to lean forward. When she did, he curled a finger under her shirt's V-neckline to caress her sternum, her cleavage. She gripped the edge of the table, savoring the lower abdomen quiver that his interest in her response gave her.

"Take it slow," he said. "Make it last."

She did, putting her lips over the tip of the spoon, drawing the ice cream in, neat and easy. As he turned his hand over, his knuckles sliding over the top of her breast, she licked the spoon and then her lips. As he withdrew the spoon slowly, her eyes half-closed. She was holding her breath, and he slid a single fingertip so close to a nipple it drew up in response. "Breathe," he murmured.

After a lingering moment, he sat back, returning control of the cup and utensil to her. Just those few seconds, and there was enough heat around the table to set the awning above them on fire. But a wet, damp wind blew over them, making the striped fabric awning above them flap. His energy settled around her, cooling her, but not too much. His other hand rested on top of hers on the table. The wrist marking was prominent under his touch, the heat of the letters branding her skin.

"You think I followed you back into the store because I couldn't see your death. I followed you back into the store because you are a beautiful woman who intrigued me. A Chaos witch who talks about grilled cheese sandwiches and wears zebra striped sneakers. Who has hair the color of sin. Who lowers her gaze when she meets a Master she wants to touch her. Kiss her. Explore her submission and cherish it."

As if he'd ordered it, she found herself lowering her gaze while he spoke. His foot pressed next to hers under the table. When he leaned forward again to wind a lock of her hair around his fingers, she couldn't think of anything but what her Reaper wanted.

But he wasn't her Reaper. Or was he?

"I've never met anyone who made me believe I could reach for that outside my fantasies," she said. "Gave me the faith that level of trust was possible. Are you sure we're not soulmates?"

He shook his head, regret on his face. "But I can be drawn to you, fall in love with you, want to be with you. Same as anyone else in your world."

"Right. No reason to put labels on things." But why did she feel he was just as disappointed about it as she was? "I guess I just thought... When you first said it, there was this leap inside my chest. Derek always knew Ruby was his, and he was hers. She knew it, too, even though she didn't acknowledge it for a long time. Raina and Mikhael... they had a rocky beginning, but their relationship was a baptism by fire that burned everything away but the obvious. They were fated for one another."

She frowned, suddenly angry. "I thought it would be the same for me, because that's the way I've felt, the whole time I've been with you. 'Yes, this is him. This is who will get me, and I'll get him.' But no. Your soulmate is still out there."

A woman she hated without knowing her. When tears sprang into her eyes, she was appalled with herself. She averted her face, swiped at it. "Wow, I'm being stupid about this. I'm sorry. Why don't you take a walk, go see what's in Cordelia's window? Leave me alone for a couple minutes. I'll pull myself together."

He shot her a look, then took the cup and napkin from her, tossing them in a nearby trash can. Recapturing her hands in one of his, he reached forward and passed a thumb over a tear track. "Leaving your side when you are unhappy is the last reason I would do so."

He was perfect. Mysterious, commanding, humorous, intelligent, scary, sexy. She shook herself, ridding herself of the negative energy like a dog shaking a wet coat. "No, I'm being worse than stupid. You're immortal, I'm not. Your soulmate might cross your path a hundred years from now, when I'm long gone to dust."

She set her jaw. "As they say, 'You may not be Mr. Right, but you can be Mr. Right Now.' Maybe I'm your Ms. Right Now for the next few decades, until I wither up and die. Which still makes you *my* Mr. Right, at least in this lifetime. So for me to act like an idiot about not being your 'soulmate' makes no logical sense. You have more right to be upset about it than me."

And he was, she could tell. It bugged him a lot. Which meant he likely wouldn't be staying long, after the mark issue was resolved. She was wasting valuable time.

She erupted from the table, intending to draw him into a walk, but abruptly swung around, almost slamming into his chest, because he'd risen to follow her. "I know why you brought it up that day, because you thought maybe...but I wish you hadn't."

Her topsy turvy logic had upended several parking meters. And the big blue postal mailbox. It had pulled its bolts free and turned over. At least there were no cracks in the concrete.

Muttering an oath and then a spell, she righted them as subtly as possible, hurrying forward to retrieve the few envelopes that had fallen out of the mailbox.

"Ramona." Silas held the slot open for her, then seized her arm and yanked her against him. The kiss was forceful enough to stop the spinning in her head. He gripped her upper arms, drawing her fully against him. When he lifted his head, his eyes were determined as the desire she could feel vibrating from him, wrapping around her.

"This is physical attraction. But my sexual needs do not rule me. Any more than I expect yours do. What is between us is important, and real. I don't care to speculate on how much time we will have that gift. I'd rather simply be glad to have been given it."

An echo of her own thoughts. But hearing him say it helped take the tension away, a sign she'd accepted the words, taken their truth into herself. When he cradled her cheek, she closed her eyes. She'd had to define herself when she knew nothing about what she was. So that was what she pulled on now, as she lifted her gaze back to those devastating green eyes.

Slaughter is in those languid eyne whene'er a glance they deal. It was from *Book of a Thousand and One Nights*, Scheherazade. Ramona wondered if the famous storyteller, who might have been real or fictional, had ever met Silas in one of the lives that predated her storytelling marathon.

"Speak for yourself on the sexual needs thing." She cleared her throat. "Mine take me over easy as a demon-possessed baby."

When he chuckled, she laid her hands on his forearms. "I'll take what you can give. And I'm not selling myself short or too cheaply, because I know you're not using me, and you care. So far, you seem wonderful and extraordinary. To turn my back on that because of bull-shit hang-ups would be foolish."

"I am glad to hear it." He gave her a look. "But do not call yourself stupid or treat your feelings as 'idiotic.'"

She lifted her shoulder. "I'm sorry I snapped at you for the soul-mate mix-up, though. Because our lives are short, mortals can get crazy while waiting for the right person. Whereas it's probably worse for an immortal, who knows just how long life can be."

His gaze flickered, suggesting the hard truth of it. She bit her lip, crossed her arms. "Okay, now that I've poked that sore spot, my place or yours? Do you have a place, when you're not Reaping souls?"

"There are many places I seek respite when the opportunity

presents itself. But our kind are travelers." He lifted a shoulder. "Another commonality we share with Guardians."

Home was a state of mind, and a fluid one. She loved her work, what she did. Being in her own skin, with her magic. Sharing company with those who loved her and whom she loved. All those things meant home to her, as much as her house and shop. When she shared that, his green eyes locked upon her.

"I don't disagree. I want to take you to your home." He tightened his grip. "I want to be in your bed, with you."

"Well, if you had said you'd wanted to be in my bed with someone else, we would have had a problem. Unless it was another equally hot male, and you wanted a threesome with me in the middle."

He gave her a somber look. "There is no one as hot as me."

It startled a laugh out of her, and he broke his serious mien with a smile. If the definition of home was a place of welcome, of comfort, joy and pleasure, then his smile now qualified as a home to her as well. She wanted to give him the same.

"Everyone needs a place they can go that they can call theirs." Sobering, she clasped both his hands, brought them up to her chest, bowed her head over them. She rested her lips on his knuckles, a formal gesture she intended to reinforce how much she meant her next words.

"As long as we last, my home is your home."

CHAPTER FOURTEEN

*W*hen they arrived and stepped over her threshold, he paused and gazed around him. Silas's expression held a poignancy that touched her heart. "No one has ever said what you did, and meant it."

"What's that?"

"That I could consider your home mine, as long as you wish to be with me."

She went to her toes, framing his face with her hands. "When and if whatever this is runs its course, my hope is we'll still care enough for one another that I can keep that invitation open. Whenever you need a place to call home, it will be here. I will be here."

He closed his hands on her wrists. "You are overly generous, witch."

Yet as he dipped his head to put his mouth on hers, she straightened a finger in front of her lips, eying him behind the barrier. "One warning. Even if I'm ninety-nine years old, and sex with me is a long distant memory, you better not darken my door if you're in some other bitch's bed."

A chuckle vibrated against her mouth as he drew her hand out of his way. When he hiked her up to wrap her legs around his hips, the kiss they shared rippled along every other place their bodies touched. The thrill of its newness coupled with the ancient familiarity of a male and female coming together. Desiring the connection, wanting it to build until only the most intimate joining would satisfy.

Her words, humorous though they were, reminded her of the bittersweet finiteness of it. The more it mattered, the deeper the feeling became, the more they'd be left wanting.

"Let's go to the attic," she said against his mouth. "I have a bedroom up there, too. I can walk."

He didn't let her down. Instead, he made the trip up the two flights a memorable experience, stopping several times to press her against the wall and kiss her even more deeply. One time he sat on a step, having her straddle him, hands cradling her backside as she clasped his neck, kissing him like she wanted to crawl inside. His hands wandered over her, learning her, bringing her body to life in ways she hadn't ever expected. He rose again, with that effortless strength, kept going. On the second landing, he put her on the railing, himself between her legs.

"The only thing giving me the patience to wait," he growled, his body urgent against hers, "is the desire to hear you beg, witch."

She wanted to beg now. But she had her own plans for that as well. He took the last set of stairs two at a time. When he let her feet touch the ground, she pushed back from him unsteadily. Her lips were swollen, body flushed, damp, nipples tight. Her hair had tumbled around her shoulders, and he pushed it back so he could stare at the aroused peaks with avid heat. He was the creator of all the dishevelment, and his pride of ownership made her tremble.

"I need to go to the bathroom," she said. "I'll be back."

"Don't be long."

She gave him a female smile as she slipped away. Though any of her bedrooms could be guest bedrooms, she also used them as hers, depending on where she wanted to sleep from night to night. The ample attic space had a third full bath and a walk-in closet, the latter containing why she'd wanted him to bring her here.

When dealing with an immortal male, a woman might wonder if the same things could stir his interest as any other man. Fortunately Ramona's two closest friends were with immortals, so she had reliable information sources.

"The 24/7 sexual drive of a teen, the experience of a porn star, and as demanding as...well, there is no comparison." Raina said about Mikhael.

"Ditto for Derek," Ruby offered, but of course Raina wouldn't let her leave her there.

"There's farm equipment that doesn't have Derek's plowing abilities," the bordello owner said.

"Oh, good Goddess. How would you know?" Ruby said.

Raina gave her an arch look. *"It's my job to know these things. A sexually confident male, a Dominant with an immortal sized libido, pretty much broadcasts it without saying a word. I just have to see how he moves, and looks at the woman he wants."*

"It makes the heart skip a beat, even if you know none of the sugar in that bowl is for you," Ramona had interjected, before Ruby could decide whether or not to grab and pull Raina's hair.

She'd decided to yank on Ramona's, too.

Though the two Guardians were committed to their women, any female with eyes could see how much they could demand—and give— if their minds went in that direction.

It was new for her, being able to smile over her friends' teasing about their lovers while feeling this spike of anticipation, knowing one was waiting for her. Probably not all that patiently. As she finished changing, her stomach somersaulted merely from the thought of that demand about to be unleashed.

Maybe it was insane, but she wanted to increase it. A witch was close to the sensual currents of the elements, so she didn't doubt her desires, or where they wanted to take her. She wouldn't let mundane insecurities and self-consciousness inhibit what she could experience with him.

Though her bedroom was quiet, the increasing intensity of the waiting energy told her he'd figured out she might be doing something...interesting. Worth waiting for.

If her stomach flipped once more, her magic would conjure a team of acrobatic circus clowns in her attic. The loosely tied lavender robe she'd donned was high on her thighs, the sheer fabric and strategically placed lace offering an ample hint of what was beneath it. She'd brushed out her hair, and when she took a last glance in the mirror, she started. It was no longer golden-blonde. For him, it was now a vibrant red-gold, the colors of fire. Just the way he'd envisioned it that first day. It swirled around her face and over her shoulders.

As she stepped out, she saw him standing at the west facing wall, which had a triangular-shaped bank of windows. Its divided lights formed triangles instead of the traditional rectangular ones. The window offered a wide view of her property, the vegetable garden, the barn. She could see the night sky, but right now it was the man standing before that view who captured her attention.

He'd removed his shirt and shoes, leaving him in jeans and bare feet, but he had his scythe in hand and was studying the blade. Perhaps a routine daily check, as those who relied on certain tools of their trade did. A way to pass the time and curb his impatience before her return. Which made her smile, and her body tighten.

However, the tension in his back, the pensiveness to his profile, told her she'd maybe left him alone too long. He was thinking about the things that could intrude upon them here. Then he turned, and saw what she was wearing.

Whatever he'd been pondering vanished from his expression. Slowly, she slipped the sash and let the robe fall from her shoulders.

The lavender lace band of the hi-cut panties was just below her navel. When she rotated on the ball of her foot, a graceful, slow twirl, she showed him the tiny satin bow centered between the dimples of her pelvis. An oblong cutout revealed the cleft and upper rise of her buttocks. Then sheer lace took over again.

As she turned to face him again, his gaze rose to the matching bra that lifted her small breasts, enough to give them an attractive quiver when she moved. The areolas were revealed over the low edge, her skin gleaming with the sheen of the powder she'd brushed across the rounded tops, another surprise waiting to be tasted.

His attention moved to her hair. It would likely return to blonde before long. However, she was almost certain one day it would permanently change to the color it was now, merely because he looked at it like that. She saw him remembering that exchange from their first meeting, then he left the scythe leaning in the corner and moved to the bed, taking a seat on the end of it.

"Come here." His voice was rough, eyes intent as wolf, dragon and anything else that hunted. If she didn't obey, he'd come and get her. But she wanted to give him something else. Something that would drive away all his worries about that mark, if just for a little while.

But with him wearing only the jeans, his knees splayed and feet braced, she could see the curve of his testicles pressed to straining fabric, the length of his erection. His cock was thickening under her regard, a rewarding response that could surely make a girl lose her resolve.

She tore her attention from it, and looked toward the scythe. "I want to dance for you. Using that."

A muscle twitched in his jaw. "Come here first. I mean it."

She came to him, though the way his gaze devoured her made her wonder if he'd let her dance after all. When she reached him, he tangled his hand in her hair, gripping hard enough to pull a little. His other hand slid over her hip and around, covering that oblong opening, thumb teasing the crease between her buttocks, fingers slipping under the lace edge. She swayed on her feet, making his eyes darken.

"You'll be careful. It's not a broom, witch."

"Here I was, planning to use it to clean my floors." The words took an extraordinary effort to form, with his hands on her conveying such obvious proprietary sexual promise. The answering gleam in his gaze made the labor worth it.

"I'll be careful," she whispered. "I want you to touch me, but I want to dance for you."

He tightened his grip. "All right. But let me know you've heard me."

"I've heard you. And I'll be careful," she repeated.

He reluctantly released her, and she approached the scythe. She half expected him to transform it into a dense foam, like the swords at her toy store. However, when she closed her hand on the handle, she felt the strength and spirit of the ash tree it had once been a part of.

She lifted it. Because it was far heavier than she'd expected, she overbalanced it. When she grabbed the upper part of the shaft to steady it, it put her close to that blade, but she'd felt the instant heat of his steadying energy. Looking over her shoulder, she saw his hand lifted, controlling the scythe's movement.

She offered him a mischievous smile. "You make it look so light. But then I forget, you're a big, strong male."

He shook his head at her teasing. But when she proved she had control of it, his power eased back. The attic was where she did her indoor ritual work, so it had space for circle casting. She brought the scythe to the center of the open floor area and spoke a quiet enchantment. Nothing that interfered with his use of it, so the weapon didn't resist her charm. Though that, too, could have been the result of his skills. Sometimes, she couldn't tell where hers started and his ended.

When she stepped back, the scythe stood upright as if it were anchored, rotating a foot over the floor. The blade changed colors when the small lamp she'd switched on cast light and shadows on it.

"Where did you get what you're wearing?" His tone had stayed husky, and his eyes glowed in the dim light.

"Raina claims she ordered it in the wrong size. But I think she intended to gift it to me, for a moment like this. I've never worn it for anyone." She lifted the weight of her hair in both hands and then let it fall as she tipped her head back. As she moved her touch down her throat over her breasts, to her hips, she spoke softly, gazing at the ceiling.

"I've practiced this here in my room, imagining a lover gazing at me."

"Not just a lover," he said. "You don't have to be shy about it, Ramona. I want to hear your thoughts honestly."

When it had been fantasy for so long, she had to work up to being brave. But nevertheless, she amended it. "I've imagined a Master sitting where you are, looking at me."

She moved toward the scythe. As she did, she pointed her toe toward the floor, letting the foot curve, brushing the top of it along the boards before she brought it forward, then did it with the other. It gave her a sensual dragging gait. No matter a woman's size, the movement was designed to draw a man's eyes to the movement of hips, thighs. Reminding him she was a woman.

"Tell me what you're doing." His body looked deceptively relaxed, a dragon's sprawl.

"Seducing a Reaper. You told me I don't have to worry about my magic doing harm while I immerse myself in how much I want you." She arched a brow, teasing him. "Or do you want to walk that back, tell me if I can do something too distracting after all? That will make a powerful Reaper lose control?"

His lips curved, eyes heating. "I am fully capable of losing control and immersing myself in you while keeping your magic from wreaking havoc. Do your worst, witch."

He'd wanted her to be honest. She would give him honest, even if her voice shook a little. "Ana and Isabella taught me how to do this.

When I'd come here and practice, I'd imagine being one of them, coming into the room with a client, facing a male whose eyes are full of me." She lifted her lashes, met his gaze briefly, then lowered them, this time a deliberate shy tease. "A Master who could take full command of me with only a word, a look that burns away the hold of any other on me, whose look tugs me to him as if he has a tether wrapped around his hand."

"I like your fantasy life, Ramona. I like seeing it come to actual life. So come here again. Let's do this right. The way we both want to do it."

～

She gave him that intrigued yet reluctant look again, like she was anticipating him overriding her intentions. He was tempted. Great Lord, the way she looked in that outfit, the cleft of her buttocks framed by lace, her gleaming breasts calling to his mouth. He wanted to take her by the waist, put her on the bed and himself in between her legs. He'd bury himself, hear her cry out as he discovered her slickness, how much of him she could take.

He placed his hand on one of the bed's wooden posts. The four of them were tall enough to support a canopy, but she'd strung small lights from post to post instead, keeping the bed open to the ceiling, papered with a mural of constellations in a night sky.

When she came to him, he glanced pointedly at the floor. The flush in her cheeks, the high beat of her heart, inflamed everything he wanted. When she followed her desires, she was answering his.

She knelt.

"What will you do to please me?" he asked.

A little noise in her throat, the reaction of a submissive who'd been asked the question she most wanted to hear. Knowing she'd had to go a single day without it, fantasizing in this room about what a Master could give her, believing she'd never have it, fucking made him ache. Even as he was ferociously, selfishly glad he would be the first to offer it.

In the way of a true submissive, giving her even a little of what she desired resulted in her offering her Master even more. She bent forward, brushed her cheek against his thigh, wrapped her fingers around his calf. He gripped her jaw, fingers whispering over her cheek, and guided her face so her mouth hovered over the straining denim, his cock throbbing behind it.

"Put your mouth on me."

She did it with reverence, a light brush of her lips over the curve of testicles, a moist press against his length, breathing heat and moisture through the fabric. He held her there, with a fistful of her hair, knuckles pressed against the nape of her neck as he leaned over her. He was gazing down the slope of her slim back, over the hooked strap of her bra, back down to the revealing panties.

A sheer, sexy confection hanging in her closet for who knew how long, waiting for a lover she could share it with. He might be the luckiest man alive.

"You dress like you want your Master to take you everywhere. Everywhere he desires."

She nodded against him, nose brushing his cock. Intentional, the little tease. The demure submissive had a healthy helping of sensual witch, mixed with playful naughty woman-child.

He'd let her know he didn't mind it, even as it wouldn't influence him. He put his hand to her mouth, pushed his fingers in there. He didn't tell her to suck on him, but she tried to do it as he thrust in and out, worked them around her tongue, the inside of her cheeks, using her mouth to get them wet.

When he removed them, he kept a palm between her shoulder blades to hold her in her forward bending position, body pressed in between his thighs. He leaned down over her, slid his wet fingers between her buttocks and found the tight entry there. He was gentle but inexorable, working his fingers around the rim to arouse her further.

"Open up for me. Push out against me."

When she did, his fingers slid in to the first knuckle, all he needed. He twitched his fingers enough that it intensified the sensations to the rim and all the nerves in that sensitive channel. A whimper caught in her throat, her hands holding his thighs as her own quivered, hips jerking involuntarily. Her forehead pressed to his belly, hot breath against his cock. He stilled his touch, moved his other hand back to her nape, squeezed.

"I don't mind if you play games with me, witch. As long as you realize you're in my playground."

She swallowed noisily. "Yes, my lord."

"Good."

He continued to work his fingers in her as she slowly came apart, trembling, pleading noises vibrating in her throat. Then he withdrew his fingers and sat back, moving his other hand to the crown of her head, a light pressure. "Stay in this position."

He rose, swinging a leg over her, and went into the bathroom. After he washed his hands, he returned to the doorway, studied her a long moment, in that kneeling position, head down. She was quivering even harder. He came back, trailing a hand up her back, brushing her neck, her cheek. She turned to put her mouth against his hand, her eyes closed, head still bowed.

"Look at me."

Her lavender eyes were huge, lips wet and parted from where he'd played his wet fingers over them when he'd withdrawn them from her mouth. "What will you do to please me?"

"I—I would like to dance for you. May I?"

"Yes." He touched her cheek, a tap. "If you remember what I told you."

"Be careful with the blade. I will."

When she rose, he steadied her. It gave him an extra moment to strengthen the buffer shield around the scythe. As she moved toward it using that distracting, fuck-me-now walk, he knew the shield should keep it from harming her, but since her magic could have a disrupting effect on his powers outside of actual sex, he wanted her taking extra care. He'd take no risks with her.

Though truth, the tool was so much a part of him he suspected it would know her importance and protect her all on its own. The energy humming around the scythe was his energy, responding to her through the shaft, through the deadly edge, so many layers of meaning to that.

She put her hand on it and did a few languid turns, a shimmy down to a squat. She stroked the ash handle as she did it. Not a blatant entendre, but like her mouth on him. Worshipful, reverent. Hungry. Cherishing.

He'd seen pole dancing in a strip club, in a Christmas pageant in a mall. In a fitness class, when it had expanded beyond the realm of strip clubs to be acknowledged as the sensual art form that kind of dancing could be.

She'd taken the lessons the demons had given her, but it was her passion that made it an expression of her fantasies, her needs. Her wishes. Her hesitancy at times, her shy expression as she'd removed the robe, had told him how much of her sex life had come from asking the sex demons questions, and exploring the answers alone when she pleasured herself.

Honora had noted that witches were practical creatures, who would balance darkness with sensuality and sex when it was needed. After the bleakness and intensity of the past couple days, this qualified as when it was needed. He'd fallen into brooding when she'd gone into her bathroom, but now his mind was out of those dark corners, fully in the center of something more natural and hopeful, pleasure beckoning.

She crooked her leg over the handle, the lavender lace stretching and riding up over her cheeks. When her hand slipped up closer to the blade, he gave her a warning look. She sent him back a teasing one, playing with him. The curves of her breasts were revealed more prominently as she brushed her tight nipples over the shaft, shifted to tighten her thigh around it. When she arched back, her lips parted and the flame of her hair caught the light. His hands closed against the edge of the bed. For an instant, the scythe wavered, looking like a broom, a witch riding it in a straight line toward the moon.

She'd brought her cunt against the handle, and was rubbing herself with a mouthwatering dexterity. Arousing herself under his gaze, the teasing intended for him, to show him what she needed. What she wanted to give to him.

"Come here," he commanded. "Dance is over."

She twisted around the handle, slid to the ground. While he made sure the scythe shifted into a safe corner, his attention remained on her. He suppressed a groan as she came those several short steps to him on her hands and knees, eyes on him, body moving like a cat's. When she reached him, he crooked a finger at her.

"Stand on your knees and remove all of it. Bra first."

She reached back, unhooked it, let the straps slide down her arms. Maybe it was the heat of his gaze that made her move slow, like a cat basking in the sun. Or maybe she just wanted to torture him. He had an answer for that. The panties were a little more challenging on her knees, but he reached out a hand, palm up so she could clasp it for balance. He could be a gentleman.

He could also be a little bit of sadist, because he tightened that grip, made her struggle and wiggle to obey him one-handed. Since that seemed to make her pupils dilate and her breath grow even shorter, she apparently was a little bit of a masochist, too.

When she was done, he slid his hands under her arms and pulled her up and onto his lap. "Open my jeans."

Her hands were shaking, so he helped, one arm wrapped around her waist as he tugged the garment past his own ass to his upper thighs, letting her sit on the folds as he pulled her fully up against him. Angling her with easy strength, he slid her down his thick length, to the root. Fucking Heaven. What he imagined it to be.

A moan hummed out of her throat. He was savagely pleased to prove to her how she'd affected him. When the friction of his broad head was rubbing against the walls of her slick channel, finding every pleasure point to unravel her, she tipped her head back into the cup of his waiting strong hand.

"There," he murmured, bringing her glazed attention back to his face.

"What?" Her breathlessness made him harder. A little feminine gasp escaped her.

"'Everyone needs a place they can go that they can call theirs.' That's what you said." He punctuated the thought with a deeper thrust. "That's what this is."

Ramona gripped his shoulders, dug her nails into his flesh. Another gasp tore from her as he lifted and lowered her again, a decisive movement he kept repeating, long, slow strokes, his biceps flexing, gaze locked upon her face. Wildness bloomed inside her, her lips parted to let in more air, her nails now seeking blood.

Ramona held onto that cliff only because she wanted to keep that suspension going as long as possible before the spiraling free fall.

Which would be glorious, too, but she wanted to see just how intense and amazing the feeling of being on the edge could become.

Plus her Master hadn't yet given her permission to fly.

She was pleading on every stroke, begging as she knew he'd desired. When her head dipped, mouth against his temple, he spoke against her throat, a growl that made her think of his Reaper form, the glowing eyes, the reaching skeletal hand that should have been frightening and it was. But the green glow of his eyes made what he'd said earlier have a different meaning for her.

Death cannot be refused.

"Silas...I need to..."

"Hold for me, witch. You're not there yet."

"Think...I...am."

"No, you're not. Hold for me. Until it feels like it is supposed to feel. Like the end of everything that doesn't matter, the beginning of everything that does."

His voice was hoarse, telling her she wasn't alone on that road. And it wasn't a road. It was water, spinning and rushing over rocks, slick and hard, crashing down to spring up and split into a million diamonds of light.

It wasn't the first time she'd invited the elements into her bedroom. The water splashed and sparkled, pelted, drops splitting, fountains churning and spiraling. It was a sky show, because their energies joined forces, keeping the water from touching down anywhere. The display gave nothing but pleasure, fueled by the magic they were creating together, with their bodies, minds, hearts.

"I rubbed myself against the place on the staff your hand has worn smooth," she gasped. "I wanted you to...think of me when you gripped it."

Arms banded around her, he brought her down on him so forcefully she felt the shock of it at depths she hadn't known she had. His mouth was on her throat, giving her a nip that added to his fiercely approving answer.

"Please..." She was begging for a mercy she wasn't sure she wanted, but she also knew it was making him more demanding, and she wanted that as well.

Mist settled on them, made damp bodies even slicker. She bit his shoulder. There was no effort to keeping the water playing and dancing. The power in the room could have called another Great Flood.

"Now," he muttered. She was all his creature, writhing and moaning in his arms, helpless and needing anything he would give her. As she obeyed, the water became as chaotic and roaring as what was within her, arcing, waves meeting in the air, splattering more drops over them.

His hair was wet under her grip as he released, driving her even higher. He worked her on his thrusting cock, and she clutched him with her inner muscles, wanting to pleasure and please him, even as her own tissues spasmed on every stroke.

He thrust his fingers in her own damp hair, pulling her head back as his mouth went back to her throat. He bit her harder this time, marking her flesh as he jetted inside her.

He kept the movement going, until he'd demanded every after-shock from her, every spasm of reaction. The water broke into tiny whorls, dancing like fairies. Spinning galaxies, the size of dinner plates, the translucent currents changing color with the lamplight's reflection. Slowly, it all became mist, wisps dissolving into the air.

She was limp, dependent on the strength of his arms to hold her. When her head fell forward to lie upon his, he dropped a kiss on her upper breast, a light suckling of her flesh that had her shuddering, holding onto him, even as her lips tipped up in a smile at his next comment.

"SweeTarts," he noted.

"Sharone makes the dust." She drew a deep, steadying breath. "The oil that helps the powder stick to the skin is an aphrodisiac."

Not that they'd needed it. Though he'd left her no doubt the experience had been as intense for him, he had a reserve she didn't have, because he was able to shift them both, lay her out on her bed. Yet when he would have moved back, she found she did have some strength, because she curled her hand into a kitten's claw over his shoulder, and managed one weak but determined word.

"No."

He gently dislodged her, but he put his mouth on her knuckles, teased the creases with his tongue, sending lovely shoots of pleasure through her.

"I'm not going anywhere, witch. I promise."

Her touch brushed his hip and thigh as he repositioned himself to stretch out beside her. After pulling the covers over them, he gathered her to him. She laid upon his chest, her ear over his heart as he held her as securely as she wanted to hold him.

Even when nothing threatened it, time was precious and limited. Though she wanted nothing to intrude on this moment, an unwelcome thought came to her.

That mark embedded in him was counting down the minutes.

CHAPTER FIFTEEN

*D*espite that one uneasy moment, Ramona slept more deeply than she'd done in some time. Not surprising, after such extraordinary sexual exertions with a virile Reaper.

When she woke, it was because something was amiss. Silas was fully awake, tense beneath her body still draped over him in peaceful pleasure. His arm tightened around her back. He was listening.

"How strange," she noted sleepily. "I don't get burglars."

The lack of concern in her tone drew Silas's curious gaze. Like her, he could detect the intruders were human, not a magical threat, so she expected that was why he didn't leap from the bed to turn that threat into ash before it could cause her a moment's distress. But he still didn't look pleased.

"They could have come up here while you were asleep," he said. "Surprised you before you could raise a defense."

"Not necessary," she assured him. "Chaos magic is absolutely outstanding at defense."

Something downstairs fell with a crash, and she made a *See?* face at him.

She slid from the bed, went searching for something to put on. The small pile of lavender lace made her smile before she tucked it into her laundry basket and found a T-shirt, cotton underwear, pajama bottoms and her sneakers. She stretched, dimpling at how it drew Silas's gaze to her, even as she could tell he was still tracking the muffled movements downstairs. Another crash, a curse loud enough to filter up to them. Then a curious repetitive thumping.

"Shall we see what they're up to?"

A tiny shriek. She shot him an impish smile. "You remember the sleeping concrete lion by the hallway? It wakes up sometimes, grabs your leg as you go by. It's a cat, after all."

She headed for the door, but he beat her there. The scythe had disappeared, so she knew he was carrying it, in whatever magical sheath he utilized for that, but he didn't look like he needed any weapon other than his intimidating expression. He put a hand on her lower back. "There may be nothing down there you can't handle," he told her, "but..."

"You're male, so no way in hell I'm going down the stairs first. I'm okay with that. I'll be your backup if you get into more trouble than you can handle."

His eyes narrowed. "I think that happened the day I walked into your shop." As he headed silently down the steps, she let her touch graze his back, her thumb hooking the back pocket of his jeans for a playful tug that had him sending her a mildly exasperated look, but he reached back, squeezed her fingers.

Since Silas had been portaling her here and there since he'd arrived, her car was still at her shop. The house had looked unoccupied. But it was more than that which had brought her uninvited guests here.

Chaos magic acted like an arcane security system, discouraging wrong doers from targeting her home. But she'd woven two additional layers of spellcraft into it.

She considered her closest neighbors her chicks to protect. There were four sets of them; two widows, one family with small children, and a newlywed couple. The first layer of spellcraft gave her a mental 911 if they found trouble. Thanks to that, she'd known the day one of the toddlers had wandered out the back door to the pond and dug up a bundle of surprised baby copperheads. Ramona had been there in time to distract and calm them, retrieve the curious child and return him to his parents. She'd also called an ambulance within five minutes of Mrs. Ruiz falling off the ladder to her attic and breaking a hip.

The second layer of spellcraft rerouted trouble that tried to find *them*. Like burglars. They would be lured to her home instead of theirs.

As she and Silas descended, that rhythmic thumping had stopped, replaced by an anxious call for help. "M, bro, where the fuck are you?" A youngish voice. Old enough to drive, but that was about the extent of his milestones.

As they reached the bottom of the stairs, Silas glanced back at her. "Stay here." Since his partner in crime was obviously stuck, Silas slipped down the hallway to stalk "M."

But Ramona found him first. Or so she thought.

"Right here, B-man." A gruffer voice came from her left. "Hold on. I found something good."

A big twenty-something male with a thin beard stood up from behind her kitchen counter. Bloodshot grey eyes, lank dirty blond hair. Body odor mixed with pizza and beer.

Those flat eyes locked on her where she stood at the bottom of the stairs. His vibes weren't like the teen's calling for his help. This male was a different kind of trouble. He was ready to escalate into felonies far more serious than simple breaking and entering, though she doubted he'd ever had the opportunity he imagined he had right now. But he'd fantasized about it. A sick creature, who would never not be sick. Never not be tormented by the demons inside him, wanting him to do and be something feared.

She felt no fear. Just pity. Then worry, because he'd drawn a gun.

"Oh, don't do that," Ramona said urgently. "That's..."

As he waved the gun at her, his finger, resting on the trigger, twitched. Ramona never ducked or flinched. The bullet hit a rafter, ricocheted, and then he was hopping around, holding his leg, banging into her kitchen table and sending chairs tumbling. "Shit, shit, shit."

She hurried forward, secured the weapon he'd dropped. "Sit down," she instructed him. "We'll call an ambulance."

"Bitch, get away from me."

"She's trying to help. Best to be courteous."

Silas was behind M, having approached through the second kitchen entrance. And now something far more dangerous than M was in her kitchen.

As they'd descended from her bedroom, she'd sensed Silas had probed the shape of her magic and accepted what she'd told him, that these humans were not an active threat to her. But M had proved he intended her harm, and that changed the landscape for her Reaper. His voice, the energy that rippled off him, contained a killing frost.

When M twisted around, he knew he was looking at Death. Trying to backpedal, he tripped over his own feet and landed on the linoleum, hard. The house vibrated from the impact.

He held up both hands. The wind had been knocked out of him, so his words came out as a wheeze.

"Hey, man, we were just checking out the place, seeing what we could grab. Didn't know you were here."

"M, what's going on? Help me, damn it. I'm fucking stuck here." At the rumble through the house, B-Man's voice morphed to full-fledged panic.

Ramona shifted into the doorway to her den and home office space. The kid was sprawled over the wide top of her horseshoe-shaped desk. His arm was caught behind it.

Poignant proof of his age, she saw he'd wanted one of the solar powered jiggle toys she kept there. The sunflower clicked along like a ticking clock, thanks to the sun that routinely spilled through the window on that side.

It had slipped from his grasp, falling behind the desk. When he tried to retrieve it, he'd leaned against the desk, making the heavy furniture move the necessary inch to pin his arm back there. The pressure on the artery had probably made his arm numb enough he'd scrambled up on the desktop to relieve the pressure. But he still couldn't free himself.

Since he had his head craned awkwardly to look toward the door, he saw her. When his eyes widened, a whispered *fuck* slipping from his lips, he renewed his struggles.

She held up both hands. Her tone was kinder to him than it would have been to his companion, though it remained firm, no nonsense. "Calm down and don't yank on it. It's probably already swollen, and you could give yourself a brachial nerve injury. We'll get you free in a minute."

"Oh shit...what the fu—"

A foreboding raised the hairs on her neck. Raising a finger to him, a silent direction to stay calm and wait, she pivoted and returned to the tableau in her kitchen.

She'd immediately known why the dangerous M was here, and the brief interaction with B-Man gave her the reason he'd crossed her path. But more was happening, and she hadn't been looking in the right direction to prevent it.

Silas was still crouched next to M. He pointed toward where B-Man was trapped. "He was here to rob things. You wanted to cause harm."

"She wasn't even supposed to be here. Thinking ain't doing. When the cops—"

M stopped mid-sentence. Stared up at Silas. Lips parted on the confession revealed through the lie, the denial.

That waft of coldness she'd felt had expanded. It contained a dark power signature, but it didn't belong to the Dark Soul magic embedded in Silas. As frightening as that energy could be, mostly because of her fear of what it could do to him, this was different.

This energy belonged entirely to Silas.

She hadn't completely understood why a Reaper would be considered on par with a Guardian, because whereas Derek and Mikhael unconsciously projected their lethal power, Silas didn't. She'd been given flashes of it, but she'd seen far more of his gentleness and humor. She'd spun all of that into the belief that he was...well, harmless wasn't the right word, not with the dangerous edge that came off his sexual Dominance. But she hadn't thought of him like this.

What vibrated off him was the energy every living thing feared most. The unknown. Complete loss of control.

Death.

Startled, heart in her throat, she shifted her gaze back to M. Eyes that had been alive with fear, resentment, calculation, held...nothing. They were filming over, the drawn curtain at the end of a stage play.

He was dead.

Like he'd told her, during a far different kind of moment, Silas had taken the man's life without touching him, as easily as... She wasn't sure anything she'd ever done in her life had looked as horrifyingly easy as that. So quick, it took her a moment to understand. She gripped the doorframe. "Silas," she whispered.

"What's going on?" The boy called out again. He kept his voice lower, maybe in deference to her suggestion that he remain quiet, but fear made the tone shrill. "M, are you okay? Bro?"

Oh Goddess. Please don't let him be his actual brother.

Silas had his scythe out, haft clasped near the blade so he could control its dip toward M's forehead. He rested the tip there, drawing blood with the lightest of touches. It reminded her of when she'd tended him, and the bare touch of the blade had drawn a bloody line across her throat. And of how he'd admonished her to be so careful last night, when they'd been doing the antithesis of this.

Another brief flash, Silas's coldness banded around a quaking pebble of heat. The life energy the male had contained, his soul. Then it was gone. So was the body, pulled into that scythe, gone in a blink as if it had never been.

Silas rose, turned toward her. She stiffened. Silas's gaze flickered in reaction, and he stayed where he was.

"Tell the boy he got away," he said, low. "In a few weeks, he'll hear M died in a car crash."

She stared at the scythe. The gold among the blue had grown and deepened to crimson. It wavered, as if what was trapped inside it was screaming. This was wrong. It was Silas, but it wasn't. It couldn't be.

"They are not brothers, Ramona. They barely know one another."

"How...how do you know that?"

"It is in the connection between them. Call the police to get the other one. I will go when I know you are safe."

She blinked. "Why? Why would you go?"

He gave her an odd look. "Because you want me to."

"I don't know what I want," she snapped. "Don't assume because you can get in my head that you know what my thoughts mean. Why did you do that?"

He inclined his head, acknowledging her desire for him to remain, though it didn't ease the tense set of his shoulders. "He came with the intent to hurt you. It was mapped all in him, and you are not the first he has harmed, or would harm, with his cruelty. It was a sickness too widespread to fix in this life. Now he can start over."

"That's not why you did it."

"No." The look in his green eyes made her shiver, a slap-in-the-face reminder that Silas wasn't human. Or maybe very human, in this particular response. "You are mine. It's my right to act toward those who intend to do you harm."

"Judge, jury and executioner?"

"There's no need for a jury when you have the ability to read someone's life, their future, and the shape of their soul. I cannot see the journey, and there is always the chance I am wrong, but in certain cases, I know I'm not."

"Someone *please, please* tell me what the fuck is going on. Please. I'm sorry, I just want to go. Don't call the cops."

She studied Silas, his impassive expression. She repeated her words and meant them, even if they were stilted. "Don't go. Promise me."

"If you do not wish it, I won't." The formal response told her she could believe him. It also put distance between them. She might need it right now.

Pivoting, she left him. She didn't have the physical strength to shift the heavy horseshoe desk. Even if her Chaos magic could be trusted—and her current state of mind made that dubious—she avoided doing spellcraft in front of humans not initiated into that world.

She could have asked Silas for help, but she didn't want that blade and cold green eyes near the kid. Fortunately, this case had a mundane solution.

Going into the nearest bathroom, she retrieved a bar of soap and filled the drinking cup before re-entering the den. The kid was still on the desk, though one of his untied oversized tennis shoes had dropped off his foot to the floor. He wore a striped blue and red sock.

"I'm going to get you loose," she told him. "But you have to be still and follow my direction. Don't try to run away."

He had thick black hair and saucer-sized brown eyes. Freckles across his nose. While her calm voice made him look a little less upset, when his gaze shifted he went pale again. That, plus the spike of uncertain emotions in her belly, told her Silas had appeared in the opening to the den. At least it solved her concern about the kid bolting.

She dipped the soap in the water, made it slippery, then ran it around the boy's lean biceps, briskly spreading out the excess water so it would drain around the captured area, lube it up. The skin was red, the area swollen from his struggles as she'd expected. "He called you B-man. What does that stand for?"

He hesitated. "Buster."

"Buster. Hmm." She set the soap aside and rested a wet hand on his shoulder blade. "Okay, try to ease it out of there. Carefully. Don't rush it."

He managed to follow her direction until he realized his arm was sliding loose. Then he reacted like a wild animal escaping a trap. Anticipating it, she'd put both hands on him and forced him to slow down, easing him into a sitting position on the desk as he inevitably found himself light-headed. The boy gazed at her warily. By tomorrow, that redness would be a ring of bruises that would get progressively more colorful.

"What compelled you to try and rob a house that looks like it's about to fall down?"

"You doing a survey, bitch?"

When she felt Silas move, she whipped around in sudden alarm, shifting in front of the boy and spreading her arms out like an angel's protective wings.

"It's okay," she told him. "Please...don't."

Silas's face went to granite. The fist of reaction squeezing her heart felt made of the same substance. She was hurting him, she knew it. But she wasn't going to let him take Buster.

"I intend the boy no harm. As long as he gives me no cause. And addresses you respectfully. Understand?" One glance his way had the boy finding words he'd likely never used in his short life.

"Y-yes, sir."

But Silas wasn't done scaring the crap out of him. If he managed it literally, she swore she'd make the Reaper replace her carpet and desk. "Did you know what your friend intended here? If you lie, it will be the last thing you do."

"No, man. No, sir. Swear to God."

Ramona closed her eyes. "If you'd wanted to be convincing," she said gently, "you would have asked 'what do you mean?'"

If the boy got any paler, he'd surpass *Twilight's* vampires. He shot a glance toward the window.

"You'll never make it," Silas said. "Try using your words instead of running."

The boy swallowed. When he spoke, he did so to Ramona, as if avoiding looking toward Silas would make the nightmare disappear. "I know he gets off on scaring people, and I didn't really want him with me, but my BF bailed. I didn't think you was here, because your ride was gone. I was gonna case things fast, do a snatch and grab, and be out of here before you got back." Another noisy swallow. "Before he found an excuse to go into his crazy psycho fucker mode."

Ramona held up a hand. The gesture was to Silas, not Buster. This one was hers to deal with. Fortunately, Silas respected her wishes.

"You're living at Rooney's old farmhouse off the main highway, aren't you? There are about six or seven of you camped out there." Rooney gave kids on the run or kicked out of their homes a place, in exchange for some rent and help around his neglected farm. He ignored what they did otherwise, because Rooney was a mean, lazy drunk.

"I live there sometimes. Sometimes not. I can be and do whatever the hell I want. I'm eighteen. Don't have to tell anyone shit about my business."

"I believe I told you to address her respectfully." Silas's silky voice could have been barbed wire, ripping across the boy's most vulnerable places. He flinched.

"I weren't saying shit about your lady, just about the way life is. Ma'am," he added on a shrill note as Silas shifted, though it was only to lean on what was now a deceptively harmless-looking staff.

Ramona studied the kid closer. As she shifted more emotional focus from what had happened in her kitchen to this, the connecting thread strengthened, giving her more information about why the magic had drawn Buster here. "Tell me your real name."

Since she'd figured out where he lived, he'd recognized the futility of evading. His shoulders slumped. "Curtis."

"Curtis. Why did you target my house specifically?"

The young man scowled. She saw him look for a lie, the easy answer, but then his brow creased. "I don't know. Just felt right. I know you run that store in town, so I guess I figured you might keep some cash here."

"Okay." She nodded to herself, aware of the kid's puzzled look, as well as Silas's bemused one. He was keeping his eye on Curtis, but the lethal death-vibe was dialing back. "What skills and goals do you have, other than the desire to see prison before you finish puberty?"

"I told you I'm eighteen," he said hotly. "Just small for my age. I'll grow."

She evaluated the thin face, the hard eyes, the wiry body, and leaned forward. Surprised, he didn't jerk back before she'd brushed a fingertip over the freckles. "Those are often a sign of interesting character. And you're fifteen."

She straightened. "I'm sure you've heard the rumors I'm a witch. They are true," she said matter-of-factly. "My vegetable garden needs weeding. You'll be able to leave when that's done adequately. Until then, the gate won't unlock, and the fence will become unscalable."

She gave him a sharp look. "Please don't get mad and destroy things when you find you can't leave until you do what I've asked. If you like doing honest work, come to my store tomorrow. I need someone to stock shelves and clean. Do inventory. Are you good with numbers?"

He looked glum. "Not really. I mix them up."

"You're dyslexic? That's excellent. Just the kind of help I need. Unless the world ends, and then an inventory count will be a moot point."

She patted his shoulder, stepped back. "There's a container of bean burritos in the fridge. Take them outside with you. They'll heat up pretty quick in the sun. The spigot water is good for drinking. It comes straight from my well. If you finish the garden and decide you want to stay, I have a shed beside my greenhouse that, if cleaned up, could accommodate the backyard hammock. There are hooks in the wall for it. You'll find a working sink and bathroom in the shed, plus a hose for showering off. If wherever you're calling home isn't a good place, you can give it a shot."

She could tell she'd upended everything in his head. The reactions he was sorting weren't all in his best interest. "Just you." She sharpened her tone again. "No one else should be here unless you have my permission to bring them. If you try to take advantage, abuse my home and hospitality, you'll find yourself back on the road and you won't be able to get back through my gate."

She leaned in close. Whatever he saw in her expression had his eyes widening. "If you try to hurt my animals, you will *run* to the man behind me to escape what I will do to you. Understand?"

Wary eyes, belligerent chin. "I like animals. I ain't gonna hurt none of them. But, um, I need to know about...is M tied up or something? Where is..."

His integrity might be teetering on a slippery slope, but it was still there. "He left you on your own," she told him, knowing it would have been the truth. "He's no one you should call a friend. Go to the garden and make yourself useful. You'll find tools in the greenhouse. Toss the weeds in the compost bed and turn over the earth on top of it so the heat will kill the seeds and it can break down. I'll be out to show you the right way to do it."

"Um, you said I could get the burritos? I mean, I can wait..."

"Yes. Give Buford a bite of whatever you take. If you don't share, he'll take it all to punish your rudeness."

"Who's Buford?"

"The one who will be in your face as soon as you produce food. Look for four legs and horns. He's your chaperone."

He rose, grumbling under his breath like the teenager he was. Low and mostly for form's sake, to not seem as rattled as she knew he was.

Silas had stepped into the room, leaving a clear route to the door. Curtis gave him a wary look, increasing his pace as he went past, like a puppy crossing the path of a watchful guard dog.

After he went to the fridge—a hungry boy was a hungry boy—he made quick work of leaving the house. She saw him reappear in the window, headed to her greenhouse to start the task she'd given him. At least while she was watching, and he didn't see an obvious line of escape. Buford appeared almost instantly, both because she'd called for his help to watch the boy, and because he was every bit of a goat.

Two things were encouraging. Though she wouldn't have begrudged him any of her food, he hadn't taken anything but the burritos. Second, he offered Buford a generous bite of one and seemed to like it when Buford allowed his ears to be scratched.

Well, that mischief was managed. For the moment. Now to deal with the male sharing the dense, expectant energy of the room with her. As she turned to face him, she had no clue what she was going to say. But she knew what she felt.

Heartbreak. But more than that—total confusion.

～

What she'd seen in Silas's eyes when he crouched beside M, yes, it was him. She'd also noted the respect Derek and Mikhael gave Silas. If Silas abused that power, he wouldn't have their respect.

She operated in a human world, and had grown accustomed to its boundaries and laws when it came to taking human life. But she was also a Chaos witch, raised by pixies in a forested world where nature handled things. Justice had a different look there, and repercussions were more decisive.

Just ask the High Fae male who'd killed her family.

Yet when she'd done it, she'd been half out of her mind with rage and grief. Silas's actions had been intensely controlled, but it was the 'intensely' that held her. She'd felt it throb off him when he'd read the male, recognized what M would have done if he'd caught her unawares.

That wouldn't have happened, because even when she wasn't aware, her magic was. But she realized even knowing that she was capable of defending herself, Silas would still have done what he did, because he wouldn't tolerate someone breathing who had harmful intentions toward her.

It is my right.

He was the alpha male and Master who'd commanded her desire, who'd unleashed it in ways she'd never experienced. Who made no apologies for protecting her by snipping a lifeline like it was a thread. But it still didn't ring true. Something was off.

"You opened your home to him."

He didn't approach her, as if he knew she wasn't sure if she wanted him to be close to her. He showed no reaction to that, yet his assumption that her witnessing M's death would end whatever had just begun between them told her what might be happening beneath the surface. But he wouldn't make her deal with that while she was dealing with her own reaction. He was used to caring for others, not asking for nor requiring that himself. Contained, solitary. Alone.

No one wanted to be around Death.

"He was led here," she said. "They both were. M was brought here to protect my neighbors. Curtis needs someone to count on in the world that isn't like M."

Silas moved to her desk, looked behind it. The staff shimmered into a crook. He dipped it behind the furniture and slid the solar toy out. When he placed it on the desk, it still had enough natural light stored that the sunflower began to rock back and forth with a languid clicking.

He lifted his eyes to her. "I should go, Ramona. Give you time to think."

"What do you think I need to think about?" She tossed him an irritated look, covering the nervous roiling in her stomach. Was it because she wanted him to go?

No. What she wanted to banish was the in-her-face experience of what his job was. "Damn it. I don't want—I don't know what I want, but you leaving doesn't make sense. I still want to get to the bottom of this, how it made me feel. Yell at you some, maybe."

"I'm at your disposal." Polite as a brick wall, while those green eyes reached into her soul.

How many times had people turned from her because of her Chaos magic? Something she not only couldn't change; she wouldn't. Because it was who she was.

Just like a Reaper was what he was, down to the very essence of his own soul. From the first, he'd expressed that life had to be lived out as the Fates, the choices of the individual, intended. He felt things for her, she knew that. But that response...

To disrupt Fate's destiny for a soul is a far greater crime.

Silas was a strong male. He could have beaten the crap out of M. Helped her hold him until the police arrived.

"My intention isn't to hurt you," she began.

"I've been a Reaper for centuries, Ramona. I'm aware of how people react to death and the taking of life. Those reactions have little to do with me and what I do."

She was tempted to slap him out of that monotone, but instead, she kept her voice just as even. "So what you just did, it's part of the job?"

"I usually use it when a first-time soul will find the death process too frightening, and that fear serves no teaching purpose. I can take the soul before the fear fully overwhelms them. Between one beat of the heart and the next."

"So you don't typically do it to expedite things? Like an obstetrician inducing labor so he or she can make a golf outing, a high school reunion?"

His gaze flickered, a brick falling out of the wall. "You have a fascinating mind," he said after a pause. "No, not usually. The Fates have a plan and a time period for everyone, and we do not...disrupt that lightly."

His hand tightened on the shepherd's crook. He'd told her that was his preferred form for it. Another brick falling. She drew closer, deliberately putting her hand over his upon the shaft. A large hand, the knuckles dusted with hair, curved fingers capable of taking her mind, holding her heart and soul. "How was he going to die?"

His gaze shifted from her touch to her face. "Morris, because that is his full first name, was going to die three million, three hundred and thirty-eight thousand, four hundred and sixty heartbeats from now. Approximately, since time continues to pass." At her blank look, he translated. "Thirty-two days. As I said, he will lose control of the car, primarily because he is drunk, roll it down an embankment, hit his head on the windshield. Death will be instantaneous."

"Oh." Had that prompted his decision, seeing that the man's time-line was short? "You've been a Reaper for centuries. You know there are bad people in the world, doing bad things, and you don't collect them until it's their time."

She felt the shift in him. So did he, because he stepped back, away from her. A clatter drew both their gazes to the window. Curtis had stumbled over a hoe.

"Silas," she pressed on, softly. "How do the Fates react when a Reaper does something like this?"

When he didn't immediately respond, her pulse accelerated, knowing what his hesitation might suggest. "I suspect they would be... annoyed. It disrupts their plans, their impact on others. Some threads must be unraveled and rewoven to follow intentions."

His green gaze flickered. "Ramona..."

"How many times have you done what you just did?"

He shook his head, and she would have given anything not to point him in the direction she was going. But she saw when he recognized it. And she ached for him.

Up until now, the mark had made itself known in blatant ways, acting against Silas's wishes, provoking a fight with him. They'd proposed it was precisely because he was strong enough to fight it that it had saved him and those like him for last, close to the execution of the plan.

This time it had used his protectiveness of her, the violence of the situation, to integrate with his personality. A sentient magic, it was learning from his resistance, who he was, trying to get around it. And it had succeeded, by undermining one of his core beliefs.

The pressure in the room changed. For the first time in their relationship, she contained his energy as it spilled out, the scythe appearing and flaming with his rage and helplessness. Revulsion.

At the Tomb, she'd noted his love for being a Reaper, that it was a soul-deep calling for him. Learning he'd just committed an act against everything it meant was too much to bear. Particularly with that curse trying to deplete and break him down in every insidious way it could.

She brought a dome of protection down over them, shielding them from view, surrounding his reaction. She also threw out a call for help over the Link to Raina and Ruby.

Then she had both her hands on him, one on his chest, one over his white grip on the scythe. As it twisted, she ducked. The tip grazed her cheek, leaving a trickle of blood. She barely noticed.

"Silas, look at me. Focus, don't let it take control. Don't let it do this to you."

Energy crackled over them. She looked up into the face of the Reaper, in cowled robe, full skeletal face, green eyes burning with fire. He shoved her from him, knocking her back ten feet, into the wall of energy that dome provided.

"I'll be rid of it, once and for all," he snarled. The scythe morphed into a short-handled sickle. Whatever matter existed inside that skeletal form, he was going to rip all of it out. Destroy his body before it could take all of his soul.

"No. Stop." She shot her own energy into that wall of rage, speared it through his arm, wrenching it back before he could swing a blow toward himself. He roared, but it gave her the opening she needed. She flung herself against him, wrapped her arms around him. All that bone, strong as the timbers of a ship.

She shielded herself with everything she could grab, and it wouldn't be enough. His power could kill her, and on top of taking M's soul before its time, causing her death would finish him off. But it was the only thing she could do quickly enough to protect him.

Then she felt Raina and Ruby's power join hers, reinforcing that shielding over her body. Silas's wash of power rammed it, made her gasp, the pressure like being hit in the chest with a cannon. But she had her sisters' Kevlar to absorb the blow, repel it.

No second blow came. Her act, the presence of the other witches' magic, had recalled him to himself. He was pulling back, trying to defuse his reaction. She held onto him, afraid he might still try to finish the job. She'd been countering a chaotic, emotion-driven response to what he'd done. If he wanted to take his own life as a calm act of deliberation, she would be powerless to stop him.

"Please don't." She kept repeating it, over and over. For five long minutes. He'd define those minutes in heartbeats, wouldn't he? She listened to his, an invisible, hollow, drumming sound inside the barrel of his rib cage.

Gradually, it started to slow. His storm of magic died back, and his fingers curled over her back. Bony, hard, but it was his sure grip. With a relieved sigh, she sent a reassurance along that Link, and a mental push of grateful thanks. She'd explain later.

"Ramona..." His voice was raw with pain.

"He's still captured in your scythe, right? He's still there." She pulled back, stared up at him. "You haven't taken him to The Gate. It wasn't his time. Can you reverse it? Fix it?"

He blinked. Considered. "There is damage to his lifeline but...it would be less. If I act swiftly."

"Okay, then." She put her hands on his face. Passed her fingers over bone. It was smoother than she'd expected. She stroked his temple, gazed into his eyes, the sockets illuminated with a shadowed green glow. "So do that. It's okay. Don't let the bastard who set that mark win, Silas. You're better than this." A pause. "Was he going to cause irreparable harm to anyone before his death?"

His jaw set. "That can't be considered, because it may serve a purpose to other lives, difficult as it is to accept."

She let out a breath. "That's the Reaper I know."

He was struggling, she could see it, trying to make sense of things. But his sense of duty was resurrecting itself. "Wait here," he said.

He was gone in a blink. Alarm filled her. Minutes ago he was considering destroying himself. And before that, he was offering to leave to give her space. He might re-consider either of those things...

He was back, standing almost where he had been. Only now he was in his human form, and the scythe blade was once again gold with a gleam of blue, rather than a full swathe of crimson staining the metal.

"Wow. That was fast."

"I released him not far from here," he said. "His memory of the act is wiped, but I left him with a deep foreboding of coming anywhere near this place. Or Curtis."

"Sounds good." She started to shake. Letting out a quiet oath, Silas picked her up and sat them down on the nearest chair, wrapping his arms around her. Sensing he needed a similar reassurance, she returned the favor, holding on to his shoulders, pressing her face to his jaw and neck.

"I could have killed you," he said. "You are reckless, witch. And brave. I am still going to beat you within an inch of your life."

"So you keep promising."

"I intend to allow adequate time to make a thorough job of it." He gave a handful of her hair a sharp tug. Tipped her face back and passed his thumb over the cut his scythe had made. His lips tightened. "How did you know?" he asked.

"Reapers can see the shape of someone's soul, but so can someone...who loves you. Is falling in love with you." She met his gaze, aware of how it stilled on her. "No matter how angry you'd be on my behalf," she said unsteadily, "how protective you are, you wouldn't have taken M's soul like that when he wasn't a direct threat to me."

His hold on her increased, even as his tone contained a bitter note. "Today, I am not deserving of your love."

She gave him a fierce look. Though the words cut her insides to say them, she could handle the pain. "I ordered one of your previous incarnations to be choked and then burned to death. Maybe I didn't deserve your love that day, but here you are. I think love has a far bigger range and deeper reach than any of us know, mortals or immortals. Plus, it's not you, Silas. It used your emotions and feelings, amplified them to take control. Even with that, it couldn't hold that control for more than a few minutes."

"This time. And mostly because of you." Expression grim, he touched her face. "I need to reach out to Honora. The affected Reapers need to be contained somewhere until this is fixed. Perhaps in the Underworld. We cannot be used against souls."

"I don't want you to go."

"I don't, either. But it is what needs to be done. Plus, you have more important matters to handle." He nodded toward the window. "Like telling him which plants are weeds."

She saw Curtis peer at an undersized purple carrot he'd pulled from the ground, rub his fingers over it.

"Oh, crap." But as he helped her from his lap, she didn't immediately go. Instead, she gripped his hands, sank to her knees between his spread thighs. As expected, the pose captured his full attention. "I know you are much older than me. More powerful. But we will figure it out. And I have a strong feeling we need you alive to do that."

She let the emotions take her, showed them to him. "I need you. I really, really need you in the world. Understand?"

He cradled her face, bent to brush his lips over her trembling ones. "I understand, witch. I will do my best to become enough of a nuisance to make you regret it."

"You're already a nuisance," she told him, and dodged his pinch. It helped her summon a smile. "I'll go talk to Curtis, then we'll call Raina so Mikhael can get a message to Honora."

Rising, she pulled away and headed for the living room, wiping at her eyes. She hadn't been aware she was crying, but it explained the quiet pain in his gaze. At the threshold to the kitchen, she came to an abrupt halt.

"Don't you dare take off. Promise."

"Promise." His tender regard was there, no matter the battering his soul had just taken. She hoped she'd done enough to remind him that this wasn't his doing. That there was only one response to someone fucking with your head.

Fight them.

Silas might be right about needing to go to the Underworld, but maybe she could go with him. Raina had been to the Underworld, after all. Ramona would reach out to Doris, the fifty-year-old widowed neighbor who cared for the animals when she was gone. Ramona would tell her about Curtis, and ask her to teach him how to help, so he could feel useful.

Knowing Silas would be feeling some urgency about getting word to Honora, she crossed her living room and pulled open the front door.

Her vocal cords locked up, her heart dropping like a stone chucked into the Grand Canyon.

As a Chaos witch, she routinely had dreams where the world rearranged itself around her. Sometimes the earth fell away beneath her feet, opening up a sink hole and plunging her into a pit of flame. Other times, she was launched into the sky, tumbled in the air currents until she put out her arms and flew. The sky dreams were good, exhilarating. The sinkhole ones were inevitably nightmarish.

This one fell in that category. In the near distance, a darkness was advancing swiftly, like a giant storm. Only it wasn't confined to the sky. The world before it was dissolving like tempered paint, vanishing into the black. Her heart jumped into her throat, chased by fear and a profound wrongness. There was no time to stop it. No time to even think.

"Ramona." Silas was at her side. Seeing from his expression that this was really happening, not a vision, made it even more terrifying.

Her neighbors' houses, the telephone poles, the faded gray of the street in front of her home, all of it was vanishing, consumed by a dark beast with a maw as wide as the horizon.

Silas let out a sharp grunt, and grabbed for the doorway. In a blink, the mark on his chest burned away the shirt he'd donned, the charred edges licked with flame. She tried to bat at it with her hands, but he thrust her away from him as his body caught fire.

He transformed again, but this was like when he'd reappeared in her shop. It was not his choice. His flesh burned away as immediately as he'd taken Morris's soul. His howl of agony pierced the flames.

"*Silas.*" Before she could grab him again, she was driven to her knees. Pressure pinned her down on her hands and knees. Her gaze snapped up. Curtis was in her garden, still looking at the carrot, completely unaware of the wall of darkness rolling toward him. He looked her way just as it reached him, a puzzled look on his face.

No...

He vanished, as did her barn, her garden. Buford was running toward her, bleating, ears flat. It rolled over him like an artist's brush, painting the canvas black. That brush was coming for her. She turned her gaze back to Silas, but she couldn't see him. She couldn't manage a scream. Something was pulling on her, a noose that choked her, body, heart and soul.

The darkness rolled over and took her.

~

She was in a desolate lack of anything, populated with a loneliness beyond what it seemed the soul could bear. She'd been there before, though, so she pushed past the feeling. She couldn't see her hands, but they were wet, she thought with blood, because they felt sliced open. She was also gripping something like rope. The two braided twists were so thin she worried they would slip free. That would be bad. Holding on seemed vitally important.

So important she started to reel them in, over her wrists, over the marks Silas had given her, over her forearms. It hurt, Goddess, it hurt. Each wrap burned itself into her arm, left her gasping as it worked its way up to her shoulder, then back down again. The left one snapped taut, making her scream. But if she opened her hand, let go, she knew it would be the worst mistake of her life.

The tension eased again, and she kept wrapping, gasping through the pain. Her mind was a whirl. What was at the end of these threads? Why couldn't she see anything?

In what seemed like eons later, she didn't have answers to those questions, but it was getting lighter. A circle of silver glass had appeared, and started to expand. Water, she realized, when it started to dominate her view. So still, it was like glass. If she wasn't floating a foot above it, she thought she could walk on it. But it wasn't the reassuring "water like silver glass," Gandalf had talked about in the Tolkien books, a resting place after death. This water would cut, slice, break anything living into a puzzle that could never fit together the same way again.

She drifted over the threat of it, carrying her trailing ropes with her. Her body started a slow spin, wrapping them around her. They burrowed into her torso the way they had her palms, cutting more flesh. The wrap worked its way down then started moving up...toward her throat.

She tried to slow the spin. It was a physical effort alone, because her magic had no response to it. Yet it didn't feel neutralized. Instead it seemed whatever was happening was the way it wanted to go. Having faith in it was a skill she'd learned a long time ago, but it could still test her. Like when the plan appeared to be to strangle her to death and leave her corpse floating in this land of nowhere.

She wheezed as the rope cut into her throat. The thing that wanted her to let go of the ropes was the wrong part, the enemy. When she refused again, the noose tightened. Pain pounded through her temples, her heart galloped. She was dying. So be it. She couldn't let go. Wouldn't let go.

"Ramona." Her name was spoken by a familiar voice, just as bodies collided with her, a tangle of limbs, familiar scents. Senses returned, awareness of color. The silver water threw light upward, creating a sky like the backside of a rainbow, dark lit hues of metallic blues, greens, reds and golds.

She felt that Link between her, Raina and Ruby, and reached for it, the oxygen that would save her.

"Help." It came out a wheeze. A moment later, the threads were loosening. She didn't know why she was suddenly calling them threads instead of rope, but it stuck in her head. She understood better when they loosened and became living flesh. Raina was clasping one bloody hand. Ruby held the other.

In the hell that life had suddenly become, she wasn't alone.

CHAPTER SIXTEEN

*S*he heard a heartrending wailing, and that was worrisome, but being able to breathe, the realization she was with her coven, was a strong improvement of her circumstances. Their trinity formed a bulwark against the darkness.

She was sitting on the beach of a tiny island in the middle of that silver plain. Ripples marked it now, lapping against a white sand shore, marked with swirls of black like doodles on canvas. It reminded her of her kitchen table. The air was cool, but contained the acrid tinge of a recent fire.

Despite the blood still wetting her palms, the cuts, Ramona didn't yet trust their surroundings enough to let go of those two essential threads. Even though Ruby's hand was flexing as if it wanted to be free.

No, it was jerking rhythmically, because Ruby was rocking herself. She was the one wailing. Screaming.

"No, no, *no*."

Raina squeezed Ramona's wrist with her other hand, a gentle but firm request to let her go. Plus a reassurance that she believed they were somewhere reasonably stable, a reality where they wouldn't be torn away from one another. When Ramona reluctantly loosened her grip, Raina moved to Ruby's other side. She sent Ramona a significant glance, a call for help to retrieve Ruby from her despair.

Having a task and a focus helped. One thing at a time.

"It's okay," Raina soothed, holding Ruby. "It's all right."

"He's gone," Ruby sobbed. "He was in my arms, and he's gone. He was afraid and I couldn't do anything."

"Stop it. Stop." Switching tactics, Raina pulled back and swung, fetching Ruby a startlingly strong clout in the face. It activated Ruby's defensive skills, as Ramona expected Raina intended. Ruby managed to half-block it and struck back, narrowly missing Raina's full lips and silky cheek when Raina ducked.

"What? Why would you—"

"We don't know what's happening," Raina told her, meeting her wet eyes. "He could be in some kind of stasis. They all could. The whole world disappeared, but obviously it's still somewhere. I was talking to Gina and Li, and then a darkness came over everything. I grabbed for them, and they were swept away. But we're here, in this place. Something still exists."

She turned a questioning gaze to Ramona. "Yes," Ramona said. "I was at the house. A boy was helping me in the garden. He disappeared, too, but didn't seem to see the darkness. Maybe those not tapped into magical abilities can't. And Silas..."

She steadied her voice, fingers curling over her throbbing palms. She realized the pain had been inflicted only upon her mind. Her skin was unmarked. Except for Silas's ink on her wrists. She closed her hands over them, a steadying cuff of pressure. "The mark came to life and fire swallowed him."

"He's dead?" Raina asked sharply.

"No. No, he can't be. I mean...I don't know, but I don't think so." She made herself believe it, even as she evaluated the possible truths. "It's more like it took him, the way the darkness took everything else."

Ruby had put her head down, forehead pressed to Raina's arm as Raina kept the other one around her back. Ruby was taking long gulps of the smoke-tinged air, fighting to contain the flood of emotions hitting Ramona like a wave. She could also feel Raina's anguish and worry for her sex demons, even if she had a better handle on it. As for Silas...

"Damn it, they're alive," Ramona told her sisters as she gripped Ruby's shoulder. "That's the only way this is going to work."

Ruby nodded, her throat working. She was getting it together, Ramona could tell. Normally Ruby was their pragmatist, strapped down, the last to show strong emotion. Probably because she carried so much of it.

"How did you know to grab hold of our lifelines and pull us in?" Raina asked. Then she shook her head. "Sorry. I should know by now not to ask why or how you do things."

"Remember what she told you when we first met?" Ruby said wanly. "'If I could tell you, it wouldn't be fucking Chaos.'"

"Right after she said we had to become a trinity coven. Remember what she said when we asked her why?"

Ruby nodded. "She gave us an 'isn't it obvious?' look, and then she said..."

"'Because our names all start with R.'"

They said the last part together, as good as a chant to help them align and shake off the debilitating effect of their worries. "And when she said we possessed the power of three, I said the first one who started to hum the *Charmed* theme song would be given crotch rot." Raina tucked a lock of Ruby's straight hair back into the band of her usual thick ponytail, then looked toward Ramona. "You okay, baby?"

Though Raina was the oldest of them, she rarely used a maternal endearment unless she knew it was needed. Then the comfort of that one simple word was immeasurable.

"Yes. I think so." Ramona got to her feet on her own steam, ran her knuckles down Ruby's upper arm as she did the same. "Okay, then?"

Ruby gave her a red-rimmed look, but squared her shoulders. "He and Derek are fine and alive. Nothing else will let me be any good to them or anyone else. Let's figure this out and kick the shit out of it."

"That's our designated badass," Raina said approvingly, then pointed. "How about we start with that?"

When she'd first taken in her surroundings, Ramona was certain the island had been nothing but a hill of black and white sand. But now there was a cottage of stone and moss, overgrown with wilted flowers. No color to them, but she had a sense there had been color. Just as she was sure the air here had been light and fresh, and the water hadn't been this still glass. The charred smell had grown stronger. It brought back to mind Silas, covered in fire. Could he be in there? Hurt, needing her?

She stumbled toward the cottage, helped and steadied by the

other two. It took longer than expected, and the cottage grew in stature as they approached. By the time they reached it, the one-story structure was twenty feet tall, with an arched doorway nearly twice their height.

"I'm getting nightmare visions of *Jack and the Beanstalk*," Raina noted.

"I don't think I brought us here," Ramona said. "I was given your lifelines, as if I was the best vehicle to do the driving, but something directed us to this place."

Ruby's brow creased. "Raina and I would know if it was Mikhael or Derek's doing."

"While Mikhael likes to surprise me with romantic trips, I'm pretty sure this isn't one of them," Raina agreed. "So we don't know if this was a bad guy or good guy move."

"Or both," Ramona said, remembering the presence of two factions in the bindings upon her.

"Regardless, going inside seems our only immediate option," Raina said. Even with the island's expanded size, they could still see the full perimeter. "And the pull I'm feeling to go in is strong. Like something needs us in there. Something...kindred."

Ramona felt it, too. "Like family."

"Family can be far more dangerous than any enemy," Ruby said dryly. "But I agree. Common sense would suggest one of us staying out here as a lookout, but I also think we need to stay in sight of one another."

"In horror films, splitting up is always a bad idea." Ramona offered one hand to Raina, the other to Ruby, and they grasped them.

The large double doors groaned and shifted.

In a blink, they'd readied whatever best first-attack spellcraft they had. Ruby had the most well-ordered arsenal to call upon, though Raina's witch skills combined with her succubus power made her no pushover in a fight. Ramona's magic had never failed to come through when needed.

But as the doors slowly creaked open, no attack presented itself. Ramona inhaled familiar scents. Fiber, dyes, wood. Weaving smells.

She exchanged glances with the other two, then stepped forward. It felt like she should take the lead, so she crossed the threshold into the cottage.

The first thing Ramona noted was that Silas wasn't there, a disappointment balanced by wonder and confusion at what lay before them. Along with a soul-deep terror that something had gone very, very wrong. Something that impacted all of them, connected to why their world had literally disappeared.

"*In the beginning...the earth was without form and void, and darkness was over the face of the deep. And the Spirit of God was hovering over the face of the waters.*" Ruby murmured it, reading her thought.

They saw a Loom, so vast it required a capital letter. It would have dwarfed her Navajo loom, making it look smaller than even her smallest loom, which she could hold in her lap as she wove with it. This Loom filled a space much larger than what the cottage had seemed to possess from the outside, even after it had expanded in size at their approach. It confirmed Ramona's witch sense that this was an in-between place, tucked into a pocket between worlds.

Parts of the Loom had been burned, a sacrilege that offended Ramona in an indefinable, gut-level way. However, the fire had gone out before it could do more than cosmetic harm, as if it was resistant to the flame. Whoever had done it had resorted to brute force, wrenching the frame with an inhuman strength to break the lap joints holding it together. Even then, one corner had defiantly held while the cracked timbers hung loose in an open, twisted rectangle.

The warp and weft yarns had been cut, sliced up, and tossed to the side before the Loom was set on fire. Someone hadn't wanted them destroyed, but they were a tangled mess.

The threads were multi-colored. Snarled like that, their tones seemed mottled and subdued, but on the Loom, Ramona thought they would have displayed every shade and vibrancy imaginable.

All the colors of the world. Which suggested to her where they might be. And made the situation even worse.

"Look." Ruby pointed. In another corner was a fountain, tumbling into a mirrored pool emitting flickers of light, like a television left on. The three women approached it, still studying their surroundings as they went. The foreboding hanging over this place was too strong to relax defenses.

As they reached the water, a cry broke from Ramona's throat. *Silas.*

The scrying pool showed him standing on a busy city street. Traffic had stopped, though. As Raina leaned in, spoke the words to zoom in for a closer view, Ramona saw people sitting motionless in their cars. Staring, empty eyes, hands fallen away from the wheels.

The image moved back to Silas. His cloak rippled around him against an ashen sky. The fabric snapped with a heated wind so evident she felt like she was drawing soot into her lungs. The cowl shadowed his smooth skull, those shadows collecting in the valleys of cheek and jawbone.

The glowing eyes piercing the darkness were red fire, not the emerald glow she knew. His scythe was planted before him, bony fingers wrapped around the haft.

As her gaze slid away from him, the pool cooperated, widening her view. Pedestrians lay where they'd fallen, staring with the same dead eyes. Her hand went to her mouth. The souls that had inhabited their bodies were marching toward him, joining those who had left their mortal husks at the wheel of their automobiles.

Silas watched them come, motionless.

"He wouldn't do this. He wouldn't take souls before they're ready." She flashed back to what had happened to Morris in her kitchen. Had that decision activated the mark, been the catalyst that activated the mark's purpose? Or foreshadowed it?

"I believe you," Ruby said grimly. "But whatever has control of him through that mark would."

While she watched, Silas turned away and began to lead the army down the street, toward a destination she was certain the Silas she knew wouldn't be leading them.

She noted his movements were stilted, awkward. Silas had a consummate measured grace, that inner calm he carried projected in his movements.

"He's fighting it." She was sure of it. "Inside, if he has any aware-ness of his actions at all, he's resisting."

"But where is he being forced to take them?" Ruby leaned over the pool, fingers clutched on the edge. The scrying magic surprised them by answering her question, the image dissolving then reforming.

They saw another Reaper, leading a much larger group of souls, as if the numbers had swelled as she proceeded toward their destination.

Though Ramona hadn't seen her in her Reaper form, she recog-nized the silver blue flame on the scythe, the symbols woven into the billowing fabric of her cloak, indicating her rank. Shock gripped her.

"Oh, Goddess. It's Honora."

She'd been unmarked the last time Silas had seen her. They had theorized that the strongest of them were being taken closest to the time the architect of all this was ready to execute the full plan. He had succeeded.

If Honora had been taken, all of them had.

Ramona leaned over the pool tensely, shoulder to shoulder with the other two. She didn't recognize where Honora was. A greyness blanketed the background and immediate surroundings. She suspected the location wasn't important. Whoever controlled this would use the closest portal to get the souls where they wanted them taken.

Honora brought them to a halt with a lifted hand. Her bones were a solid, ebony black, the red glow of her eyes casting a blood shadow on the face of her skull. She drew a line before her with the scythe. The witches watched closely when she sketched a symbol with a stiff hand, as if someone was holding her wrist, forcing her to draw it. The Wake leader would be fighting the control, just as Ramona knew Silas was.

But they hadn't had time to tell Honora the mark would try to integrate with her behavior, wash the will away in the belief a Reaper was acting as intended.

The line thickened, burst forth with light, tearing open a doorway. Or not a doorway.

The water in the scrying pool sizzled, startling them into a quick flinch. Though they didn't draw away, they overlapped hands, Ramona's fingers over Ruby's, Raina's over hers. They put the bond in place to shield them from any recoil that might come through their connection to the scrying magic. Forewarned was forearmed, as Ruby might say.

"Merciful Goddess." Raina's golden-green eyes were stark.

The Pit. Silas had briefly mentioned it, and Ramona expected it would be considered the antithesis of The Gate. Living in the subconscious of them all, artists had called it forth in countless depictions. Often it was confused with Hell, the network of redemption chambers in the Underworld, administered by Lucifer.

Knowing The Pit was merely the gateway to the demon realm of the Underworld didn't make it less terrifying. Fear, pain and acts of evil held dominion beyond it. Even through a reflection, Ramona could feel the hunger that lived in those flame-licked depths, waiting, wanting what the Reaper was bringing them.

Souls.

"Honora." She wanted to scream at her, wake her up, stop her. She was beckoning her souls toward that edge, lemmings who couldn't resist the Reaper's pull. Worse—they trusted it.

Once we connect to their lifeline, they cannot leave us.

Honora was using that tether. The first line of souls came forward, docile, obedient. Ramona pressed her fist to her mouth as they simply stepped into space and were gone. Ruby and Raina watched with matching helpless anguish.

Ramona spun away. As the souls dropped into The Pit where they would be devoured, shredded and cease to exist, she watched that tangled galaxy of threads. She saw the shimmer, the spark, the waver of light before certain ones simply vanished.

Silas had been willing to throw himself in that place for Cal, rather than face the agony of losing even one soul to a Soul Collector. They had to stop this.

Ramona turned back to the pool, knowing she needed to see what Honora did next. Her gaze was flat stone as the souls passed her, dropped in. They were crowding one another now, the pace picking up. It was like watching cereal pour into a bowl, an obscene thought. Then Ramona cried out. Because the Reaper turned and stepped out into the same space.

"Honora."

Unlike the souls, who simply disappeared into the gaping maw, flame shot up and enclosed Honora, a sickly white-blue-green that was no normal fire.

Ramona saw the robe burned away in a blink, the skeleton figure arching up in agony, a scream breaking from Honora's lips. Then she was gone, a spiral of ash and snapping embers.

Gone. Destroyed. Irrevocably.

"Enough of this shit." Raina pulled her and Ruby away from the pool, jerked them around so they were looking at the broken Loom. "We weren't brought here to watch. We were brought here to fix this. If we fix this, we help. So that's what we focus on."

Ramona knew she was right, but she had to say his name. "Silas."

Somewhere in those advancing armies of souls was her Reaper. If Reapers had threads here, as she was sure every living thing did, she wanted to find it, wrap it around her and hold it as fiercely as she'd held Raina and Ruby's, even if it cut down to her very bones.

But if he survived, and his souls and fellow Reapers didn't, she knew he'd prefer the oblivion of those flames.

"Derek, Jem," Ruby said, echoing her.

"Mikhael, Gina, Li, Ana, Saul..." As Raina chanted off the names of her demons, they linked hands again, formed a circle and held tight. They spoke the names of those loved ones three times, Ramona adding in Buford, dear Buford, and the other two adding in names as well. With each repetition, a determined calm settled on them. They'd been through darkness before.

"The fight's only over if you give up," Raina said. Dropping hands, they faced the Loom again.

"This is where the Fates weave the path of souls," Ruby said, her eyes hard and mouth taut. "So where are they?"

"Something took them," Ramona said. "And Raina's right. We've been brought here to fix this."

She pointed to the wall, to a plaque embroidered and framed like a grandmother's needle point. The words glowed as Raina read them aloud. "When darkness reigned, a Loom was formed by the Goddess. The spun life of every soul, connecting with all others, created the pattern of Life itself. The Goddess gave the task of operating the Loom to a trinity of Hecate's daughters. So it is that only a Hecate's trinity can operate the Loom."

"It makes sense," Ramona told the other two. "The Fates have to have a backup plan if something goes wrong."

"And we're the backup plan," Raina said. "Apparently all other Hecate trinities had schedule conflicts with the apocalypse. But other than us being witches, *why* would the Fates think we could do this?"

"You're Passion, Ruby's Order. I'm Chaos. The life spark." Ramona answered her. "Everything related to creation, to the way we live our lives, is a mix of those things."

Keep it simple. Ramona gazed at the broken Loom. That was the starting point. Stepping forward, she laid her hand on the corner that was still attached, because she had a suspicion. One that turned into hope as she felt what was in the wood.

It was a living, breathing magical artifact. Despite the cracks in the massive beams from the tearing loose of those joints, it could repair itself. With their help and guidance, plus a solid shot of healing energy, it could bring itself back together.

Repair it, then the warp threads—which contained the individual souls—would need to be strung back on. Her gaze went to the tangle, and she couldn't stop her heart from sinking.

She would have to splice countless warp threads to re-join them. Then would come the wefts, the most challenging part. Because the threads would need to be seamless and smooth in the pattern for this to work, she had to hope the ones that needed to be reconnected could be felted. When she felted wool, it was almost a magical process, the way a bit of water could bring a broken strand back together, so it was smooth in the tapestry once more.

They were surrounded by water, so they had a good supply of that. Hell, she'd even used her saliva for the occasional quick repair on her own weavings.

However, when she knelt, touched the threads, she realized it wasn't going to be water they needed. She pressed her chin to her chest, listening to what the fibers were telling her. Every type of thread felt different. Silk and wool blends, cotton...the texture of these reminded her of all of those fibers, but they were also infused with pure creation energy, soul energy. She saw a face in her mind when she touched this thread, a soul. Part of the warp threads. When she touched another, she saw an event, a relationship formed. A pattern, formed by the weft threads. She would be able to tell warp from weft based on the images she was given.

As she drew her hand away, she noted there was a tiny smear of blood on her fingertip where she'd touched a broken piece of the weft. Testing, she reached for the other ragged end of it, pinching the two together. The tiny fibers moved under the pressure of her touch and the blood, coming together to form an unbroken thread again.

She stared at it, the significance of the information flitting through her heart. Then her gaze lifted to encompass the vast pile of tangled, cut and torn threads. It seemed impossible to do it in the limited time they had, and that was even estimating the amount of thread she could see. A humming vibration, a presence, told her that her human eyes were only processing how many she could conceive of before her. There were an infinite number of threads that had been on that Loom, that were part of that mess. Waiting.

But she, Raina and Ruby wouldn't have been brought here if it couldn't be done.

"Well, thank Goddess you showed us how to use that loom of yours, so we know the basics," Ruby said, breaking her out of the thought.

Ramona recalled that rainy afternoon, where she'd shown them how to weave on her simpler looms, in the ways Crescent had taught her. Ramona had been nine and reluctant, afraid, at the height of her fear of what was within her. But once the pixie had taught her the skill, and how to make the thread itself, she'd told her to have at it.

Ramona's thread, the patterns she created, always ended up something different than expected, but when Crescent made her really look at what she created, Ramona had realized it was...perfect. The best mix of Order and Chaos.

The warp was the order, the straight line. The constant. The weft, the pattern, provided the element of Chaos, while all the pieces to the weaving process...that was the skill and faith, adding to the elements that contributed to the end results.

While she'd have to take point on that process, Ruby and Raina knowing the basics *was* important, so they'd understand what she was doing, and tailor their support and energy toward her for it accordingly.

Her gaze went back down to her finger, the smear of drying blood. She understood what it meant. But it didn't matter. All that was relevant was it needed to be done.

This wasn't just about one woman's son, lover, family. Countless numbers of souls faced destruction, and there was no telling how that would change the face of the world they knew. It also might not be the end goal; just the beginning of an eternal nightmare on earth.

"Ruby," she said, rising. "The Loom knows what it needs to repair itself. Tap into it and let it guide you. I will start working on repairing the threads, so as soon as the Loom is back together I can start warping it."

"Okay." Ruby gestured toward the doorway to the cottage. "I'll cast a shield first, an alarm system in case we come under attack. Something came for the Fates here. If we start fixing things, we may attract its attention again."

"Leave it to the gun shop owner to think about our defenses," Raina noted, then added, "and one of us can reach out to Mikhael and Derek. Since they're on the trail of the mind that set this in motion, what we know might help them. If we can reach them."

"Your non-human blood gives you the farthest range. Plus, I don't think..." Ruby straightened her back, firmed her voice. "You need my shit together, and if I heard Derek in my head right now, asking about Jem, I'd lose it. I'm not doing that to you two again."

Raina squeezed her shoulder. "You didn't this time. Sometimes a woman has to have a good cry before she can do her best work."

Ramona gripped Ruby's hand as well, though her mind was still on that tangle. And what they'd seen in the scrying mirror. "Raina, once you make your call, if you can reinforce what Ruby's doing, that will move us even quicker to the warping." She took a breath, met their gazes. "Once I start working on that and repairing and starting the weft pattern, I won't be able to do anything but that. I can use whatever energy you can lend me, to help me go as fast as I can, and not falter, but if something attacks us... I'll be able to hold my own with the weaving while you deal with it, but I'm not going to be able to stop and help."

"We'll handle it," Ruby told her.

As Raina dropped to her heels, one hand on the floor of the cottage, the other on her temple to aid the focus she needed to reach out to her mate, she nodded. As well as tossed out one more encouraging thought. "Remember, we're not fighting this battle alone. There are hounds who envy Mikhael's tracking ability. With that and a teaspoon of luck, he and Derek may have already cornered this bastard."

When darkness swept the world, Mikhael and Derek were in the vast depths of the Underworld, using its pathways to get to their goal, since navigating the Earth's surface would take longer. Now it had become impossible to do otherwise.

So deeply bonded to the energies of the earth, they felt the magnitude of the disruption. Then it became worse. The bond that connected them to their witches, and Derek to his son, simply... vanished.

The primal need to abandon what they were doing, go in search of those threads, was as strong as what had gripped the Earth in darkness. But with over two thousand years of life and experience between them, they knew obeying that compulsion wasn't the right course.

It didn't change the pain of it.

They also knew what to do with that, and how to channel it. Their focus on their goal reached a lethal intensity, their usual banter silenced. Shadows shrank from the swiftly moving men. A glance at their garb—one in cowboy hat, jeans and boots, carrying a staff, the other dressed in black Armani, his dark talon-edged wings spread to add to his speed—might not have inspired that reaction alone. But one glance at the ice blue eyes of the Light Guardian and the death gaze of the Dark Guardian, and any Underworld mischief-makers decided to stay in their cracks and crevices and await easier prey.

The power gathered around the two Guardians wouldn't blast obstacles out of their way—they'd be turned to vapor.

Mikhael could tell Derek's heart was roaring for Ruby and Jem. He himself was trying not to think of his irascible, passionate witch, but it was impossible. Especially when he detected her life thread, reaching out to touch him. Seeking him. Faint. So fucking faint.

He grasped Derek's arm, bringing them to a halt. "Raina," he said. Derek's gaze speared him as the Dark Guardian tuned into it.

"Ruby and Ramona are with her. The Fates...they are on the Isle of the Fates."

Derek's brow creased. "No one can access that place. It's one of the most secure places in all the universe."

Mikhael lifted a shoulder. "Nevertheless, they are there. Reapers are pulling souls from bodies before their time. They are leading them to The Pit and then they are being destroyed by flame themselves. Something has damaged the Loom, but our witches are putting it back together."

"If the souls can be returned to their bodies, the reversal might create a recoil on the spellwork. It could weaken whatever is controlling the Reapers and trying to pull them to The Pit."

"Yes." Mikhael paused, then his expression tightened. "I was able to communicate that much, but she is gone. Giving us the bare essentials was difficult. Things above are bad."

Derek swore, then tightened his hand on his staff. He didn't ask about Jem. If Raina knew his status, or Derek could do anything for him, she would have communicated it. "Let's get to the source."

"We're almost there."

Knowing the witches were alive would have to be enough, for both of them. A few minutes later, after covering miles in barely a blink, with a complex mix of portaling and sheer determined speed, they surfaced.

This part of the world seemed unaffected by the darkness, but perhaps that was because it was already hellish enough as it was. The frigidly cold mountain region was remote from human civilization. Derek studied what lay before them. "It looks like something out of Grimm's fairy tales."

"There's a reason they wrote those stories."

The cottage had gingerbread embellishments, flower boxes out front with brown husks of plants that never could have survived here, even to grow and die. It was a pitiless, cold fortress of spellwork, intended to repel with extreme prejudice anyone who tried to breach its walls.

"Allow me," Mikhael said, setting his jaw.

"I have your back."

Mikhael spoke the words as Derek readied himself. The cottage quivered, shimmered, twisting, resisting the Dismantling and Neutralizing magic. The Reveal spellcraft Mikhael injected into it contained an artistry and ruthless determination Derek appreciated. They had different styles, but they'd learned the building blocks shoulder to shoulder.

With their lifespan, those thirteen years in the elite Guardian school should have been a dot in a thousand-page volume, but the intensity of that training, how it had broken them down and rebuilt them, never faded.

The most important lesson they'd learned was no matter how big and bad they became, there would always be something bigger and badder. So Derek kept all his senses on full alert, watching every attack point that might disrupt Mikhael's efforts.

He didn't have long to wait.

He lunged forward as spiraling shoots of poisoned flame erupted from the ground. He swept out a dousing flood of water with one hand, raised his staff and sketched an arc in the air that repelled the jagged metal pelting them like blood-hungry hail. He knew when he was being tested, distracted, so he wasted no time calling the craft to hand he needed to electrify the air, transforming the metal into a fluttering fall of flower petals.

Though Mikhael was intent on breaching the entry, Derek heard his appreciative chuckle. *I think you've been learning from the Chaos witch.*

A Guardian who stops learning is a dead Guardian.

Worse. A boring one, who might as well be dead. And you're already a tedious Boy Scout.

A rumbling earthquake split the ground. While Mikhael went smoothly airborne, hovering as he worked the unlock enchantments, Derek brought the crack back together, sealed and reinforced it.

Energy work was about seeking the deeper levels, understanding the nature of what the sorcerer needed to do his work. Those who sought to manipulate it to their own ends often made mistakes. This one didn't cut corners. But then, Ramona had speculated he'd spent decades preparing this. He wasn't impatient.

A wall of fire shot up around the cottage and Mikhael used his wings to take him up higher. He had his eyes closed, lips barely moving as he sought to understand the shape of the barrier keeping them from entry. Derek shifted in front of him as the wall of fire crackled and danced. A roar, and a dragon the size of a Boeing burst through it.

Shit. Derek threw up a shield, modulating it so Mikhael could keep working through it. No point, since the dragon shredded it. Fine, he'd take the cowboy approach.

He tossed out the lines of energy, wrapped them around the creature's thick neck and legs, giving the lines barbs that speared the flesh and wings. As the thing howled, Derek went left, yanking it into a spin toward him, away from Mikhael.

The dragon wasn't an actual dragon enslaved to a master. It was a Frankenstein construct, put together from pieces of living tissue and a complex level of spellwork. Which made it three times as dangerous as a real dragon, and those were no picnic, if they were of a mind to be an enemy.

His boots had been sourced from one of those.

This thing was a weapon capable of bludgeoning, poisoning, ripping and decimating whatever it contacted. It had teeth, armored scales and breathed fire that cooked Derek's renewed attempt at shields.

So Derek once again dropped them and leaped to meet the dragon, leading with his staff. He shot lightning into its composite heart, followed by a tsunami of water. The electrocution illuminated its insides as it screamed and writhed. Grabbing a handful of scales for leverage, he slid over its back and behind it, avoiding the slash of the giant tail. When the beast crashed down a hundred feet away from the left side of the cottage, he crouched on its motionless back.

No time for a coffee break. The next barrage included basketball-sized mortar shells that exploded in the air when he blocked them from ground impact. He lost sight of Mikhael in the resulting detonations, flashes of fire and choking smoke. Shrapnel sliced over his face and shoulders, because he was having to divert more energy to protecting Mikhael, but it would heal. His witch would put her hands on it and scold him for not being more careful.

There were perks to this kind of shit.

Slowly, things quieted. The smoke cleared. Either they'd exhausted the outer defenses, or Mikhael's success had deactivated the trigger for them.

Both apparently. Derek grimly appreciated Mikhael's faith in him, for the Dark Guardian had let none of it distract him from finding the right entry point for the cottage. Only now did his dark eyes open, wings folding back as he touched back to ground. He'd had to exert himself enough he'd shed the Armani and wore more serviceable clothing. Black jeans and a T-shirt. When it came to color, Mikhael embraced the Underworld clichés.

"Didn't want to get your expensive shoes dirty?" Derek asked him.

"I take care of what matters to me."

"Must be why I'm all beat to hell."

Mikhael's lips twitched, but their gazes turned toward their goal. The cottage veneer was gone. They were looking at a shack dipped in poorly spread and hardened tar. Bare ground led to the single door, the wood scarred as if a tiger had tried to scrape its way inside. Next to the door, on a too-short hook, a set of chimes beat against the wood on a listless but bitterly cold wind. A ragged cloth fluttered at one tiny open window.

Despair and a lack of mercy formed the siding and foundation for this place. Whatever lived here had nothing left to give the world. It only wanted to take from it, so keenly that Derek suspected the desire to inflict suffering was what kept the walls standing. It certainly wasn't the architecture.

Mikhael glanced toward the dragon, a bundle of melted metal and sparking spell remnants. "While I did the work, you had all the fun." He gave Derek an assessing look, taking in the blood on his face. "You're getting slower."

"You're uglier."

"Not what your wife says."

"On the day we die," Derek said in a measured tone, "you'll still find a way to poke that wound. I shouldn't have blocked that poison fire spell from reaching you. Maybe there would have been boils to mess up that pretty face."

"Missed opportunity."

"Fine. I'll tell your mate you obsess over my wife, then."

"Don't. She worries about it. With no cause for it in the slightest, but it is a vulnerable spot in her heart."

The unexpected straight comment had Derek meeting the Dark Guardian's gaze. He offered a short nod, nothing more needing to be said. In their uneasy alliance that occasionally flirted with actual friendship, they drew lines. Those that protected the women they loved wouldn't be crossed by either. Not consciously or willingly.

"Heads up."

"I feel it."

Their quarry wasn't done. The shack had its own protections, and crossing the threshold would set them off. More subtle defenses this time. Mind-magic, to render the shack invisible and scramble the mind. The enemy would think the shack was to the left—forty yards into the open air over the rocky edge of the cliff. Before they realized it, they'd be splattered on unforgiving ground below.

Or, since a quick glance showed that the bottom wasn't visible, it might be a vertical portal, taking the disoriented attacker somewhere else entirely. Where, with their mind scrambled for an indeterminate time period, they would be uncertain where they were or how to get back.

"It's ingenious craft, but he's not fueling it anymore," Derek murmured, coming back to Mikhael's side. "Either because he can't spare the energy to keep fueling it, or..."

Because his objective had been accomplished. They were both connected to the currents of life in the world above. Even without Raina's message, they knew things were worsening.

Derek met Mikhael's gaze again. They'd both had enough. Not only were they out of time, they might already be too late.

"*Obliterate.*" Mikhael could apply the spell with the precision of a neurosurgeon, or the blunt effectiveness of the Jolly Green Giant's fists. This time it was the former, as capturing their quarry alive might be vitally useful.

The flash that passed over the threshold was crimson red. When it blasted away the mind-magic, Derek had added a backup buffer to absorb the recoil. He handled housekeeping, wrapping up the dangerous residue of the craft and shooting it out over the cliff edge, letting it shred and turn to ash. The cold wind blew it away.

Once again, what they saw around them changed. They were no longer above ground, nor even in the mountains. They stood in the cheerless hallway of a Cold War relic bunker, based somewhere in Europe. Bare concrete walls flickered with anemic lights in rusted metal cages.

Mikhael exchanged another look with Derek, and the two advanced, their senses covering every angle and dimension. Though removing the sorcerer's defenses told them their powers eclipsed his, Derek referenced the corollary to that #1 rule. Stronger didn't mean smarter.

This male had proven himself an exceptional spell crafter. The Underworld demons using him hadn't had to do much more than seize the handle of the weapon the sorcerer had *wanted* to create, load and aim.

They'd reached a steel door, marked with symbols. Derek traced the unlocking over them with his staff. A quiet flash, and the door creaked inward in an uncertain way.

The room's interior matched the study of any modern-day

sorcerer. Old books, scrolls, crystals, a functioning lab for mixing potions, plus a high-end computer with several screens, including one mounted on the wall. Disuse clung to it, though. As they'd suspected, its purpose had been served.

Mikhael drew Derek's attention to a door at the other end of the space. A wooden one, more fitting with the original cottage they'd seen. It had a wreath on it. Its flowers were spelled to stay fresh. Everything else they'd faced had reeked of death and rage. The green aura misting around this brought the scent of fresh earth and growing things.

Once they stood before it, Derek touched a flower. Mikhael rested a hand on his shoulder to increase the clarity of the image transmitted between their minds. A fortyish woman in a garden, wearing a straw hat and pulling weeds, a smudge of dirt on her soft cheek. She had brown hair, friendly eyes. She was tired but content with her day, the sun soaking through her clothes, the results of her labors blooming around her.

The door moved, opening several inches. A voice came from within. "It's not polite to watch someone's home movies without permission."

Derek pushed the door back. The space within was narrow. A bunk bed was bolted to the far wall. The man lying on the thin mattress was on his side, facing the wall, his arms wrapped around himself and legs drawn up, head tucked down. His shaggy hair hung to his shoulders. When his head turned in their direction, he showed an untended beard of about two weeks' growth. His eyes were cold. Fixed. If he hadn't spoken, Derek would have called them the eyes of a dead man.

In this case, a man who'd died while his body yet lived.

"It's not polite to end the world without the permission of the populace," Derek answered coolly.

Raina referred to Guardians as cosmic cops. The bite to it had softened since she'd mated with one, but she still liked to tease them with her distaste for authority. They didn't argue with the description. Like all cops, he and Mikhael knew motives mostly fell under three categories. Love, power or money. Based on that wreath, Derek was going with love. Which sucked, because a wrong act motivated by love was the hardest to derail.

Both he and Mikhael had creative tools to extract information, universally effective. But a sorcerer of this power could make getting that data far more difficult. Derek suspected he might even have some form of self-destruct to take it beyond their reach. This male cared little about surviving to see his efforts succeed. As his next words confirmed.

"You're the only thing left on my list. Be killed by those who think that they're doing the right thing. You can't stop it, though. There are too many links in the chain. The weight will pull everything over the edge."

That indifferent gaze slid over them. "Guardians. Soldiers of the Underworld and Heaven. When I was a Reaper, I brushed paths with you now and again. Odd that you two work together. Do you have names?"

"Derek. Mikhael." Derek gestured. "And you are?"

"Bryan. First names work. Just like on a playground, because that's what we all are. Children on a playground. That's where the biggest dreams happen and most brutal games are played." Bryan's gaze held Derek's. "I'm not ending the world. I'm destroying the Fates' control of us."

"Did you kill the Fates?"

"Impossible. They are like...air." He barked a pitiless chuckle. "You can't starve air of air. Can't kill an element, can you? But what you can't destroy, you can trap. And the way to trap something powerful is to make them think they're not trapped at all. They're somewhere they can no longer fuck up people's lives. Oblivious for now, and fine. When they figure out they've been removed from the ability to do harm, it will be far too late to try and reclaim their tyranny over our souls. The Reapers have been blocked from collecting them at the appointed times."

Mikhael frowned. "But they are collecting them. Well before the appointed times. You should have taken a closer look at that fine print. The demon world figures out every loophole. Look."

At his glance, Derek opened a scrying screen, using his tracking of the energies on the earth above to lock onto the most concentrated point of the disruption, correctly assuming it would illustrate the point.

Bryan turned over, pushed himself up heavily. The smell that wafted to them was of a body that hadn't seen soap for quite a while. With bloodshot eyes, he stared at the sight of a cowled Reaper marching forward, portaling souls out of the mortal world and into the grey-cast tunnel provided for them. To the edge of The Pit.

Raina had told them what was happening, but it didn't dilute the horror of seeing it. As the souls tumbled over, Derek steeled himself not to move, not to distract Bryan from the watching, even as his reaction mirrored the rage he felt from Mikhael.

Bryan stared a long moment, then his face hardened. "So dark forces are mucking with my plan. Fits with their usual MO, doesn't it? The demon world can have their pound of flesh. There will be people who escape them. Life will go on."

Derek let the image dissipate. Bryan locked gazes with Mikhael, not an easy feat for anyone, but the accomplishment spoke to the will of what burned in his tormented soul, the husk of what he once was.

"I feel your contempt." His attention drifted to the wreath. "But Reapers are given a soulmate once. Just once. Our lives are lonely and long. You are Guardians. You understand, for it's the same for you. It's how we're designed, how we're made. Have you found yours? I can see you have. Everything you are is about her, and it becomes more and more that way every day. She *is* your heart. Now what would you do if the Fates you serve took your heart away?"

His expression transformed to cold fury. "Made her suffer before she died. You can hear her crying your name, crying out for your help, every night when you sleep. A help that came too late. She'd have had every right to die believing you'd failed her, but she didn't. Her last thought of you was love, because that was what she was. She took all the love you had inside you with her."

"Your loss was grievous," Derek said. "And Reapers serve the Fates in a way that often isn't easy. But is this a way to honor that love?"

Bryan shook his head. "You don't understand. They took those memories away. I served the Fates for hundreds of fucking years, all the while not knowing they took that from me. On the threshold of dissolving into peace, it was revealed to me. A big *fuck you* for your service. You lose everything that matters to you, feel that pain, day after day, and try not to go mad from it. Try not to answer it with revenge, fury, destruction. Destroy the cause."

He shifted to Mikhael. "Do not lie. If you lost what mattered most to you, you'd burn down the world that did that to her, to you, to the love you shared. Wouldn't you?"

"Yes. But he would stop me." Mikhael tipped his head to Derek. "As I would stop him if it happened to him. Because there must always be balance. Else there would be no room to find that love to begin with."

How many times had he and Mikhael debated the point, why Mikhael chose the Dark, and Derek served the Light? Though Derek might not understand Mikhael's choice, what he found in that darkness, in this kind of moment, confirmed they served the same purpose.

"The Fates don't make those decisions," Derek said quietly. "They are like the artist, the writer, the actor, looking for inspiration, suspending thought or intention to let the magic come to them, to guide them."

"You are going to instruct a Reaper on what the Fates decide?" Bryan scoffed. "Try to make me believe it's something outside of them. Like a God or Goddess?"

"Yes. But it is us, too," Derek responded. "All of us. Every soul, all the energy that gives us life and movement, it chooses the threads we follow, for reasons buried beyond our reach, but there, the knowledge is there, under the sorrow and fear and pain." Derek felt Mikhael's gaze on him, wondered if those endless debates between them were in his mind as well. "Love knows all things *aren't* possible. There is no escape from the horrible and unimaginable. But love has an endurance that exceeds the horrible, the unimaginable, if your faith in it is strong enough."

"You think you're that powerful?" Bryan scoffed. His eyes burned, on the verge of tears he was no longer capable of shedding. "You are about to find out. You think I didn't know the Fates would call others to their Isle? Who better than daughters of Hecate bonded to Guardians? Plus a Chaos witch, bonded to one of the strongest Reapers? That piece was unexpected, a last moment gift." His face twisted with vicious irony. "Some might call that...Fated."

The triumph in his eyes, that he'd succeeded in giving them some of the poison that infected him, was fleeting. He laid his head down on the pillow, wrapped his arms around it. His fevered gaze lingered on Mikhael. "That Dark Guardian look could kill me if I wasn't already so far gone. Or give me pain, if it wouldn't be just one more drop in this blood-filled sack of it." He looked at Derek. "Your words are just what you hope, and it all means nothing. Chaos or order, it means nothing."

He closed his eyes, the energy he'd found for the conversation ebbing. But he had enough for his next words. Derek expected he'd always have enough for them.

"She used to make breakfast for me. She would wear one of my shirts, her hair tangled on her shoulders, her feet bare. She would smile at me, distracted because she had things to do, but she would still make breakfast for me. I didn't realize what a miracle that was. Someone who loved me, in my kitchen, making breakfast for me."

He didn't smile, he was well beyond that capacity, but they saw the far distant echo of it. "She was a terrible cook. She could only do toast and scrambled eggs, but she made those for me, an act of love. Of service to that love. She was so pleased when she figured out scrambled eggs come out better if you take them off the heat when they're still a little uncooked. Let the heat of the pan finish it up, keep them from drying out."

Derek approached the bunk, trusting Mikhael to keep a lookout for any treachery, though they both sensed the man had no objective at this point other than death. "Bryan, do you want to know why I believe you should tell me where you put the Fates?"

Bryan's eyes opened, considered. He'd spent decades studying, researching. An unanswered question was likely the only thing that could tug at his logy mind.

"You know that the demon world will take your purpose for their own," Derek told him. "But it runs deeper than that. When you use Dark Soul magic, you walk a line along the abyss. What clings to its edge are forces that will wrap around you, sink into you, capture your purpose and use it for their own ends, often without you realizing it, because your own pain blinds you."

It resurrected the memory of how he'd nearly lost Ruby to it. He felt Mikhael's awareness of where his mind went, a mix of emotions touching him from the Dark Guardian. Yes, it would always be both bond and sore point between them, the pain and regret, the sacrifice and debt. But it also included things that ensured they would also be brothers.

Brothers that more often than not wanted to beat the shit out of one another, but brothers all the same.

"Your intent was to free souls from what you felt was the imprisonment of their lifeline." Derek held the sorcerer's gaze. "But those lifelines are not imprisonment, as we told you. They are a series of experiences, a mix of Fate and choice." Which, as a Reaper, before his grief pushed him to an unfortunately brilliant calculated madness, he'd known. Derek was counting on that bank of memories being in there, as closely tied to that woman as his pain was.

Though his expression didn't show any of that awareness, at least Bryan was listening. "By taking them off those roads, away from the guidance of Fates," Derek continued, "you have missed that below the Loom is the abyss. Waiting to take those souls, devour and use their energy for a purpose that has no regard for their light, their desires or choices. Yes, some may survive, get away from that end, but was that really your initial intent?"

Derek leaned forward, dominating Bryan's vision. "It has been decades since her death. Souls are reborn into other lives when and if they are ready to do so. Her soul could be one of those being led to that Pit."

Bryan stared at him, the gears in his mind visibly grinding, trying to un-muck what had been salted and sanded in there. His hand tightened on the pillow. "No. She wouldn't...she stayed in Heaven. You're lying to me, trying to trick me. I'm not...no. Try to break through my shields, Guardian, and I will ensure everything behind them disintegrates before you can touch what lies there."

He spat the words, drew out of Derek's reach. Flipping over to face the wall, he huddled against it. He started rocking, muttering equations. Likely shoring up the defenses on those shields.

We are out of time, Derek. Though they could speak in one another's minds if needed, Mikhael used the subtle shorthand gestures they'd developed during Guardian training. No speech had been allowed during those thirteen years except by instructors. *We are losing too many souls.*

Plus three women's lives were on the line. Their women.

Mikhael was willing to take the lead on what needed to happen next. But Derek was the Light Guardian. He'd do it.

"Bryan." He spoke to the man's tense back. "I am going to give you something. The way you felt before she died."

Bryan turned his chin to his shoulder. Puzzlement crossed his face, suspicion. "You think throwing me an illusion as a gift will help—"

"It's not a gift." Derek closed his hand on Bryan's shoulder. When his fingers wrapped over the bony upper arm, he shot the full force of the "gift" into Bryan.

Bracing himself, he opened the path. In order to take Bryan down it, he had to join him. He wished he could have tried to break through Bryan's shields, made it a fair fight. There would be nothing fair about what he was about to do.

When they reached that strongest memory, Bryan and his soulmate in her kitchen, he stood silently at Bryan's side. Through Bryan's eyes, Derek saw her beauty. Her hair more lustrous, eyes brighter. The lines of her face, the plump body he'd known intimately. The soul that knew him and his heart. Nothing in the universe felt like that connection except divinity itself, because they were one and the same.

She had a woman's distracted look, as she balanced the daily to-dos. Like Ruby, when she was holding Jem on her hip while talking to her gun store manager on the phone, plus scribbling out a grocery list. All while Jem played with her ponytail and Derek lifted his morning coffee from the counter, pressed a kiss to her throat. She'd dip her head toward his, brush her hair against his face, and offer him an absent smile.

Derek would have smiled at the memory himself if what he was watching didn't cut him to the bone as a result of what those kinds of memories meant.

Bryan and his soulmate had had chickens. She was talking about feeding them. Bryan fell to his knees, held her tight. Everything he'd missed came back to him, a storm created out of all the elements. Overwhelming.

Tears were born again, squeezing out of his eyes as she bent over him, put her arms around him, confused but giving comfort. Derek didn't tune into their words. Not just to give Bryan privacy, but because he was closely monitoring the course of energy inside the former Reaper, staying aware of when he would step back mentally, when reality would penetrate and detonate like a dirty bomb.

Though his conscience had been bludgeoned into numbness,

Bryan had possessed one. In her arms, he began to remember what their love had truly meant, all the layers. Its connection to his choices and how he'd intended his life to be lived, the purposes he'd intended to serve. The truth began to grow within him.

Be ready, Derek sent the gesture to Mikhael. He blocked out everything else, the inevitable route this would take. He could have probed Bryan's mind during the distraction, seen if he could break through those shields Bryan had said would avail him nothing, before this went too far, but he wouldn't risk it. What was at stake was too important.

Ironically, a reason Bryan would understand.

It was not the first time Derek had had to do something like this, but his bonding with Ruby and the birth of his son had made him far more aware of what Bryan himself had pointed out. Little separated him from this male except Derek's heart, his woman, still lived. He would do anything to protect her. Ruby knew that.

When she'd broken free of the Dark Soul magic, she'd needed his help to do it. But she'd realized how far Derek would go to keep her from being lost to it. She'd held onto who she was, enough to know the right thing to do. Even though she'd thought climbing out of that despair would destroy her, she had, because she'd had him to clasp her hand, stand with her and heal.

Bryan was getting the illusion of that rescue. But though he'd scoffed at it as such, he couldn't resist the power of Derek's training. When he recognized it was an illusion, it would be because the truth of his soul and conscience had been opened by it. And then things would get ugly.

He rose, stepped back from his wife. She was gazing at him, that half smile on her face. As she began to shimmer, Bryan looked through her, saw the route he'd followed. Nights working on the right formula, chasing down texts he'd needed. Coming up with the spells, mapping every clue until he found out where the Fates were, and how to take them from the Loom. Open the protections on the Isle so the demons could attack it, hold up their end of the bargain.

In his rage, he would have killed the Fates if he could have, but he'd known that was beyond his strength. Instead, with cold calculation, he'd embraced his madness, recognizing an escape from the force of the pain in pushing himself to the limits of his genius, with no moral boundaries.

He'd wanted the Fates to suffer, but he'd been controlled enough to keep his wits, shift them into a contained environment where they thought they were still working the Loom. They were stuck in a loop of awareness where they never progressed beyond a single fixed point in time, an extreme form of short-term memory loss.

The spellcraft was fucking amazing. In other circumstances, his soul would have been marked as a candidate for Guardian training. The Underworld would have offered it to him as an alternative path when he was ready to shed his Reaper mantle. This loss had derailed him. A soul learned and grew, and he hadn't grown enough. He hadn't been able to cope with the loss.

Whether mortal, Reaper or Guardian, the will could be broken. Everyone had something they couldn't bear to lose.

Got it? Derek asked silently, knowing Mikhael was seeing the same formulas he was seeing, the location of the reality shift for the Fates.

Got it. Coming?

I'll finish this.

Do you wish me to stay until it is done? Mikhael wasn't sentimental, so the offer was a surprise.

No. Every moment counts. I'll rendezvous with you.

Mikhael disappeared. A chill tapped Derek's spine, either from his exit, or foreboding about what lay ahead.

Bryan stared at the unfurling path he'd taken. Experiencing the full, vibrant memory of the love that had started it years ago, under the gaze of the woman who'd adored him, he saw with clear eyes where he'd ended up. And the point in his timeline when his actions had resulted in the deaths of others. Those he'd pulled from their own lovers and families.

Then what Derek had showed him revealed itself again. The souls falling into The Pit, those already lost to the abyss, those marching toward that edge. The possibility that Bryan's soulmate could be one of them.

Derek hoped not, but there was no guarantee.

Bryan tried to avert his eyes, began to mutter again, but he was inside his mind, no shutting it out. A denial choked from him. Now back in the desolate room where Mikhael and Derek had found him, he dropped to his knees. "No."

It didn't take long. Derek felt the knowledge bludgeon Bryan's heart, blow after agonizing blow. An immortal could be killed, if one knew how to do it. In this case, the immortal had taken himself to that threshold, by allowing Dark Soul magic to drain his lifeforce.

Derek watched life die out of Bryan's eyes, but not the horror, the knowledge that he couldn't change what he'd done. Redemption would be a long road for him. But like death itself, it was one they all walked.

Let them who are without sin cast the first stone.

CHAPTER SEVENTEEN

*O*ne, two, buckle my shoe. Three, four, shut the front door. Five, six, pick up sticks. Seven, eight, don't be late. Nine, ten, start all over again.

A reminder that child's play symbolized Chaos magic. It only had to make sense to them. It had been an important revelation as to why the Fates gave a Chaos witch her magic at such a ridiculously young age. She'd had to understand that, make the connection. Every time she used the magic, learned something new, it was reinforced.

Witches who relied on order, like Ruby, might have lost time, trying to figure out the best approach to unsnarling and repairing a galaxy of soul threads. A Chaos witch simply plunged her arm into it, fingers seeking, and found the first thread to touch. A soul currently a young girl, whose biggest concern was whether the boy who'd smiled at her in class liked her. But now that young soul was in a perplexing limbo that didn't feel right, a feeling that would turn to fear as she faced The Pit.

Millions of threads, millions of lives. She couldn't think of how daunting the task was, how long it might take, how little time Silas might have, or about the souls that were even now falling into oblivion.

She was vaguely aware of Raina and Ruby recrafting the Loom. As they'd noted, the life imbued in the grain aided them in bringing it back together, healing the cracks, re-lapping the joints. Everything in this room had a voice, if they listened. Though beaten up and damaged, the Loom was as immortal as the Fates that guided it. With the witches' aid and care, it was restoring itself. It knew its job.

Ramona started warping the Loom as soon as they were done, levitating herself as needed to go back and forth because of its height. Not seeing any weights for the purpose of ensuring the tension of the warps was correct, she used her magic for that as well. It was all about energy and feel. There were no marks on the loom, nothing to indicate the sett, the required spacing between the warp threads, how many yarn ends per inch, but there wouldn't be, would there? She was dealing with lives, souls, tapestry patterns that would change based on what the threads told her, the path they wanted to take, the stories they wanted to tell.

Which meant the warp tension was trickier on this Loom, because it was connected to the universe, and the universe breathed in, breathed out. When it breathed in, it contracted. But that would contribute to the pattern, too.

Over the years, sitting at Crescent's loom and then her own, she'd thought a lot about the Fates, how they were said to guide souls. She had always thought it a metaphor, but now it made sense. The soul followed a path from birth to life to death, and the weft threads that crossed it connected it to other lives, other experiences, becoming the tapestry that was all their lives. A universe of lives.

The splicing didn't require as much blood, just skill, and she applied her Chaos magic to it, pulling the cut warp pieces up out of the snarled mess, re-fusing them hundreds at a time, bolstered by the energy Raina and Ruby sent her while they simultaneously kept an eye on what was happening around the cottage, any threat to Ruby's shielding.

When she got the warp done, she didn't give herself pause, plunging into felting the broken weft threads. Doing it with only her hands was too slow. She went sky clad, stripping down to bring the threads over her arms, her shoulders, letting them take the sips of blood they needed to reconnect them, and use her as the needed conduit back to their place on the Loom.

On the day she'd given Ruby and Raina that weaving lesson, she'd shown them a pattern could be changed with a touch, a pressure, a different thread.

On some looms, the piece that guided the weft thread through the warps was appropriately called a boat or shuttle. A flat piece of timber, a sword, helped spread out the upper and lower warps, forming the "shed" the boat passed through. She found it when she finished the warping, the golden gleam of the worn-to-silk-smooth wood resonating with an energy that said it had likely been donated by a tree of power at the beginning of time. But it was meant to do a job, and there was no time for ceremony. Even so, she kissed it, said a blessing, then swiftly inserted it back into the warp. Over under, over under.

"Something's coming."

Ruby's sharp tone drew her gaze briefly toward the open doorway. The rippling waters on the beach were getting choppy, the sky starting to darken above it. "Whatever wanted this destroyed knows we're trying to put it back together."

Ruby pointed to the scrying mirror. "In more hopeful news, those threads you just repaired and attached, I think a couple belonged to the souls about to take that final step. I saw them act like they woke up from a dream. Confused-looking, but very much alive. They turned away from The Pit, at least for now, though they still seem bonded enough to their Reaper they're not going far."

A promising sign that Mikhael and Derek's theory was correct. If they could reattach enough souls at a swift pace, the building of that momentum in the opposite direction the demon world wanted them to go might help the Reapers break the lock of those marks within them.

She had to redouble her efforts. Triple them. It was too much to hope her sisters wouldn't notice how that worked. Raina frowned and drew closer, reaching toward Ramona's arm, where a dozen threads shimmered. "Ramona, it's cutting your flesh."

"They need to make contact to talk to me, find their path." Blood was always the quickest way. Sacrifice.

She felt Raina hovering, wanting to say more, but then Ruby distracted her.

"Incoming," she snapped.

Ramona glanced toward the windows to see the darkness spawn a legion of monsters she'd seen in a nightmare.

"Soul Collectors," she said.

"Not today," Raina said grimly, but her gaze came back to Ramona.

"Ruby and I will hold them off, as agreed. You're the master weaver. But Ramona, don't…"

"I've got this." She thought of how the Collectors had mangled Silas. "Send them back to whatever hell they came from." She met Raina's eyes, then Ruby's. "Whatever happens, happens. We can't let them win."

Then she turned back to her task. She had to shut it all out, couldn't think about losing Silas, Ruby or Raina. As the two witches ran out the tall doorway, sealing it behind them with a solid thud that shuddered through the cottage, she poured her focus into the threads. Over and under, over and under. Keeping them steady, her energy guiding them to what they needed. The threads she repaired gave her the lives of hundreds, a split-second view of the world unfolding through their eyes before they left her body, looping through the air like slender, determined birds, diving down to weave themselves into the warp.

She hadn't found a boat, a shuttle of any kind, which made sense as tapestry looms often didn't use them. But in this case, its absence had told her the Fates did the weaving with the mind, using it or brief touches with their hands to make adjustments to the Loom as needed.

The threads flashed in and out, weaving the lives that had restarted. Their million stories, faces, eyes, laughter, tears, were in her head, against her flesh. She wiped blood off her hands, kept working. Stumbled and fell, got back up. Stumbled again.

When she dared a look toward the scrying pool, she cried out in despair as more souls went into The Pit. But she also saw a percentage of them milling, moving in different directions. Showing that confusion Raina had noted. But when her gaze shifted and the pool accommodated her with a wider view, her heart choked her.

Even at a distance, she knew him. He was getting closer to The Pit, and thousands of souls followed, spread out behind him like a sea of starlight. But he was carrying the crook, not the scythe. Evidence he was still fighting the mark's hold.

A glance toward the windows showed a storm raging outside. A flash of light revealed a Soul Collector, flying straight for the glinting glass, teeth bared, clawed hands outstretched as if it already had her in its grasp.

Raina intercepted it. Ramona bit back a cry as she risked physical contact, her hands upon it, the black tendrils of the beast covering her as they hit the ground, plowing up sand. Raina reared up, her fangs bared, vampire sharp. The succubus energy glowed, that wild passionate red. Before the creature could use its own debilitating power on her, she'd trapped its life force, was yanking on it, intending to shuck it like an oyster.

Usually Raina used her spell casting to fight a foe. She'd told them, *"My skills as a witch give me a creative armory. My main power as a succubus is fucking someone to death."* But in this instance, she'd brought the two abilities together to make her close combat skills even more impressive.

Ruby joined her, thrusting a wicked-looking long blade into the thing, stabbing with deadly precision and frightening speed until it broke contact with Raina and rolled away. Ruby leaped after it, cleaved its head from its batlike body. The Soul Collector's malevolent energy hadn't affected Raina. She'd already spun to throw an electrified net at another descending Soul Collector. It wrapped around it like barbed wire and tightened, slicing it into millions of pieces. Ruby took out three more Collectors with a concentrated spell that seemed intended to rearrange atoms.

They'd both learned from the diabolical fighting styles of their Guardian mates. A good witch used anything she could put in her arsenal.

As Ramona continued to weave, keeping contact with the threads, she looked back at the scrying pool. Her heart jumped. In just the few seconds she'd taken to seize those impressions, Silas's distance to The Pit seemed to have decreased by half.

With a wild, desperate noise, she threw herself back at the thread remaining. No more half measures. She called *all* the remaining threads in the corner to her. She dug down into the deepest levels of her consciousness, unleashed whatever reservoirs she could find there to connect to those souls, repair the threads, get them on the Loom.

On her own looms, if the weaving became longer than the loom, she fed the excess over a roller. Here, the excess shimmered in the air, disappearing as if through a doorway above the Loom. She could gauge how fast she was going by how quickly that excess was advancing.

Sparks of her magic flew through the air, swirling around her. Her tears of pain baptized the thread, adding to the blood staining them.

The barbed wire Raina had put around that Soul Collector felt like it was wrapped over every inch of Ramona's body. She wasn't crying because of that, though. She was crying because she had to do this right, to make it all work again, but every second it took, souls spilled over the ledge of The Pit, into the clutches of the Soul Collectors. Souls lost to the web, to the Loom, to how they might have influenced other threads in future lives. Gone forever.

No one had the right to do that.

Then there was the crime that would strike her even more personally. She wanted to know how Silas would change her own life, her path. She refused to let him be lost to her. Even if she had to give this life to ensure future possibilities, future path crossings, with his.

Silas was getting closer and closer to that Pit. She could feel it, in the way the bands on her wrists throbbed, in how her heart screamed with a pain greater than what was being slashed into her flesh.

There were three Fates for a reason. This was more than the job of one, even with the Loom and its pieces assisting as much as they could.

Help...need help, soon as you can manage it.

She didn't know how much time passed after she made that call, because that was becoming meaningless except as an hourglass of diminishing sand. Then Ruby and Raina burst through the cottage doors.

A hail-driven blackness concealed everything beyond the threshold. As they backed in, Ruby chanting a protection spell, clawed hands came through it to swipe at them. Raina shot an arc of fire above Ruby's gesturing hands, a starburst that gave Ruby the extra second to lock the spell in place. As something hit the protection wall with force, Ruby flinched at the impact but held, continuing to chant, her face a dispassionate mask, rigid like a knight's shield. Raina joined her voice to it, a weaving as intent and thorough as what was happening on the Loom behind them.

The doors slammed shut, the windows sealing, creating a fortress. "Fucking hell." Ruby let out a breath. "They've emptied the demon world on us."

Which meant they had to be doing something that would fuck up the bad guy plan. When Ramona had time to appreciate that, she would.

Both women had sustained damage. Ruby was limping and Raina had a wound in her side that had spilled an alarming amount of blood on her clothes, but she'd slapped a temporary seal on it.

"That'll hold for now," Ruby said, her expression intent, testing the shape of her shield, looking for weak points. "But we're going to need reinforcements before it's over."

"Mikhael and Derek will come as soon as they can. Or send other Guardians if they can't." Raina turned to Ramona, blanched. "Ramona."

They were beside her in an instant, as close as they could get. They couldn't touch her, but their worry was a physical contact, their alarm coursing over her like a tropical ocean wave. Her magic used the thought to send that sensation through the threads, which was a nice reassurance for them, even if she couldn't afford the indulgence.

"Tell us how to help," Ruby said urgently. "You have to get free."

"Can't." She was inside the maze of countless moving threads, passing around and through her as she fed them to the Loom. Reforming lives, their intended paths. The colors were incredible, more than she'd ever seen. So many lives and journeys resuming.

"This is...quickest way." Her gaze moved to Ruby then back to Raina, peered at them through that maze. "They're all...connected. The Reapers, the souls... We have to get it done. Silas. Have to do... what's necessary. Direct your energy toward the Loom. Help the threads keep moving, help the Loom...reinforce it."

She was going so fast now the threads were sometimes getting in one another's way, and the Loom was creaking at the force of the energy striking it, the plucking against the tension of the warp.

Though their concern pressed in on her, the frustration, they immediately complied. They stayed out of the path of the threads, but they directed power toward them and the Loom, steadying her guidance, giving the Loom strength.

A thunderous vibration shook the cottage. Ruby staggered, telling Ramona something had hit her shielding with force. Distantly, they could hear the howl of the Soul Collectors. Ruby and Raina had to break off, reinforce the shielding together.

Because the pain was getting too distracting, Ramona projected her spirit into the matter around her. She left her body standing in a growing pool of her own blood.

When she fully re-inhabited that form, she was going to hurt like a son of a bitch. Despair gripped her, knowing she was fooling herself about that, but that was okay, too. All those souls in the dark, crying out, she could hear them through the threads. Their fear. She remembered what Silas said, how he'd take them before the moment of death, if the fear got to be too much. He was gentle, her fierce Reaper.

The souls would remember none of this if she got it right. If they all got it right. A body was made up of all the elements, including Light. She could offer any and all of it to them. Every soul reattached meant one less in The Pit, and maybe, just maybe, if the energy reversal became strong enough, Silas and his fellow Reapers could break the demons' hold, retake control of the souls and restore them to their bodies.

"You're going to lose," she muttered through cracked lips.

Raina and Ruby's power was back, twining over hers as the threads left her, helping them get to the Loom, strengthening it. They offered her strength as well, though she diverted almost all of that to the souls. She thought of the two of them fighting the Soul Collectors. Warriors, witches, sisters. They knew death was not the worst thing a person could endure.

She managed glimpses of them while they did their part. Set jaws and determined eyes, windows to beautiful, enduring souls. Their command of craft was awe-inspiring. She felt so much love for them, her two sisters who had drawn her into their triangle, allowing it to become the stable force that could do this, give the world back to itself.

She hoped the Fates were okay. She hoped Mikhael and Derek had found them.

In the impressions of the lives lived by those threads, she caught flashes of what was important, the connections that were being woven back into the tapestry. As Raina adjusted the sword to push the wefts tighter together, she hoped those echo memories would hopefully be retained in the pattern, not lost.

The fabric continued to roll off the Loom, disappearing into that slash of light. Somewhere in all of this would be Jem's sweet lifeline.

Ramona couldn't contemplate Ruby returning to her son's lifeless body, knowing his soul was lost to The Pit. She wanted to say the Fates couldn't be that cruel, but that destiny had been taken from their hands. It was in her hands now. Hers, Ruby's and Raina's.

She thought of the boat her mother had put her in, to give her a chance to live her life. As she watched the threads weaving through the warp, she knew her mind was the boat. Just like the one that had carried her to Crescent, carrying her forward in her life, so she was doing the same for the souls. The ink on her wrists was concealed by blood, but she knew the words. *For only she that has my soul can engage my sword.* Her gaze slid to the sword, holding the warp open to make the weaving move faster.

Her Chaotic energy had expanded to cover everything. She didn't have to look toward the scrying pool's image anymore to tune into it; it was suspended in her head. The pool was a channeling tool only. At some point, she'd adopted the Fates' apparent ability to project what was happening in that pool into their minds, use it to set the pattern while keeping their attention on their task.

Silas was close enough to The Pit she could distinguish his tall, fine form. But something had changed. His cloak flapped, its ragged points snapping, a menacing expression of the male himself. The shepherd's crook was gone, his scythe so sharp even a look could cut.

That would have worried her, but his eyes weren't crimson. They were green, burning like hellfire. She imagined the tightness of his jaw, the way the muscles would flex when he was determined to prevail.

Her heart leaped. Her Reaper was digging in, fighting that mark, a battle of one against a force intending to break him for it. He was moving slower, dragging. A harrowing fifty feet from The Pit's edge, all those souls behind him, he dropped to a knee. She could smell the charring of bone as that mark burned into him, to force him to do its bidding.

No one forced her man to do anything. He'd endured The Pit to protect one single soul.

From the west, another Reaper was approaching The Pit, a multitude of souls on his heels as well. Silas's head rose, his eyes focusing on that advancing group.

Something dark twisted in the air around him. Then she realized he was doing it intentionally. Like a man grasping the enemy's blade embedded within him, suffering the pain to jerk it free with his bare hands, Silas siphoned that dark energy out of the mark. He pulled it into himself, to use for his own purposes. But dark energy could only be used for dark purposes, which was when she knew what he was going to do.

Oh, Goddess. Silas. Anguish ripped through her.

He crouched and sprang, hurtling through the air, covering the ground between him and the other Reaper.

The Reaper didn't look up. His mark had him solidly in its power, leading the souls toward that edge. The first line was mere steps away from the hungry flame.

Silas landed just past his fellow Reaper, rolled and came up on one knee, his head down, the scythe at his side. Gleaming with a golden-red wetness. The Reaper's body dropped inside its cloak. Such was the sharpness of the blade, the cowl had been severed with the head. The cloth-covered bundle bounced twice and rolled a few feet away.

Like a puppet's strings being cut, the souls were released. They stumbled, scattered. She bit back a cry as two accidentally fell into The Pit. They clawed at the sky, but no purchase existed on apathetic air.

Silas would have lunged for them, she was sure, but he couldn't do anything that close to the edge without bringing his souls with him. They were pushing against the scattered ones, trying to reach him. The numbers were great enough to herd released ones over the edge if they came too near it.

Silas had been given no respite from the mark. He remained hunched over, fighting it. The agony of killing a fellow Reaper might give him more strength to resist...or drain it away.

It had been a last resort. *You wouldn't have done it otherwise. Fight, Silas.*

Silas lifted his head, stared toward the souls, his grip on the scythe tightening. Then his gaze turned toward the east. Another Reaper was coming, moving ponderously toward that edge with souls in tow. *No.*

He couldn't fight what had him, but he'd recognized he could steal enough energy from it to stop the souls' advance. By killing his brethren. Eventually he would turn the scythe on himself, to protect the souls that only his will alone was keeping out of The Pit.

She gave herself to her magic, to its will. She offered it all her faith, no doubt, a belief that Chaos was the source of all creation, that it could ultimately make things right because no one could control it, not even a Chaos witch. She was merely the channel for it.

She thought of the Fates, here day after day, weaving those lives, the way it was meant to be. For all that people railed against their fate, the choices they were given or opportunities missed, or considered Chaos something to fear, Chaos served nothing but life and love itself. One just had to surrender oneself to it.

The way one surrendered to a Master. The way Silas had been teaching her she could trust him enough to do.

She remembered the Oscar Wilde story about the Nightingale, giving its heart's blood to create the perfect rose, a rose for a young man to give to his lover. In the story, the young man and his lover were both unworthy, oblivious to the momentous sacrifice that had gone into the gift, the preciousness of it. But the trees, the other animals, the wind and water, they all knew. They always knew, bearing silent witness to pain and joy, carrying it to the hearts that needed to hear its powerful song. Yet the most powerful part of it was delivered in silence, because words couldn't frame it.

She knew how to finish this. How to free the Reapers. Their soul lines were here as well. All of it was getting sharper, more obvious. A wrenching shriek came from her own soul as she called forth the effort. She brought all the remaining threads toward her at once, opened herself fully to them. The roof was getting taller and taller, as was the Loom, accommodating the cyclone of threads. All those brilliant colors. The threads slashed over her, barely pausing as they took what they needed and plunged toward the furiously working Loom.

Raina, Ruby...keep helping the Loom, the threads... Don't stop for anything.

She was almost all spirit now. Her body was lying on the floor, below the threads, her spirit dancing above it, twirling. She knew they could see her there.

Dance with me in the storm. I will never cause you harm. Trust me beautiful souls...

She glimpsed her sisters' faces, the knowledge in their eyes. Ruby's tears, Raina's broken expression. She thought she'd spent most of her life alone, but she'd never been alone at all. She had to give her heart to this, for Silas and the others. It was the purpose Crescent had told her to look for.

I was falling in love with him. I wanted to love him forever. I can love him forever. Love was the energy that could never be destroyed.

～

What he would give for silence. The mark's roar was like being trapped against a subway tunnel wall while the train passed. Plus the lament in his heart hadn't ceased since he'd taken Petruso's head. The two souls who'd toppled over the edge were more notes of pain. If he could use his other magical abilities, he could have caught them without having to physically approach the edge. But the only magic available to him was what he'd charged into his blade to kill a Reaper. The mark hadn't anticipated needing to prevent that.

Or that Silas could use his focus on stopping the Reapers to help him fight the will of the cursed mark. A dark purpose used against a dark purpose. His insides had become a battleground, the mark trying to torture him into taking his souls to the edge.

Fuck that. Those souls were his. They'd walk over the ash of his existence before going to that Pit.

Brenner was coming toward Silas, a benign army of souls behind him. His honorable brother, walking toward death.

Silas readied the scythe, grimly determined. Brenner would want him to do it. The alternative was unthinkable to any of them.

A thunderous noise, even louder than the roaring in his head, shook the ground, rolling up under his feet. It sent a painful vibration through the air, rippling the sky above in a sonic wave. The souls jittered with it, many stumbling or falling to the ground behind Brenner.

Everything stopped. The agony that exploded inside him was worse than anything so far. This was it, the end. The cry that tore from him seemed to come from some other creature. Maybe Brenner, because it looked like he was screaming, too.

Amid the delirium of pain, Silas managed to identify the source. The mark was digging in more ferociously than it had before, with a violence that suggested...desperation.

Something was pulling it free. Something determined as fuck, and it was working. The mark was weakening. His own magic was almost...within his grasp.

If he could lay hold of it for even a second, the mark might be weak enough he could Obliterate it and survive the experience, though the latter was no longer a priority. Opportunities offered during an apocalypse were a gut-instinct, few-seconds-window. Sometimes sticking a grenade into the enemy wrapped around you was the way to go. If nothing else, his souls would be safe from that Pit, long enough for his other brethren to hopefully regain control.

Grabbing the shaft of the scythe just below the blade, he twisted it around, shoved the tip at his chest. It went through his robe, between bone. He snarled the spell out loud, trying to give it every bit of leverage he could.

The magic activated, praise God and Goddess. And it felt exactly like he'd shoved a grenade under his rib cage.

Howling, hammering pain, then all went black. He swirled through it, insensible to everything but the smell of raisins, the brush of wavy, flame-red hair with touches of golden sunlight. Lavender eyes.

Then it all disappeared. A long pause. *The universe breathes in, breathes out. And when it breathes in, it contracts...*

Those words floated through his head. As he slowly regained awareness, of himself and his surroundings, he had the sense it had been a while, not a swift blackout. A lot of things had changed around him. Or maybe he was somewhere else entirely.

He was lying flat on his back, arms and legs spread wide as if he'd been flung. But he felt the comforting hardness of his scythe's handle in his grip. It was the only comforting thing. Everything else was painful, including breathing.

He couldn't get up. He needed to get up, to see if the souls were all right. If Brenner was. He'd also have to think about what he'd done. What he'd failed to do. Who they'd lost.

The knowledge was there, threatening to swamp him, and he couldn't afford to be overwhelmed. Not yet.

Souls often used denial as a coping tool for the agony of change and loss. He'd see if it would work for a Reaper.

A hand gripped his shoulder, a flood of Light energy accompanying it. As it swept through him, he could feel the unimpeded flow of it. The mark was gone, a relief he seized with both hands. The Light energy chased out any residuals, helping his immortal body heal the damage it had done, and he'd done to himself, getting rid of it.

"How do you feel?"

"Like a bug crushed by an anvil." He wasn't sure how long it took him to reply. The words came out hoarse.

"Mikhael is helping your friend," He recognized Derek's voice. Ruby's mate. Light Guardian. "Give yourself a minute. That mark was damned determined to take you with it."

"The souls…"

"We can't see them, but your friend said most appear to have been drawn back to their bodies."

Silas tried to lift his head, but it took the courteous strength of Derek's palm cupping it to help him look. The gathering of souls was down to a milling handful. Still confused, needing additional guidance to get back to their bodies—he needed to deal with that—but no more Pit.

The opening to the demon world had seemed to sit on a vast wasteland, but that had been illusion, to minimize distractions. A rift could be opened almost anywhere. They were actually at the lower end of a Walmart parking lot. Silas lay on the grass behind an eighteen-wheeler with a Dunkin' Donuts logo, and an RV with a map of the United States on its bumper. The driver had been to all but five states.

Between the two vehicles, he could see the rest of the lot. The store was having a sale on bedding plants. The cheerful array of nodding blooms rested under a vast white pavilion. People were shopping. They couldn't see him, the Guardians, or the confused souls.

The view was surreal. It confirmed that the reset had left the human world mostly oblivious to the near catastrophe. Until they became aware of the souls that hadn't been saved.

A woman dancing in zebra sneakers, her hair a ripple of gold. Her gaze, seeing so much. Always a little sad. He'd thought that was because of how alone she'd often been. He thought now it was because of how deeply she understood the power she'd been given.

He put his head against the ash wood of his scythe. Derek's hand tightened on his shoulder.

"You found the architect of this, then," Silas said, before the Light Guardian could speak.

"We did. You were right. It was a former Reaper." Derek helped him up, kept a light hand on Silas's shoulder as the world righted itself. "The Fates were found. They were already halfway to figuring out how to release themselves, but thanked us courteously for our help. Before returning to their island."

He could feel it, in the restoration of the communications conduits Reapers used to know the Fates' will. The Reapers who had survived were out there, connected to him as they'd been before the insidious possession mark. They were like those remaining souls, disoriented but figuring it out.

Maybe like him, they weren't eager for full awareness. The Reapers who'd been destroyed in The Pit might have been granted a mercy, instead of having to wake up to how many of those in their charge had been lost.

Silas stared at the flowers. His scythe seemed the only stable force in his universe, so he kept holding it. "The women, the witches, they did it."

"They did," Derek said quietly. "The Fates chose well. When they restored enough souls to reverse the tide, it broke the strength of the sorcerer's mark and destabilized the demon power reinforcing it. That earthquake you might remember feeling was The Pit being resealed, and the demons responsible being shut back in it. Our fellow Guardians also sealed the rift that gave the demon world access to the Isle."

"Good. We'll take steps to ensure it will never be that vulnerable again." From here forward, the Reapers would also serve as the Fates' personal guard. Everyone needed someone to watch their back. Evil was always watching.

You killed a Reaper. You almost took Brenner's head. Marching toward the Pit, he'd watched at least four more drop into the fire. Including Honora. How many had they lost? How many souls?

"Silas." Brenner was beside him. Silas frowned as he dropped to a knee, bowing his head.

"What are you..."

"You are Wake commander now. My lord." The Scotsman's voice held a wealth of pain.

Silas stared at him. A storm still roared in his ears, but it came from his own soul, not that cursed mark. Stiffly, he put a hand on

Brenner's shoulder. When the other Reaper rose, they gazed at one another.

For his very first act as Wake leader, Silas would give himself, Brenner and the other Reaper survivors a way to exorcise their pain, spill it from their hearts like blood.

"The souls lost were far more than Collectors can consume at once," he said. "Our Wake will lead an extraction. If there are souls to retrieve, we will do so."

As Brenner stared at him, Silas knew he was thinking what they'd all been taught. *Never go into The Pit. Never enter the demon world.* Well, fuck that. The demon world was a place, which meant it was navigable. He'd been there,. And this time he wouldn't be alone, one against many.

"I will gladly rip souls out of their gullets." The Scotsman was on board. His eyes brimmed with grief he was trying to suppress. Eventually there would be no tasks left, and they would all have to face the enormity of what Silas also refused to think about right now.

He turned to Derek. "Would you and those fellow Guardians care to accompany us?"

"Try to keep us away." Derek made that grim declaration as Mikhael joined them.

"I can take you to the best entry point from the Underworld side," the Dark Guardian added.

"Good." Reapers were materializing around Silas, responding to his silent call. He didn't have to look to know who was there. And who wasn't.

"Silas, do you wish—" Derek spoke.

"No." Sparks shot off his scythe, sending a ripple of tension through the Reapers. He had risen from the ground in human form, but in the space of that half-asked question, he'd gone to his full Reaper form again. He felt as stripped down as that skeleton made him appear. "We do what we need to do now. The rest is for later."

He spoke to the Reapers. "We follow the Dark Guardian to the best entry point of the demon realm. Once we accomplish what is possible, we rendezvous at our usual spot. Then we grieve and determine what remains to be done. Yes?"

As the Reapers nodded, Silas turned toward Derek. "Forgive me for not asking," he said in a measured tone. "Is your son well, Light Guardian?"

"He is," Derek responded carefully. "Thank you. He is with his mother."

"All is as the Fates will it." Silas paused. "The witches have done the world a great service. You are fortunate males. Lead us when you are ready, Dark Guardian."

When he turned away to speak to Brenner and several of the others, Mikhael met Derek's somber gaze. "He knows."

"He's locked it down, because to let it loose would paralyze him," Derek said, low.

"Our women are going to need us." Mikhael's expressionless voice spoke volumes. "They need us now."

"They'll understand he needs us more. As do those souls."

Silas was obviously already gripping the reins of leadership, giving direction and reassurance. A lifeline for himself, as much as the rest. "The sorcerer was wrong," Mikhael commented, watching him. "Our witches give as much of themselves to keep the world safe as we do, and trust the powers the Goddess gave them to carry on. They expect us to remain defenders of this world, no matter what is taken from us...or them. So none of us dishonor what, or who, is lost."

"As Silas said, we are fortunate men." Derek tightened his grip on his staff. "Let's go help him. Then we go to our women. I want to hold my son."

CHAPTER EIGHTEEN

*I*mmortality's bounce-back time could be jarring, how quickly one was restored to normal strength. Even after a traumatic possession experience that could have landed him in the clutches of an Underworld fire that burned his essence back to a mote in the collective unconscious.

It felt like there should be a pause, a gathering of one's composure, something that marked how potentially disastrous the experience had been.

But no. The sun was shining on another day. The vast majority of the world had resumed without any awareness of what had happened, waking up from darkness as if they'd merely taken a power nap. Yet as Silas had predicted, a terrible number of beings had been found simply expired, no real explanation. They'd recovered many, but almost a third of the souls who'd dropped into The Pit had been consumed. Lost to the Loom forever.

They'd cut a bloody swath in the demon world, administering a grim lesson. The Reapers and Guardians had made a formidable purpose-driven army. Still, the loss of that one-third made it an empty victory.

When someone died, those left behind often felt that spirit near them for a certain amount of time. Even when the soul had passed through The Gate, the emotional impressions they left on a loved one formed an echo that lingered, a song whose music still vibrated around and through them.

A woman chanting seemingly nonsensical rhymes, her image dancing in his peripheral vision, hair shimmering around her like a cloak as she turned. Like the wind itself.

His Wake was at the rendezvous point, Gettysburg. He'd been at that Reaping, the terrible battle that had happened well over a century ago. All the confused souls, emerging from mostly young bodies. It was an appropriate spot, since the Reapers there today were trying to make sense of what had happened, deal with their own losses.

Honora. He held the name in his head, let it pass through all of them, a silence surrounding it to pay tribute to her. He would miss her for a long time.

His Reapers looked across the field at him. The blade of his scythe gleamed a clean blue-gold as always, but his robe bore the symbols of a Wake commander.

Honora had often seemed so impassive, but being a Reaper required a concentrated and balanced amount of compassion, empathy, anticipation, wisdom and justice. An appropriate dismissal of self. A Reaper leader required even more of that.

Emotion expressed too overtly is an expression of ego. A declaration of "look at me, notice me." Is there anything more useless? Self-absorption is an oversaturated sponge, taking away awareness of the world unfolding around you. That awareness transforms one into a vessel capable of handling anything, keeping perspective, and ensuring your unconditional love for all souls is always within reach.

He honored her, grieved her. But he wasn't reviewing her early lessons because of that. He was sorting through them as a meditative exercise, hoping to find what he needed.

She'd told him he too often let his emotions rule him.

The normal Reaping schedule had resumed. The Fates were back in their place. There were many to thank for that. No war was won with only one person, but by reattaching the threads to the Loom, using her Chaos magic to do the impossible, Ramona had restarted the Loom, and her sisters had helped get the Pattern back on track. Countless lives had been pulled away from The Pit.

She'd paid for it with her life.

Honora's loss had staggered him. The souls lost to The Pit, those they couldn't recover, skewered him like a hundred spears, and they'd haunt him for a thousand sleepless nights. As would the many hours they spent in that hellish place, searching every corner, fighting Soul Collectors and whatever else that world could throw at them.

The worst and most hopeless emotions had congregated in that realm, the beings that inhabited it soaked in despair, hatred, malevolence, greed and rage. The choking smoke and stinking sulfur smell would forever be curdled in his gut. Plus the memory of that ceaseless white noise roar which seemed to come from nowhere, but was capable of stealing a stone's sanity. All of it, never ending.

Just like loss, loneliness and grief itself could seem.

They'd stayed until they were certain they hadn't missed a single surviving soul. They'd lost six Reapers, but this time it was in the cause of fighting to rescue souls. And a message had been sent.

A Collector normally had no desire to fight with or capture a Reaper. It had always been more of a competition, since a Collector couldn't get at the soul until it was rising. Not without magical help, like Bryan had provided.

It would be a long time before that realm tried to fuck with souls or Reapers again. If anything from the demon world came after souls in the future, they'd have no retreat point. The Reapers wouldn't be stopped by any threshold in the effort to retrieve them.

This Wake had a new kind of leader. From what he'd picked up from the Cast leadership, the other commanders felt the same.

When he returned from the demon realm, he'd made a direct request to the top ranks. Though, in his mind, it hadn't been a request.

He'd never Reaped the soul of a Reaper, because Reapers handled their own endings. But not in this case. Upon arriving at that desolate bunker, Silas wasn't sure if his intent was to help with that end. But when he found Bryan's soul, still curled up inside his rotting body, staring at a blank wall, Silas had thought of Ramona.

He'd thought about her holding the wax heart, telling the customer that melting it would soften her own heart, a vital step in doing the same for the spell's target.

Bryan had been driven mad by the loss of his soulmate. Silas had never realized the depth of his desire to find his own, until he'd believed Ramona was it, and then found out she wasn't. He supposed the Fates were kind in that way, because if that longing for one made itself known too early, took over the heart the way she had his, a Reaper might lose his or her purpose, seeking it.

But Bryan had found and lost it. And Silas was looking at the results. *No.* The result for one soul. One soul driven by its own pattern on the Loom. Silas pulled that thought to him, Honora's wisdom. But it wasn't until he thought again of Ramona, the things she'd said to him, that he was able to look into the true depths of Bryan's battered life energy.

The magic of Chaos rested in letting go of everything, every scrap of control, even the deceptive and fleeting control of vengeance. He would do no harm to this pale, sickly being.

"When everything of value we have, all that matters, is taken from us, why must we take anything more from one another?" Silas said quietly.

The sorcerer stared at him, and Silas could almost see the erratic pounding of the broken heart, the rundown state of it since the day Bryan had learned of his past, lost all that made his present and future worthwhile. His heart had been bleeding poison instead of grief, the grief hoarded inside.

"Good-bye, brother." Silas took up the scythe and cleaved the soul open. The Reaper's energy spilled out, a wavering, drifting mist that filled the narrow, dank room. Silas moved into the sorcerer's study, sat down on the battered desk chair, watched until his very last essence vanished. Perhaps it would find and cleave to other Reaper energies, like Honora's. Find healing, a way to redemption.

It was said that hatred and revenge brought nothing but more hatred and revenge, and forgiveness brought peace. He knew the first part was right, but he sure as hell didn't feel peace. Silas still had that one task left. He'd willingly accept any torment to put it off.

It didn't have to be his job. Even now, alongside the edge of the Gettysburg battlefield, Brenner drew him out of his contemplation. The Scotsman was his new right hand, as Silas had been to Honora. Brenner didn't speak his offer as he'd done the couple times before. But he showed it in his proximity. Silas only had to give him a single gesture, and he would take the burden.

His witch would never forgive him for that. He'd kept her waiting for three days, known where she was at all times. She had no fear as some souls did. She'd made good use of her time—spending part of a day with Buford and her animals, drifting to favorite places she'd known in her lifetime. Gone to the river where her mother had left her and where she'd washed the ash of her pixie family off her. But time was getting short. No Reaper would let it go beyond three days unless the soul was a wanderer, approved to be a ghost for a time.

She wasn't.

He hadn't put it off because he didn't want to see her. He wanted to see her more than anything he'd ever wanted in his centuries of life. It was knowing that when he saw her, the clock would start ticking toward the end. Same as for all ephemeral life.

He looked at Brenner, shook his head. "Resume your duties. Life and death go on as they must."

Honora had told him that countless times. They were a front row witness to it every day. It always went on. It didn't care how much things hurt.

His tone sounded flat to him, an emotionless response. Love at its deepest core, when taken away, was the same kind of darkness as any other, leaving no energy to give to anything other than the pain. It made him wonder if Honora had suffered more losses in her lifespan than any of them knew. But unlike Bryan, she had turned that into a life of service, of love. He would honor and serve her memory, honor and serve Ramona, the way both women deserved. No matter what it cost him.

"So we saved the world. Not something most people ever get to say."

It was the first thing she said to him.

He found her at the Tomb of the Unknown Soldier, watching the sentinel slowly pace the twenty-one steps. It was a woman this time. Tall and straight, about five-ten in height. One billion, six hundred thirty-eight million, four hundred twenty-two thousand and eighty-six heartbeats. Eighty-five, eighty-four... She'd drown in her eighties, rescuing a man who'd fallen into a river. She'd be hiking, almost as tall and strong as she looked now.

Ramona sat under the tree where they'd had their picnic. She looked much as she always did, telling him just how comfortable and confident, how closely she had bonded to her identity, in her most recent life. Just as he'd anticipated. it was her truest self, the Chaos witch who'd drawn him into that life, accepted him there. A purple skirt with green sequined embroidery fluttered around her ankles, her arms loosely linked around her knees.

Her hair was that beautiful fire-hued red, like it had been the memorable night in her attic. The wind rippled it over her back like fall leaves as she rested her temple on her knees, gazed at him with her large lavender eyes. All she needed were wings to look like the Fae who'd raised her.

He sat down next to her. She slipped her hands around his upper arm, put her cheek to his shoulder. The contact, the wonder of it, made him shudder deep inside. He closed his hand over hers, unable to speak. She continued, covering the pregnant silence.

"Of course, people save someone's world every day. They just don't know they've done it. Like that commercial where the person grabs someone's arm to keep them from stepping out when the light changes, because they see a car is still coming." Her fingers tightened on him. "Or listens to someone when they really need to be heard, before everything inside them blows up. Or when someone consciously doesn't step on a bug."

She stroked her hand up and down his arm, over his forearm, fingers briefly tangling with his before she stroked upward again. He sat under her touch like a statue, suffering, unable to move, but savoring her touch like fire devouring its fuel.

"Crescent told me that. Pixies being so small, a carpenter ant was the size of a guinea pig to us. She said size isn't significance. Just because I'm so much bigger doesn't mean I should think it's okay when I step on a bug and squash it. She said 'What if the Powers That Be felt that way?'"

"What did you say?" He pushed the response through emotions so thick the words came out heavy, ragged. She touched his face. He didn't look at her, but felt her fingertips slide over his cheek, down to his jaw, following the tears that were making silent, bitter tracks.

"I was not in a good place. I missed my mother, felt abandoned, even though I knew my mother hadn't had much choice. I said how do you know the Powers That Be *don't* feel that way? Because it seems things get regularly squashed every day, as if they don't matter."

Ramona put her head on his shoulder again. Pressed her face against it. A gesture that told him she was feeling things just as large and overwhelming as he was. "She said for some things, there's no point believing the possible darker truth. Doing that just keeps you from doing good in the world. Making others happy."

He wanted to turn to her, hold her, but that would make things more difficult. He wanted to be inside her once more, and that would make it impossible to survive.

"I'll miss these conversations," she said.

Now at last, he looked at her face. So lovely and earnest. He wished he could block the overlay, but it was there. When they'd first emerged from the demon realm, he'd gone to Raina's. They'd taken her there, prepared the body to lay out for three days, in the old tradition. Raina and Ruby's spellwork kept her in stasis, like Snow White. Only instead of a glass coffin, this was a mist of energy that didn't prevent him from grasping her hand, though the lifeless cool stillness of it was terrible to him.

They'd cleaned her up, but grooves had spiraled over her limbs, her throat, everywhere flesh was visible. Badges of honor, evidence of how she'd opened herself to the souls. Her blood had drained onto the floor of the Fates' cottage, her flesh torn and sacrificed to bring the world back to order. She'd ultimately died of blood loss and internal injuries caused by the depth of those wounds.

Those grooves had dug into her wrists, but above and below the words. They were still there. Which meant how she'd felt for him had preserved them to the very last breath.

He'd put his forehead to hers, held her body close, but he was too much of a Reaper. He knew she wasn't here. This body, lovely as it had been, and no matter the joy it had given him, had drawn him because of the soul inhabiting it.

When he'd lifted his head, Ruby's tears were reabsorbing the salt of those that had already dried on her face. Raina was a tearless witch, but all her pain was in her eyes, in the choking agony he felt from her. He was glad they had Mikhael and Derek, plus all the incubi and succubi who pressed close to both women, ready to comfort them, help them through the grief of losing their bonded trinity.

He couldn't lay her back on the table. He just couldn't. Ruby understood, coming forward and letting him slip Ramona into her arms. Raina came to her other side, steadied her body as he stepped back.

"Buford. Her animals...Curtis."

"All her animals are coming to live here," Raina assured him in a raw voice. "Li and Gina are going to organize a barn building. The boy that just started helping her, Derek met him. We'll take care of him."

"Buford is having a hard time," Ruby said. "As all familiars do. But we'll help him."

Silas managed a nod. "I'll escort her soul to The Gate on the third day. I expect she will want to linger, touch each of you in some way, give you a remembrance of her spirit."

Then he'd fled. No other word for it.

But here, on the third day, she'd come to one of his favorite places. She'd been sure he'd be strong enough, that he wouldn't abdicate the right to be the one to escort her.

There were no guarantees with reincarnation. A soul subconsciously knew what it needed to be and do. That might not include him in a subsequent life, though their connection was strong enough he had no doubt they would see one another again. He just didn't know if it would be the next life or centuries from now. He wasn't sure he could bear that thought.

"Of course, how do we really know if we save a life?" she asked thoughtfully, still on the same thread. "Plenty of people believe the day you die is written down somewhere and nothing changes that. Seems like I spent an eternity reweaving those threads. Each one had a certain length. They also didn't break, become any shorter. Except..."

Her breath hitched. "The ones who were pulled out of their bodies and taken into that Pit. Their thread burned black and then dissolved, as if they'd never existed. How many..." She was holding a terrible pain over it, one with a throbbing echo in himself.

"Don't." He brought her into his lap. Oh, Lord and Lady. To hold her was Heaven and Hell together. He tried not to crush her with the fierceness of his grip. He'd told her he'd protect her, care for her. Despite feeling he'd failed in that, he wouldn't back away from this. "The numbers are far less than they would have been if you and your coven sisters hadn't done what you did. We were able to recover more as well."

"I couldn't go see Ruby and Raina. I just couldn't."

"There is a reason there is a Veil between the living and the..."

"Dead," she finished, and his arms constricted around her. "So that we don't hang around too long and they don't hold on so tight they don't live their lives. It's the danger of the Mirror of Erised. The Harry Potter books—"

"I've read Harry Potter."

She smiled. "You're really a soft-hearted nerd. Even if you are scary and badass with your oversized knife and that kill-someone-with-a-look thing."

"Don't tell anyone I'm a soft-hearted nerd. I'm in charge of the Wake now."

"You'll be excellent at it." She swallowed, a little tremor going through her. "Ruby and Raina... Do they seem all right to you? No lingering effects from the Isle?"

"They are well. They will grieve you deeply, but they'll have each other. And their mates."

A little sob took her, sharing their pain. "Can we...can we be together one more time, Silas? You and me? Would it be too hard for you?"

He hadn't expected it until she said it, and then he knew it made complete sense. Because as difficult as it would be, he wanted it, too. He lifted his head, and when she turned her face to him, he put a hand with its own tremor against the softness of her cheek. "It is a pain I will willingly bear," he told her roughly

It didn't matter they'd met and known one another in his life for a blink of time in the reckoning of the universe. They'd been shown one previous life where their paths had crossed. A horrible one, but he believed there'd been more. It was the only thing that explained the depth of this loss.

Rising, he took her hand, guided her away from the Tomb. He was afraid to use a portal, afraid it would pull them closer to the inevitable destination they had to face, so he went to a part of the park where another group of trees gave them privacy. No one could see them, even as they stood in plain view, so it was for them, the lack of distraction. The grove screened the outside world from them.

She turned to face him. "Take control," she said softly. "Show me I belong to you."

"If that's what you want." He pushed past the ache in his throat to claim that role with both hands. It was there, as it always was with her. "Ask me. Don't tell me."

Her soul trembled in his hands. "Please," she said softly.

He removed her shirt, pushed the skirt down to her ankles and she got rid of the sneakers. "Odd, to have clothes in this form," she said.

"The soul is just another expression of who you are," he said. "Until now, you needed and wanted clothes."

Because of that, if she'd simply desired to be naked, they would have faded away, but often a soul wanted to hold onto the familiar act of removing them. Since that transition helped keep her on this plain, he wasn't arguing with it. He didn't remove his yet, reinforcing the reminder she wanted.

He put his hand to the side of her throat, a squeezing pressure to hold her in place as he took her mouth. The pleasure of it was an agony, and he countered that with a fierceness, showing her how much she meant to him.

The kiss was a branding, demanding everything from her with tongue and teeth. She met that with full, sweet surrender, leaning into him, trying to get even closer. Her hands were on his upper arms, nails biting into his biceps, then shifting to hold onto his back as he cinched an arm around her waist and took her to the ground, putting himself between her legs.

He stripped himself of his clothes, the robe over them, but he sensed she was cold. That happened, when the mortal life was seeping away from the soul. So he draped the robe over them, let it fall on either side of her as he brought his bare body fully against hers, every inch of its heat against her coolness.

Her hands on him had the strength of desperation, and he would take that, fuel that energy with his own. He shoved into her, brutal, but he already knew she was damp, ready for him. She had been, the moment he'd demanded that she ask. She needed to be able to surrender to his control. Something she'd never had her entire life, until the two of them came together.

The surge of emotions he felt translated right to her mind, because when she was pure soul energy, they could do that. *I can no more explain why your surrender is so important to me, why I feel the fierceness of the conqueror, the need to protect you, than...*

Than I can explain why I want and desire to be conquered by you, why I feel safe with you, everything I am held within your grasp. Her thoughts finished the rest. She stared up at him.

"I don't give a damn where you go," he told her. "You will never stop being mine." To prove it, he grasped her wrist, showed her. Even in her soul form, the ink was there, the ribbons coming to life to spiral over her arms, glowing with the power he gave them. They'd burn their way into her soul's body. She'd carry them into whatever life she next inhabited. When they found one another again, he would recognize those marks on her soul.

And hope the Fates would be kind enough to let her recognize him.

They portaled to The Gate in silence. The route was sometimes the same, sometimes different. In her case, he wasn't surprised it was different. A soaring route through clouds, like a bird riding the wind currents. A spin through a rainbow, so they felt the energy, were splattered by the rain droplets that had created it.

A brief touchdown in a field of purple wildflowers, startling a trio of deer, and then they were passing a bridge of light. She gazed off the edge of it, seeing forms in the far distance, against a broad glittering band like a river. Her hand was in his, hadn't let go. Then she tensed as they passed through the final barrier.

He understood her trepidation, since everything became dark. But then The Gate appeared in the distance, drawing them forward. He held her hand as they walked toward it, following a path invisible yet solid beneath their feet. They were only energy here, but the need to make sense of it created substance. He'd seen the surroundings become a horse pasture, a snow-topped mountain. Even a bingo hall, The Gate a curtained doorway at the back.

For a witch like Ramona, it was no surprise The Gate appeared close to its true form, framed by an arch of ancient stone, vines growing over the rough surface. The tall doors of solid oak had a carving of a tree on them, with spreading branches and a thick, detailed canopy of leaves.

He brought her to a stop a few feet from it. As he stared down at their joined hands he knew, just like when he'd held her body at Raina's, he couldn't let her go. Realizing it as a truth he'd have to turn his back on didn't change it.

Immortals had a complicated relationship with time. Some things came around again and again, such that they viewed them the way a person did the beeping of their alarm clock on Tuesday, after going through the same cycle on Monday. But other things were like being stuck on that precipice of the sun rising and never seeming to move forward, straining for the light to come.

"Fuck it," he said suddenly. "Why should Fate decide you're my soulmate? What if I feel it, in my heart, in my soul? We've assumed its Fated. How do we know it's not us changing the color of the thread, making that decision at the fork of the road?"

The glint of tears in her eyes had the brilliance of that sun spilling over the horizon. "Thank Goddess," she said. "I was hoping you'd figure that out."

At his startled look, her lips tugged in a painful smile. "Isn't it possible both things are true?" she asked gently. "The Reapers couldn't see my death because I'm a Chaos witch, but *you* couldn't because I *am* your soulmate?"

He'd never felt like an idiot standing in front of The Gate, but then, Ramona had brought him a lot of firsts. He held both her hands, thumbs rubbing against her wrists. "Why didn't you say anything?" he said at last.

"Because you're the centuries-old one. If you didn't come to that conclusion, my say-so wasn't going to change your mind. I hoped, though." Her eyes filled with tears again, and she clutched his shoulders. "I feel it pulling me. I don't want to go. Oh, God, Silas, I don't want to leave you. I can't bear the wait to find you again. I feel like I waited forever, and when I saw you, when you held me, I knew I would never be alone again. I wanted to believe that so much. That's the cruelest thing about this, and all of it is cruel."

He pressed his face in her hair. He would be strong. He would be the Master she needed him to be. "I've lived a long time, and never realized that empty place inside me had someone waiting to fill it. I just accepted it being empty. You will never leave it, Ramona. You're there. You're part of me. We will bear it. We will find one another again."

"And maybe you'll be less clueless this time," she snuffled against his shoulder.

"Maybe," he agreed, the laughter too jagged for him to manage it. He just held her closer. But he could feel the tug, too. It wasn't going to lessen...or get any easier.

He moved them two steps closer, so he was still holding her, but she could reach out, touch the panel, all that was needed for entrance. She would be pulled out of his arms, but that was the way he wanted it. He wanted whatever lay on the other side of that door to know he'd held onto her as determinedly as he could, until the very last moment.

"I can't," she said. "I can't do it."

He summoned all the willpower he had to do the unimaginable. What a Reaper was meant to do, that had to be done, for the world to be what it was supposed to be, no matter his own feelings. He closed his hand around her wrist, gentle but firm.

For only she that has my soul... He felt the texture of the words under his grasp.

He stretched their arms out together, side by side, and held her palm just above the surface of The Gate. The tree canopy disappeared, the entry becoming a wall of silver-blue water, readying itself for her passage. Ripples would glide out from her fingers when she touched it, the energy tingling through them both. But he wouldn't be able to follow her.

Her gaze was on his face, her hand gripping his neck. She had a leg wrapped around his hip. She felt the same way he did. They would be ripped apart, because neither one would accept a passive parting. Whatever witnesses there were to a life, she wanted them to understand what he meant to her, what saving the world had cost her, though neither of them would have done anything differently.

He kissed her with all that feeling, all his desire. He was glad he'd had her soul, had that ability to mark his claim on her in spirit as well as flesh. Wherever she went, she would hold onto that, know he considered her his. And he was hers. All hers.

As he kissed her, he brought her palm to that transient surface, let the liquid energy ripple over their joined flesh. He braced himself for it, deepened the kiss, if that was possible, held her tighter, though he was ready to let the grip slip before it could harm her soul.

"Silas," she spoke against his lips, a whisper. "What's happening?"

He lifted his head, and what he felt, what he saw, had his brow creasing.

Nothing. Nothing was happening.

After a long moment, Ramona offered him a tremulous smile through her tears.

"Did you forget to bring the key?"

"The debate has raged since the beginning of time. How much of its path is chosen by the soul, and how much by the random Chaos of the pattern? I expect no one will ever know. A question with a ready answer, a story without unexpected twists, is as boring to the author as it is to the reader."

Silas turned quickly, putting Ramona behind him, but in the same instant, he recognized the voice. Dropping to a knee, he bowed his head. His movement drew their tangled hands away from The Gate, but he didn't release Ramona. He couldn't, not even to pay proper respects to the Fate approaching them.

Her hair, a mix of gold and brown, lay thick and wild over her shoulders, draping over a substantial bosom. She wore a tiara shaped like the tree of life, the trunk studded by blue stones. Her green robe flowed into colors of blue sea and golden-red flame together at the hem and open draped sleeves, where gold rings adorned her strong hands. Gray eyes the color of storms washed waves of crackling power over Silas and Ramona.

She went by the name of Asherah. She wasn't the actual Asherah, but a manifestation honoring the Goddess energy the name represented. Her two Fate sisters were the same, calling themselves Astarte, goddess of passion, and Anath, the warrior goddess. An alliteration trinity.

Like Ramona, Ruby and Raina.

Asherah inclined her head to Ramona. "You have our thanks, Chaos witch. It was not intended that you would serve as a Fate so early, and yet you met the challenge bravely and with no regard for your own survival." Her gaze flicked to The Gate. "Obviously. There are many threads on the Loom that will carry your blood. Those souls you saved should have interesting lives to watch."

A shadow crossed her expression. "A life is a thread of incredible fragility and resilience. When it passes through our hands, we feel the texture of it." She met Ramona's gaze. "As a weaver, you understand that."

"Yes, my lady." Ramona had dropped to her knees beside Silas. A witch would always recognize and honor a manifestation of the Lord or Lady.

"I can even tell how long or brief a life will be, when nothing unexpected interferes." Asherah's broad face was somber. "As it has."

"Are the consumed souls forever lost?" Silas asked quietly, need and responsibility surfacing as a spoken wish.

Her expression turned even more thoughtful. "It is an unknown. But I expect time will share that, if we keep our minds to it. Reapers, Guardians, Fates...plus the wishes from the hearts who connected to those souls, in this life or the next. My presence here is not to address that."

She lifted her hands, showed them a strand of energy. Like wool becoming thread, it spun itself out over her fingers, narrowing. As Asherah spread out her hands, palms facing a foot apart, that thread began to go back and forth, back and forth, weaving in and out over her knuckles.

Silas noticed Ramona's gaze had stilled on the motion. Slowly, she rose to her feet, her hand caressing his before she let go, moving toward the Fate. As Silas stood, she took another step. When Asherah sent him a meaningful glance, he forced himself to remain where he was.

"She will come to no harm from me, Reaper," the Fate said, her voice holding the strength and power of the Earth, but the tenderness of a mother as well.

Because as Ramona got closer, their relative sizes changed. So did Ramona's age. By the time she reached Asherah, she was a small child, perhaps the age she'd been when her mother had to abandon her to the river. Asherah was ten feet tall. She dropped to one knee, leaning forward and extending her hands with the thread woven over them.

"Do a cat's cradle," Ramona's childish voice insisted.

Asherah smiled. The grey world around them brightened, and they were in a meadow. Silas could still feel The Gate behind him. Pulsing. Waiting.

Asherah twisted the threads over her large fingers until it formed the bow-like shape. Ramona held out her hands.

Asherah's gaze went to Silas. "You know this game?"

When he shook his head, she explained. "The task is to transfer the weaving to another's hands, without breaking the pattern. Children hold all the secrets to the universe, you know. Aware of it without question or analysis, a blessing they leave behind far too soon, though it always lies within them. A Chaos witch keeps it closer than most."

Everything within him stilled. The possible import was too fragile. He didn't dare speak it in his mind.

As a child, Ramona had the same thinness she'd carried into adulthood. A waif who would blow away in a good wind, except she enjoyed that wind on her own terms, choosing to fly or hold fast to the earth with the deep roots of her will.

Carefully, her small fingers tunneled under the threads on Asherah's. As she managed the transfer to her own hands, her fingers changed, as did the rest of her body. When the task was done, an adult Ramona stood facing Asherah, both human-sized again.

Asherah's ancient eyes held pain and joy, the mix that made life what it was. "You gave the world back to itself. In return, the Loom is giving your life back to you, the way it was intended to be lived."

Reaching out, she cupped Ramona's face, stroked. "You and your sisters will come to us again. When our time is over, you will become the Fates, transitioning to immortal lifespans."

At Ramona's look of shock, Asherah raised a bold stroke of a brow. "It makes sense, does it not? Why else would all three of you be mated to immortals?"

She turned to Silas, the glint in her gaze hinting at the woman she'd been before she'd become a Fate. "She was correct, about how clueless even immortals can be. If your heart said you and she belonged to one another from the beginning, nothing should have convinced you otherwise. We know much, but only a soul knows its own heart."

He executed a silent bow, that heart too full to form words.

Asherah kissed Ramona's forehead, then she turned and walked away. The meadow vanished, and she walked a path of blue-silver water much like the transitioning substance of The Gate. She faded into it, a ripple of water herself.

Ramona turned to him. The threads had vanished, and he had her hands again, almost too overwhelmed to remember not to hold them too tightly. But she blinked up at him. "I have a feeling I'm about to return to my body. It's going to hurt like hell. Can you kiss me before that happens?"

She let out a pleased and surprised noise as he was already a step ahead of her, holding her close, taking over her mouth, her mind, and everything else his passion could reach, until she was pressing hard against him, wanting not to be parted. Never.

But as she started to be drawn back to her body, and those paroxysms of pain started, he made sure his expression, his touch, gave her his promise. When she woke, he would be there.

CHAPTER NINETEEN

"*F*ucking hell."

Raina's exclamation would have made her laugh out loud, except returning to her body was every bit as excruciating as she'd expected it to be.

Ramona drew in a ragged breath, punctuated by a moan.

"Shit, get...go get Matilda and Isabella," Raina barked the order. "And anyone else who knows anything about healing. Or painkillers."

Ramona sensed people scampering to do Raina's bidding as she tried to hold her eyes open. It was difficult, because they were flooded with tears, a mix of the good, the sorrowful and *holy hell*, this hurt.

Though even rolling her eyes caused agony, she glanced down. They'd laid out her body in a dress made of a fabric she'd woven herself, out of silk and merino wool, dyed in swirling colors. It swished around her hips but had a shaped bodice and embroidered V-neckline. Silas would like it. Her feet were bare, and her toenails had been painted. Her fingernails hadn't, because of how torn up her hands had been.

That was part of the pain. Restoring her life had restored her physical body and was healing it at an accelerated pace, but it was a little like having band-aids ripped off of mortal wounds. Over and over again, by gleeful imps. She wondered if she'd have scars grooved in spirals along her upper arms and legs, a memory of the soul threads. That would be kind of cool. Especially overlaid by those ribbons Silas could summon when he was feeling particularly... Masterful.

"You were going to cremate me in my favorite dress," she said. "And bare feet. Very appropriate."

"I'm going to slap her," Ruby said.

"Wait until everything doesn't hurt. Though a hug would be nice." Her voice was raspy. It sounded almost as sultry as Raina's.

Her sisters leaned over her, filling her vision. She reached up to touch Raina's collarbone, her sable hair. Ruby's ponytail twined around her other fingers. Even though the effort made her gasp, she needed to touch them. "We did it," she murmured.

"We did. Though you did a lot of the heavy lifting."

"My eyes tell me otherwise."

Raina's left arm was in a sling and she had bent over Ramona gingerly, favoring that wounded place in her side. Ruby was sitting in a chair, as if standing was a problem. Both displayed bruises and scratches, burns. "If you two hadn't guarded The Gate, and helped keep the Loom going, I couldn't have done anything."

She closed her eyes, shuddered. "Shit, it hurts," she whimpered. "I'm glad it hurts, because I'm alive, and I'm going to stay alive, but it really hurts."

"We're getting something that will help," Raina promised. She pressed a kiss to Ramona's forehead, and Ruby did the same to her hand, holding it gently. "Glad you didn't leave us," Raina added, her voice uneven. "We promised we'd be three old crones together."

"I think we're going to be more than that," Ramona said. "Our retirement may be different than we planned."

They exchanged curious looks, but there'd be time to tell them. Right now, she needed something else. "Silas?"

"He's not...oh wait." Amusement threaded through the tearful relief in Ruby's voice. "A storm just blew all the furniture off Raina's porch. I'm betting that's him."

"Damn immortal males," Raina grumbled. "No respect for property."

"Buford..."

"I'll send Derek to get him. Poor guy's been beside himself. Cathair's been keeping him company, though."

Drawing in a breath was overwhelming enough, let alone finding words. But she nodded, because it was important. So was what she could feel now.

He was in the room.

He was being kind and considerate enough to give her friends time with her, to celebrate her being alive, even as the energy of his impatience to be near her took up all available space.

Raina made a subtle gesture to Ruby, and they withdrew. Then he was there, his green eyes concerned for her, her protective Master wanting to take away her pain, but there were good kinds of pain in the world. This was one of them.

"Being dead felt better, at least from a physical standpoint," she noted. He picked up her hand, laid it on top of his palm and curled his fingers loosely around hers, just to let her feel the connection. It took her back to The Gate, when they'd touched it together, when he'd been the strong one, trying to help her go through, even though she could already see the desolation in his gaze. It made her grip his hand tight, no matter the cost. The message she was sending made it worth it.

"You're back," he said quietly, amusement in his warm gaze. She wasn't sure what he meant until he tilted his head, drawing her attention around them. There were fireflies, butterflies, hummingbirds, and yes, dragonflies, cutting circles around the room. Raina was firing orders at Li and Saul to open windows to shepherd them out, while closing the doors to the parlor so they didn't get lost in the house's many rooms.

Ramona couldn't stop herself; waves of magic kept coming from her like she was a bubble machine. Which meant now there were also bubbles.

Bubbles of happiness, touched with colors, rainbows of blues, silvers, gold and more. Wind rippled through the room, moving the curtains, lifting Raina's hair and swirling it around her like a cloak. She shot Ramona a look of mock exasperation, but there was so much love and joy in her friend's green-gold eyes, Ramona knew she'd be forgiven.

Normally they'd put shielding in place to help her modulate her magic, keep it from disrupting their homes, but today Raina and Ruby seemed to be celebrating the unexpected things her magic was tossing out into the world. Like the unexpected yet welcome things that could be thrown in one's life path. Her attention went back to Silas.

Isabella approached her other side, had her sip from a tonic. "You taught me how to prepare this, remember? It will put you to sleep, help the healing, while giving you a break from the pain. It will be less when you wake up. You'll feel better."

"I can't imagine feeling any better than I do now." She tapped a weak finger against his palm. "Silas."

"I am here. Always."

"Don't neglect your souls while I sleep. Help them. And figure out how to help the ones that are still lost."

He held her gaze. Love united in purpose might make separation no less painful, but it made the bond itself all the stronger. "I will do anything you wish. But I will sit with you a while first. Soulmate."

They were just beginning this life together, and would have much to learn about one another. But now she was certain he would be with her, throughout every life she lived.

The bond between them would be as strong as the thread of a soul itself.

EPILOGUE

$\mathcal{H}$e was home. Ramona had felt it, as soon as she left the barn.

Sometimes he had to be gone a couple weeks, sometimes a few days. Sometimes only a few hours. If his return happened during business hours, he might show back up in her shop, sit on the stool behind the counter and watch her. Depending on his mood, the shoppers might or might not see him, but she could.

Or she'd be in the barn with the animals, and he'd come help her, tell her about the souls he'd Reaped, what the members of the Wake were doing. She'd tell him her news, as well as what was happening with Raina and Ruby, the people in their lives.

Like couples throughout the ages, coming home after the workday to exchange stories. Share.

The thing was, he usually came to find her. Something about this, making her come to him, started her heart pounding, not in a bad way. It was a very Dom thing to do. And suggested he had something particular planned.

Especially since he was in her attic bedroom. When they had time together, he didn't waste it, finding ways to show her just how demanding he could be. How creative.

As she came up the two sets of stairs, the silence in the house was compelling. His presence vibrated in the air. She stopped on the second landing, the creases of her palms moist, her stomach wobbling.

This was about sex, yes, but it was interlaced with messages of need and possession, such that he wanted her to feel it in every corner, expanding, filling the space with heat, life...desire.

Her Master was home. There was no escaping Death. No refusing it. Surrender was the only option, and the reward for that...her heart pounded.

When she reached the doorway to her bedroom, she saw three things.

A folded blanket in the center of the floor.

Him sitting on the end of her bed and wearing only a pair of jeans.

A belt being threaded between his fingers.

His green gaze pinned her where she was. "Take off your clothes and jewelry," he said. "Right there."

"I've been taking care of the animals, so I should—"

"Take them off."

The words died in her throat. Because her body was suddenly quivering madly, a herd of marbles appeared from nowhere. They vanished before the notes of their rolling progress could reach her ears. He'd absorbed the magic, same as he'd taken the fire into his palm from her hair.

He'd done it while threading that strap through his fingers. No hesitation, no break in rhythm. As she continued to stand there, he stopped though, green gaze boring into her.

Hastily, she removed her clothes, put them aside. Laid the jewelry on the nightstand. Then she stood before him as his gaze slid over her, at a pace that made it clear what he was looking at was his to take his time perusing. Inside and out.

"Turn. Spread your legs and bend over."

She pivoted, her bare feet sliding along the worn wood. She thought he would come to her then, but he didn't. He issued another knee-weakening command. "Lift your backside, part the cheeks so I can see my choices. See how wet your cunt already is."

She complied. Unsteady, she almost teetered forward, but something pressed against her shoulders, her nape, as she dropped her head forward, her hair brushing the floor. The steady wall of energy held her like his hands, his strength and power caring for her.

"Straighten and turn." When she did, he pointed to the folded blanket. "Kneel there."

As she obeyed, her hand fell to it to stroke. Incredibly soft, it was a mix of creamy colors, like chocolate and vanilla swirl ice cream.

Again, he balanced the surge, so she wasn't sitting in ice cream, though the idea of him licking it off of her wasn't so bad...except she really liked the blanket and didn't want it ruined. Fortunately, her magic agreed.

"I crossed paths with an alpaca farmer who cares for her animals like they're her children. She weaves the blankets from their wool herself. I thought you would like one. I'll take you to meet her one day."

He frequently brought her gifts like that. Things that said he was thinking of her. The power of a man who gave such consideration to what he offered a woman, wanting to earn her smiles, her delight, was overwhelming.

Her smiles were a gift she'd give to him a million times a day if he needed it. And he needed it more these days.

He was more serious now. The losses of the recent past, the weight of the leadership he carried, had taken some of his levity. But he still smiled for her. Still made her laugh and offered her plenty of chances to do the same for him.

Though she wasn't glad for the reasons, the way he could wield that additional seriousness and authority toward her in particular ways was sexy as hell. Like now.

He passed the strap through his fingers again. Over, under. Her gaze followed it, lowered when he looked her way. That belt was making her nervous. Really nervous.

"I'm afraid."

He rose immediately, dropped to his heels to touch the side of her face. A command to keep her gaze down, even as he also did it as a reassurance.

"Tell me why. You know I would never hurt you."

She had no doubt of that. The mark had possessed him, but it wasn't him. That wasn't the core that loved, cherished, protected and considered her his.

"I'm afraid of how much I want this. And I've never had it done to me. I'm worried my magic will think you're causing me harm. Or that my feelings will get out of control."

"Look at me."

When she did, she saw a wicked glint in his eye. "You being out of control is my fondest wish. Eyes back down."

Another quiver went through her thighs at that measured tone. He straightened and returned to the bed. The density of his power increased, pressed against her, made her get wetter. Her nipples grew taut and that spiraling tingle in her stomach expanded.

She listened to that slow whisper of sound as he threaded the strap through his fingers again.

"My fondest wish is that we reach the point where you have no fear, no worries that I can't handle whatever your reaction is when we come together like this. I believe we're getting there, aren't we? Remember the week I told you that you couldn't touch yourself without my permission?"

"Yes, sir. I remember."

During that week, no matter where he was in the world, he'd relentlessly sent her thoughts about what he intended to do to her. Channeling her reactions to the constant arousal should have kept her busy enough to calm her down, but no. When he'd finally come to her, she had the kind of intense release she would have denied herself before she was with him. She'd clung to him, weak in the aftermath, cherishing his approval, his deep appreciation of her efforts.

And trusting the shelter of his magic.

"Surrendering the right to your pleasure to me," he said to her now, "and me giving you punishment for your worries, your fears, will reinforce how much you can rely on my control."

While things like denying her permission to touch herself indulged the Master in him, she'd sensed it was part of a bigger plan he had, to build that structure around her. Until he stated it as he did now, she hadn't dared to look at it too closely, in case she was imposing something that wasn't there, a wish rather than a truth.

Yet the truth was here, and she was ready to accept and believe in it. When it came to intimacy, not just her body was learning to surrender to him, but also the Chaos magic threaded through her heart and blood.

"Thank you for the blanket, Master," she said quietly.

It was the first time she'd called him that, outside of her head. There was a pause in the movement of the strap, then it continued. His voice deepened. Roughened.

"You are brave. Fearless. You've sacrificed yourself for the world, for its many souls. You care for and protect your friends, and those who need you, like Curtis. But for any risks you take with your mental or physical wellbeing, you answer to me. How many strikes will fit the act? I suppose the number of souls you saved wouldn't work. Even my arm would tire from that."

Though the quaking stayed, she hid a tiny smile at his musing tone. "Ah, well," he continued. "I'll decide based on your shrieks. Get on the bed on your hands and knees, facing the headboard."

She rose from the alpaca blanket and moved to do his bidding, keeping her eyes down since he hadn't instructed otherwise. Yet when she put her knee on the bed, he was there, hand grasping her elbow to steady her. Her body acted without thought, turning against him, her face to his chest.

Both arms closed around her, the belt brushing her hip and upper thigh. He hugged her close, responding to her need for that. He stroked her back, fingers tangling in her hair. "My beautiful witch," he murmured, the deepness of his voice vibrating through her. "I missed you."

"I missed you, too."

He kissed the top of her head, held her tight. "I love you. You know that."

His demanding tone prompted another half-smile. "I do." But she said nothing else, the silence drawing out as her smile deepened.

"You will get a worse punishment for teasing me," he threatened.

"Oh, I suppose I love you, too. I hadn't given it much thought."

She laughed as he scooped her up and tossed her on the bed. She bounced and rolled, but when she came up on her hands and knees, his touch was on her hip. A reminder of the position he wanted her in, which brought her nervousness back.

As often as he'd threatened, and given her the occasional teasing smack, he hadn't gone this far. If the wetness he explored between her thighs was any indication, she suspected this was going to open the door to him doing it much more.

She bit back a whimper as he curved his hand over her labia, fingers resting with firm pressure there. No matter what play they did, he always started with this. A reminder of whose physical touch alone was allowed upon her and in her most intimate regions.

He stroked her buttocks, the curve of her back, her shoulder blades. She dropped her head forward, hair pooling over her braced hands as he moved to her nape, gripped her there. He put a knee on the bed, and her breath quickened.

He slid the strap against her thigh. "I love your ass," he murmured, then his hand slid under her to follow the line of her belly to her breasts. He cupped one with deceptive gentleness, thumbing her nipple. "All your curves. Down on your elbows. Put that lovely ass higher in the air, and spread your knees. If I want to spank your cunt, I want it accessible."

She complied, wetting dry lips again. Her heart might just roll up into her throat and stay there. His large hand gripped her hip, holding her steady. "The anticipation is the knife edge, isn't it? Like that moment before I thrust into you. I want to hold there forever, watch you grow more needy, pant for it, a plea in your throat, your gaze on my cock, the petals of your sex glossy like your lips that you keep wetting with your tongue. But I also don't want to wait. I want to plunge in and keep thrusting. I want to literally fuck you to death."

He liked to make observations like that, in a calm, conversational voice, as if he was giving Brenner instructions or remarking on the weather. He'd keep doing it, until the kind of whimper he'd described came from her. Like it did now.

"There's my bird, ready to fly." His hand moved to the back of her neck again, holding her as he stopped trailing the belt along her skin. Instead, he gave her the first strike with it.

She jumped, but it was merely a lick, one he followed with similar strokes, a weight and pace intended to warm her up. She suspected he would escalate when he knew she was ready. His controlled tempo was unbearably arousing, her Master giving her a punishment, telling her it was his right to do so, just as he'd said. She was willing to climb to higher levels of pain and intensity to give him what he was demanding. What he was letting her know was for them both.

There. That one was harder, sending a sting through her upper thigh. Then she let out a little cry as he switched tactics, using the flat of his hand to spank her sex between her spread legs. Three fast slaps that had her jerking, trying hard not to move away, and coming back to center quickly when she did. He would tie her up if she moved too much.

One night, he'd done a forced orgasm session with her, a torment so intense and incredible it had taken hours for her knees to regain strength afterward. He'd carried her, bathed her, fed her, and had delighted in it. She might ask him to do it again—when she was feeling particularly brave.

Sometimes sacrificing oneself to save the world took less courage than indulging her Master's more demanding moods. A thought that would amuse and please him to know, she was sure.

Immortal, powerful males. Now she understood what Raina and Ruby had explained was most frightening about their Guardians' sexual appetites. They couldn't resist letting them pursue them to their fathomless depths. Silas brought his skill and experience as a Master to her as gifts, helping to fuel her own ever-deepening needs for more.

He'd returned to using the belt. Her skin was tingling, and she was gasping. He moved his grip to her thigh, the reminder to hold her legs open, her ass up to take every blow.

"The right strikes can make the capillaries bloom like a garden across pale female skin. I want to see the bruises from my belt here," he said. "Watch you gaze at them in the mirror, be fascinated with them. Wanting more."

She would. He knew her. She wasn't a pain slut. It had to do with her desire to carry his marks, whether temporary or the more permanent kind. The ones on her wrists were blazing gold, and as he continued to administer her punishment, they were spiraling up her arms, up her thighs, holding them wider, his magic as well as hers reflecting what they desired to give one another.

It was starting to hurt. "Sir...I'm...it's painful."

"More than you can bear?"

"Almost."

"When you get past almost, wait another five strikes. Then ask me for mercy."

He'd told her that before, that he would take her past what she could handle, just past, to remind her he was the one who made the call. A structure he would reinforce in a million ways, so she could have the true surrender she'd always craved. That she'd believed was a fairy tale.

Her thighs and ass were on fire, and she was flinching from every strike. Was it enough? Could she handle more? Maybe, but she wasn't sure and oh, Goddess, how it hurt...

She was whimpering again, and when he stopped, her knees would have failed her if they weren't firmly braced on the bed, her elbows helping. She had her face pushed against her hands, the heat of her magical wrist bindings stroking her face, the sides of her neck, emanating out to her shoulders.

"My sub is overly ambitious in her desire to please her Master. She should have asked for mercy ten strikes ago. But luckily, I'm here to watch over her."

She quivered as he put his mouth on the sore spots, teased her gently with a stroking tongue. Then he put the belt before her, stretched it out. "Hold it in both hands. Feel the heat my grip and your stinging flesh gave it."

She did, pressing her palms against the tingling warmth the strap held. She heard the sound of his zipper, the jeans being removed, and he was behind her, gripping her hips.

"Slow and easy, a boat ride in wet heat." When he eased into her cunt, he was stretching her, more of the same reminder as she lifted her hips up and down, adjusting to his size. To take him deep as he wanted to go.

As he pressed himself fully against her ass, another noise came from her throat, her fingers tightening on the strap. "I bet my healing witch has a cream I can rub into your skin later," he said. "I'll lay you on the bed, care for you. You take care of your Master, and he will take very good care of you."

"Thank you," she managed, and earned another approving grunt. Her nails dug into the belt. Oh, Goddess. He was so...damn...good at this. He could almost make her forget that she wanted to give him just as much pleasure in return. Though she knew he wanted her to lose her mind like that, how she felt for him was every bit as powerful as his control over her senses...one fed the other, just like the wrist marks themselves.

She gripped him with her inner muscles, worked them against his length as he pulled out, drove in. When he stilled inside her, she kept doing it, letting him feel the squeezing grip, how it could send sensation along his length. He muttered an oath, dropped down over her, pressed a wet kiss with teeth against her back.

"Siren and witch in one," he told her roughly, then he was back to stroking again, this time with determined thrusts that could have moved her along the bed if he didn't anchor them, his hands on her waist as he drove in and out, pushed them up to that edge.

"Oh...please..."

"Hold," he told her, a growl.

She couldn't. He was taking her there too fast, her body spiraling, and her milking of his cock was affecting her, too. But she didn't stop doing it, didn't stop trying to hold back. Didn't stop begging him for mercy, until he granted it to both of them.

"Now."

She cried out, a note she was sure the animals heard in her barn, that Buford absorbed in every fiber of his magical being, the Chaos energy feeding all of them as it was thrown out like sunlight and pummeling rain. Sensation roared over her, his seed jetting inside her body, making her hips buck up, so he slammed into her even harder, and she shrieked, just as he desired.

He groaned with her, their bodies moving in tandem, though of course he held out longer than her. Eventually, she just rested limply in his grasp as he finished, coming back to a slow thrust and retreat. As the aftershocks rippled through her, she made quiet contented noise.

It was like a slow boat ride, as he'd said. Getting slower, the sun beating down on their replete bodies, seducing them into a lazy afternoon nap.

Which suddenly sounded like a perfect idea.

When they finally came down, her head rested on her forearm and then his as he dropped over her, pressing her closer to the bed, her cheek to her comforter. He spread kisses along her neck and shoulder, making sounds of approval. Slowly, he eased from her, but when he would have left her to get washcloth and lotion to cosset her with, as he'd promised, she found his hand, clung to it. What she needed right now was him. Her Master, surrounding her, holding her, while she was still shaking, her foundation split apart by his will. His holding her would put it all back together.

He understood. Silas settled himself on his back against the pillows, bringing her up to drape over his body as he wrapped his arms around her. She rested there, no need to think or feel anything, the motes of their magic drifting in the air. Like the spirits of the pixies who'd loved and taught her to believe in herself and her magic. That path had brought her to this confident, strong male, who wanted to honor her own strength, everything she was, even as he asked her for everything.

Dreams did come true. Crescent had been right.

Her Master wasn't done with what he needed from her. Silas reached over to the nightstand, picking up the Reaper jewelry Saul had given her. After he examined it, he touched the top of her hand, waited until she turned it over to put the heavy man's ring in her palm. "If you desire to do so, put it on my finger, and tell me I'm yours, witch."

Her startled gaze came up to his, and his lips quirked. "You said you found it sexy, how Derek wore the proof of his belonging to Ruby. If you prefer a different kind of ring for me to show that, you may choose it at your leisure, but I will wear this one until then. I will not take it off."

She drew an unsteady breath. "Won't it fall off when you transform?"

"I can spell it to stay in place. Trust me. I will ensure it is welded there if necessary."

Pushing herself up to her elbow, she removed the stabilizer she'd used for her smaller finger and then slid the ring onto his lefthand ring finger. Her heart thudded as she saw it fit as if it was made for him.

He studied it, then brought his gaze back to hers. Those green eyes took her over as he cupped her chin, slid fingers along her jaw so she could feel the coolness of the ring pressing against the pulse of her throat. He put his lips on hers, a slow, lingering kiss, then drew back.

"You remember when we went to New Orleans?"

Some time ago, she'd had to help Ruby, Raina, Mikhael and Derek with a problem there, and Silas had decided to accompany her. He liked the beignets. "Yes."

"I think we should go back. Not to save the city again, unless of course it needs saving. I want to see you dance on the railing in front of the Aquarium. Take you to the sculpture garden at the art museum. There's a mirror labyrinth piece there now, where I could enjoy your body, watch your face in a million different reflections as I bring you pleasure."

She liked that idea. Liked doing anything with him, including this.

Listening to his voice, a rumble against her ear, promising to change fantasies into reality for her.

He could also find solace for the things that troubled him in her body, in her open heart, which embraced everything he wanted and needed from her. She could be his reminder that while life might always have to give way to death, love kept life returning, again and again, to explore the endless patterns the Fates—and the souls themselves—wove.

Chaos was the source of love and life itself.

WANT MORE? *How about a crossover Arcane Shot series novel?*

Before Joey wrote *Arcane Chaos*, she did a bonus novel, where Raina, Ramona, Ruby and their men were called to help out with a threat to New Orleans (as mentioned in the epilogue). This situation needed the help of some of Joey's contemporary characters from the Knights of the Board Room series as well.

While the timeline feels a little off for the progression of Silas and Ramona's relationship as laid out here, we hope you enjoy this adventure with the Arcane Shot series characters!

CLICK HERE TO READ NOW
ARCANE KNIGHT

Reading this in print format?
Look for it at your favorite book vendor!

ABOUT THE AUTHOR

Having penned over fifty acclaimed BDSM contemporary and paranormal titles, which includes six award-winning series, *Joey W. Hill* has been awarded the RT Book Reviews Career Achievement Award for Erotic Romance. A submissive herself, Hill brings authenticity to her intensely emotional love stories.

She is grateful for the support of a wonderful and enthusiastic readership, which allows her to live on her beloved Carolina coast with her even more beloved husband and menagerie of animals.

- On the Web: https://storywitch.com
- Twitter: https://twitter.com/JoeyWHill
- Facebook: https://facebook.com/JoeyWHillAuthor
- Facebook Fan Forum: https://facebook.com/groups/JWHMembersOnly
- MeWe: https://mewe.com/i/joeywhill
- GoodReads: https://www.goodreads.com/author/show/103359.Joey_W_Hill
- BookBub: https://bookbub.com/authors/joey-w-hill
- Amazon: https://amazon.com/Joey-W-Hill/e/B001JSCIW0

ALSO BY JOEY W. HILL

Mirror of My Soul

Mistress of Redemption

Rough Canvas

Branded Sanctuary

Divine Solace

Worth The Wait

Truly Helpless

In His Arms

Ignition Sequence

Naughty Bits Series

Naughty Bits

Naughty Wishes

Vampire Queen Series

Vampire Queen's Servant

Mark of the Vampire Queen

Vampire's Claim

Beloved Vampire

Vampire Mistress *(VQS: Club Atlantis)*

Vampire Trinity *(VQS: Club Atlantis)*

Vampire Instinct

Bound by the Vampire Queen

Taken by a Vampire

The Scientific Method

Nightfall

Elusive Hero

Night's Templar

Vampire's Soul

Vampire's Embrace

Vampire Master *(VQS: Club Atlantis)*

Vampire Guardian *(VQS: Club Atlantis)*

Vampire's Choice

www.ingramcontent.com/pod-product-compliance
Lightning Source LLC
Chambersburg PA
CBHW061309170626
46817CB00001B/122